Praise for The Cazalet Chronicles

'If I were sent to a desert island with one book this would be my choice'   HRH The Duchess of Cornwall

'Charming, poignant and quite irresistible . . . to be cherished and shared'   *The Times*

'She is one of those novelists who shows, through her work, what the novel is for . . . She helps us to do the necessary thing – open our eyes and our hearts'   Hilary Mantel

'The Cazalets have earned an honoured place among the great saga families . . . rendered thrillingly three-dimensional by a master craftsman'   *Sunday Telegraph*

'Like Ferrante, Howard's fictional sphere is domestic and yet reveals deeper truths about human nature. Her characters leap from the page like living, breathing people and her acutest insights are reserved for what makes us flawed yet lovable. She is the most amazing storyteller because she makes you care'   Elizabeth Day

'Superb . . . hypnotic . . . very funny'   *Spectator*

'Evocative and gracefully written'   *Cosmopolitan*

'A family saga of the best kind . . . a must'   *Tatler*

'A dazzling historical reconstruction'

Penelope Fitzgerald

'This chronicle will be read, like Trollope, as a classic about life in England in our century'   Sybille Bedford

MARKING TIME

Elizabeth Jane Howard was the author of fifteen highly acclaimed novels. The Cazalet Chronicles – *The Light Years, Marking Time, Confusion, Casting Off* and *All Change* – have become established as modern classics and have been adapted for a major BBC television series and most recently for BBC Radio 4. In 2002 Macmillan published Elizabeth Jane Howard's autobiography, *Slipstream*. In that same year she was awarded a CBE in the Queen's Birthday Honours list. She died in January 2014, following the publication of *All Change*.

MARKING TIME

Volume Two of The Cazalet Chronicles

ELIZABETH
JANE HOWARD

PAN BOOKS

First published 1991 by Macmillan

This edition published 2021 by Pan Books
an imprint of Pan Macmillan
The Smithson, 6 Briset Street, London EC1M 5NR
EU representative: Macmillan Publishers Ireland Ltd, 1st Floor,
The Liffey Trust Centre, 117–126 Sheriff Street Upper,
Dublin 1, DO1 YC43
Associated companies throughout the world
www.panmacmillan.com

ISBN 978-1-5290-4943-5

3 5 7 9 8 6 4 2

A CIP catalogue record for this book is available from the British Library.

Printed and bound by CPI Group (UK) Ltd, Croydon, CR0 4YY

Visit **www.panmacmillan.com** to read more about all our books
and to buy them. You will also find features, author interviews and
news of any author events, and you can sign up for e-newsletters
so that you're always first to hear about our new releases.

For Dosia Verney

CONTENTS

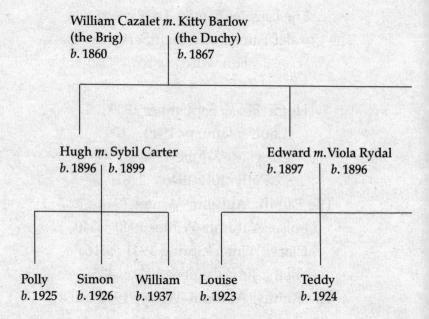

William Cazalet *m.* Kitty Barlow
(the Brig)   (the Duchy)
b. 1860   *b.* 1867

Hugh *m.* Sybil Carter
b. 1896   *b.* 1899

Edward *m.* Viola Rydal
b. 1897   *b.* 1896

Polly   Simon   William   Louise   Teddy
b. 1925   *b.* 1926   *b.* 1937   *b.* 1923   *b.* 1924

THE CAZALET FAMILY TREE

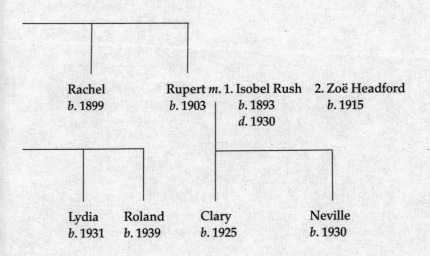

Rachel
b. 1899

Rupert *m.* 1. Isobel Rush   2. Zoë Headford
b. 1903   *b.* 1893   *b.* 1915
                d. 1930

Lydia   Roland   Clary   Neville
b. 1931   *b.* 1939   *b.* 1925   *b.* 1930

THE CAZALET FAMILY
AND THEIR SERVANTS

WILLIAM CAZALET, known as the Brig
    Kitty Barlow, known as the Duchy (his wife)
        Rachel, their unmarried daughter

HUGH CAZALET, eldest son
    Sybil Carter (his wife)
        Polly
        Simon
        William, known as Wills

EDWARD CAZALET, second son
    Viola, known as Villy (his wife)
        Louise
        Teddy
        Lydia
        Roland, known as Roly

RUPERT CAZALET, third son
    Zoë (second wife)
    Isobel (first wife; died having Neville)
        Clarissa, known as Clary
        Neville

JESSICA CASTLE (Villy's sister)
  Raymond (her husband)
    Angela
    Christopher
    Nora
    Judy

Mrs Cripps (cook)
Ellen (nurse)
Eileen (parlourmaid)
Peggy and Bertha (housemaids)
Dottie and Edie (housemaids)
Tonbridge (chauffeur)
McAlpine (gardener)
Wren (groom)
Billy (gardener's boy)
Emily (cook)
Bracken (Edward's chauffeur)

FOREWORD

The following background to this novel is intended for those readers who are unfamiliar with *The Light Years*.

William and Kitty Cazalet, known to their family as the Brig and the Duchy, have shut their London house, and spend all their time in Sussex at Home Place. The Brig's sight is failing, so he is less active in the family timber firm which he heads. They have three sons, Hugh, Edward and Rupert, and one unmarried daughter, Rachel.

Hugh is married to Sybil and they have three children. The eldest, Polly, does lessons at home with a cousin and is fourteen at the opening of this novel; Simon is thirteen and has joined his cousin Teddy at a public school; and William (Wills) has just had his second birthday. The middle son, Edward, is married to Villy (Viola Rydal, whose widowed mother, Lady Rydal, is something of a martinet). They have four children. Louise, aged sixteen, has ceased to do lessons at home with her cousins, and has spent one term at a domestic science school; her brother Teddy, who is very athletic, has been at a public school for two years now, while Lydia, who is eight, has been going to a small day school. Roland, the baby, is four months old.

The third son, Rupert, was married to Isobel by whom he had two children: Clary is the same age as Polly and is doing lessons with her, and Neville, now eight, has been attending a day school in London. Rupert's second wife is Zoë who, at twenty-four, is twelve years younger than he. They have no children.

The unmarried daughter, Rachel, who occupies herself looking after her nearly blind father, also helps to run a charitable Babies' Hotel that at the start of this novel has been evacuated for the second time to a nearby house owned by the Brig, her father. Her great friend is Margot Sidney, known as Sid, who teaches the violin and lives in London, but pays frequent visits to Home Place.

Edward's wife, Villy, has a sister, Jessica, who is married to Raymond Castle. They have four children – more cousins for the Cazalets. Angela, whose first, hopeless love was for Rupert Cazalet, is now twenty, and works in London; Christopher at sixteen is passionately interested in nature and against war, and Nora, a year older than Christopher, has been at the domestic science school with Louise. The youngest, Judy, is nine and goes to a boarding school.

At the end of *The Light Years* the Castles came into a house and some money inherited from a great-aunt of Raymond's, as a result of which they were able to move from mean accommodation in East Finchley to the great-aunt's house in Frensham.

Miss Milliment is the very old family governess: she began with Villy and Jessica, and now teaches Clary and Polly.

Diana Mackintosh is the most serious of Edward's many affairs. She is married with three sons.

Apart from the grandparents' house, Home Place, the Brig has bought and converted two other nearby houses: Mill Farm, which is now used by the Babies' Hotel, and Pear Tree Cottage, which serves as an overflow for the

FOREWORD

Cazalet and Castle families. In addition they have a house in London, Chester Terrace, now more or less shut up.

The three Cazalet sons also have London houses. Hugh and Sybil's is in Ladbroke Grove, which Hugh is still using during the week when he is working in London. Edward and Villy's home in nearby Lansdowne Road is used by them during the children's term time. Rupert and Zoë have a small house in Brook Green.

There are a number of servants working for the Cazalets, but the principal ones in this novel are: Mrs Cripps the cook, Tonbridge the chauffeur, McAlpine the gardener and Billy the gardener's boy, Wren the groom, Eileen the parlourmaid – all of Home Place – and Ellen, Rupert's nurse for Clary and Neville, who finds herself busier than ever after the late births of Wills and Roland.

The Light Years ended in 1938 with Chamberlain's speech after Munich – 'peace with honour'. *Marking Time* begins a year later, after the invasion of Poland when war is clearly imminent and unavoidable. Children are being evacuated from the cities and everybody is waiting for Chamberlain to announce the result of the British ultimatum.

HOME PLACE

September 1939

Someone had turned off the wireless and, in spite of the room being full of people, there was a complete silence – in which Polly could feel, and almost hear, her own heart thudding. As long as nobody spoke, and no one moved, it was still the very end of peace . . .

The Brig, her grandfather, did move. She watched while – still in silence – he got slowly to his feet, stood for a moment, one hand trembling on the back of his chair as he passed the other slowly across his filmy eyes. Then he went across the room and, one by one, kissed his two elder sons, Polly's father Hugh and Uncle Edward. She waited for him to kiss Uncle Rupe, but he did not. She had never seen him kiss another man before, but this seemed more of an apology and a salute. It's for what they went through last time there was a war, and because it was for nothing, she thought.

Polly saw everything. She saw Uncle Edward catch her father's eye, and then wink, and her father's face contract as though he remembered something he could hardly *bear* to remember. She saw her grandmother, the Duchy, sitting bolt upright, staring at Uncle Rupert with a kind of bleak anger. She's not angry with *him*, she's afraid he will have to be in it. She's so old-fashioned she thinks it's simply men who have to fight and die; she doesn't understand. Polly understood everything.

1

People were beginning to shift in their chairs, to murmur, to light cigarettes, to tell the children to go out and play. The worst had come to the worst, and they were all behaving in much the same way as they would have if it hadn't. This was what her family did when things were bad. A year ago, when it had been peace with honour, they *had* all seemed different, but Polly had not had time to notice properly, because just as the amazement and joy hit her, it was as though she'd been shot. She'd fainted. 'You went all white and sort of blind, and you passed out. It was terribly interesting,' her cousin Clary had said. Clary had put it in her *Book of Experiences* that she was keeping for when she was a writer. Polly felt Clary looking at her now, and just as their eyes met and Polly gave a little nod of agreement about them both getting the hell out, a distant up and down wailing noise of a siren began and her cousin Teddy shouted, 'It's an air raid! Gosh! Already!' and everybody got up, and the Brig told them to fetch their gas masks and wait in the hall to go to the air-raid shelter. The Duchy went to tell the servants, and her mother Sybil and Aunt Villy said they must go to Pear Tree Cottage to fetch Wills and Roly, and Aunt Rach said she must pop down to Mill Farm to help Matron with the evacuated babies – in fact, hardly anybody did what the Brig said.

'I'll carry your mask if you want to take your writing,' Polly said while they hunted in their bedroom for the cardboard boxes that contained their masks. 'Damn! Where did we put them?' They were still hunting when the siren went again, not wailing up and down this time, just a steady howl. 'All Clear!' someone shouted from the hall.

'Must have been a false alarm,' Teddy said; he sounded disappointed.

'Although we wouldn't have seen a thing buried in that awful old shelter,' said Neville. 'And I suppose you've heard, they're using the war as an excuse not to go to the beach, which seems to me about the most unfair thing I've ever heard in my life.'

'Don't be so stupid, Neville!' Lydia said crushingly. 'People don't *go* to beaches in wartime.'

There was a generally quarrelsome feeling in the air, Polly thought, although outside it was a mellow September Sunday morning, with a smell of burning leaves from McAlpine's bonfire, and everything looked the same. The children had all been sent away from the drawing room: the grown-ups wanted to have a talk and, naturally, everyone not classed as one resented this. 'It isn't as though when we're there they make funny jokes all the time and scream with laughter,' Neville said as they trooped into the hall. Before anyone could back him up or squash him, Uncle Rupert put his head round the drawing-room door and said, 'Everyone who couldn't find their masks bloody well *go* and find them, and in future they're to be kept in the gun room. Chop chop.'

∞ ∞ ∞

'I really resent being classed as a child,' Louise said to Nora, as they made their way down to Mill Farm. 'They'll sit there for hours making plans for all of us as though we were mere pawns in the game. We ought at least to have the chance to object to arrangements before they're *faits accomplis.*'

'The thing is to agree with them, and then do what one thinks is right,' Nora replied, which Louise suspected meant doing what she wanted to do.

'What shall you do when we leave our cooking place?'

'I shan't go back *there*. I shall start training to be a nurse.'

'Oh, no, don't! Do stay until Easter. Then we can both leave. I should simply loathe it without you. And anyway, I bet they don't take people of seventeen to be nurses.'

'They'll take me,' said Nora. 'You'll be all right. You're nothing like so homesick now. You're over the worst of all that. It's bad luck you being a year younger, because it means you'll have to wait to be really useful. But you'll end up a much better cook than me—'

'Than I,' Louise said automatically.

'Than I, then, and that'll be terribly useful. You could go into one of the Services as a cook.'

A thoroughly uninviting prospect, Louise thought. She didn't actually *want* to be useful at all. She wanted to be a great actress, something which she well knew by now that Nora regarded as frivolous. They had had one serious . . . not row, exactly, but heated discussion about this during the holidays, after which Louise had become cautious about her aspirations. 'Actresses aren't *necessary*,' Nora had said, while conceding that if there wasn't going to be a war it wouldn't matter so much what Louise did. Louise had retaliated by questioning the use of nuns (Nora's chosen profession, now in abeyance – partly because she had promised *not* to be one if there hadn't been a war last year, and now ruled out in the immediate future because of the need for nurses). But Nora had said that Louise had no conception of the importance of prayer, and the need for there to be people who devoted

4

their lives to it. The trouble was that Louise didn't care whether the world needed actresses or not, she simply wanted to be one; it put her in a morally inferior position *vis-à-vis* Nora, and made a comparison of the worth of their characters an uncomfortable business. But Nora always pre-empted any possibility of covert criticism by hitting a much larger and more unpleasant nail on the head. 'I do have awful trouble with priggishness,' she would say, or, 'I suppose if I ever get *near* being accepted as a novice, my wretched smugness will do me down.' What could one say to that? Again, Louise really didn't want to know herself with the awful familiarity employed by Nora.

'If that's what you think you are, how can you bear to be it?' she had said at the end of the row/heated discussion.

'I don't have much choice. But at least it means that I know what I've got to work against. There I go again. I'm sure you know your faults, Louise, most people do, deep down. It's the first step.'

Still wanting to convince Nora of the worth of acting, Louise had tried her with the greats like Shakespeare, Chekhov and Bach. (Bach she'd added cunningly – he was known to have been religious.) 'You surely don't think you are going to be like any of *them*!' And Louise was silenced. Because a small, secret bit of her was sure she *was* going to be one of them – or at least a Bernhardt or Garrick (for she had always hankered after the men's parts). The argument, like any argument she had ever had with anyone, was quite unresolved, making her doggedly more sure of what she wanted, and Nora more determined that she shouldn't want it.

'You judge me all the time!' she had cried.

'So do you,' Nora had retorted. 'People do that with each other. Anyway, I'm not sure that it is judging exactly; it's more comparing a person with standards. I do it to myself all the time,' she had added.

'And, of course, you always measure up.'

'Of *course* not!' The innocent glare of denial silenced Louise. But then, looking at her friend's heavy beetling eyebrows, and the faint, but unmistakable, signs of a moustache on her upper lip, she had realised that she was glad that she didn't *look* like Nora, and that that was a judgement of a kind. 'I judge that you are a much better person than I,' she had said, not adding that she would still rather be herself.

'Yes, I suppose I could be a cook somewhere,' she said, as they turned into the drive at Mill Farm where, until two days ago, they had been living. On Friday morning it had been decreed that all the inhabitants move to the Brig's new cottages, now made into a quite large house and called Pear Tree Cottage because of one ancient tree in the garden. It had eight bedrooms, but by the time it had housed Villy and Sybil, with Edward and Hugh at weekends, Jessica Castle, paying her annual visit with Raymond (who had gone to London to fetch Miss Milliment and Lady Rydal), there was only room left for Lydia and Neville and the babies, Wills and Roland.

The shift to Pear Tree Cottage had taken all day, with the older children being moved into Home Place, where Rupert and Zoë were also ensconced, together with the great-aunts and Rachel. On Saturday, the Babies' Hotel had arrived: twenty-five babies, sixteen student nurses, with Matron and Sister Crouchback. They had arrived in two buses, one driven by Tonbridge and the other by Rachel's friend Sid. The nurses were to sleep in the squash court, now equipped with three Elsans and an extremely reluctant shower. Matron and Sister occupied Mill Farm with the babies and a rota of student nurses to help out at night. On Saturday afternoon, Nora had suggested that she and Louise go and make supper for the nurses, an offer most gratefully received by Aunt Rachel who had been up since dawn and was utterly exhausted with efforts to make the squash court a place in which people could not only sleep, but keep their personal effects. The cooking had proved extremely difficult, as the kitchen utensils from Mill Farm had been moved to Pear Tree Cottage, and the Babies' Hotel equipment – brought down in a Cazalet lorry – had lost its way and did not turn up until nine in the evening. They had to make the meal at Pear Tree Cottage and Villy took it down with them in a car. This meant cooking under the almost offensively patronising eye of Emily, whose view of ladies and their children was, of course, that they couldn't boil an egg to save their lives; she was also unwilling to tell them where anything was on the twofold grounds that she didn't know whether she was on her head or her heels with all the upset, and didn't want them using her things anyway. Louise had to admit that Nora was wonderfully tactful and apparently insensitive to slights. They made two huge shepherd's pies and Louise a batch of real Bath buns because she had just learned how to do them and was particularly good at it. The supper had been most gratefully received and Matron had called them two little bricks.

Babies could be heard crying as they reached the house. Nora said that they must have had their morning sleeps interrupted by the air-raid warning and having to be carried into the air-raid shelter that the Brig had had built. 'Although how the nurses are going to get there from the squash court in time if there are raids at night, I can't imagine,' she added. Louise thought of bombs dropping from nowhere in the dark, and shivered. *Could* the Germans do that? She thought probably not, but she didn't say anything, not wanting really to know.

Matron and Aunt Rach were in the kitchen. Aunt Rach was unpacking kitchen things from tea chests. Matron sat at the table making lists.

A student was measuring out feeds from an enormous tin of Cow and Gate and another one was sterilising bottles in two saucepans on the cooker. An atmosphere of good humour in a crisis prevailed.

'Needs must when the devil drives,' Matron was saying. She had a face like a sort of outdoor Queen Victoria, Louise thought: the same rather protuberant pale blue eyes and little beaky nose, but her plump and pear-shaped cheeks were the colour of flowerpots crazed with little broken veins. Her shape, on the other hand, was pure Queen Mary – upholstered Edwardian. She wore a long-sleeved navy blue serge dress and a crackling white apron and cap with starched veil.

'We've come to help with lunch,' Nora said.

'Bless you, darlings,' Aunt Rachel said. 'There is some food in the larder but I haven't really sorted it out. A ham, I think, somewhere or other, and Billy brought down some lettuces.'

'And there's the prunes Sister put in to soak last night,' said Matron. 'I do like my girls to have their prunes – it saves such a fortune in Syrup of Figs.'

'They'll need stewing, though,' Nora said. 'I don't know if they'll get cool in time for lunch.'

'Beggars can't be choosers,' Matron said, clipping her

fountain pen into the top of her apron and creaking to her feet.

Louise said she would stew the prunes.

'Don't take those bottles off the heat yet. If they've had their twenty minutes, I'm a Dutchman. Where should we be, Miss Cazalet, without our little helpers? Oh, don't do that, Miss Cazalet, you'll get a hernia!' Rachel stopped trying to move a tea chest out of the way, and let Nora help her. More babies could be heard crying.

'We've had our routine upset by Mr Hitler. If he goes on like this I shall have to send him a p.c. The morning's a ridiculous time to have an air raid. But there you are – *men!*' she added. 'I'll just see if Sister has anything to add to this list – of course, it's Sunday, isn't it? No shops open. Oh, well, better late than never,' and she glided out of the room, to be met in near collision at the door by a student carrying two pails of steaming nappies. 'Look where you're going, Susan. And take those outside when you soak them or nobody will be able to fancy their dinner.'

'Yes, Matron.' All the students wore short-sleeved mauve and white striped cotton dresses and black stockings.

'See if you can find Sid, my pet, would you?' said Aunt Rachel. 'We must get as many tea chests out of the kitchen as we can before the nurses' lunch. She's upstairs, doing blackout.'

∞ ∞ ∞

The blacking out of all the windows of all three houses and the inhabited outbuildings – which included the roof

9

of the squash court – had been occupying the Brig for some days now, with the result that Sid and Villy had been put to making wooden battens onto which blackout material could be nailed. Sybil, Jessica and the Duchy, who each possessed a sewing machine, were set to making curtains for those windows that precluded battens, and Sampson, the builder, had lent a long ladder from which the gardener's boy was to paint the squash court roof, but he had quite soon fallen off and into a huge water tank which McAlpine had described as a slice of luck he wasn't entitled to, dismissing Billy's broken arm and loss of two front teeth as mere cheek. Sampson had been told to deal with the squash court roof along with so much else that it had not made much progress by Saturday morning, the day that the Babies' Hotel was due to arrive. Teddy, Christopher and Simon were all roped in to help one of Sampson's men with the scaffolding and then to cover the sloping glass with dark green paint while inside the stuffy and darkening scene, Rachel and Sid erected camp beds with Lydia and Neville watching sulkily from the gallery (they were supposed to be messengers but Aunt Rachel was letting them down by not thinking of enough messages). Everybody worked hard on that Saturday, excepting Polly and Clary, who slipped off in the morning on the bus to Hastings . . .

'Who did you ask?'

'Didn't *ask* anyone. I told Ellen.'

'Did you say I was going too?'

'Yeah. I said, "Polly wants to go to Hastings, so I'm going with her." '

'You wanted to go too.'

'Of course I did, or I wouldn't be here, would I?'

'Well, why didn't you say *we* wanted to go?'

'Didn't think of it.'

This was Clary being slippery, which Polly didn't like, but experience had taught her that saying so only made a row, and if this was going to be the last day of peace she didn't want to have a row or anything to spoil it.

But somehow, it wasn't a good day. Polly wanted to get so fascinated by what they were actually going to do that she wouldn't have the chance to think of what might be going to happen. They went to Jepson's, ordinarily a shop that she loved, but when she found Clary was taking ages over choosing which fountain pen she was going to buy (part of the outing was to spend Clary's birthday money) she felt impatient and cross because Clary could take something so trivial so seriously. 'They're always squeaky and hard at first,' she said. 'You know you have to *use* the nib to get it good.'

'I know that. But if I get a wide nib now, it will probably get *too* wide, but the medium one doesn't feel as though it will ever get right.'

Polly looked at the assistant – a young man in a shiny worn suit – who was watching Clary while she licked each nib before she dipped the pen in a bottle of ink and scribbled her name on small pieces of paper on the counter. He did not seem impatient, only bored. He also looked as though this was his most usual expression.

They were in the stationery department of the book shop – rather a backwater since it only sold writing paper, and printed things like addresses on the paper, At Home cards and wedding invitations, and sold fountain pens and pencils. 'It's very important to lick new nibs before you use them,' Clary was saying, 'but I expect you tell people that. Could I try that Waterman – the maroon one – just to see?' It cost twelve and six and Polly knew she would not buy it. She watched the man while Clary tried pen after pen, and he ended up just looking into the distance. He was probably worrying about whether there would be a war.

'What do you see,' Polly asked him, 'in your mind's eye, I mean?'

'I haven't got a mind's eye when I'm trying pens,' Clary said quite crossly.

'I didn't mean you.'

They both looked at the assistant, who cleared his throat, passed his hand over his heavily Brylcreemed hair and said he didn't know what she meant.

'I don't blame you,' Clary said. 'I'll have the Medium Relief—'

'That'll be seven and six,' he said, and Polly could see he was looking forward to being shot of them.

Outside they quarrelled mildly about what Clary described as Polly's idiotic remark. 'At the best, he thought you were patronising him,' she said.

'I wasn't.'

'He *thought* you were.'

'Shut *up*!'

Clary looked at her friend – well, more of a cousin, really; she wasn't *feeling* like a friend . . .

'Sorry. I know you're feeling het up. Look here, Poll. It could still be all right. Think of last year.'

Polly shook her head. She was frowning; she looked suddenly like Aunt Rach when she was trying not to cry over Brahms.

'I know what,' Clary said gently, 'it isn't just that you want me to understand you, you just want me to *feel* the same. Isn't it?'

'I want *someone* to!'

12

'I think both of our fathers do.'

'Yes, but the trouble with them is that they only count *our* feelings up to a point.'

'I know what you mean. It's as though our feelings were simply the size of our bodies – smaller. It is idiotic of them. I suppose they can't remember being children.'

'Not at *their* age! I shouldn't think they can remember more than about five years back.'

'Well, I'm going to make a *point* of remembering. Of course, they cash in by saying that they're responsible for us.'

'Responsible! When they can't even stop a ghastly war that might kill us all! That seems to me to be about as irresponsible as people can get!'

'You're getting het up again,' Clary said. 'What shall we do now?'

'I don't mind. What do you want to do?'

'Get some exercise books and a present for Zoë's birthday. And you said you wanted to buy some wool. We could have doughnuts for lunch. Or baked beans?' They both loved baked beans because Simon and Teddy had them quite a lot at school, but they never got them at home, as they were regarded as rather common food.

They had been walking towards the front. There were not many holidaymakers about although there were some on one bit of beach, sitting uncomfortably on the pebbles with their backs to silvery wood breakwaters, eating sandwiches and ice creams and staring out at the grey-green sea that heaved back and forth in an aimless, surreptitious manner.

'Do you want to bathe?'

But Polly simply shrugged. 'We didn't bring our things, anyway,' she said, although Clary knew that that wouldn't have stopped her if she'd wanted to. Further along – past that bit of beach – some soldiers were hauling huge rolls of barbed wire out of a lorry, and positioning them at regular intervals along the shore where they could see that what looked like concrete posts were sunk in a line at intervals half-way up the beach.

'Let's go and have lunch,' Clary said quickly.

They had baked beans and toast and lovely strong Indian tea (they didn't get that at home either) and a jam doughnut and a cream horn each. This seemed to cheer Polly up, and they talked about quite ordinary things like the sort of person they would marry. Polly thought an explorer would be nice if he would explore hot parts of the earth as she loathed snow and ice and would naturally accompany him, and Clary said a painter because that would fit with writing books and she knew about painters because of her dad. 'Also, painters don't seem to mind so much what people look like; I mean, they like people's faces for quite different reasons, so he wouldn't mind mine too much.'

'You're fine,' Polly said. 'You have beautiful eyes, and they are the most important feature.'

'So have you.'

'Oh, mine are far too small. Awful really. Little dark blue boot buttons.'

'But you have a marvellous complexion – frightfully white and then pale pink, like a heroine in novels. Have you noticed,' she continued dreamily as she licked the last remnants of cream off her fingers, 'how novelists go on and *on* about how their heroines look? It must be frightful for Miss Milliment when she reads them, knowing she could never have been one.'

'They aren't all beautiful as the day,' Polly pointed out. 'Think of Jane Eyre.'

'And you're tremendously lucky with your hair. Although coppery hair does seem to fade with age,' she added, thinking of Polly's mother. 'It gets more like weakish marmalade. Oh, Jane *Eyre*! Mr Rochester goes on like anything about her being so fairylike and small. That's an ingenious way of saying that she looked charming.'

'People want to know that kind of thing. I do hope you aren't going to get too modern in your writing, Clary. So that nobody knows what is going on.' Polly had pinched *Ulysses* from her mother's books and found it very hard going.

'I shall write like me,' said Clary. 'It's no good telling me what to write like.'

'OK. Let's get the rest of our things.'

Lunch cost four and sixpence, which was more than they had bargained for, and Clary handsomely paid it all. 'You can pay me back when it's your birthday,' she said.

'I think Miss Milliment must be used to all that by now. Wanting to marry people wears off quite young, I think.'

'Gosh! Does it? Well, I don't suppose I *shall* marry, then. I don't feel at all strongly about it now, and women over twenty age very rapidly. Look at Zoë.'

'Grief ages people.'

'Everything ages people. Do you know what that drawly lady, Lady Knebworth, Aunt Villy's friend, said to Louise?' When Polly was silent, she added, 'She told her never to raise her eyebrows 'cos it would put lines on her forehead. Quite a good thing for you to know, Polly: you're always frowning when you try to think.'

15

They were outside the tea shop by now, and Clary said, 'What shall I get her for her birthday?'

'Aunt Zoë? I don't know. Soap, I should think, or bath salts, Or a hat,' she added.

'You can't buy people hats, Poll. They only like the awful ones they choose themselves. Isn't it odd?' she continued as they wandered back from the front towards the shops again, 'When you see people in shops choosing their clothes and shoes and stuff, they take *ages* – as though each thing they choose will be amazing and perfect. And then, look at them. They mostly look simply terrible – or just ordinary. They might just as well have chosen their clothes out of a bran tub.'

'Everyone will be wearing uniforms of one kind or another any minute,' Polly said sadly: she was beginning to feel rotten again.

'I think it's an interesting observation,' Clary said, rather hurt. 'I expect it could be applied to other things about people – and turn out to be a serious reflection on human nature.'

'Human nature's not much cop, if you ask me. We wouldn't be in such danger of having a war if it was. Let's get the wool and things and go home.'

So they bought their things: a box of Morny Rose Geranium soap for Zoë, and the exercise books, and Polly bought some hyacinth-blue wool to make herself a jersey. Then they went to wait for the bus.

∞ ∞ ∞

After lunch that Saturday, Hugh and Rupert had gone on an expedition to Battle armed with a formidable list of shopping. Rupert had volunteered for the job and then

Hugh, who had had what nearly amounted to a quarrel with Sybil, offered to accompany his brother. Lists were collected from all three houses of the many and varied requirements and they set off, with Rupert driving the Vauxhall that he had acquired since joining the firm the previous January.

'We shall look pretty bloody silly if it's peace after all,' he said.

After a short silence, he looked at his brother, and Hugh caught his eye. 'We shan't look silly,' he said.

'You got one of your heads?'

'I have not. I was just wondering . . .'

'What?'

'What you had in mind.'

'Oh. Oh – well, I thought I'd try for the Navy.'

'I thought you might.'

'It'll leave you holding the fort on your own, though, won't it?'

'I'll have the Old Man.'

There was a short silence; Rupert knew from his months in the firm that their father was both obstinate and autocratic. Edward was the one who could manage him; Hugh, when he disagreed with an edict, confronted his father with direct and dogged honesty: he had no capacity for manipulation, or tact, as it was sometimes called. They had rows that ended, as often as not, in an uneasy compromise that benefited no one – least of all the firm. Rupert, who was still learning the ropes, had not been able to be much more than an unwilling witness and this summer, when Edward had been away on a volunteer's course, things had seemed much worse. Edward was back, temporarily, but he was simply waiting to be called up. Rupert, whose decision to go into the firm had been made just about the time that Zoë had become pregnant, still wondered whether it had been the right choice. Being an art master had always seemed a stopgap – a kind of apprenticeship to being a full-time painter; becoming a businessman had turned out to preclude his ever doing any painting at all. The imminent prospect of war, providing the opportunity for escape, excited him, although he could hardly admit *that* – even to himself.

'But of course I'll miss you, old boy,' Hugh was saying, with a studied casualness that suddenly touched him: Hugh, like their sister Rachel, always became casual when he was most moved.

'Of course, they might not take me,' Rupert said. He did not believe this, but it was the nearest he could get to comfort.

'Of course they will. I wish *I* could be more use. Those poor bloody Poles. If the Russians hadn't signed that pact, I don't think he'd dare to be where he is.'

'Hitler?'

'Of *course* Hitler. Well, we've had a year's grace. I hope we've made good use of it.'

They had reached Battle and Rupert said, 'I'll park outside Till's, shall I? We seem to have a hell of a lot to get there.'

They spent the next hour buying four dozen Kilner jars, Jeyes Fluid, paraffin, twenty-four small torches with spare batteries, three zinc buckets, enormous quantities of green soap and Lux, four Primus stoves, a quart of methylated spirit, six hot-water bottles, two dozen light bulbs, a pound of half-inch nails and two pounds of tin tacks. They tried to buy another bale of blackout material, but the shop had only three yards left. 'Better buy it,'

Hugh said to Rupert. They bought six reels of black thread and a packet of sewing-machine needles. At the chemist they bought gripe water, Milk of Magnesia, baby oil, Vinolia soap, Amami shampoo, arrowroot and Andrews' Liver Salts and Rupert got a tortoiseshell slide for Clary, who was growing out her fringe and spent much of her time looking like a faithful dog, he said. They picked up two boxes of groceries, ordered by the Duchy and Villy respectively that morning. They bought Goldflake and Passing Cloud cigarettes – for Villy, again, and Rachel. Rupert bought the *Tatler* for Zoë, and Hugh bought a copy of *How Green Was My Valley* for Sybil – she loved reading the latest books and it had been well reviewed. Then they consulted the list again, and realised that the shop hadn't included the order for Malvern water for the Duchy.

'Anything else?'

'Something that looks like ships bras?'

'Sheep's brains,' Hugh said knowledgeably. 'For Wills. Sybil thinks he'll die if he doesn't have them once a week.' So they went to the butcher, who said that Mrs Cazalet Senior had just rung and wanted an ox tongue of which he happened to have one left and he'd only just put it in the brine so it wouldn't need much soaking, tell the cook. 'If you don't mind, sir,' he added. He was used to Mr Tonbridge coming in for the meat if the ladies didn't come themselves, which was seldom. If anything was needed to make him feel that things were in a funny old state, it was gentlemen doing the shopping, he thought as he wrapped the brains in greaseproof paper and then brown. The boy was sweeping the floor – they'd be closing soon – and he had to speak sharply to him not to get sawdust on the gentlemen's trousers.

Outside, the street was fuller than usual: several pregnant mothers with pasty-faced children in tow were wandering up and down, staring disconsolately into the shop
windows, and then moving on a few yards.

'Evacuees,' Rupert said. 'I suppose we're lucky not to
have any of them. The Babies' Hotel is a much easier bet.
At least babies don't have nits and lice, and don't complain about it being too quiet and not being able to eat
the food.'

'Is that what they do?'

'That's what Sybil says Mrs Cripps says that Mr York
says Miss Boot says.'

'Good Lord!'

When they got into their laden car, Hugh said, 'What
do you think about the children staying where they are?'

Slightly startled, Rupert said, 'You mean our lot?'

'Yes.'

'Well, where else can they go? They certainly can't be
in London.'

'We could send them further into the country. Away
from the coast. Suppose there's an invasion?'

'Oh, honestly, I don't think we can look that far ahead.
Light me a cigarette, would you? What does Sybil think?'
he went on when Hugh had done so.

'She's being a bit awkward about it all. Wants to come
to London herself to look after me. I can't have that, of
course. We nearly had a row,' he added, surprised again
by the awful, unusual fact. 'In the end, I shut her up by
saying I'd live with you. I never meant it,' he said, 'I
knew you wouldn't be in London anyway. But she didn't.
She's just a bit on edge. Much better for the family to stay
together. And I can get down at weekends, after all.'

'Will you keep your house open?'

'Have to see. It depends whether I can get anyone to look after me. If not, I can always stay at my club.' Visions occurred of endless dreary evenings eating with chaps he didn't really want to spend the evening with.

But Rupert, who knew his brother's home-loving habits, and briefly imagined poor old Hugh on his own in a club, said, 'You could always come up and down in the train with the Old Man.'

Hugh shook his head. 'Someone's got to be in London at night. That's when they'll drop their bombs. Can't leave the blokes to cope with the wharf by themselves.'

'You'll miss Edward, won't you?'

'I'll miss both of you. Still, old crocks can't be choosers.'

'Someone has to keep the home fire burning.'

'Actually, old boy, I think people will be keener on me putting them out.'

A moment later, he added, 'You're the only person I've ever met who actually hoots when he laughs.'

'It's awful, isn't it? I was called Factory at school.'

'Never knew that.'

'You were away most of the time.'

'Oh, well, the position is shortly to be reversed.'

Hugh's tone, both bitter and humble, touched Rupert, who instinctively glanced at the black stump that rested on his brother's knee. God! Think of going through life with no left hand because someone else had blown it off. Still it *is* his *left* hand. But I'm left-handed – it would have been worse for me. Slightly ashamed of his egocentricity, and wanting Hugh to feel better he said, 'Your Polly is a pearl. And she's getting prettier every day.'

And Hugh, his face lighting up, said instantly, 'Isn't she just? For the Lord's sake don't tell her.'

21

'I wasn't thinking of doing that, but why not? I always tell Clary things like that.'

Hugh opened his mouth to say that was different, and shut it again. It was all right in his book to tell people they were beautiful when they weren't; it was when they *were* that you had to shut up. 'I don't want her getting ideas,' he said vaguely, and Rupert, knowing this was Cazalet for getting above oneself, the only-pebble-on-the-beach syndrome with which he too had been brought up, deemed it better, or easier, to agree.

'Of course not,' he said.

∞ ∞ ∞

Raymond Castle sat with his eldest daughter in Lyons' Corner House at Tottenham Court Road.

'Daddy, for the hundredth time, I'm perfectly OK. Honestly.'

'I dare say you are, but your mother and I would prefer you to be in the country, with us and the rest of the family.'

'I do wish you would stop treating me like a child. I'm *twenty*.'

I know that, he thought. If he'd been treating her as a child, he'd simply have *told* her she was bloody well packing her bags and getting into the car with him and the old trout and the governess. Now he was reduced to *preferring* . . .

'And anyway, I couldn't possibly come today: I've got a party tonight.'

There was a silence during which, in going through the familiar, and often unsuccessful, motions of not losing his temper, he recognised wearily that he had no temper

22

to lose. She defeated him – by her appearance, a confusing blend of Jessica when he had married her but missing the romantic innocence and sheer untried *youngness* that had so enthralled him. Angela's golden hair, that a year ago had hung so engagingly in a long page-boy bob, was now drawn back severely from her forehead, with a centre parting and secured by a narrow plait of her own hair (he assumed) exposing her face with its perfectly plucked eyebrows, smooth, pale make-up and poppy-red mouth. She wore a pale grey linen fitted coat, and a wisp of amber chiffon scarf at her white neck. She looked fashionable (he called it smart), but utterly remote. That was the other way in which she defeated him: by her manner of completely and indifferently withdrawing from any communication with him at all beyond the meaningless, well-worn clichés in response to any questions. 'I'm fine', 'Nobody *you*'d know', 'I'm not a child', 'Nothing much', 'What does it *matter*?'

'Good party?'

'I don't know. I haven't been to it yet.' She replied without looking at him. She picked up her cup and finished her coffee, then looked pointedly at his. She wanted them to go – to put an end to what he felt she saw as merely idle curiosity. He called the nippie over and paid their bill.

The idea of calling on her in the flat that she shared with an unknown girl friend and taking her out to lunch had occurred to him as he drove over Waterloo Bridge on his mission to collect Lady Rydal and the governess. 'Your good deed for about a week, I should think, old boy,' Edward had said that morning, but he had been quite glad to take on the task: he did not like situations where he was not in control, and in Sussex it was the Old

Man who ran the show. If he just turned up, he might find out what was going on because he could not see for the life of him why she would be so secretive unless there was something to be secretive *about*. He'd wondered whether he'd better telephone first, but decided that that would defeat the object. Which was . . . ? Well, he *was* her father and really she shouldn't be left in London on her own in the circumstances. He must try to get her to come down with him. *That* was why he was going to see her. He'd feel pretty bloody terrible if he'd come all this way, and then simply left her in town with the chance of getting blown up. Virtue succeeded the slightly uncomfortable feelings; he was somebody for whom self-righteousness was often a boon. He'd rung the top bell of the house in Percy Street and waited an age, but nobody came. He put his finger on the bell and kept it there. What the hell was going on? he kept asking himself as various hellish on-goings occurred to him. By the time a girl – not Angela – stuck her head out of an upper window and shouted 'Who is it?' he was feeling quite angry.

'I've come to see Angela,' he shouted back, as he limped down the steps in order to see the girl.

'Yeah, but who is it?' she replied.

'Tell her it's her father.'

'Her *father*?' An incredulous laugh. 'OK. Whatever you say.' He was just about to mount the steps again – trying, because of his leg – when he heard the girl's voice again. 'She's asleep.' She made it sound as though that was that.

'Well, let me in and wake her up. In that order,' he added.

'OK.' The voice sounded resigned now. While he waited, he looked at his watch as though he didn't know the time. Well, he didn't, exactly, but it was well after twelve. In bed at noon? Good God!

The girl who opened the door to him was young with straight brown hair and small brown eyes. 'It's quite a long way up,' she said as soon as she perceived his limp.

He followed her up two flights of stairs that were covered with worn linoleum and smelled faintly of cats, and finally into a room that contained, among much else, an unmade bed, a tray on the floor in front of the gas fire that held the remnants of a meal, a small sink with a dripping tap, a sea-green carpet covered with stains and a small sagging armchair in which crouched a large marmalade cat. 'Get off, Orlando. Do sit down,' she added. The gas fire, filled with broken and blackened elements, was roaring. 'I was making toast,' the girl said. She looked at him doubtfully, not supposing that he would want any. 'It's all right. I've woken her. We went to a party last night and were jolly late, only I got up early because we hadn't any milk, and, anyway, I was starving.'

There was quite a long silence.

'Do go on with your meal,' he said.

At once she began hacking at the sloping loaf of bread. Then, without looking up, she said, 'You really *are* her father, aren't you? I recognise you now. Sorry,' she added. For what? he wondered. For the incredulous laugh? For Angela, having this old crock of a father who turned up without warning?

'Do a lot of mock fathers come flocking to the door?'

'Not exactly *flocking*—' she began, but was interrupted by Angela, miraculously – it seemed to him – made up and with her hair elaborately done. She wore a dressing gown and her feet were bare.

'I've come to take you out to lunch,' he said, trying to sound assured and festive about it.

She allowed him to kiss her, then, looking at the room with a certain distaste, said she would just get dressed and they could go.

In the street, he said, 'Where shall we go?'

She shrugged. 'I don't want any lunch. Anywhere you like.'

In the end they walked down Percy Street and along Tottenham Court Road to Lyons' Corner House, where he worked his way through a plate of roast lamb, potatoes and carrots, while she sipped coffee.

'Sure you couldn't fall for a Knickerbocker Glory?' he asked. When she had been goodness knew how much younger, these fearful concoctions had been her greatest treat. But she simply looked at him as though he was mad, and said no thank you. After that, he chatted feverishly, telling her about collecting her grandmother and Miss Milliment, and it was when her face cleared at the mention of this last name that he realised how angry she had been throughout the meal. 'I did like Miss Milliment,' she said, and some indefinable expression crossed her face and was gone almost before he saw it. It was then that he apologised for turning up without warning.

'Why *did* you come, anyway?' she said. It was some sort of faint acknowledgement of the apology, and he launched into it having been on the spur of the moment, and thence to his wanting to get her out of London. Now they were about to go, and the whole meeting had been a wash-out. When they reached his car, parked outside her house, he said, 'Well, perhaps you'd ring Mummy up, would you? She's at the new house. Watlington three four.'

'We're not on the phone, but I'll try. Thanks for the coffee.' She presented him with her cheek, turned and ran up the steps to her house, turning in the doorway only, he felt, to be sure that he was really going to get into his car and leave. Which he did.

During the rest of that arduous day – which he mismanaged in a number of stupid ways: fetching his mother-in-law *before* Miss Milliment was the first (Lady Rydal seemed to feel that even being driven in a motor car to Stoke Newington was some kind of insult) and getting Miss Milliment, whose luggage was singularly difficult to pack into the car with Lady Rydal's (he had to fix up the roof rack which took ages), and then running out of petrol before he even got through the Blackwall Tunnel, and then getting a puncture on the hill just before Sevenoaks (not his fault this, but regarded by Lady Rydal who was an authority on them, as the last straw) – during all this awful, cumbersome day, he ruminated on the miserable encounter with his eldest daughter. In her behaviour to him he saw a reflection of himself that he could neither bear nor discountenance: a middle-aged man, irascible and disappointed, good for nothing that interested him, bullying people in order to infect them with his discomfort – particularly, he knew, his own children. Jessica he did not bully; he lost his temper with her, but he did not bully. He loved her – adored her. He was always contrite on those occasions, would spend the ensuing hours, or even days, paying her small, devoted attentions, castigating himself to her about his wretched temperament and luck, and she, bless her angelic heart, would always forgive him. Always . . . How alike these occasions were to one another now struck him; there had become something ritual about them. If either had forgotten the next line the other could have prompted. And had he not noticed, in the last year or so, that there was something mechanical about her responses to him? Did she really care? Had he, perhaps, become something of a bore? All his life he had been afraid of not being liked: he hadn't been brainy enough for his father, and his mother had only adored Robert, his older brother, killed in the war. But when he had met Jessica, fallen instantly and wildly in love with her, and she had returned his love, he had not cared at all about whether other people liked him or not: he had been entirely fulfilled and overwhelmed by this beautiful, desirable creature's love. Dozens of people would have wanted to marry Jessica, but she had become his. How full of dreams and ardour to succeed for her sake he had been then! What schemes he had had to make money, to give her a life of luxury and romantic ease! There was nothing he would not have done for her but, somehow, nothing had worked out as he had planned. The guest house, the chicken farm, growing mushrooms, a crammer for dull little boys, the kennels venture: each plan had become smaller and wilder as it succeeded the previous failure. He was no good at business – simply hadn't been brought up to it – and, he had to admit, he was not very good with people, with anyone, excepting Jessica. When the children had come along he had been jealous of them for the time they took away from him. When Angela was born, only a year after he was invalided out of the army, Jessica seemed unable to think of anything else; she had been a difficult baby, never sleeping for more than an hour or two at a stretch throughout, which meant that neither of them got a proper night's sleep, and then when Nora arrived, Angela resented her so much that Jessica could not leave them alone together for a minute, and of course they'd never been able to afford a nurse, or more than a bit of daily help. When Christopher was born, he thought, at least he had a son, but he'd turned out the worst of the lot – always something wrong with him, bad eyesight, a weak stomach and he'd nearly died of a mastoid when he was five, and Jessica had spoiled him so he'd become more namby-pamby than ever, afraid of everything – and nothing *he* did made any difference. He remembered how he'd staged a fireworks show for them when they were small, and Christopher had howled because he didn't like the bangs, and how he'd taken them to the zoo and for a ride on an elephant, and Christopher had refused to get on the animal, made a frightful scene – *in public*. Jessica kept saying he was sensitive, but he was simply a milksop, which brought out the worst in Raymond. Somewhere, in the depths, he knew that he had bullied Christopher, and hated them both for it. The boy *asked* for it: his shaking hands, his clumsiness, his white-faced silences when gibed at provoked Raymond to irresistible fury that he could only temper to irritation. When *his* father had got at him, for not being brainy, he'd just gone off and done something else – damn well. He'd got his blue for rugger and for rowing; he'd been a first-class shot, the best diver in his school, so there had been plenty of things for his pater to be proud of if he'd cared to. He never had, of course, had simply continued to make him feel a fool about not knowing things he hadn't cared about. The army had been a wonderful way out for him. He'd done jolly well, had become a captain by the outbreak of the war, then become a major, got decorated, married Jessica and had a heavenly fortnight's leave in Cornwall with her – and then Ypres, the third battle, which was when he lost his leg. That had felt like the end of the world; it had certainly been the end of his career. He'd fought endless battles about not being sorry for himself and, on the whole, he thought he had won, although he supposed it had made him harder on other people – all those fortunate chaps with two legs who could do what they liked; he had never felt that any of them had the slightest notion what it was like to be *him*. They hadn't meant to have Judy at all: he'd had to take a job in the school to bring down the school fees (schoolmasters got very reduced rates) and it had helped with Christopher, at least. Aunt Lena had helped a bit with the girls from time to time; the only trouble about that had been that she never told him in advance what she was going to do, so he and Jessica never knew where they were. At least now, with Aunt Lena dead, they'd got some money and a far nicer house, but it was a bit late in the day to make the difference it would once have made. His children who, when younger he realised now, had been afraid of him, were becoming indifferent.

They did not behave in the same way about this: Angela snubbed him, made it clear that he bored her; Christopher avoided him whenever possible and was studiously polite when he could not; Nora and Judy both had special voices for talking to him, bright accommodating voices – he suspected Judy of copying Nora, and both of them of imitating Jessica, who employed a kind of determined serenity whenever he became at all touchy. The effect was to make him feel isolated from the family life that they had with each other, and which he seemed excluded from sharing.

By now he had changed the tyre and wedged the punctured one into the overcrowded boot and got back into the car with its silent occupants. Miss Milliment smiled at him and murmured something about being sorry not to have been of any use, and Lady Rydal, to whom the idea of being of use to anyone had never occurred in her life, said crushingly, 'Really, Miss Milliment! I do not think that mending the puncture of a *car* can be said to be part of a governess's repertory.' After a pause, she added, 'A puncture is nothing to what we must expect to put up with.' All the remaining journey he wished, with savage hopelessness, that he was on his own, driving to Aunt Lena's house in Frensham, where Jessica (and no one else) would be waiting with tea for him on the lawn, instead of chauffeuring the old trout and a governess back to the Cazalet Holiday Camp.

∞ ∞ ∞

By four o'clock on Saturday afternoon, Sybil and Villy had to stop their blackout activities as they had run out of material. Sybil said she was dying for a cup of tea, and Villy said she would brave the kitchen to make some.

'Brave was the right word,' she said some minutes later as she brought a tray out onto the lawn where Sybil had put two deckchairs for them. 'Louise and Nora are cooking a vast supper for the nurses and Emily is simply sitting in her basket chair pretending they aren't there. They're really very courageous; I don't think I could stand it. I've already told her it was an emergency, but she simply looks at me as though I make it up.'

'Do you think she'll give notice?'

Villy shrugged. 'Quite possible. She's done it before.

But she adores Edward so she's always changed her mind. But, of course, Edward won't be *here*, and I doubt if a combination of the country and cooking for a whole lot of women and children will have much lasting appeal.'

'Edward really will go?'

'If he possibly can. That is to say if they'll take him. They won't take Hugh,' she added as she saw her sister-in-law's face. 'I'm sure they will say he's needed to run the firm.'

'He says he will be living in London, though,' Sybil said. 'I've told him I won't let him live in that house alone. I should go mad worrying about him.'

'But you couldn't have Wills in London!'

'I know. But Ellen could look after Wills and Roland, couldn't she? And you'll be here, won't you? Because of Roland?' The idea that anyone could leave a six-month-old baby seemed out of the question to her.

Villy lit a cigarette. 'I honestly haven't thought,' she said. Which was not true. She *had* thought, constantly, during the last weeks, that if only she hadn't saddled herself with a baby, she could now do all kinds of useful – and interesting – things. She loved him, of course she *loved* him, but he was perfectly happy with Ellen who was delighted to have babies to look after, instead of Neville and Lydia who were becoming too much for her in some ways and nothing like enough in others. To spend the war being a grass widow and ordering a household seemed both dreary and absurd to her. With all her Red Cross experience, she could easily nurse, or train VADs, or run a convalescent home or work in a canteen . . . It would be far better if Sybil held the domestic fort: she had no ambitions beyond looking after her husband and her children. Villy looked across the tea table at Sybil, who sat, with the blue socks she was knitting on her lap, twisting a small white handkerchief in her fingers.

'I *can't* leave Hugh in London by himself,' she said. 'He doesn't like clubs and parties like Edward, and he can't manage in the house on his own, but when I try to talk to him about it, he just gets shirty and says I think he's useless.' Her rather faded blue eyes met Villy's and then looked away as they filled with tears. 'Oh dear,' she said. 'I'm about to make a fool of myself.' She stabbed at her eyes with the handkerchief, blew her nose, and drank some tea. 'It's all so *beastly*! We've almost never had a row about anything. He almost accused me of not minding enough about Wills!' She shook her head violently to negate such an idea, and her untidy hair started to fall down.

'Darling, I'm sure there will be a solution. Let's wait and see what happens.'

'There's not much else we can do, is there?' She picked some hairpins from her lap and out of her head and began twisting the tail of her hair into a bun.

'What makes it *worse*,' she said, through a mouthful of hairpins, 'is that I can perfectly well see that it's a trivial problem compared to what most people are going to have to endure.'

'Thinking of people worse off than oneself only makes one feel worse,' Villy said; she was familiar with this situation. 'I mean, you simply feel bad about feeling bad, which doesn't help at all.'

Louise came out of the house with a plate on which were two steaming Bath buns.

'I thought you might like to try my buns,' she said. 'The first batch has just come out of the oven.'

'I won't, thank you, darling,' Villy said at once. Since Roland, she had put on weight.

'I'd *love* one,' Sybil said: she had seen Louise's face when her mother refused. She should have taken one, she thought.

She shouldn't eat buns, Villy thought. Sybil had also put on weight after Wills, but she did not seem to mind – just laughed when she couldn't get into her frocks and bought larger ones.

'Goodness! How delicious! Just like the shop ones, but better.'

'You can have them both if you like. I'm making masses for the nurses. Emily wouldn't have one either,' she added, putting her mother firmly into Emily's category which she hoped would annoy her. 'She can't bear me being able to make them. She's being horrible to Nora about her shepherd's pies, but Nora has the back of a duck. I wish I did. She doesn't notice people being horrible to her at all.'

'You will clear up properly, won't you?'

'We've *said* we would.' Louise answered with the exaggerated patience that she hoped was withering and went back into the house, her long, glossy hair bouncing against her thin shoulders.

'She has shot up in the last year, hasn't she?'

'Yes, she's outgrown practically everything. I'm afraid she's going to be too tall. She's dreadfully clumsy. Apparently she broke the record for smashing crockery at the domestic science place.'

'That's part of shooting up so fast, isn't it? They aren't used to the size they have suddenly become. It's different for you, Villy, you've always been so small – and neat. Simon is just the same: accident prone.'

'Oh, well, boys! One expects them to knock things about. Even Teddy breaks things a bit. But Louise is simply *careless*. She's always been difficult with me, but she's even rude to Edward now. It was quite a relief to get her away to school, although whether that place will be much *use* to her, I don't know.'

'Well, the Bath buns are a triumph.'

'Yes, darling, but when have you ever been expected to make Bath buns? At least they teach them how to interview a servant, but things like goffering a *surplice* – I mean, *really*! When could that be said to be a useful accomplishment?'

'Invaluable if you married a clergyman.'

'I feel that Nora is the most likely to do that.'

'She would be wonderful, wouldn't she? Kind and good and so *sensible*.' They could at least be in agreement about all other virtues being accorded to plain girls.

'But Louise would be far too selfish,' Villy finished. 'Where do you think those children can have got to? I told them to be back for tea.'

'Which ones?'

'Lydia and Neville. They seem to spend all their time at Home Place; they're hardly here at all.'

'Well, they were furious at being put here with the babies—' Sybil began, but Villy interrupted, 'Yes, I know. But I didn't want there to be room for Zoë and Rupert because I thought being with our babies would be so hard on Zoë.'

'You're quite right. Poor little Zoë. I must say having the Babies' Hotel evacuated onto us isn't exactly going to help, though, is it?'

'No. But perhaps she's—'

'Do *you* think so?'

35

'I don't know. But Edward told Rupert that the best thing would be to get on with having another one, and Rupert seemed to agree, so it's possible.'

'Oh, good.' Sybil did not say that Rupert had asked Hugh what he thought, and that Hugh had advised a six-months gap to give Zoë time to get over her loss, and that Rupert had seemed to think that this was a capital idea.

But Villy caught her eye and said, 'I expect he asked Hugh, who told him exactly the opposite?'

'How did you guess?'

'Darling old Rupe,' said Villy as she collected the tea things.

'All the same, I think it would be better if he simply asked Zoë,' Sybil said.

∞ ∞ ∞

Zoë had been given the task of picking the quantities of ripe Victoria plums of which there was a glut. 'But they mustn't be wasted,' the Duchy had said that morning. 'So, Zoë dear, if you strip the kitchen garden trees, we can have plum tarts and bottle the rest. Do mind the wasps.' She had found the largest trug there was in the greenhouse, and the small ladder which she had lugged to the kitchen garden wall and methodically stripped each espaliered tree. It was better than sewing with the aunts, and better than trying to write her weekly mean-ingless letter to her mother who was paying a visit of indefinite duration to her friend in the Isle of Wight. Since last year, Zoë had tried to be kinder to her mother, to pay her more attention, but the most she seemed able to manage was not to be *un*kind. Ever since June when she had lost the baby she had been sunk in an apathy so entire that she found it easier to be alone. Alone, she did not have to make any effort to be 'bright' as she called it; she did not have to contend with sympathy or kindness that either made her feel irritable or want to cry. It seemed to her as though for the rest of her life she was going to have to endure undeserved attentions, to attempt insincere responses, to be seen continuously in the wrong light and also, she could foresee, be expected to 'recover' from what everybody excepting herself perceived as a natural tragedy. Pregnancy had been quite as arduous as she had imagined; nothing they predicted happened as they said it would. The morning sickness that was supposed to last only three months persisted throughout, and did not confine itself to the mornings. Her back ached for the last four months so that no position was ever comfortable, and her nights were broken every two or three hours by trips to the lavatory. Her ankles swelled and her teeth developed endless cavities, and for the first time in her life she experienced both boredom and anxiety in equal proportions. Whenever she was feeling really bored, not well enough to do anything that interested her, the anxiety began. If it was Philip's child, would it *look* like him? Would everybody immediately see that it was not Rupert's child? How would she feel about a child whom she would have to pretend was Rupert's if she knew that it wasn't? At those times, the desire to tell somebody, to confess and be berated, even *not* to be forgiven, but simply to *tell* someone, became overwhelming, but she managed never to do that. She was so depressed that the notion that it could as well *be* Rupert's child hardly ever struck her. And Rupert had been so sweet to her! His tenderness, his patience and affection had continued

throughout her sickness, her frequent tears, her with-
drawals into sullen bouts of self-pity, her irritability (how
could he understand her when he knew nothing?), her
reiterated apology for being so hopeless at the whole
thing (this when her guilt was its most oppressive) – he
seemed willing to contain anything that she was through
all those months, until at last she'd had the baby, at home
with the midwife that the family always used for their
births. Hours and hours of agony, and then Rupert, who
had stayed with her, had brought the bathed and
wrapped bundle to lay in her arms. 'There, my darling
girl. Isn't he beautiful?' She had looked down at the small
head with its shock of black hair, at the tiny wizened
yellow face – he was born badly jaundiced – framed by
the lacy white shawl the Duchy had made. She had stared
at the high forehead, the long upper lip and *known*. She
had looked up at Rupert, whose face was grey with
fatigue, and unable to bear the innocence of his anxiety,
and concern, and love, had shut her eyes as scalding tears
forced their way out. That had been the worst moment of
all: she had not imagined having to accept his pride and
joy. 'I'm dreadfully tired,' she had said. It had come out
like a whine. The midwife had taken the baby away and
said that she must have a nice rest, and Rupert had kissed
her and she was alone. She had lain rigid, unable to sleep
due to the thought that she would never now be free of
this consuming lie: that little, alien creature would grow
and grow, and become more and more like Philip, whom
by then she had begun to hate, and the thought that only
its death would have released her had horribly occurred.
Or mine, she had thought: it had felt slightly better to
wish for one's own death rather than someone else's. And
then, in less than a week the baby *was* dead. It had always

been sickly, had never thrived, either would not feed from her abundance of milk, or if it did, threw up, hardly slept because it was always crying weakly – from colic, they said – but afterwards the midwife had said something about a twisted intestine, and that it had never had a chance. It had been Rupert who had told her that it had died (she had refused to think of a name for it); his distress for her had been the last piercing thing before a great bleak calm descended upon her. It was over. A terrible thirst and pain for days until the milk went, leaving her with stripes all over the beautiful breasts she had once prized so much. She had not even cared about that; she had not cared about anything at all. Her relief was too dangerous for her to accept it – had she not wished it to die? – and so she remained in the isolation of withholding the only things that she wanted to say to the only person who loved her. She took a long time to recover – was tired all the time, slept long nights and heavily in the afternoons, waking exhausted by her stupor. She was surrounded by kindness from the whole family, but curiously it had only been Clary who had reached her. She had woken from a sleep on the sofa one afternoon in their drawing room to find Clary carefully setting a tray of tea on the table beside her. She had made some scones, she said, her first scones actually; she wasn't sure that they were much good. They hadn't been: rock hard and surprisingly heavy. 'It's the thought that counts,' she had said mechanically.

The atmosphere had been full of rather watery goodwill, but Clary had answered, 'Yes, but it only counts for the person who thinks it, doesn't it? I mean, it's a good thing other people don't know a lot of one's thoughts. I used to wish you were dead, for instance. It's quite all right, I don't any more. It was pretty bad for me thinking that – just sometimes, of course – but it would have been worse for you if you'd known. I hated you for not being my mother, you see. But now I'm awfully glad you never tried to be her. I can think of you as a friend.'

Her eyes had filled with tears – and she hadn't cried for weeks – and Clary had sat quite still on the stool by the low table, and the silent warmth and steadiness of her gaze were a wonderful relief. There was no need to try to stop crying, nor to explain or apologise or lie about it. When she had finished, she couldn't find a handkerchief, and Clary slid the tray cloth from under the tea things, spilling the milk a bit, and handed it to her. Then she said, 'The thing is that with mothers and babies, they can go on having them, but with children and mothers they only get one.' She put a finger on one of the beads of milk on the table and licked it. 'I hope you don't think I'm trying to minimise your bereavement. All I mean really is that one can get better from almost anything. It's just one of those amazing things. That's why people like Hamlet were so frightened of hell. It not stopping, and personally, that's why I don't believe in it. I think everything changes while you're alive, and simply stops when you're dead. Of course I may change my mind in the years to come, but there's plenty of time. Even *you* have quite a lot of time, because if you really *are* only twenty-four, you're only ten years older than me.'

She got called by Ellen soon after that, who told her to come and clear up the mess she'd made in the kitchen.

'Sorry about the scones,' she said, as she collected the tray. 'They tasted quite nice before I cooked them. The metamorphosis was unsatisfactory, I can't think why.'

After Clary had gone she lay thinking about what had

been said – and not said – but when she reached the point where Clary had said, 'I can think of you as a friend,' she found she was crying again. She had no experience of friends.

She had made various resolutions after that: to look for a new house (they had not moved after all, partly because of her pregnancy and partly because although Rupert was paid more by the family firm than he had earned as a schoolmaster, it was not yet enough to finance a move), to entertain for Rupert; but here she ran into the difficulty that Ellen, who had taken over the cooking since the children were now both at school all day, was not really up to more than plain nursery food, ill-suited to the sophisticated occasions she had in mind. Somehow, nothing came of any idea or plan and it did not seem to matter very much that it didn't. She sometimes thought that perhaps there were other more serious or difficult resolutions to be made, but they seemed at once so far-reaching and amorphous – intangible to her mind – that she was afraid that if she even understood them they would turn out to be possible only for someone quite different from herself. Some things were better. She no longer resented Clary and Neville, who in any case seemed to need less of Rupert's time and attention. Neville, who was now at a day school, kept her at courteous, breezy arm's length – it was Ellen he talked to or his father. With Clary it was different. She sensed that Clary did try, had good intentions, never failing to notice and admire any new clothes that she wore. She responded by trying to help Clary with her appearance, but, except for one party dress that she made herself for her, Clary had no interest. When she took her shopping, Clary never wanted the things she chose: 'I just feel silly in it,' she said when Zoë

41

had found her a perfectly sweet serge sailor suit with brass buttons. In any case, she tore, split, got ink on and outgrew everything. She was hard on her clothes, Ellen said, as she endlessly washed and ironed and mended them.

With Rupert, she was in limbo. All the feelings that he had had for her, she had accepted without question. He thought she was beautiful and desirable, so of course he loved her. But all last year she had been neither of those things and, humiliated by her gross appearance and the nauseating symptoms that had gone with that, she also felt humiliated by his kindness. She wanted him to adore her, but this – no one knew it better than she – was impossible: nobody who was pregnant could be adorable. She had not even wanted him to make love to her, and as soon as he realised this he had desisted: 'It does not matter in the least,' he had said. In the least?

She had agreed to come to Sussex for the children's holidays, had not even minded very much that Rupert, due to his new job, no longer had the same free time but, like his brothers, was only able to take two weeks off and come down at weekends. It was easier to be alone. She read a great deal: mostly novels – G.B. Stern, Ethel Mannin, Howard Spring, Angela Thirkell, Mary Webb, Mazo de la Roche – and some biographies chiefly, when she could find them, of kings' mistresses. She read Agatha Christie, but could not get on with Dorothy Sayers. She read *Jane Eyre* and quite enjoyed it, tried *Wuthering Heights* but could not understand it at all. Since being in the country, the person she found it easiest to be with had surprisingly turned out to be the Duchy, who asked her one day whether she would do the flowers. Up until then, her relationship with her mother-in-law had consisted of calm courtesy and her own slightly over-careful politeness, but this summer she had sometimes found the Duchy's eye upon her with a look of reflective kindness that was not in the least intrusive since it seemed to need no response. She had recognised that the offer for her to do the flowers was a gesture; she tried very hard and found that she enjoyed doing them and was actually good at it. From there, she picked with the Duchy and began to learn the names of different roses and so forth, and later, at her request, the Duchy taught her how to smock – another skill which she acquired. The Duchy never mentioned the baby – Zoë had been afraid that their increased intimacy might lead to that, and that she would have to say things she did not feel or mean under that direct and honest gaze, but this never happened – nor did the Duchy, by any remote implication, suggest that she should have another baby. Because the thought of this, which sometimes seemed her only future, hung heavily over her, unmentioned but somehow implicit. In the Cazalet family, wives had children – several of them – it was normal and expected. Neither Sybil nor Villy appeared to have the horror that she felt about the whole business; they seemed to her blessed with the full set of maternal feelings, disregard for their own bodies or discomfort or pain and, what was more, they seemed invariably delighted by the results, whereas she found babies mildly disgusting, and most children, at least until they reached Clary's age, a nuisance. It was these feelings that held her in thrall; she was not like them, and while a year ago she had felt superior, more beautiful and therefore interesting, now she felt inferior – a coward, a freak, somebody they would all be horrified to have in their midst if they knew. So she clung to her convalescence,

'Why not, pray?' said Lydia, imitating her mother at her most formidable.

'Because every time your hair gets longer, you'll get taller. It'll sap your strength,' he warned. He had heard Ellen saying that. 'Ladies have been known to die of having too long hair. They get weaker and weaker and on the fifth day they are dead.'

'You didn't make that up, I know where it comes from. It's Augustus not eating in that frightening book. *I* know. Mr York has got evacuees. Why don't we go and see them?'

'We might as well. We can't go back past the cottage. They might see us. We can go on our stomachs through the corn in front, or through the wood and round the back.'

'Quicker round the back.' Lydia knew that going through corn any old way made people cross.

'What *are* evacuees?' she asked, as they trotted through the small copse and into the field at the back of Pear Tree Cottage.

'Children from London.'

'But we're children from London.'

'I should think children from London whose parents can't be bothered with them in a war.'

'Poor *them*! You mean their mothers just – let them go?'

'*I* don't know. I should think policemen take them away,' he added vaguely. He knew that Lydia could be boring on the subject of mothers. 'I manage perfectly well without one,' he offered. 'I have all my life.'

There was a pause, and then Lydia said, 'I don't think I'd like to be looked after by Mr York. Or horrible housekeeping Miss Boot. Although they have got a sweet little outdoor lav.'

They climbed the five-barred gate that led into the farmyard. It was very quiet excepting for two or three brown hens who were walking about eating very small things they suddenly found. A large tortoiseshell cat was crouched upon one of the posts of the smaller gate that led into the farmhouse garden. The gate was shut; they looked over it into the garden, which was full of cabbages and sunflowers and white butterflies and an apple tree so drooping with fruit that its branches were hunched like someone carrying heavy shopping. There was no sign of the evacuees.

'They must be in the house.'

'Go and knock on the door.'

'*You* go.' Lydia was rather frightened of Miss Boot, who always looked to her as though she might really be somebody else.

'All right.' Neville lifted the latch and walked softly up the narrow brick path to the white latticed porch. He knocked on the door. Nothing happened.

'Knock louder,' Lydia said from the other side of the gate.

He did; the door flew open and Miss Boot stood there – like a jack-in-a-box.

'We heard you had some evacuees,' Neville said politely, 'and we've come to see them.'

'They're out. I told them to stay out till I call them to their tea.'

'Do you know where they've gone?'

'Gone? It won't be far. They don't go far. I shouldn't go worrying after *them*. I'd go home to my mother if I was you.'

'I don't have one,' Neville said gravely. He knew from experience that this always made a difference with ladies. It did: she suddenly looked much nicer, and went and fetched him a piece of cake.

'But I can't eat it,' he said to Lydia, as they walked back into the yard. 'It's got seeds in it. And – *she's* got a seed growing out of her face. It must have fallen onto her when she was making the cake.'

'It can't be a seed.'

'*Yes!* It was a sort of brown blob with little sprouts. It was a seed, you bet. Want some?'

'I'm not hungry. Let's give it to the hens, but round the cowshed in case she sees.'

In the cowshed they found the evacuees – two boys and a girl. They sat huddled in a corner, quite silent, and apparently doing nothing at all. They stared at each other for a bit, then Lydia said, 'Hallo. We've come to see you. What are your names?'

There was a further silence. 'Norma,' the girl said at last; she was clearly the oldest. 'Tommy, and Robert.'

'I'm Lydia, and this is Neville. How old are you?'

'Nine,' the girl said. 'And Robert's seven and Tommy's six.'

'We're both eight.'

'We don't like it here,' Norma said. Tommy started to snuffle. She boxed his ear, and he was instantly quiet. She put a protective arm round him.

'Nah,' Robert said. 'We want to go 'ome.'

'Well, I don't suppose you can,' Neville said. 'Not if there's a war. You'd be bombed. I expect in a few years you'll be able to go back.'

Tommy's face contracted. He took a deep, shuddering breath and turned bright red.

'Jeepers!' the girl said. 'Now you've ruddy well gone and done it.' She banged Tommy on the back and a wail burst from him. 'Want to go 'ome *now*,' he wept. 'Want my mum.' He drummed his heels on the ground. 'I want her *now*!'

'Poor boy!' Lydia cried, as she flew to him.

'Mind,' Norma said, 'he bites people. When he's upset.'

Lydia withdrew a little. 'I'm sure it won't be years,' she said. 'Neville, where's the cake?'

Neville held out his hand, but before he could get it anywhere near Lydia, Robert had snatched it, and seemed literally almost to swallow it whole. Norma looked at him with disgust. 'You got worms,' she said. 'Didn't I tell you?'

''Aven't.'

'You 'ave. I shall tell Miss in the 'ouse.'

'*Worms?*' Neville said. 'Where? I can't see a single worm.'

'They're in his stomach,' Norma said. ''E never stops eating. 'E needs a good dose.'

Tommy, who had watched the appearance and disappearance of the cake, had now put his head into his sister's lap which muffled his sobbing.

'What a pity they're inside you,' Neville said to Robert. 'It means you can never get to know them.'

''E got stung by a chicken,' Norma said, 'trying to take an egg off of a nest.'

'Chickens don't sting,' Lydia said. 'It must have been a bee. What does your father do?' she added, feeling she should change the subject.

''E drives a bus.'

'Gosh! Does he really?'

'I said 'e did.' She pulled up her dress which was

made of blue shiny stuff, like satin, and wiped Tommy's nose on her knickers. 'What do you do down 'ere, then?' she said.

'We go to the beach and have picnics and swim—' Lydia began.

But Robert interrupted her. '*I* bin to the seaside,' he offered. 'I bin, and I touched the sea with both 'ands.'

'Yes, and you was sick in the bus on the way 'ome,' Norma said crushingly. She had been absently picking at bits of Tommy's very short tufted hair; it was extremely short, almost like mown grass, Lydia thought. Robert's was just the same. She caught Lydia looking at Tommy's head. 'Nits,' she said. 'Miss in the 'ouse said they 'ad nits, so she cut it and then she washed them in some 'orrible stuff – didn't 'alf stink.'

'You 'ad them as well,' Robert said, and she flushed.

'I never,' she said.

'What are nits?' Neville asked. He squatted down beside Norma. 'Have you got any left? Can I see one?'

'No, you can't. They've all gone. You're rude,' she added.

'You're rude,' Robert echoed; they both glared at Neville.

Lydia said, 'He didn't mean to be, did you, Neville?'

'I'm not absolutely sure,' Neville answered. 'I might have, and I might not.'

'Shall we play a game?' Lydia said; things didn't seem to be turning out too well.

'There ain't nowhere to play,' Robert said.

'What do you mean?'

'Ain't no pavements. No canal – no nothing. Just *grass*,' he finished with intense scorn.

'What do you do at a canal?'

'We go up on the bridge and when the bargees go through underneath we spit. We call them and they look up and we spit right in their eyes.'

'*That's* rude,' Neville said triumphantly. 'That's *in*be*liev*ably rude.'

'No, it isn't,' Norma said. 'Mum says they're only diddies. Serve 'em right. It's a boy's game, anyway. *I* don't do it.'

'What's diddies?'

'Gypsies. I thought everyone knew that. Don't you know that?'

'We know different things,' said Neville. 'We know an enormous amount of different things.'

'Let's go to the pond,' Lydia said desperately; she couldn't think why they couldn't all be friends.

They agreed, rather reluctantly, to go to the pond which lay at the bottom of a steep slope in the field next to Mr York's house. It had rushes growing round it, and at one shallower corner the earth was encrusted with the hoofmarks of the cows coming to drink.

'Look, there are dragonflies,' Lydia said rather hopelessly: she had a feeling that they wouldn't much like them.

'If they come near me I'll kill 'em,' Robert said. He scratched a scab off his knee and ate it. The rest of his legs were as white as fish, Lydia thought, and they were so thin that his black boots looked too big.

'Is your father going off to fight in the war?' Neville asked.

Robert shrugged, but Norma said, ''E might and 'e mightn't. Mum says if 'e does it'll be good riddance. Never trust a man. They're only after one thing.'

'One thing?' Neville said as they trudged home later

for their tea. Miss Boot had called the evacuees in for theirs and it had been quite a relief. 'What one thing? I want to know, because when I'm grown up I suppose I'll be after it too. And if I don't like the sound of it, I'll think of some other thing to go after.'

'I can go after things just as much as you.'

'She didn't say ladies went after it.'

'I don't care. I shall.'

They quarrelled gently all the way home.

∞ ∞ ∞

'What do you want with your grouse, darling?'

Diana looked down at the large hand-written menu. 'What are you going to have?'

'Cauliflower, French beans, broccoli, peas—' the waiter towering above them intoned.

'French beans, I think.' It was awful: here was Edward giving her a slap-up lunch at the Berkeley, probably the last she would have for ages, and she wasn't in the least hungry. It would not do to say that, though: Edward, like Louis XIV about whom she had been reading recently, liked his ladies to eat and drink heartily. Ladies! During the last year she had felt a chilling certainty that someone called Joanna Bancroft, whom she had met at a dinner party, had been one of Edward's flirtations, if not an actual affair. When Edward's name had come up during dinner, the young woman – younger than Diana, hardly more than a *girl* – had said, 'Oh! *Edward! He would* say that!', as though he was a very old friend, but when they were powdering their noses in their hostess's bedroom and she had asked her if she knew Edward well, the girl had answered rather distantly that she had simply met him during a weekend at Hermione Knebworth's, and the reply, elaborately casual, had roused her suspicion. When, later, she had asked Edward about Mrs Bancroft, she had recognised at once that he was lying. He had been suave and hearty, and had not met her eye. She had had the sense to shut up about that, but it had exacerbated her feelings of insecurity which had been thoroughly kindled by his revelation, a few weeks before the Bancroft episode, that Villy was having another child. Up until then, he had given her to understand, or rather had not stood in the way of her understanding, that all intimate relations between him and Villy had finished long ago. Her jealousy had been such that she had not been able to stop questioning him about it: had, she realised after-wards, more or less driven him into saying that it had been Villy who had *wanted* another child, and that he had felt unable to deny her. It was then that she had under-stood that he could not bear confrontations of this kind – of any moral kind, she suspected – and as her respect for him diminished (his attitude about the new baby and his wife continuing to be presented to her in a light she knew not to be true) so, curiously, her conscience shrank, and her intentions, her determination, emerged. If he was a poor thing, she had more right to call him her own.

She raised her glass of champagne cocktail to touch Edward's.

'Happy?' he was saying.

'What do *you* think?'

Their caviar arrived – a prim, thick-lipped pot nestling in a bed of chipped ice, accompanied by thin triangles of toast that came warm and shrouded in a napkin, and a young waiter served them with chopped egg, onion and parsley, while the wine waiter poured vodka into tiny glasses from a frosted bottle.

'Darling, I shall be utterly tipsy!'

'Never mind, I shall be driving.' This, she knew, did not refer to their journey to Sussex later in the day, but to the interlude before it at Lansdowne Road. As though he sensed her – faint – anxiety about this, Edward said, 'I really swear we shall be perfectly safe there. The family are all in Sussex, immersed in getting ready for the Babies' Hotel arrival. Villy is in charge of the blackout. Anyway, she has . . . other things to look after.' This, she knew, was a tactful reference to Roland, the new baby, born in April, precisely two months after she had first heard of his existence.

'Of course I trust you,' she said, and he smiled and took her hand.

'I know you do,' he said, giving it a little squeeze. 'You're a marvellous girl, and I'm the luckiest man in the world.'

While they finished their caviar, they watched a neighbouring couple being served with *canard en presse* – an oldish couple who hardly spoke to each other. The man screwed his monocle into his eye to watch the carving of the duck breast, while the woman looked distastefully at her mouth in a tiny mirror. The pieces of breast were laid on a silver dish over a spirit lamp. Edward said, 'Do you know the story of the woman here who was wearing a very *décolleté* dress?' Diana shook her head. 'Well, one of her, you know, breasts fell out, and a young waiter saw it and popped it back.'

'What *savoir faire*.'

'Oh, no, it wasn't. The head waiter came up to him

and hissed, "In this restaurant, we use a slightly warm tablespoon."'

'Darling! You made that up!'

'I didn't. A chap I know saw it all.'

The juices of the carcass had now been pressed and were being heated in a silver sauceboat over another spirit lamp.

'Supposing everybody ordered that,' Diana said, 'what would they do?'

'They'd be up a gum tree. I don't much care for it myself – it's too rich. I like plain food.'

'Plain food! You really can't call caviar and grouse plain food! It's party food!'

'Well, this is a very small private party. It's my birthday.'

After a second of horror that she might have forgotten, she said, 'Your birthday's in May!'

'I have one every month.'

'It must make you frightfully old.'

'Yes, I'm marvellous for my age.' The wine waiter brought the claret and poured a little into Edward's glass; he thrust his nose into it, and nodded. 'That's fine. Pour some now, would you?'

'What is it?' She knew he liked her to be interested in wine.

'Pontet Canet 'twenty-six. I thought it would suit our grouse.'

'Lovely.' One of the differences between her husband and Edward, she thought, was that Angus kept behaving as though he was rich when he wasn't, and Edward behaved as though he was only a little richer than he was. It was wonderful to be with somebody where a treat of any kind didn't involve pinching for weeks on everything else. It was also lovely to be with somebody who didn't pretend to be bored by the good things in life. Angus thought it was the thing to seem weary about any pleasure or extravagance, as though he had really had too much of it all, whereas Edward, who seemed to have a pretty good life all the time, never stopped enjoying it and saying so.

'This is *fun*, isn't it?' he was now saying, as he attacked his bird. 'It was rather bright of me to have to spend the morning at the wharf. A really cast-iron alibi. And then, of course, I *have* to collect all kinds of stuff from Lansdowne Road for Villy, and then the traffic will be dreadful getting out of London.'

'It probably actually will be.'

'Well, we'll worry about that when we get to it. The great thing is to enjoy the present and let the future take care of itself.'

But it doesn't, she thought, several hours later, lying on her back in the bed in Edward's large dressing room; or, rather, perhaps it does, but it doesn't take care of *me*. Her own future stretched drearily before her and she felt she was simply being keel-hauled in its wake. If there was a war, and even Edward seemed to think that there would be, she would spend the winter and beyond stuck in that damp, oaky little cottage in Wadhurst with Isla and Jamie. She loved Jamie, of course, but her sister-in-law bored her beyond belief. The alternative was spending the winter – or, indeed, the whole *war* – in Scotland with Angus's parents, who had never liked her and where she would be miles away from the slightest chance of seeing Edward. Angus, who was as usual staying with them till he brought the other boys back down south for their prep school, had said that he was joining the army, which would keep *him* out of the way most of the time, but then Edward might be away too. He had already tried for the Navy and been turned down, but he'd get into something. She remembered feeling like this last year, but last year there had been a wonderful reprieve; it was too much to hope that that would happen again. Edward was asleep. She turned to look at him. He lay, turned towards her, his left arm thrown across her, his hand loosely clasping her right breast – his favourite, he called it. She had unfashionably large breasts, but he liked them: his lovemaking always began there. His face, in repose, had a kind of simple nobility: his wide forehead with the widow's peak that was just off centre; the rather large and beaky nose, whose nostrils were each adorned by one silky, even more voluptuously curling hair, only visible if his head was thrown back; the faintly purple bloom below his cheekbones (he shaved twice a day if he was going out in the evenings); and the chin with a faint cleft above which the neat and bristling moustache, kept as carefully clipped as a little hedge, barely concealed the long, narrow upper lip that contrasted so oddly with the full lower one. One saw people who were asleep quite differently, she thought. It was the open eye that distracted one from being able to be sure what the person *was*. Now, because they were soon to part, and the sex had been good – the best ever for him, he had said – and he lay, handsome and defenceless beside her, she felt a surge of love that was both romantic and maternal. 'Wake me up if I drop off,' he had said earlier. 'If we are *too* late getting off, I'll be in hot water the other end.' A boy's remark.

She moved and touched his face. 'Wake up, old boy,' she said, 'it's getting late.'

But later still, in the car going down, they quarrelled. By the time he had loaded the car, it was half past five, hours later than they had meant; he had opened the front door for her to get in, and then said, 'Good Lord! I've forgotten Villy's jewellery,' and gone back into the house. When he returned, he had been carrying a large Victorian jewel box. He got in beside her, couldn't find the car key and in order to feel in his pockets, shoved the box onto her lap carelessly. It was not locked and the contents spilled onto her skirt and the floor. 'Dear me, how careless!' he said, as he pushed the key into the ignition. For what seemed like hours, she retrieved pieces of jewellery, much of it in little battered leather boxes that also opened since many of them had broken clasps. Silently she put garnet earrings, paste necklaces, brooches and an entire set of topazes and pearls back into their places – all Villy's stuff, that he had given her; not stuff that she wanted to see or even to know about at all. The box had a small Bramah key attached to its handle by a red ribbon. She untied this and locked it, and then twisted round in her seat to put the box in the back. She was conscious of ungovernable envy and fear, and was unable to stop herself asking, 'Which did you give her for the last baby?'

'The topazes,' he answered shortly. Then, 'Good Lord, Diana, what on earth made you ask that?'

'I was curious.'

'Well – don't be. It has nothing to do with you. With us,' he added in a more conciliating tone.

'It has, rather, hasn't it? I mean, you told me that you only had the baby because Villy wanted it so much. So it seems rather odd to give her a whole lot of jewellery for it as well.'

'I always gave her a piece after each of the children. I

57

couldn't very well change about that.' After a silence, he said, 'Could I?'

'Obviously not.'

Her sarcasm was either lost on him or he ignored it, as he said, 'Well, I bet Angus gave you things after you had the boys.' Then, with what seemed even to her incredible stupidity, he added, 'Let's close the subject, shall we?'

Pictures of Angus, drunk and maudlin after their firstborn, and the idiotic fur coat he had bought her occurred, and she said bitterly, 'Oh, yes. After I had Ian, he bought me a fur coat – a full-length skunk that I had to take back to the shop as soon as I could go out.'

'Why on earth?'

'Because he did not have the money to pay for it. The cheque had bounced by the time I got it back.'

'How perfectly beastly for you. Poor sweet!' But then he added, 'I expect he meant well, though.'

'He didn't mean anything. Except that he wanted to be the kind of man who gave his wife a fur coat. He'd told masses of our friends, and when people asked to see it, he told them that he had had to send it back because I had ridiculous principles about not wearing fur.'

Edward did not reply. They were driving down Whitehall, and lorries loaded with sandbags were being directed by police into Downing Street and to the doors of the government offices. There was not much other traffic.

'And so,' Diana continued – she felt both nettled and reckless – 'of course he gave me nothing after Fergus. Or Jamie.' This is idiotic, she thought. Why am I saying such unattractive, unimportant, *stupid* things? She began to feel frightened. 'Edward—'

'Since you brought the subject up,' he said, 'it seems

rather funny to me that you should make such a fuss about Villy having a child while we are going to bed together, when you did exactly the same thing yourself.'

'I never told you that I didn't ever go to bed with Angus! I told you that I didn't *want* to! And, anyway, it was different about Jamie.'

He did not want to pursue the difference. 'Well, come to that, I can't remember ever telling you that I never went to bed with Villy. I didn't talk about it because—'

'Because what?'

'Because it simply isn't the kind of thing one talks *about*.'

'You mean, it might be embarrassing?'

'Yes,' he said doggedly, 'it certainly might.'

Outside Waterloo Station there was a queue of buses all full of children waiting to get into the station. As they drew alongside one of them they could hear the shrill voices in a kind of singing shout: 'Jeepers creepers! Where d'yer get those peepers? Jeepers creepers! Where d'yer get those eyes?' over and over again.

'Poor little beggars,' Edward said. 'Some of them must be going to the country for the first time in their lives.'

This touched her; she put a hand on his knee. 'Darling! I don't know what came over me! I've been feeling so blue. And it's the end of our lovely time. I suppose I'm terrified that you'll be sent away somewhere and I'll never see you. It's ridiculous to quarrel when everything's so awful, anyway.'

'Darling! Here – have my hank. You know I can't bear you to cry. Of course we won't quarrel. And I promise you one thing.'

She took her nose out of the voluptuous handkerchief that smelled so deliciously of Lebanon cedar. 'What?'

'Whatever I do I'll find a way of seeing you. Wild horses wouldn't keep me away.'

She blew and then powdered her nose.

'Keep the handkerchief,' he said.

'Really, you encourage me to blub,' she said; she felt lightheaded as people sometimes do after a near accident. 'You always tell me to keep your splendid handkerchiefs. I have quite a serious collection.'

'Have you, sweetie? Well, I like you having them.'

They were all right after that, discussed how they could meet. Diana had found a girl in the village who would look after Jamie for a day sometimes: if he telephoned and got Isla, he would pretend to be an old friend of her father's who, since widowed, lived in the Isle of Man with a gigantic clockwork railway apparatus which he played with from morning till night. 'Well, not too old a friend,' Diana said. 'Daddy's seventy-two, and you wouldn't sound like a contemporary of his. You'd better be the *son* of his oldest friend.' Edward said he could sound old if he tried, but when challenged to try sounded, as Diana said, exactly like someone of forty-two, which he was. Why would the *son* keep ringing her up? They invented an ingenious but totally unconvincing fantasy about that, and everything became far more light-hearted. 'And, of course, we could write to each other,' Diana eventually said, but Edward made a face, and said writing was not much in his line.

'I did so many lines at school,' he said, 'that I invented a system of tying ten pens together, not in a bunch but in a string, so that I could write ten at once. But they caught me and I had to write more than ever.'

'I can't imagine you at school.'

60

'Nor can I. I loathed every minute of it. Never out of hot water.'

They parted at the gate of Plum Cottage. A hurried embrace in the car.

'Look after yourself,' he said.

'And you. God bless,' she added, she was feeling tearful again, but determined not to cry.

When she was out of the car and had walked round it to the gate, she turned, and he blew her a kiss. This made her want to rush back to the car, but she smiled as brightly as she could, waved, and walked up the brick path. She heard him start the engine and go, and stood listening until she could no longer hear the car. 'I *am* in love with him,' she said to herself. 'In love. With him.' It could happen to anyone, but once it did, they had no choice.

∞ ∞ ∞

That Saturday evening, all the grown-ups from Pear Tree Cottage – that is to say, Villy and Edward (only he was late), Sybil and Hugh, Jessica and Raymond, and Lady Rydal – dined at Home Place, as the Brig had decreed that they should. Only Miss Milliment was left there to dine with the older children, some of whom had been swapped from Home Place for the meal. By the time Edward arrived, the adult party were starting upon their roast veal, with Mrs Cripps's delicious forcemeat balls and paper-thin slices of lemon, mashed potatoes and French beans. They were fifteen round the long table that had had its fourth leaf put in for the occasion, and Eileen had got Bertha to help hand round the vegetables. Sid, who realised that she was the only outsider – a situation in which on different levels she often found herself – looked round at them with an affection that apart from her usual irony had something of awe. Everybody had worked hard all day in preparation for war, but now they all looked – and talked and behaved – as though it was just another ordinary evening. As they were either talking or eating or both, she could rove round the dark polished table. The Brig was telling old Lady Rydal some story about India – frequently interrupted by her: both considered themselves to be experts on that subject; he on the strength of a three-months visit with his wife in the twenties, she for the reason that she had been born there, 'a baby in the Mutiny'. 'My ayah carried me out into the garden and hid me in a gardener's hut for two days and thereby saved my life. So you see, Mr Cazalet, I cannot consider all Indians to be unreliable, although I know that that is a view that those less well informed might take. And,' she added to put the finishing touch to this munificence, 'I cannot believe that the Indian nature has *changed*. There was a great deal of loyalty that was most touching – my father, whose experience was unrivalled, always said that he would trust his sepoys as he would his own brother.'

This both made Jessica and Villy exchange a glance of suppressed amusement – only they knew that Lady Rydal's father had quarrelled so fiercely with his brother that they were not on speaking terms for at least forty years – and gave the Brig the opening he needed: armed with the slightest coincidence, he could breach a small gap in anyone's conversation, and now he was in with how interesting that she should mention sepoys, because a remarkable man he had met on the boat – extraordinary thing – both going over *and* coming back had said . . . Sid moved on to the great-aunts, who sat side by side in their bottle-green and maroon crêpe-de-Chine long-sleeved dresses placidly sorting out the food on their plates: Dolly regarded forcemeat as indigestible, and Flo could not bear fat, while each deplored the other's fussiness. 'In the last war we were grateful for anything,' Flo was saying, and Dolly retorting, 'I have not the slightest recollection of *you* being grateful for anything; even when Father gave you that nice holiday in Broadstairs after you had to leave the hospital you weren't grateful. Flo was useless as a nurse, because she simply could not stand the sight of blood,' she remarked rather more loudly to anyone who might be listening. 'She ended up with other VADs having to look after *her* which, of course, was not at all what the doctor ordered . . .'

Sybil, wearing a rather shapeless crêpe dress – she had put on weight since having Wills – was telling the Duchy how worried she was about him.

'It's only a phase,' the Duchy said placidly. 'Edward used to spit whenever he lost his temper as a little boy. He used to have the most ungovernable rages, and, of course, I worried about him. They all have tantrums when they're babies.' She sat, very straight, at the end of the table, dressed, as she always was, in her blue silk shirt with the sapphire and mother-of-pearl cross slung upon her discreet bosom – breasts, Sid thought affectionately, would not figure in her anatomy or her language – her frank and unselfconscious gaze directed now at her daughter-in-law. Now she began to laugh, as she went on, 'Edward was the naughtiest of the lot. When he was about ten, I suppose it was, he once picked every single daffodil in the garden, tied them in bunches with his sister's hair ribbons, and sold them at the end of the drive. He had a notice that said "Help the Poor" on a board, and do you know who the poor were? Himself! We had stopped his pocket money for some other crime, and he wanted a special kind of spinning top!' She took the tiny lace handkerchief from under the gold strap of her wrist-watch and wiped her eyes.

'And did he get it?'

'Oh, *no*, my dear. I made him put it all in the box on Sunday at church. And, of course, he got a spanking.'

'You must be talking about me,' Edward called from across the table. He had been listening to Jessica.

'Yes, darling, I was.'

'I was hopeless at school, too,' Edward said. 'I don't know how you all put up with me.'

How self-confident he must be to say that, Sid thought, but any further thoughts were interrupted by Jessica saying, 'I wish you'd tell that to Christopher. He feels he is such a failure at school.'

'He feels that because he *is*,' Raymond said. 'I've never known a boy muff so many opportunities.'

'He *is* good at Latin,' Jessica said at once.

'He *likes* Latin. The test is whether a boy works at anything he *doesn't* like.'

'And natural history. He knows a lot about birds and things.'

'I don't think anyone works much at things that they don't like,' Villy remarked. 'Look at Louise. I really think that all those years with Miss Milliment all she did was read plays and novels. She has the most rudimentary idea of maths and Latin. And Greek.'

'Does Miss Milliment teach them Greek?' Rupert asked. 'She is an amazing old thing, isn't she? Who educated *her*, I wonder? She knows a hell of a lot about painting.'

'I suspect she largely educated herself. But I expect you know, don't you, Mummy?' Villy turned to Lady Rydal, who looked at her in some surprise before she answered.

'I haven't the slightest idea. She came from a respectable family, and Lady Conway said she had been very good with her girls. Naturally, I didn't enquire into her personal life.'

'Well, I think whoever it is, it's better for girls to be educated at home,' Hugh said. 'You hated your boarding school, didn't you, Rach?'

And Sid, at once directed towards Rachel, saw her flinch at the memory before she said, 'I did, rather, but I expect it was very good for me.' She was almost too tired to eat, Sid saw, and longed to say, 'Darling, give up for the day – go to bed, and I'll bring you anything you feel like on a tray,' but it's not my house, she thought, and she is not supposed to be my love, or anything near it, and I have no power at all. After that, she could observe and think of nothing but Rachel. She realised that the Duchy was bringing Zoë into the conversation, drawing attention to the centrepiece of roses on the table that apparently Zoë had done, but all the time she saw Rachel trying to eat what was on her plate – the family did not approve of people picking at their food, and the Duchy deplored waste. She saw Rachel cutting off a sliver of veal and putting it into her mouth and then, eventually, swallowing it, picking at the mashed potato with her fork, crumbling the piece of bread on her side plate and eating tiny pieces between sips of water. Rachel had not only had endless and arduous administrative problems in moving her Babies' Hotel, she had borne the brunt of her parents' conflict about it, although that part of it had been considerably worse last year when there had been no accommodation for them but the squash court. Practical considerations had not then, as now, impaired the Brig's patriarchal generosity, but they had offended, and still to some extent did offend, the Duchy's sense of what was sensible and proper. Rachel, who hated conflict, had had the unenviable task of carrying messages about all this between her parents, softening them *en route* from the arbitrary and sweeping plans of her father and the awkward, not to say unanswerable questions from her mother, which, as Sid could see, suited both parties: the Brig would brook no interference of his arrangements, and the Duchy would never actually oppose them; the presence of a daughter therefore enabled them to continue a bland relationship in public. But this, as so much else in her filial life, was at Rachel's expense, and in this case, it was *her* charity that was at stake and so naturally she was even more driven and dutiful. What is to become of us? Sid thought, and could find no answer. At least Evie, her sister, was out of the way, safely ensconced in Bath, being the secretary for yet another musician she had fallen for – at least, that was what it had sounded like the last time she had telephoned. But what was she, Sid, to do when the war finally started? She could not simply continue teaching music in schools, surely? She should join some women's service, but every time she thought of that, as she had been doing with increasing frequency in the last few weeks, she had also to think that this would mean leaving Rachel, completely and for an unknown amount of time, a prospect so chilling and awful as to paralyse her. So far she had been able to retreat from this dilemma because it still lay precariously in the future, a possibility, a last and uncertain resort, but since yesterday with the news that the Germans had invaded Poland, had knocked out the Polish air force and immobilised their railways, she knew that it was on the brink of not being the future any more. She ached to talk alone with Rachel, if she needs me, she thought, but Rachel did not acknowledge need in relation to herself of any kind, would only consider her – Sid's – duty as earnestly and sincerely as she would her own. Anyway, tonight was out of the question. Tonight, at the Duchy's instigation, they were to play the *Pastoral Symphony*, her beloved Toscanini's performance, on her splendid new gramophone. 'I think we need that kind of music tonight,' she had said before dinner, the only allusion made by any of them to what lay in store. And after the Beethoven, Rachel would be utterly worn out, even supposing she stayed the course. She looked across the table now to catch Rachel's eye, but she was talking to Villy, and as she looked away, it was Zoë's eye that she caught, and Zoë gave her a small, hesitant smile – almost as one outsider to another, Sid thought, as she returned it. She had used to evade Zoë, distrusting the extraordinarily pretty but, she thought, vacuous face, but Zoë's habitual expression had changed: it was as though before she had known everything she thought she needed to know, and now knew nothing. The effect was to make her mysteriously younger, which was odd, because Sid had thought that sorrow – and she had, after all, only recently lost her baby – made people look older. She had observed that the family treated her differently from a year ago; they seemed now to have accepted her, as, in a way, they have me, she thought, but, then,

'Edward, give her your handkerchief,' Villy cried, as Flo stopped coughing and began to sneeze.

Edward felt in his pockets. 'Can't seem to find it.'

Raymond proffered his; Villy got up with a glass of water and ministered to Flo, whose face had suffused from mulberry to beetroot.

'You'll be lucky if you ever get your hanky back,' Dolly remarked. 'I've never known Flo return a hanky. In her entire life.'

'At least I have some sense of humour,' Flo returned between sneezes, 'which is more than could be said for some.'

Rachel caught Sid's eye then and winked; to Sid it felt like a caress. She winked back.

∞ ∞ ∞

At dinner, or rather supper, in Pear Tree Cottage, however, the war – beside much else – was discussed with varying degrees of anxiety and cheerful abandon. In this last camp were Teddy, Simon, Nora, Lydia and Neville (Lydia and Neville had wheedled themselves dinner in the dining room on the twofold grounds that it would be less trouble for the servants, and that they hadn't had a treat for weeks). Their presence was deeply resented by Polly and Clary who had only recently been promoted to supper downstairs and that not always. 'They haven't got a shred of justice in their bodies,' Clary had said earlier of her father and Aunt Villy. Christopher and Polly were united in their disapproval and dread of war; Louise was poised uncertainly between all of them: disapproval of war was one thing, having one's career utterly wrecked was another; on the other hand, it was all being, or feeling as though it was *going* to be, terribly exciting. Miss Milliment, who had earlier sensed that Villy would be relieved if she did not seem to expect to go out to dinner with the rest of the family and had said how much she should like to have supper with the children, preserved an interested equanimity. She sat now in her dark brown stockinette skirt and cardigan – which she had that morning discovered right at the back of her wardrobe; she could not have worn it for at least two years, and it had been casually attacked by moths, but fortunately only in places that did not show very much – her small grey eyes glinting with amusement behind her steel-rimmed spectacles.

'If only Hitler could have waited another three years,' Teddy was saying, 'I could have gone slap into the RAF and had a wizard time dropping bombs on *him*.' His voice had broken during the summer term, and now sounded too loud, Louise noticed.

'I thought you said you wanted to be a fighter pilot,' she said.

'I do, really, but I might have to be a bomber.'

'And what does Christopher want to do?' Miss Milliment enquired; she thought he was being rather swamped by Teddy.

'Oh – I don't know,' he muttered.

'Christopher's a cautious objector,' Simon said.

'You mean conscientious,' Nora snubbed.

'What is that? What do you do if you are it?' Neville asked.

'Object, of course, you fool.'

'Don't say "you fool" to Simon. I agree with him anyway, Miss Milliment.'

'Do you, Polly? I didn't know that.'

'You mean you object to war? What an extraordinary thing to object to!'

'It isn't. You don't know anything, Neville, so shut up.'

'I think Neville is trying to find out,' Miss Milliment said mildly.

'Well, you could drive an ambulance, or something boring like that,' Teddy said.

'Or you could simply be an evacuee,' Neville said. 'We met some this afternoon.'

'Who's we?'

'Lydia and me.'

'Lydia and *I*,' Clary corrected him.

'They were rather disgusting,' Lydia said. 'One of them ate a scab off his knee.'

Neville turned on her. 'I've seen you do that,' he said.

'You never have!'

'I certainly have. It's not a thing I've often seen,' he explained to Miss Milliment. 'So I wouldn't be likely to forget it, would I? In your *bath*!'

Lydia went pink. 'I simply didn't want it to fall off into the water and go back into blood,' she said.

'Who's being disgusting now?' Nora said.

'It's difficult not to be disgusting about things that are that,' Lydia said.

'If you simply weren't *here*,' Clary said, 'we wouldn't be talking about disgusting things. We'd be having a far more interesting conversation.'

There was a silence while everyone ate their fish pie and runner beans.

'When is Judy coming back?' Clary asked at last. She didn't much want to know but felt she had to show that other conversation was possible.

'Dad's fetching her tomorrow. She's at Rottingdean with a school friend. She had her tonsils out at the beginning of the hols, and Mummy thought some sea air would do her good.'

'And Angela?' Miss Milliment enquired.

'Oh, she's got some sort of job and she lives in a flat with a friend. We hardly ever see *her*. She simply hates it at Frensham. Mummy wanted her to be a deb now we've got some money, but she wouldn't.'

'Do you call that interesting conversation, Miss Milliment?' Neville asked.

'One of the evacuees had worms,' Lydia said, before Miss Milliment could reply. 'And they had to have their hair cut because little animals lived in it. Medically speaking, they weren't much cop.'

'They were a lot of cop,' Neville said. 'I should think doctors would far rather have a few people with a lot of things wrong with them than everyone with one wrong thing. Supposing you got chicken pox and measles and mumps all at once,' he added, warming to the subject, 'you'd be so spotty you'd just be one large spot – they wouldn't show because there'd be no skin in between. And,' he added, 'the other good thing would be that then you could just be well for the rest of your life. If I was a doctor, I'd give people all the things they hadn't got—'

'Shut up! I knew it was a mistake having them down for supper—'

'That is the principle of inoculation,' Miss Milliment said. 'That is why people in this country, at least, do not get smallpox any more. You were all given a little dose of smallpox when you were babies.'

'Well, that's something,' Neville said. 'All our side has

got to do is give all the Germans smallpox and they'd be too ill to fight. Can you die of it?'

'People used to die of it, yes.'

'You see?'

'Don't put your plum stones on the table, Neville,' Clary said crossly; she could see that Polly became tense every time the war was mentioned, and perhaps Miss Milliment noticed that too, because she launched into an account of Dr Jenner and his experiments with cow pox.

This impressed Christopher very much. 'It must have saved thousands of people's lives,' he said, his spectacles misting up as his face became red with excitement. 'I wish I could invent something like that!'

'Discoveries of that nature usually come about from sharp observance,' Miss Milliment remarked. 'There is no reason why you should not discover something, Christopher, if that is what you most want to do.'

'Rich man, poor man, beggarman, thief,' Lydia muttered. She helped herself to another plum, gouged out the stone with her spoon and went through the ritual again. 'Rich man!' she exclaimed with artificial surprise.

'I don't do my stones like that,' Neville said. 'I do them quite differently.'

'How?'

He screwed up his eyes and held his breath.

'Engine driver, pirate, zoo-keeper, burglar,' he announced at last. 'I don't cheat about stones like you, because I wouldn't mind being any of them.'

'You always miss the point,' Clary said. 'The whole *point* is that there are some things you wouldn't like.'

'Like being married to a thief,' Lydia said.

'I don't know, that might be quite exciting,' Polly said.

'They'd come home in the evening with all kinds of things you'd never thought of. If it was a thief with the same *taste* as you, you could furnish your whole house.'

Teddy, who had eaten his share of pudding, and there wasn't anything else, said could he and Simon please go back to Home Place now as they were in the middle of something they had to finish. 'All these women and children,' he explained to Simon as they ran back, 'give me the pip,' and Simon said he quite agreed. He didn't actually feel like that about the older girls, but he recognised that it was a bit feeble of him, and knew that it was only a matter of time before he'd feel like Teddy.

'What are we in the middle of?' he asked. He was worrying a bit about Christopher being left out of whatever it was.

'You'll see.'

They reached the end of the track and emerged onto the road. It was nearly but not quite dark. When they reached the drive to Home Place, Teddy did not go in but continued to run along the road up the hill. Then he slowed down, and started to explore the hedge that bounded the little wood by Home Place. 'There's a place through here somewhere,' he said, 'Christopher showed me last year.'

'It'll be jolly dark in the wood.' Simon began to feel a bit nervous.

'No, it won't. You'll see. Ah! This is it.' He plunged through a gap in the hedge and Simon followed, through brambles and old man's beard and the rattling seeds of old cow parsley. Just as he began to feel that he would rather be with Christopher looking through his collection of Peter Scott cigarette cards or feeding his owl, Teddy stopped.

'Here we are,' he said, and sat down. Simon sat beside him; they didn't seem to be anywhere much. He watched while Teddy produced a night light and a box of matches. 'You make a flat bit of ground for it,' he said, and Simon obediently scraped away at leaves and twigs until he'd cleared a small bit of ground. I hope it's not going to be witchcraft, he thought, but he didn't say anything.

'Now, then.' Teddy next pulled out his bulky and businesslike penknife.

'What are you going to cut?' He was beginning to be afraid that Teddy might be going to cut them and mix their blood like Red Indians in pacts.

'This.' It was a rather battered cigar.

'Where did you get that?'

'Easy. The Brig left it in the ashtray. I think he'd forgotten it. It wasn't stealing, it was just taking.' He put the cigar on his knee and began sawing it in half. 'I thought it would be more fun if we could both smoke at once,' he said, and Simon was torn between pride at being included, and dread of what he was being included in.

'You suck one end and get it really wet,' he said as he handed Simon his half. Then he struck a match and lit the night light which lay between them. Simon could see Teddy's face which was hot from the run. 'You light yours first,' Teddy said, handing him the box of matches. Simon tried: he used three matches, but it didn't seem to light, and the bit in his mouth felt crumbly and like very old leaves with a bitter taste.

'Here, I'll do it for you. Give it to me.'

When he had handed back Simon's half, now glowing, he said, 'You'll have to keep smoking or it'll go out. Now, for the best of all.' From under his flannel shirt he pulled a small bottle. Simon could see the label that said 'Syrup of Figs' on it. He put it carefully on the ground and pulled out another bottle that Simon recognised as tonic water. Then he produced one of the Bakelite picnic mugs.

'We're going to smoke *and* drink,' he said. 'And propose some toasts. That sort of thing.'

Simon felt immensely relieved: no witchcraft, no blood-letting.

'Although actually,' Teddy went on, as he poured equal quantities from each bottle into the mug, 'it isn't tonic water – I couldn't find any, they'd drunk it all. So I mixed up some Andrew's Liver Salts with water. It'll come to much the same thing.' He lit his cigar, took a drag on it and was momentarily speechless. Simon realised that his had gone out. While he relit it, Teddy took a deep swig from the mug, and handed it to him. 'It's a bit warm,' he said, 'being next to my chest and, of course, I couldn't manage ice.'

Simon took a cautious drink. It was nothing like as nice as orange squash or, indeed, any other drink he could think of.

'I'm afraid the fizz has rather gone out of it,' Teddy said. Simon couldn't reply. He had taken a drag on his cigar which made him feel as though he was falling off something.

'Now. Here are the toasts. Death to Hitler.' He drank, and handed Simon the mug. 'You have to say it as well before you drink.'

'Death to Hitler,' Simon said. It came out like a croak, and it felt as though the first drink was surging up his throat to meet the second. He swallowed several times, and things settled down.

'Don't we have to drink healths as well?' he said.

'Good idea. Strangways Major.'

Strangways Major was a prefect and captain of rugger, and altogether so exalted that Simon had never spoken to him.

'You're not taking very big swigs – go on, there's lots more.'

He had another go, hoping he would have got to like it, but he hadn't.

'I think I'll stick to smoking,' he said, but Teddy said don't be silly, took back the mug and filled it up again.

He went on with toasts. They drank to Laurel and Hardy, Bobby Riggs, Mr Chamberlain, Cicely Court-neidge and, finally, the King, but when they got to him, Teddy said that they must stand up, which turned out to be surprisingly difficult. Teddy was swaying about and laughing. 'I think I'm a bit drunk,' he said. He helped Simon up, but the moment he let go of him, Simon found himself sitting down again very suddenly and hard, and then he was terrifically sick which made his eyes stream although he wasn't crying as he told Teddy. Teddy was wizard about it, said it was probably something he ate, 'The fish, I expect – it comes all the way from Hastings in a van,' and that it didn't matter in the least. 'It doesn't matter anyway,' he said. 'In fact, I don't think anything matters very much.' When Simon felt better, they blew out the night light and went home.

∞ ∞ ∞

'It's a funny old world.' He sounded as though he was trying to be as nice about it as possible, but it was clear that he thought it could do better if it tried. Mrs Cripps, who was never quite sure when he was referring to personal matters, about which she had fervent curiosity and interest, or world matters, about which she had neither, trod warily.

'Well, there it is, I suppose,' she answered. She poured a little tea into her cup to see if it had stood long enough, and it had.

'It isn't as though they're anything to do with the Empire, after all.' He watched as she filled his cup; the dark liquid mixing with the creamy milk turned it the colour of beech leaves. His chauffeur's hat, a smart grey with a black cockade, lay on the table beside a plate of Bakewell tarts.

'Mind you, I've nothing against Poles. As such.'

Her heart sank. What did he *mean*? There was a silence while he stirred three lumps of sugar into his tea – he always made a proper job of that; he never left any sugar wasting in the cup like some.

They were in the very small sitting room off the kitchen, where she sometimes put her feet up in the afternoons. By common but unspoken consent, it was not used by the other servants, excepting Eileen who sometimes took tea with her there. The dining-room dinner was over, and she could hear distant sounds of Madam's gramophone and, nearer, the sounds of the girls washing up in the pantry.

'Would you fancy a tart, Mr Tonbridge?' she said.

'Seeing as it's your pastry, Mrs Cripps. After you.' He handed her the plate and she took one, just to be sociable.

'Close was it, in London?' she asked. It was London she wanted to hear about, and what had happened to him there.

'In more ways than one,' he replied before he could stop himself. He drank some of his tea – she did make a nice cup of tea – while he endeavoured to overcome the sudden urge to tell her the awful things that had been going on. But no, he still felt too shocked and humiliated – tell her anything of that and it might be the end of her respect.

'There's no doubt we're on the brink, Mrs Cripps, like it or not, that's where our politicians have landed us – Polish Corridor or no Polish Corridor.'

The poles he had earlier alluded to now became people instead of something to prop up the hops, but the corridor defeated her. How on earth could a corridor have anything whatever to do with starting a war? She composed her features to cautious concern. He'd been sent to London for the day to collect some things from the London house, and there'd been a rumour (gleaned from Eileen waiting at breakfast) that he'd been invited to bring *her* and the child back down with him, but he hadn't or he wouldn't be sitting here now.

She fell back on one of his favourite statements. 'It's my belief, Mr Tonbridge, that you can't trust politicians.'

'Now there I agree with you.' He moved his cup a fraction nearer to her, and she at once rinsed the tea-leaves out of it into the slop bowl and poured him another one.

'And half the time, they don't know what they're doing.'

'They do not, Mrs Cripps, and that's a fact. They don't tell us the half of it either, if you ask me.' She pushed the plate of tarts towards him and his hand reached out for one, but he paid no attention to it and therefore did not have to thank her. 'But when, as they say, the balloon goes up, Mrs Cripps, who pays the tune?'

She flashed him a smile so that he could see her gold

stopping, which, like other things about her seldom seen or not seen at all, he found definitely attractive.

'You tell me,' she said as she leaned towards him and her bust shifted slightly under her overall.

A fine figure of a woman, he thought – not for the first time either. 'You have a remarkable mind. For a woman. And I tell no lie,' he said. 'I don't need to tell *you*. You know it all. It's a real pleasure to converse with you. Unlike some.'

This glancing, but gratifyingly uncomplimentary allusion to Mrs Tonbridge was the nearest she came to appeasing her curiosity, but from it she guessed that there *had* been a visit, and that it had not turned out well. And if there was a war, which naturally she wasn't in favour of in *itself*, it would mean that the family would stay down here, which in turn would mean more work, but would also mean that Frank (as she privately called him) would be about. So it would be worth having a perm to her hair, she thought later, as she eased her aching legs between the sheets – her veins were really bad at the end of the day with all the standing she did at work.

But Tonbridge, after he had hung his uniform carefully on the back of the chair in his dark little bedroom next to the gun room, unstrapped his leather gaiters, and unlaced his boots, found himself standing in his vest and drawers by the small casement window after he had shut it for the night, frozen with the terrible memories of his day. Naturally, he'd done his work first, hadn't got to Gosport Street till well after two. The house had seemed very quiet, and he'd noticed that the curtains upstairs were drawn: it had struck him with sudden hope that she might be away visiting her mother. He'd let himself in, but after he slammed the door behind him, he heard sounds from above. He'd started to go upstairs but the bedroom door opened and there she was – not dressed – just pulling her dressing gown round her, her mules clacking on the lino. 'It's *you*!' she said. 'And what do *you* want?' He'd told her straight of Madam's kind offer for her and the kid, and she had launched into her sarcastic 'Oh, thank you so very bloody much for condescending to consider *me*' type of thing and stood barring his way on the stairs. 'What's going on?' he had said – not wanting to know but he had to say something.

She had folded her arms across her bony chest and begun to laugh. Then she'd called, 'George! You'll never guess who's here!' The bedroom door opened again and out came one of the largest men he'd ever seen in his life. Well over six foot he was – he had to stoop coming out of the bedroom – with curly ginger hair and a moustache. He wore a sleeveless singlet and was buttoning his flies over a beer belly, but his arms were like two legs of mutton with tattoos all over them. 'George is looking after me now,' she said, 'so you can vamoose.'

'Spying on us, is 'e?' George said. 'A Peeping Tom, is 'e?' He took a step forward, and the floorboards creaked.

'I'm here to take her away from the bombs. And the kid,' he said, but his voice came out weak.

'The kid's gone. I sent him off with his school.'

'Where?'

'Never you mind where. What's it to do with you?'

He started to say something about it being his kid, but she laughed again. '*Your* kid? You must be joking! Why did you think I married you – a little runt like you?'

It was out. Something he'd always wondered about, and shied away from as a wicked notion he shouldn't believe in.

'I'll just get my clothes, then,' he said, and moved blindly up a stair but his legs were shaking and he had to get hold of the banisters.

'Don't you dare lay a finger on me!' she cried, and George moved down to her and laid a hand like a bunch of pork sausages on her shoulder.

'Get 'im his clothes, Ethyl,' he said. 'I wouldn't have no use for them, would I? 'E'll go outside and wait for them as quiet as . . .' he paused and his light blue eyes were full of considering contempt, 'a *mouse*,' he finished.

So that was it. He'd gone down the stairs and into the street, and she'd opened the upstairs window and just flung the stuff down at him – socks, shirts, two pairs of shoes and his winter uniform – all thrown onto the pavement and the street, in the gutter, and he'd gone about, picking them up and putting them into the back of the car while George stood massively in the doorway and watched him. He'd never felt so humiliated in his life; the whole street might be watching, so all he could do was collect everything as quickly as possible, get into the car and drive away. But as soon as he'd got to the end of the street and turned a corner, he had to stop, because he found he was sobbing, he couldn't see a thing, and one thing he'd always been was careful with Mr Cazalet's cars. He always says there's no one to touch you for care of your vehicle. 'I'd trust you with a brand new Rolls if I had one,' that's what he'd said and not so long ago. He remembered this twice. He'd been with Mr Cazalet for twenty-one years now, and few could say the same. It wasn't only the driving, it was the upkeep, and he'd defy anyone – anyone at *all* – to find any dirt, anything wrong with the engine, any polishing neglected. He blew his nose, and felt with trembling fingers in his pockets for his packet of Weights and lit one. And with Mr Cazalet losing his sight, he depended on him more than ever. 'I depend upon you, Frank,' he'd said not so long ago – last summer it had been when it had first looked like war – 'I know I can always rely on you,' he said. A gentleman like Mr Cazalet wouldn't say that for nothing. And even when he'd had that trouble with Mr Cazalet driving on the right-hand side of the road because that's how he rode his horses, 'I put my foot down,' he said aloud. 'Either you drive on the left, sir, or I'll do the driving.' Now he always drove him, and Madam, and Miss Rachel, who was a really nice lady, not to mention Mrs Hugh and Mrs Edward. 'You're part of the family,' Miss Rachel had said when she visited him in hospital after that trouble with his ulcer. 'I think you're very brave,' she had said. Very *brave*. Miss Rachel would never tell a lie. He'd glanced into the back of the car; he'd have to get a box or a case or something to put his stuff in – couldn't turn up at Home Place with the car looking like that; he had his pride, after all.

He was sniffing loudly now by the window. He flexed his biceps and looked at his arm to see if it made a difference, but it didn't much. Scrawny, she'd called him. 'You're bow-legged,' she'd said on another occasion. He had such narrow shoulders, Mr Cazalet had had his uniform made. We can't all be the same, he thought miserably. He looked at the case with his stuff in it lying on the floor still not unpacked. He'd do that tomorrow. He wouldn't think about *any of that*, except, now, he was glad he hadn't told Mabel – as he privately called her. She respected him, looked up to him, as a woman should; it felt quite natural when he was with her. As he got into bed he realised that he hadn't got a home any more – not with that man in it – and then he thought this was his home, where the family was; always had been. He thought he'd lie awake, with his insides churning, but the Bakewell tarts had settled his stomach, and he was asleep before he knew it. And that was the last day before the war.

∞ ∞ ∞

When Mr Chamberlain had finished, and the children had been sent out of the room, the Brig suggested that he and his sons – and Raymond, of course – should repair to his study to discuss plans, but the Duchy said no, if plans were to be discussed she thought that everyone should be present to discuss them. She said it with such surprising asperity that he gave way at once. Everybody settled down; Miss Milliment wondered quietly whether they would like her to leave, but nobody seemed to hear her, so she crossed her ankles and looked rather anxiously at her shoes, the laces of which had already come undone. The Brig, who had lit his pipe very slowly, now said that obviously everybody should stay put: the London houses could be closed, or possibly all but one . . . 'What about the children's schools?' Villy and Sybil said at once. Surely they would remain open – they were in the country, after all, and it would be a pity to interrupt their education. It was decided that Villy should ring Teddy's and Simon's school, and that Jessica would find out about Christopher's school and whether the domestic science establishment attended by Nora and Louise was to continue or not. There was then a pause, eventually broken by Villy, who said what about the Babies' Hotel? She didn't think the nurses could get through the winter in the squash court: the glass in the roof would make it perishing cold, apart from the fact that the poor things had no real facilities for washing or keeping their clothes, 'Or even anywhere to be when they aren't working,' she added. The Brig said that he'd been considering modifications to the squash court that would deal with all that, but the Duchy said sharply that it was out of the question to modify a place that people were having to sleep in. There was a silence; everyone recognised that she was upset, but only Rachel knew why. Raymond then announced that kind though they all were, he and Jessica and their brood had a perfectly good house of their own at Frensham which they would repair to, as they had always been going to do, in a week's time. Rupert said that he was going to have a crack at joining the Navy, and he knew that Edward had made his arrangements; Hugh would be in London, the older boys and girls at school, so why couldn't they let the nurses have Pear Tree Cottage and all live here at Home Place? This idea, while it seemed to have no valid objection, met with covert resistance. Neither Sybil nor Villy relished the idea of having no household of their own; the Duchy had serious misgivings about whether Mrs Cripps would stand the numbers to cook for; Rachel felt anxiety about turning her sisters-in-law out of their house for her – Rachel's – charity, and the Brig did not wish to be baulked of his ingenious schemes regarding the squash court. Nobody voiced their reservations, and when the Duchy had said that they would cross that bridge when they came to it, some of them felt able to acknowledge the scheme as a good idea. Rachel then said that she and Sid *must* get back to Mill Farm where they had been in the midst of unpacking and settling in Matron and the babies. Then

'Because you're much smaller, and your legs will get scratched.'

They'll get scratched above our wellingtons just as much.'

'Yes,' Neville said, 'and the blood will run down into our boots and mingle with our sore heels.'

'I think everyone should wear them, or no one,' Clary said. It was rather sickening, she remarked to Polly, how those two pretended to be grown up when they weren't.

'And why aren't Teddy and Christopher being made to do it?' Clary demanded, as they waited in the scullery while Eileen provided them with receptacles.

'Because the Brig wants them to do things to the squash court,' Louise said.

'And it's none of your business, anyway,' Nora said. Neville put out his tongue, but Nora saw him. 'That's extremely rude, Neville, you should apologise at once.'

'It just happened to come out,' he said, retreating from her. 'I don't think I need to apologise for something which simply *happened*.'

'Yes, you do. Apologise.'

He thought for a moment. He had put the large colander that Eileen had given him on his head so that it was not possible to see his expression.

'I'm so frightfully sorry that I can't come,' he said at last. 'That's what people say when they don't want to do something,' he added.

Clary saw his eyes gleaming through the holes in the colander. 'It's no good,' she said to Louise. 'Much better to pretend he never said it.'

Louise entirely agreed. She felt Nora often got far too bossy, but she was also obstinate and would never give way in front of the other children. 'Look, Neville, just say you're sorry. Quietly.'

He looked at her; she was much nicer than Nora. She saw his lips move.

'I said it,' he said. 'So quietly that I should think I was the only person who could hear.'

'Well, that's that,' Nora said, slinging her basket over her shoulder. 'A lot of fuss about nothing.'

'Mincemeat out of a molehill,' Neville agreed. He had taken off his colander, and his face was bland.

'Oh, come *on*!' Clary cried. It was awful how long people took to get started on anything.

The best blackberry place was at the far end of the large meadow beyond the small wood at the back of the house. The grass was high and bleached, as it had not been cut for hay; the few large trees were turning, the Spanish chestnuts laden with their yellowing spiky balls. This year, Polly thought, they would really be able to roast chestnuts; last year they had thought they would, but in the end they had all gone back to London the same as usual. 'What's going to happen to us, do you think?' she asked Clary.

'I should think we'll stay here and have lessons with Miss M. They wouldn't have got her down here if we weren't. But the boys will go to school, I should think – after all, their school is in the country, and I suppose *they* will go to their domestic science place. Neville ought to go to a boys' school as well,' she added. 'He's getting awfully spoilt.'

'But – if we're *here*, and our fathers are in London or somewhere else, what happens when we're invaded?'

'Oh, *Poll*! Our fathers will be in London. They'll come

down for weekends. And we won't be invaded. We have a navy. They'll stop all that sort of thing.'

Polly was silent, not from conviction, but from the hopeless sense that the more people tried to be reassuring, the less you could trust their views. They had reached the wide sloping bank that inclined towards the next wood – the one where she had imagined the tank blasting through towards her and Dad last year. The brambles festooned the clumps of hawthorn that were scattered on this piece of land, which also contained many rabbit holes, molehills and in one place the end of a dewpond, now simply a dampish declivity surrounded by a few disconsolate rushes. In the Easter holidays it was a good place for primroses which clustered round the clumps, and in the early summer they had found little purple orchids. Now the large trees in the wood were burnished in the golden, windless light, and the clumps glistened with bramble, briony and hawthorn berries, and there were swags of old man's beard.

'Everybody spread out and start picking!' Nora called. She made it sound like a school outing, Louise thought, as she noticed the others moving quickly as far from Nora as possible, which left her, Louise, feeling that she'd have to stay with her cousin or it would look rude. They put up a cock pheasant between them, but before it flew, it ran, with its drunken, stilted gait, a few yards away; then, when Lydia ran after it, it rose in the air and whirred away.

Neville soon got tired of picking and upset his colander, which discouraged him even more. He went exploring the rabbit holes: he had a secret desire to see the inside of a warren, and thought that if only he could widen the entrance, he'd be able to slip in. He did not even want to tell Lydia this plan; it would be far more fun to mention it casually when they were having their baths. 'I went into a warren today,' he would say. 'It was just like Beatrix Potter – little frying pans hung up on sticky-out roots from the walls, and the floor all smooth and sandy. The rabbits loved me coming to see them.' He imagined them hopping onto his knees, all soft and furry with their lovely ears lying down on their backs and their bulging eyes looking up at him in a trusting way. But he couldn't make any headway with the digging at all. He tried with the colander, but it simply wouldn't *dig*, and then he tried scooping earth up with one of his wellingtons, but it was too floppy. And then when he put the wellington on again, it seemed to be full of little sharp sandy pebbles, so he took it off again. He'd have to pinch a trowel out of McAlpine's shed, he thought, as he limped towards the others thinking of what he would say about not having any blackberries, and then, of course, he trod on a bramble and thorns went into his foot, and when he tried to go on walking it really hurt.

This made everyone not notice about his not having any blackberries and Nora was really nice to him. She made him sit down and took his foot and found where the thorns were, and squeezed and squeezed and got two of them out, but the last one was too deep. 'It could be sucked out,' she said, and everyone who was standing round looked doubtfully at his grimy foot. 'He's your brother,' Nora said to Clary who did not seem very keen.

'Although if he'd been bitten by an adder and would die if I didn't, of course I would,' she said, 'but just a *thorn* . . .'

'It's only a *bramble*,' Louise said.

'No, it's a rose thorn and quite a big one. It's broken off. If he walks on it, it'll simply go in deeper and deeper.'

'Then it might come out the other side,' Lydia said, 'come sprouting out of the top of his foot.' They were full of unhelpful suggestions.

'All right,' Nora said. 'Give me your foot again.' She sat down opposite Neville and took his foot in her hands. Then she spat on it and rubbed it with her dress, which wouldn't show, Louise thought, because it was a rather nasty mixture of orange and black in sort of stripes and blobs – a cross between a zebra and a giraffe. Then she sucked for a bit, and then squeezed, and finally the thorn, black and quite large, came out.

'You should have worn socks inside your wellingtons,' she said mildly. 'There you are. Has anybody a sock to lend him?'

Lydia obliged. 'Although if there'd been an air raid, I bet you could have run,' she said.

'Let's go home,' Polly said at once, and Clary could see that this idea hadn't occurred to her, but that now that it had she was definitely nervous.

'Thank Nora,' Clary said.

'I was just going to,' Neville said sulkily. 'And now you've spoiled my thanks. I'll thank you on the way home,' he said to Nora, 'when I start to feel like it again.'

An ordinary afternoon, Polly thought, as they made their way back. How many more of them would there be? She looked at Clary trudging beside her. 'What are you thinking?'

'I was trying to describe that pheasant. You know – exactly how it looked – *you* know – like a bird in fancy dress – a bit military, and the way it ran – a sort of swaggery stagger . . .'

'Why? I didn't think you were interested in birds.'

'I'm not, particularly. But I might want to put one in a book, and I have to keep remembering things for that.'

'Oh.'

Aunt Rach weighed the blackberries and altogether they came to eleven pounds three ounces, and the Duchy gave them each a Meltis Fruit after tea, and Dottie cried because Mrs Cripps said she hadn't cleaned the preserving pan properly, and that now it might catch. In the early evening, the nutty fragrance of the hot seething blackberries seeped into the large hall and could even be detected on the top landing by Great-Aunt Dolly as she went to the bathroom to put water in her tooth glass for soaking her senna pods.

Everyone was summoned to hear the King broadcast at six o'clock, and remained motionless and silent listening to his strained and halting speech as he battled with his stammer. 'Poor King!' Lydia said. 'To have to speak when you hardly can!' And Louise said how lucky it was that he hadn't wanted to be an actor, because that would have been a tragedy; he would just have to walk on in plays carrying a spear. Then there was someone called J.B. Priestley who read from something he'd written, and just as there was wonderful Sandy Macpherson on the cinema organ, the maids were told to get on with laying dinner which they felt was very bad luck, and the children were told to go off and have their baths, whereas the grown-ups, who didn't have to do anything, switched off the wireless and didn't even listen to him.

'They won't let us listen to what they don't even *want*,' Clary complained. She had once seen Sandy Macpherson coming up out of a pit playing his organ in a large cinema in London and had been looking forward to boasting about it. 'And we have to listen to *them* playing for hours. Sometimes,' she added, as she recognised that this was not quite true.

'Anyway, France has come into the war,' Teddy remarked cheerfully. 'Oh – sorry, Christopher, but you know what I mean. It makes it all more *friendly*.' They were watching Christopher, who was kneeling on the floor wrapping small pieces of liver round bits of rabbit fur. The owl, a tawny, sat on the top of the wardrobe watching him. Christopher had found him as a baby on Hampstead Heath: he had a broken leg and had been in a poor way. Christopher had put the leg into splints and nursed him back to health and now he was very tame. Simon longed for one, but he knew that he wouldn't be allowed to keep it at his school. The owl suddenly flew down and landed on Christopher's shoulder with a papery thud. Christopher held up a piece of food on the palm of his hand, the owl took it and flew back with it to the wardrobe: its expression of inscrutable outrage did not change.

'Do you ever let him out?' Teddy asked.

'I tried once, but he just flew into a tree and stayed there all day. And in the evening, when I brought him his food, he flew down and came back into the house with me.' He did not add that he had only done that once, as a token towards the owl's freedom; secretly he wanted him to stay for ever. But now, he'd been boarding at his school ever since they moved to Frensham, and his school might be evacuated into another school, and he knew that this might make keeping an owl difficult, although some-how he'd have to manage it. The owl flew down for another piece: this time he nearly lost his balance, and dug his talons in to get a firmer hold on Christopher's shoulder. Christopher had permanent claw marks, Simon had noticed, but he didn't seem to mind.

∞ ∞ ∞

The first evening of the war was spent like so many other evenings: the succession of bedtimes mechanically contested by each child as a matter of pride. 'Any minute now we'll be going to bed *before* Wills and Roland,' Lydia grumbled, 'and Wills is only two, and Roland is *nought*.'

'Yes,' Judy said, 'and at Berkeley Court Monica and I didn't have our baths until after supper which made it about nine o'clock.'

She had been fetched by her father that afternoon from staying with a school friend, and had been insufferable, the other two thought, about how grand and wonderful it had been. They'd already heard about how Monica had two ponies, and there were éclairs for tea, and a fridge that made ice and a swimming pool, and a lake with a rowing boat, and Monica had had her hair permed and possessed a necklace of real pearls.

'Swank, swank, swank,' Neville muttered. He was sitting on the floor of the room they shared seeing whether he could have sucked out the thorn from his foot himself. He could.

'Whatever are you doing?' Judy cried.

'Just biting my toenails. To make a change.'

'How repellent! Lydia, don't you think that is simply repellent?'

'They're Neville's feet – he can do what he likes with them,' Lydia said loftily. She did privately think it both clever and disgusting of Neville, but they were now united in their dislike of and boredom with Judy's treat.

'Monica had her very own bathroom,' Judy went on, as Ellen appeared to say their bath was ready and hurry up.

'Yes, and I suppose she had her very own head and nose and teeth—'

'And bottom,' Lydia finished and Neville burst into hoots of laughter.

At Home Place, the older children had supper in the hall, as they were too old to have milk and biscuits upstairs, and the grown-ups wanted the dining room to themselves, so there was a sense of grievance that no two of them were to have the usual privilege. They were eating mince and mashed potato and runner beans and the sky in the domes above them turned from violet to indigo segmented like a melon by the struts between the glass which, Clary noticed, were dark when the sky was light and seemed pale when the dusky dark began. Upstairs they could hear baths running, doors being opened and shut, general sounds of the grown-ups getting ready for their dinner. Bessie, the Brig's large black Labrador, lay at Christopher's feet, her brandy-snap eyes fixed on his face with a terrible greed that she thought she concealed by sentiment. He stroked but did not feed her. A year ago, he thought, he had his camp in the woods, a dream of adventure and escape. It now seemed impracticable, and therefore childish to him, but there also seemed nothing to take its place. The reality of being a pacifist had been brought home at school to him during this last year: the teasing, the downright bullying contempt in which he was held by almost everyone.

Only Mr Milner seemed to understand. Mr Milner was the classics master, and Christopher, who had started by not liking Greek very much, had found he was liking it because he liked Mr Milner, and the way in which he talked about what he thought so much. Christopher was always drawing things, mostly birds and sometimes animals, and he often did it in his exercise books that were meant for homework. When Mr Milner came upon a portrait of Tawny, with some sketches of simply his talons, or an unfurled wing, he hadn't been sarcastic or condemning about it, had just exclaimed, 'I say, that's awfully good, you know, really awfully good! Do you do much of that sort of thing?' And when Christopher had mumbled, quite a bit, he'd said, 'Absolutely right. If you want to be an artist of any kind the great thing is to practise *all the time* – that's what being a practising artist means. I've never been able to abide those slim volumes, that single cello concerto. However good they are, one knows perfectly well that if the chap had done more he'd be better.' And then, just before the summer holidays and after the exams, he'd suddenly given him a block of the most beautiful paper, very thick and white with a lovely feel to it. 'I just happened to have it,' he had said, 'and you could make far better use of it than I.' Mr Milner *knew* he was a pacifist, and was literally the only person who behaved as though that was a perfectly natural thing to be – had simply asked him why he was one, and listened to the reply. Then he had said, 'Well, Christopher,' (Christopher had noticed that he only called people by their Christian names if he liked them, otherwise he would have been Castle) 'principles are very expensive things – or can be . . .' He was fat and rather bald, which made his eyebrows look even bushier, and had a sort of wheezy voice that cracked when he got excited, which he did about a lot of things. He always wore the same tweed jacket with leather patches on the elbows and the sort of boots that were for going up mountains, and his ties were never very clean, and when he laughed it was 'Ho ho ho!' followed by more wheezing. Boarding had meant being free from Dad getting at him, but certainly not good in other ways, except for Mr Milner.

My being against it won't make the slightest difference to it happening, he thought, because I don't really count, and then he heard Mr Milner's voice saying, 'Everybody counts, dear boy, if only to himself. Don't turn yourself into an abject exception.'

'What are you smiling at?' Neville asked.

'Nothing much,' he said, and then he thought, That's a lie and I hardly noticed. He decided to count them up all the next day just to see how often it happened. Only, of course, he thought, if I know I'm counting them up there won't be so many of them. It was a bit like what Mr Milner had said that somebody had said about the state of mind in which people wrote diaries.

∞ ∞ ∞

Polly was abstracted: she left a lot of her mince, and when it came to apple amber, she said she didn't want any. She, too, was thinking of last year, when Oscar had been alive and got lost, and then found, just in time for peace. But Oscar had been found stretched out, stiff as a board at the end of the back garden. He had been run over, the vet had said: his back was broken. Another serious funeral, and after that, she had decided that she had better not have another cat until she had her house and everything. Now, she was glad of that decision. At least she did not have to contemplate whoever she might have had being gassed to death. Dad had wanted to give her another for her birthday, but she said she was too old for a cat. 'At least, I've reached a middle age when it wouldn't be advisable,' she had said, and he had said, 'Well, Poll, you know best,' and she had wondered afterwards why people always said that when they disagreed with one. Actually, she felt sad about not *wanting* a cat, but now, she thought, perhaps she had always known that the war wouldn't go away, had been simply waiting, and looming all the time. And here it was, and everything, on the face of it, seemed to be much the same. If only Dad wasn't going to be in London, she thought. If only they could all stay together, then whatever happened couldn't be so awful. At least she didn't have to go on trying to believe in God.

Bessie was between her and Christopher. She had quickly realised that Polly had food on her plate and had leaned her bulk against Polly's knee and chair. Christopher had turned to her and smiled and said, 'Don't give in to her, she's far too fat for her age. It wouldn't be a kindness.'

'I know,' she said. Bessie wouldn't have a gas mask. Human beings were only kind to them up to a point, she thought, they weren't *really* kind. Teddy and Simon were talking about cricket. They talked more and more about things that didn't interest her. If she had children, she'd have them all educated in the same place, then they'd go on knowing each other and doing the same things. This idea cheered her up and she asked Christopher if he agreed, and he did, and then Nora, who had heard them, chipped in saying there was a frightfully modern school like that in Devon called Dartington Hall where the children were all terribly spoiled.

'What do you mean, spoiled?' Clary asked.

'Well, you know, allowed to do what they like all the time. And they do crafts, things like woodwork which doesn't strike me as an educational subject at all.'

Clary said, 'I can't see that doing what you like would spoil you. It makes me far nicer when I do.'

'Everybody needs discipline,' Nora said. 'I know *I* do.'

'Well, we can't all be the same,' Clary said. Christopher suddenly choked with laughter, but Nora just went rather red.

An evening, just like any other evening, Polly thought, as Aunt Rach came downstairs dressed in her blue moiré dress with a little cape round her shoulders. 'Hallo, darlings! Having a nice supper?'

Simon said, 'What would you say if we told you it was horrible?'

'I should say, "Serve you right, silly old aunt, for asking such a daft question."'

She was on her way to the drawing room, but the Brig had heard her voice and now called to her: 'Rachel! The very person I wanted to see,' and she turned and went to his study.

'Poor Brig,' Clary said. 'Think of not being able to read.'

'Or ride. Or drive,' Teddy said, which seemed far worse to him.

'He hasn't driven for ages. Tonbridge won't let him. But he goes on the train all by himself.'

'Bracken meets him at Charing Cross.'

'Bracken is getting so huge that Dad says he'll have to buy a larger car to fit him into. And in the end he'll only fit into a lorry. I expect he'll be called up and they'll have to put him in a tank to drive. Come on, Simon, let's finish our game.' They went off to the billiard room.

'Let's play cards,' Clary said, not because she specially wanted to, but she wanted to get Polly's mind off the war. She looked at her now. 'Pelmanism?' she coaxed; she was particularly good at that game. Polly wrinkled her white forehead. 'Racing demon?'

Louise, who also realised about Polly, said what a good idea, so they went up to the old nursery, where Polly and Clary now slept, and got out the packs of cards and made Christopher join them, but he never won, and so he left, saying that he was going to read.

∞ ∞ ∞

At dinner, in the dining room, nobody talked about the future; all general ruminations had been exhausted and everyone had withdrawn into their own personal uncertainties which most of them felt, for various reasons, it would sound both selfish and pusillanimous to discuss. They ate their asparagus soup, made from the last pickings from the beds for that year, the Duchy remarked, and oxtail with beetroot in a white sauce and carrots chopped up with peas and mashed potato, followed by charlotte russe, a pudding dear to Mrs Cripps's heart – she loved arranging all the little upright sponge fingers in the pudding mould – but Edward called it wet cake and thought he would wait for cheese. Even he was at a loss for conversation; the precious hardwood logs had been dumped in the river again, but the men never talked about the business except when they were alone together. He wondered how Diana was doing, and whether she had been joined by Angus, and if she had, whether she would let him sleep with her or not. He hadn't got a leg to stand on there because, after all, he and Villy . . . but he didn't exactly relish the idea. He looked at Villy, who was wearing a plum-coloured dress with a sort of draped neck that didn't suit her at all. They had had the beginnings of a row at Pear Tree Cottage when they were getting ready for dinner because she had said that she wasn't prepared to spend the entire war tucked away in the country looking after one small baby; she would go mad, she said. If there was to be one London house kept open, she thought it should be Lansdowne Road. 'Hugh could live in it during the week, and the rest of the family could come up whenever they needed to.'

This had silenced him: he knew that the chances of seeing Diana would be halved if Villy was in London, but he could hardly raise that as an objection. 'We'll have to see how things turn out,' he had said.

He noticed that his father wanted some port, which stood at his right hand, but that he was unsure where his glass was. He got up and went round to pour it for him, and then pushed the decanter round the table to the next person.

'Zoë, the port is with you,' he said, and she gave a little start, and moved it on to Hugh. How attractive she looked. She was wearing some sort of housecoat affair, long, pale greeny-blue brocade woven with little apricot flowers, with her hair swept smoothly back from her face into some kind of net so that it looked like a huge bun – a sort of Victorian effect. And she had a complexion that made all the other women look weather-beaten or faded, although these days she was very pale. He wondered whether Rupe had taken his advice about starting another baby as soon as possible.

The Duchy knew perfectly well that the men wanted to talk on their own so as soon as the pudding was eaten (the Duchy disapproved of cheese at night), she suggested that the women withdraw. When they were settled, and Eileen had brought the coffee, Rachel said, 'Before you start any music, Duchy dear, I think I'd better distribute these. The Brig wants them put on every bedroom door.' She handed them round.

'"Instructions in case of an Air Raid,"' Sybil read aloud. 'Goodness! Who did all this?'

'I did. Matron said she must have them for the nurses, and the Brig said they should be for everyone. I'm sorry that my typing is so bad – I type like a two-toed sloth.'

It must have taken her hours, Sid thought, and Villy obviously thought the same, because she said, 'Wasn't there even any carbon paper?'

'There was, but it was frightfully old and, anyway, if you make as many mistakes as I do, it isn't actually much quicker.' The instructions were very sensible, and told people what to do either during the day or night. 'Although, of course, they won't have air raids in the dark. They won't be able to see where they are,' Villy said.

'As long as we all do the blackout properly.'

They spent a little time deciding which children they would be responsible for, and then there was a silence.

The evening, filled, as in a way it was, by small domestic activity – by Sid and the Duchy playing Mozart sonatas, by the men coming out from the dining room – was, none the less, punctuated by these small, dead moments, when the minute sound of Sybil's knitting, or a log subsiding in the fireplace, or sugar being stirred into a coffee cup only accentuated those times when each person was engulfed by their private anxieties.

As she was shutting the piano, the Duchy remarked, 'Do you remember how, in the last war, it became unpatriotic to play German music? Such a ridiculous notion.'

'Not everybody thought that, surely?' Sid was putting her fiddle away, but Rachel could hear that she was shocked.

'Only the sort of people who gave white feathers to men with flat feet or bad eyesight, Duchy dear,' she said.

'I'm sure the Germans will be worse about that sort of thing,' Hugh said.

'But, then, they will have far less to lose. Composers aren't our strong point, compared to them,' Rachel said, then put her hand over her mouth and looked at Villy whose father had been a composer, after all. How lucky, she thought, that Lady Rydal had opted for dinner in bed that night.

But Villy, who had loved her father dearly, perhaps more than anyone else in her life, was suddenly remembering him writing in one of his diaries that going to Germany as a young student, and dazzled by the quantity of music available, had been like being a dog let out into a field of rabbits.

'Hitler is reputed to like Wagner,' Sybil said; she had finished the second sock, and pulled its pair out of the bag before handing them to her husband. Thank goodness *that* pair was finished: she was really bored of knitting socks, but Hugh seemed so pleased with them that she felt she had to keep him supplied.

'I can well believe it.' The Duchy disliked Wagner immensely: he went, she felt, too far in directions that she did not like to consider at all.

'Bed!' Edward cried. 'We've got an early start.' He

looked at his brothers. 'Better if you give Rupe a lift, I've got a call to make on my way.'

∞ ∞ ∞

Rupert had been faintly dreading the moment when he would be alone with Zoë in their bedroom. When he had gone up for his bath before dinner, she was sitting at the dressing table doing nothing. He put his hand under her chin and tilted her face up to him; he could see that she had been crying because her eyelids were swollen, their whiteness a faintly translucent blue. To his surprise she smiled at him, took the hand that now lay on the shoulder of her kimono and thrust it under the silk. As he gazed into her astonishing cloudy eyes, that were not, he had long discovered, the green of anything else, she moved his hand from her shoulder to her breast. Startled, charmed, he bent to kiss her, but she put her hand on his mouth and made a little backward, provocative move-ment with her head, indicating the bed. He felt a sudden surge of light-hearted excitement and pleasure – his old, young Zoë was back.

Now, as they walked quietly up the stairs and along the gallery landing to their room, that brief, idyllic half-hour that had been – perhaps fortunately – interrupted by Peggy knocking on the door and coming immediately into the room to turn down the bed, seemed like a dream, either only to have happened to him or not to have hap-pened at all. Peggy had gasped and blushed with embar-rassment, but without her they would never have made dinner on time. They had both dressed with lightning speed, laughing – Zoë had bundled her hair, still faintly damp from being washed, into a chignon and buttoned herself into the housecoat he'd bought her last Christmas. 'Haven't even time to do my face,' she said. 'Will I do?'

'You're so—' he began, then 'I love you,' he said, 'that's the long and short of it. You'll do for *me*.'

But now, at the end of what had been rather a sticky evening *en famille*, he began to worry about having said earlier to her that they would talk about the future; his going into the Navy (if he could), and how she felt about things, and he was afraid, because it would lead to an argument. She was no good at arguments, and her inability to understand things that she didn't want or like usually irritated him to the point where he accused her to himself of wilful incomprehension; aloud he would be aggressively patient and she would sulk. He dreaded ending the day on such a note, and since they had made love, which until the last few months had been the resolution of such times, he felt the outcome might be a tense, sleepless night.

He was wrong. What happened was pretty much the same as before dinner, and this time, because he was not so startled by her light-hearted ardour, he realised how much more enjoyable it all was when he wasn't either feeling sorry for her because of the rotten time she'd had, or anxious that he was no longer able to give her pleasure. When they were lying quietly in what felt to him the most blissfully companionable silence, she said, 'Rupert, I've been thinking.'

His heart sank, then rallied. He was full of the most tender regard: he would be patient, and gentle, and somehow get her to understand that some things had to be outside and beyond their own wishes. He settled her into the crook of his arm. 'I'm listening,' he said.

'I'd like us to find a desk for Clary for her Christmas present. You know, one with a secret drawer, a beautiful old one that she can have for her writing. I thought we might try that place in Hastings that Edward goes to – '

'Cracknell.'

'Yes, him. Don't you think that's a good idea?'

'A marvellous idea,' he said. Tears came to his eyes. 'We'll go next weekend.'

'But it's got to be a secret.'

'Of course. You don't think I'd *tell* her, do you?' He was delighted to be outraged on this scale.

'It's a long time till Christmas.' She wriggled free of him and sprang out of bed.

'Where are you off to?'

'Putting on some clothes for Peggy in the morning,' she said, pulling her nightdress over her head.

It was odd, he thought, as he got into his pyjamas, opened the window to let in the cool, misty air, and went back to bed, odd that the piece of future they *had* talked about should be simply the next weekend. And then, perversely, after he had kissed her and turned out the light, he wished that they *had* talked – seriously, but without fighting – about what lay ahead, and then cursed himself for always wanting something more, or else, of her than he got.

∞ ∞ ∞

'You are. Well, you are to me, anyway.'

Edward and Villy had taken Jessica and Raymond back to the cottage by car as Raymond was so lame, and Sybil and Hugh had said no they would love the fresh air, and were walking back. Sybil had a torch that she shone so carefully in front of Hugh that she stumbled and he put out his arm to steady her. 'Come round the other side of me,' he said, 'and then I can hold your hand.'

'Beauty is in the eye of the beholder,' she said, half laughing at herself for saying it.

'I don't think that's true. Anyway, whatever I think you look like, and whatever *you* think you look like, I love you – always have – always will. Whatever happens.' It slipped out, that last bit. Why the hell did I say that?

There was a silence during which he began to hope that she hadn't noticed. But then she said, 'I could bear anything that happens if we could all be together. But with Simon miles away at school and you in London by yourself – Hugh, it *would* make sense if we kept our house open. Wills and Polly can stay here and we could come down at weekends. Don't you see?'

'I wouldn't have a second's peace all day worrying about you in the house alone and if anything like an air raid happened, I'd be too far from you to look after you. It's out of the question.' He squeezed her hand. 'I'll be down at weekends, regular as clockwork.'

The retort that it was to be *she* who was not to have a second's peace all week worrying about what might happen to *him* nearly escaped and was swallowed down in silence. If one of them had to be anxious, it must be she. She could not bear the thought of him worrying. She shut up.

When they were in bed, he said, 'But, you know, I think quite possibly it will all be over much sooner than we think. I don't think that Hitler will find the Maginot Line much fun – it won't be like last time. And this time,

Elizabeth Crofton-Hay, who went on and on about coming out, being a débutante, being presented, etc. Her only other topic of conversation was Ivor Novello with whom she was madly in love; she had been to *The Dancing Years* fourteen times, but she had no real *artistic* interest in the theatre at all. She had left, and this term it would be someone else but they hadn't arrived, so she quickly chose the nicest bed by one of the windows. The room was exactly the same. Two iron bedsteads with blue covers; two chests of drawers with a small square mirror hung on the wall behind them; two narrow wardrobes; and two cane-bottomed chairs. The floor was covered with dark blue linoleum so polished by the inmates that the small woollen rug placed beside each bed slipped about the room at the slightest touch. She sat on her bed still in her coat: it was too cold even to smell the furniture polish. She had only discovered that she had stopped minding – stopped feeling homesick – about half-way through last term. Before that, although sometimes she had begun to recognise that she wasn't, she had been afraid to think about it too much, in case she started feeling awful again. (This had happened a lot during the first term. She would be putting suet crust into a pudding basin, or sitting in the dining room with everyone chattering away, and just as she thought that it wasn't too bad being away from home, misery would engulf her; she would have to stop whatever she was doing and rush up and lie on this bed and cry.) But then, she gradually realised that she was getting used to the whole thing. She had stopped breaking china, and feeling sick; for hours, days sometimes, she didn't think about home at all. She had wondered why this didn't make her feel elated, but when she had talked to Polly at Christmas (because, after all, Polly was in the same position: after years of worrying about there being a war, war was turning out to be much like ordinary life so far as frightening things were concerned) Polly had said that not worrying so much about it hadn't made her feel wonderful either. But she had added that she thought this was because she didn't really believe that the war would go on simply being a bit gloomy and tiresome, and Clary had interrupted by pointing out that if one was a Finn one would undoubtedly be frightened – she was quite without tact, Louise thought. But really, it was more that she had other things to be frightened about: her audition, for instance. She had managed to persuade her parents that she should have one – to one acting school, and if she failed to get in that was to be that. She would have to learn typing and do some boring job in an office. They had agreed, she thought, largely because her mother had been so set on sending her to France to learn French with some family (clearly out of the question since the war had started) that they had not thought of any alternative, and at her age – she would be seventeen in March – she was too young to join up or anything frightful like that. Thank God! It seemed awful to have had to spend years and years doing lessons and being treated as a child and then to have one's burning ambition set aside as selfish and frivolous. The Wrens or the ATS would be like some vast boarding school, she imagined. So, *if* she got in to the acting school she was to be allowed a year, and anything could happen in a year. She was selfish, of course. The 'holy' term with Nora had showed her that. The Miss Rennishaws were very High Church: church-going was practically compulsory, although you were not made to go to their church – had the choice of another one where they did not burn

111

incense, and conduct confessions, et cetera – but Nora had taken to all that with her usual ardour and more or less swept Louise along with her. Every week, all that term, Louise had knelt in the little box and although initially she had found it hard to think of things to confess – had even, on one occasion, made a few things up – she found it got easier and easier – in fact, her character worsened by the week. 'I am very proud, revengeful and ambitious,' was how she had started, but Father Fry had picked that up at once, and said Hamlet had only been *wishing* that that was what he was like and, in any case, the remarks were too general to constitute confession. So then she had had to get down to things like admitting that she didn't think she ought to have to clean lavatories or scrub floors – things that when they were doing their week as a housemaid at the school they were made to do – and they were on to pride at once. When she had complained to Nora that it didn't seem to be making her a better person but rather the reverse, Nora had replied that one could not evolve at all until one recognised what a rotten weak character one was to start with, and she had tried to make Louise have sort of practice confessions with her every night. To be fair, Nora thought of endless faults – or sins, she called them – about herself and every time she mentioned one, Louise realised that she did that too, and once or twice it got almost like a competition to see who was the worst. Everyday life had become a minefield. A single moment's inattention to one's character and one sinned. 'That's what makes it so important and exciting!' Nora had cried, but privately Louise had felt that it stopped anything being fun. She had decided that although she did now believe in God, she certainly didn't love him, she didn't even *like* him very much, but this was clearly a sin on a scale that she felt would be too much for Nora, although Father Fry had been surprisingly calm about it, saying mildly that he had felt much the same as she when he was her age, a remark that contrived to make her feel both comforted and snubbed.

But then Nora had left, to work in Aunt Rach's Babies' Hotel, which had moved back to London. Elizabeth Crofton-Hay had not been at all religious, although she had gone to church every Sunday. To begin with she had enjoyed learning about make-up and finding out that Elizabeth washed her stockings in Lux every night, and wore a pearl necklace that was composed of single pearls given her every birthday by her godparents, but the more interesting experiences of Elizabeth's life – a term in Florence and a long weekend at Sandringham – seemed not to have made her in the least exciting to talk to, and Louise quickly got bored with the rhapsodies about Ivor Novello. She went to the door to see who her new companion might be. The piece of paper pinned to it said, 'Louise Cazalet and Stella Rose'. For some reason this made her think of a pale blonde girl with straight hair streaming down her back, an illustration from the fairy books – a heroine's name. She decided to unpack and find a thicker jersey.

But supper was nearly finished before Stella arrived. She had missed the train, and consequently the school taxis, and had had to wait until another taxi turned up. Supper was provided for her, and Miss Rennishaw suggested that Louise should stay and keep her company while it was eaten. So eventually they were alone in the large dining room, sitting at one of the eight round tables. She was not in the least like a princess. Her hair was black and fine and curled all over her head; her skin was olive with no trace of colour; she had long narrow eyes of a greenish grey above high cheekbones, a prominent bony nose and a pale, surprisingly elegant little mouth with a small dark mole set to one side and slightly below it. By the time she had noticed this much, Louise realised that Stella was observing her with an equal curiosity. They exchanged faintly embarrassed smiles.

'You're not homesick, are you?'

'Homesick?'

'I mean, feeling a bit strange – your first evening.'

'Oh, no! I was just thinking how glad I am not to be at home now. When my father hears I've missed the train, he'll go through the roof. If I was home, I'd never hear the end of it.'

'Would your mother mind?'

'She'd mind *him* minding, which comes to much the same thing. What's it like here?'

Louise said truthfully that it was not at all bad. But that did not satisfy Stella, and by the time she had finished her apple charlotte, she had cross-examined Louise about everything and knew about there being four different categories of work – cooking, parlourmaiding, housemaiding and laundry – and that they changed their jobs every week, that two mistresses taught cooking, an Old Girl called Patsy superintended the parlourmaids, that the smaller Miss Rennishaw taught them how to clean, and that an ancient, sardonic Irishwoman, Miss O'Connell, ran the laundry. They worked each morning, had the afternoons off, and then started at five, after tea, until supper was served and washed up. 'Miss O'Connell's the worst: she made me goffer a surplice *three* times last term. Each time I finished it, she crumpled it all up, dipped it in the starch and made me do it again.'

Stella stared and then burst out laughing. 'I haven't the least idea what you're talking about.'

'Well, you know what a surplice is? The white, smocky thing priests wear in church.'

'Oh. Right,' she said quickly.

'Well, a goffering iron is a sort of—'

But here Miss Rennishaw the Smaller put her head round the door and told Stella that her father wished to speak to her, and Stella made a comic face of fear, but Louise could see that she was also actually alarmed, leaped to her feet and followed Smaller out of the room, who returned a moment later to tell Louise that she might clear Stella's supper things away and put them in the pantry. When she had done that, she hung about the hall. She could hear Stella's voice between long pauses. 'Yes, Father, I know. Yes, it was. I said I'm sorry. I don't know. It just got sort of late. I know. Yes, it was. Oh, Father, it's not the end of the world! Sorry. I've said I'm sorry. I don't know. I don't know what else to say.' It seemed to go on and on until it sounded as though Stella was in tears, and Louise began to feel awfully sorry for her. A minute later, Stella appeared, and as soon as she had shut the Rennishaws' sitting-room door made the comic face again, rolling her eyes and shrugging her thin shoulders in a parody of despair.

'Jeepers!' she said. 'I've given my mother a sick head-ache, dinner was delayed because of all the telephone calls, I'm not fit to be allowed out because I'm so selfish and irresponsible, and he's a good mind to stop my allowance for the whole term.'

'I thought you were—'

'Crying? Oh, I had to sound like that. It's the only way to stop him. *Fathers!* Do you have trouble with yours?'

'Not – well, sometimes.'

'I can't wait to be grown up,' Stella said as they climbed the stairs to their attic.

'Oh, I absolutely agree with you there!'

The first bond between them. It was even better when Louise discovered that Stella, unlike all the others, had no wish to be a deb – 'I hardly know what they are!' she said with entrancing scorn – but wanted to *be* something, although she hadn't decided exactly what, which led the way into Louise's ambitions about the theatre and the impending audition. Stella was pleasingly impressed. 'You can practise on me,' she said. 'I simply adore being acted to or played to – or anything like that.'

'In fact, I might join you at the acting school,' she said much later. 'I think I'd rather enjoy that.' This shocked Louise, who felt that this was an irreverent approach to her sacred art.

'You can't just *decide* to act,' she said.

'Why not?'

'Why *not*? Because it's not just a job, it's more of a calling. I mean, you have to be some good at it in the first place.'

'Like you, you mean?'

'I never said I was.'

'But you *think* you are. Perhaps you just want to be famous. I don't care about that. I would do it just to find out what it was like. If you're interested in things, it doesn't matter too much if you turn out to be no good at them. It's doing it that's fun.'

'Oh.'

'You don't agree with me?'

'I just haven't thought about it like that.'

They were to have many conversations of that kind during the term, which was the coldest, the Miss Rennishaws said, that they could remember. Everybody had hot-water bottles and wore bedsocks, and shut their windows at night after the taller Miss Rennishaw had been round to say good night to them. She believed in fresh air of any temperature. There was a coal fire in their sitting room, which meant that half a dozen of them could get warm at a time. There were plentiful meals in spite of the rationing that had begun before the term started. Recipes were being changed. To begin with, it didn't seem to make much difference: their four ounces of butter was doled out to them on individual saucers, but bacon and sugar were pooled – cooking was done with margarine and lard. Meat was not rationed until the end of the term, but it had become more expensive, and they were taught to make more stews and pies and to use offal, the latter being generally unpopular. Louise stopped going to confession, but she felt too nervous of Miss Rennishaw's disapproval if she gave up church as well, so she went. Stella came the first Sunday with her, and stood and sat and knelt, but was mute. 'I don't know the words,' she said, when Louise asked her afterwards why she hadn't joined in. 'I shan't come again, anyway,' she added. 'I just wanted to see what it was like.'

'Don't your family ever go?'

'Never.' She answered so repressively that Louise dropped the subject.

Stella's curiosity seemed to embrace everything, and to be insatiable. It led her to trespassing: 'Let's see where this path *goes* to'; to examining the contents of people's chests of drawers when they were housemaids together ('Barbara Carstairs has a box with false *eyelashes* in it – black – not at all like her sandy ones, and Sonia Shillings-worth has a photograph of someone in her underclothes drawer that definitely isn't her brother,' whereupon Louise, although shocked, would fall into the trap of asking, 'How do you know?' 'She hasn't got one – I asked her'). It led her to dipping her fingers into jars and tins to taste the contents, to experimenting with pots and bottles of cold cream and astringent lotions – even lipsticks were tried and then hastily rubbed off. At the same time Louise discovered that she could be intensely and unexpectedly private and resented questions of any kind. She was very funny: in a few weeks she could imitate anyone in the school, not only their voices but everything else about them. But she was also a wonderful audience: weeping at Louise's Juliet, and laughing until the tears ran down her face at her sketch of a dancing-class teacher. 'Angelic Louise! Oh, I love people who make me laugh. And cry. You're the only person here who could do that.' She was wonderfully sympathetic about Louise's parents being so uninterested in her career. 'Although,' she said, 'it can be worse if they have definite ideas for one.'

'Do your parents have ideas for you?'

'*Do* they! Sometimes my mother wants me to go to university so that I can thereafter be a teacher or work in a library or something. But my father simply wants me to make a good, suitable marriage. And then sometimes it's the other way round. They have rows about it and then they make up and blame it all on me.'

'What about your brother?'

'There was never any question about him. Peter's always been going to be a musician. As soon as he left school he went to the Academy. The only thing is, he'll get called up before he's finished his training. He got deferred to finish his first year because he had a double scholarship. So he'll only have one more term.'

'Perhaps the war will be over before then. Nothing much seems to happen.'

'It will.'

'How on earth do *you* know, Stella?'

'I just do. My father says Hitler's become unbelievably powerful – and he's insane.'

Louise noticed that many conversations ended with Stella quoting her father as though there was nothing more to be said. Sometimes, as now, she found this irritating. 'Well, it doesn't seem as though much is going to happen. I mean, all our evacuees have gone back to London and there haven't been any of the air raids we were told would be so frightening. And my father says that with every month that goes by, we're getting more aeroplanes and ships and everything, which makes it less and less likely that the Germans would dare to attack us. So honestly, it is possible, Stella, that your father may be wrong.'

But Stella's face – her whole body – implied the utter impossibility of this. Louise dropped the subject. By now, they loved one another enough to disagree, to disapprove, to snub each other, but they never actually quarrelled.

'I'm so lucky you were here!' Stella would say. Sometimes this exclamation would be followed by a list of Louise's attributes: she used her mind, she'd *read* things, she was determined upon a career, she was 'a serious person', until Louise, blushing with pleasure at being so appreciated, would disclaim the virtues, aware all the time that she neither read nor thought enough to be so extolled, and she would counter-attack with Stella's talents, which seemed the greater to her because they were so lightly borne (Stella could not only play anything she heard by ear but had perfect pitch; she also turned out to be fluent in both French and German and to have a photographic memory – she could read a recipe once and remember every detail of it). Sometimes it was how lucky it was that they had met, and Stella proceeded to outline the boringness of the other girls: one could see them all, she said, and proceeded to *enact* the seven ages of the deb. 'All horsy to begin with, with shining, healthy pink faces and Harris tweed jackets talking about cubbing and fetlocks, and then simpering away in tulle and white net with little pearl necklaces and tight perms, and then all soppy and radiant in creasy white satin being married, and *then* in cashmere with larger pearls holding some ghastly baby – oh, I left out being *presented* with those idiotic white feathers in their hair and long white gloves – and then looking much fatter in a suit with a complicated hat at their child's speech day, and then looking completely *passé* in beige lace at their daughter's coming-out dance . . .' Her caricatures of all these phases were accompanied by wonderfully comic expressions, and her hands delineated the appropriate clothes until Louise was helpless with laughter.

'Henrietta's not so bad,' she would say eventually.

'She *is*! She sleeps on her back so that her face will stay smooth when she's old.'

'How do you *know*?'

'Mary Taylor told me, because she's always having nightmares and Mary has to wake her up.'

'Well, there are the Seraphic Twins.' Angelica and Caroline Redfern were identical: ash blonde with velvet brown eyes and amazingly long, elegant legs, and widely regarded as the height of glamour.

'Oh, *them*! It's only there being two of them that impresses people. You know, like pairs of things being more valuable than one of them from the collecting point of view. Two minds without a single thought is more like it.'

Louise, after she had laughed, said she thought Stella was in danger of being priggish. 'I mean, we aren't actually that much more marvellous.'

'I never said we were. But we make the most – well, more – of ourselves. We *want* to be more.'

Somehow, Stella always had the last word. As, Louise recognised, Nora had also often done. Perhaps I am a weak character, she thought incredulously. Surely not! All the same she knew that Stella was her best friend, and as she, unlike Stella, had never been to schools, boarding or otherwise, this was a new and exciting experience, and the only sad thing to dread was that after this last term they would be parted, as Stella was staying on to complete her course. 'Although I might not,' she said. 'You never know. I loathe cooking, and I'm certainly never going to do any housework, and what's the use of me learning how to interview servants when soon there won't be any?'

'Stella, don't be so *mad*! There'll always be servants.'

'There won't. They'll go and do war work and then they won't want to come back. Would you?'

'That's different.'

'Now you're relying on the old class structure.'

'So what? That's what we've got.' But here she had hit on a new and hitherto entirely concealed vein in her friend, as Stella launched into her political views. What did Louise think class structure depended upon? Educating people so badly that they could only do the dull and menial jobs, *or* relying upon them having some vocation, like nursing, where they wanted to do whatever it was so badly that they would put up with being very poorly paid. There was nothing like making sure people were half educated and not paying them properly to keep them in a place where nobody else wanted to be, she finished. They were lying head to tail on Louise's bed, eating Walnut Whips and wrapped in their eiderdowns, and for a moment or two they were both silent, although the storm outside, a shrieking wind and rain slamming against the windows, felt to Louise like her own thoughts, chaotic and noisy – and aghast.

Then Stella said, 'You've never thought about these things, have you?'

'No, not in the way you put it.'

'Your family don't talk about things like that?'

'Well, not much.' She thought of her father inveighing against people who were too lazy to work for their money. 'My father told me once that he drove a bus in the General Strike.'

But Stella simply laughed, and retorted, 'There you are then. Conservative to the bone.'

'And my mother has done a lot of work for the Red Cross. And charities and things.'

'Charity is just another way of keeping people in their place.'

Louise was silenced. Everything that Stella said amazed her; she had no experience, no knowledge, no machinery of thought to contest, to deny or even to contribute to these ideas. Much later, after they had cleaned their teeth and Miss Rennishaw had been to say good night and told them that a tree had fallen down across the drive, she said, 'But who *will* do it if *you* don't want to and you don't think anyone else will?'

And Stella, who knew at once that she was talking about housework, said, 'I don't know. I should think most of it won't get done. Most of it is unnecessary – look at all the pointless polishing we do.'

This answer did not seem entirely satisfactory, but she was too unsure about everything to argue. Because it was disturbing (and exciting), and she knew nothing compared to Stella, she decided to find out more, only she felt it was going to be quite difficult to choose anyone else to ask.

They were both going home for the same weekend, and then on the Friday before it, her mother rang Louise. 'I'm afraid this weekend will have to be put off, Louise. Grania has suddenly become not at all well, and I have to take her to a nursing home.'

'What's happened to her?'

'As I said, she's not at all well. She's been very forgetful lately, and now she doesn't seem to know what is going on at all, and the servants can't manage her. So I'm taking her to a very nice place near Tunbridge Wells where I'm told the nursing is good and she will be properly cared for. And of course Daddy's away – he never seems to get any leave – so could we make it next weekend instead?'

'But I'd be perfectly all right at home by myself. And it won't take you more than one day, will it?'

'I'm afraid it will, because I've got to go to Frensham to collect her from Aunt Jessica and then take her to the home, and *then* go and shut up her house in London – deal with poor Bryant who is practically having a nervous breakdown. Grania's been ordering enormous meals for dinner parties and then not asking anyone because, of course, she doesn't really know anybody any more and then she gets very distressed and thinks it's all poor Bryant's fault.'

'Goodness! She's sort of gone off her head!'

But her mother repeated repressively: 'She's simply become very confused.'

When she told Stella, Stella said, 'Well, I'll have to ask, of course, but perhaps you could come and stay with me.'

Which, after what they both considered was a lot of fuss, is what happened. Stella's mother said yes, and then Miss Rennishaw said that Louise's mother must give her consent, and then Louise's mother wanted Mrs Rose's telephone number . . . 'What on earth *for*?' Louise cried. 'It's really awful the way they treat us, as though we were babies.'

'I entirely agree with you. Particularly when, if we were boys, in a year's time we'd be considered old enough to go to France and die for our country. Well, I would, anyway.' Stella at eighteen was a year older than Louise.

'Do your family talk about politics a lot?' she asked in the train.

They talk about everything a lot. They talk so much that they hardly have time to hear what each other says, and then they accuse each other of never listening to anyone else. Don't look so worried. We'll do things on our own.'

The Roses lived in a large, dark mansion flat in St John's Wood. It was on the third floor and was reached by a lift, like a cage, that made mysterious noises when in motion. The front door had an iron grille in front of stained glass. It was opened by a small squat woman who looked, Louise thought, as though she was sick and tired of being so tired. She had black eyes with paler dark circles under them and a mouth that seemed compressed with tragic resignation. When she saw Stella, she smiled and patted her effusively, before kissing her. 'This is my aunt Anna,' Stella said. 'This is my friend Louise Cazalet.'

'The other way round, Stella. How many times have I told you that you tell the older person to whom they are being introduced?' Stella's mother emerged out of the gloomy passage that seemed to stretch for ever in front of them.

'But a child,' Aunt Anna murmured and, nodding to Louise, she pushed past Stella's mother and disappeared.

'How do you do, Louise? I am so glad that you can keep my girl company this weekend. Take Louise to her room, Stella. Lunch will be in a quarter of an hour and Papa is coming back for it.'

'That means "don't you dare be late",' Stella murmured. 'Have you noticed how they hardly *ever* say simply what they mean?'

All the same she was ready in no time and hanging about in Louise's doorway.

'Is your mother French?'

'Good Lord, no. Viennese.'

'She's fantastically beautiful.'

'I know. Come on. Papa's back – I heard the front door.'

She led the way to a large sitting room very full of fat, upholstered chairs and sofas, glass-fronted bookcases, and a grand piano. One whole side of the room was adorned with huge gilded mirrors in front of which, on a pair of marble-topped tables, were plaster busts of

Beethoven and somebody she didn't recognise. The tall windows on the opposite wall were partly obscured by dark velvet curtains that were looped back with thick silk tasselled rope to reveal inner curtains of elaborate white lace. A coal fire burned in the grate, glowing distantly in the crowded twilight. The room was very hot. Stella took her by the elbow and guided her through the furniture to the far end where Mrs Rose stood beside her much shorter husband.

'This is Louise, Papa.'

As he shook hands with her he remarked, 'When you introduce people, Stella, you should use their full name. Your friend is not a housemaid.'

'Sometimes she is. It's one of the things we have to do at school.'

'Ah ha!' It came out like a snort. 'Peter is late. Why?'

'He has a rehearsal, Otto. He said not to wait.'

'We must, of course, *obey* him. Come, Miss Louise, and have some lunch.'

He led the way through the room to another door beside the one they had come in from, which proved to lead to a smaller room where a table was elaborately laid: a white cloth, silver, rather heavy, old-fashioned-looking china and tall, straight-backed chairs with velvet seats. This room was curtained in the same manner, but lit by a large chandelier with parchment half-shades on each candle bulb. Stella's parents sat at each end of the table and Louise and Stella were placed each side of her father. After a moment, Aunt Anna appeared, followed by a little maid who seemed almost overpowered by the enormous soup tureen she carried on a tray which she set before Mrs Rose, who proceeded to ladle it into plates that were set in a pile before her. Louise was not used to soup. It smelled strong but inviting, and contained dumplings bobbing about in the broth and she was not sure how to eat them.

Mr Rose observed this at once, and said, 'You have not had *Leberklösse*, Louise? It is very good.' He took a spoonful which included a dumpling and popped it into his mouth. Louise copied him. The dumpling was scaldingly hot and, without thought, she spat it back into her spoon. Everybody noticed this, and she felt herself blushing.

'It is Otto's fault. He can eat food hotter than anyone in the world,' Mrs Rose said kindly. Louise drank some water.

'You are a sensible young woman not to burn your mouth. A burned mouth, and you can taste nothing.' Just as she was thinking how kind he was, he put his spoon down with a bang, and almost shouted, 'This soup is without its celery. Anna! Anna! How is it possible that you have forgotten an ingredient so important?'

'I did not forget, Otto, I could not find any. All the celery was just white stalks with the leaves already cut. What could I do?'

'Make another soup, of course. I know that you have in your repertoire fourteen soups, many if not all of which do not require celery leaves. Don't look like that, woman, it is not a tragedy. I am just telling you that it is not as it should be.' He picked up his spoon again and smiled at Louise. 'You see? The smallest criticism and I am treated like a tyrant. Me!' He laughed fondly at the absurdity.

In spite of this, he – they all – had a second helping of soup, and while Stella was cross-examined about the school, Louise could look at her friend's parents in peace. Mrs Rose, although probably quite old – at least forty –

was not somebody who had been a beauty once – she still was one. She was immensely tall with wavy iron-grey hair fastened with a slide at one side. All her features were large, but so beautifully arranged that looking at her was like a close-up in the cinema. She had enormous dark brown eyes set very wide apart below a broad forehead from which her hair sprang in a widow's peak. She had cheekbones like Stella, but her nose although large was not bony like her daughter's: it had exactly the right quantity of flesh and she had sharply delineated and flaring nostrils. Her mouth was wide, and when she smiled these statuesque proportions were lit with a beautiful gaiety that Louise found bewitching.

Peter Rose arrived just as the soup plates had been cleared from the table, and her father was telling Stella that it was absurd that she could not read Italian when he had so often offered to teach her.

'You trying to teach me things means you losing your temper and me bursting into tears,' she said.

This, Louise could see, was about to provoke another outburst, quelled only by Peter's arrival. He slipped into the room and his seat at table very much as though he wished he was invisible. All eyes turned to him; he was bombarded with attention, disapproval and questions. He was late; why was he so late? How had his rehearsal gone? Would he like soup – Anna had kept some hot specially for him – or would he like to go straight to the meat course? (A vast, savoury stew had been brought in by the maid.) He had not had his hair cut in spite of the appointment being made for him; he would have to go after lunch . . . but this only branched out into a myriad other suggestions of how he should spend his afternoon. He should rest; he should take a bracing walk; he should go to the cinema to take his mind off the concert. Throughout, he sat, his myopic eyes gleaming behind heavy spectacles, his capable very white hand brushing back the lock of hair that fell constantly across his forehead, a nervous smile starting and being suppressed. He opted for soup and Aunt Anna rushed out of the room to procure it. At the same time his father observed that he seemed so full of himself and this concert that he had not even had the common politeness to notice their guest. It seemed astonishing to him, he ruminated, at a volume suited to someone soliloquising in the Albert Hall, how – considering the enormous trouble taken by their parents – two children should seem apparently devoid of any decent behaviour at all. A daughter who answered back, answered her *father* back, and a son who utterly ignored the presence of a young lady who was a guest in their house. Could Sophie understand it? But his wife merely smiled and continued to serve the stew. Could Anna? – 'Otto, they are *children*.' He turned to Louise but, filled with nervous embarrassment, she began to blush: he observed it, and let her go.

Peter said: 'Hallo! I know you're Louise, Stella has told me.'

While the stew, accompanied by red cabbage (another thing that Louise had never had before in her life) and excellent mashed potato, was being eaten, Stella's father cross-examined her about what she was going to do with her friend during the weekend.

'We'll go to Peter's concert, of course.'

'You enjoy music?'

'Oh, yes! Yes, I do.'

'Louise's grandfather was a composer,' Stella said.

'So? And who was he?'

'He was called Hubert Rydal. I think he was only a minor composer.'

'Indeed? I do not think,' he said, chewing furiously as he spoke, 'that I should much like your children, Stella, describing me as a minor surgeon. What could they know of surgery to make such a pronouncement?'

'I only meant that that's what people call him.' Louise felt herself blushing again and, worse, tears starting in her eyes as she remembered how much she had loved him – how his habitually noble face, hawk nose, snow-white beard and large blue, sad, innocent eyes would crumple and dissolve into uncontrollable giggles when he thought something was funny, how he would take her hand, 'Come with me, little dear,' and lead her to some treat kept tacitly secret from her grandmother who seldom found anything funny, how when he kissed her, his beard had smelled of sweetbriar . . . 'He was the first person I knew who died,' she said unsteadily, and looked up to find Mr Rose regarding her with a sharp and comprehending kindness.

When their eyes met, he smiled – a curious smile that she would have described as cynical had there not been so much understanding and affection mysteriously there as well – and said, 'A worthy granddaughter. And tomorrow, Stella? What do you propose to do with your guest?'

Stella muttered that they were going shopping.

'And in the evening?'

'I don't know, Pappy. We haven't thought.'

'Very well. I shall take you to a theatre. And then I shall take you out to supper. You will enjoy yourselves,' he commanded, smiling ferociously round the room at all of them.

The plates were removed and a platter of cheeses brought. Louise, for whom cheese at home consisted invariably of Cheddar for the nursery and servants, and Stilton for the grown-ups and people of her age at Christmas, was amazed to see such a collection. Mrs Rose, who saw this, said, 'Stella's father adores cheese, and many of his patients know it.'

Stella said virtuously, 'Cheese is rationed, Pappy. At school, we get only two ounces a week. Imagine you, Pappy, living on that!'

Peter said, 'At the National Gallery concerts, you get cheese and sultana sandwiches.'

'Is that what you go for, you greedy boy?'

'Of course! I have no interest in music at all; I just *adore* sultanas.' As he said this, he imitated his sister.

All the same, Louise noticed that none of the family ate much of the cheese excepting Mr Rose, who, helping himself to three kinds, cut them into smaller pieces, screwed black pepper liberally over them, and then popped them into his mouth.

The cheeses were replaced by a delicious-looking con-coction of paper-thin pastry which proved to have apples and spices in it, that Louise, although she felt she had eaten far too much already, was unwilling to resist and, as it turned out, quite unable to – since, with the remark that nobody could refuse Anna's strudel, Mr Rose ordered his wife to pass her an enormous slice. During this course, a furious argument broke out between Peter and his father on the merits of various Russian compos-ers, whom Mr Rose provocatively dismissed as producers of schmaltz or fairytale music, which made Peter so angry that he stammered and shouted and knocked over a glass of water.

It was only after very black coffee served in tiny, brittle red and gold cups that Louise and Stella were allowed to go off by themselves, and then only after much questioning and criticism about how they were to spend the afternoon.

'*Are* we going for a walk?' Louise asked. She felt sleepy after the huge meal, and dreaded the raw freezing air.

'Good Lord, no! I just said that because it's the one thing they never seem to mind. We'll just get the hell out, and then think of some lovely indoor thing to do.'

In the end they took a 53 bus to Oxford Street and spent hours in Bumpus, where after much cheerful browsing, they decided to buy each other a book. 'Something that we think the other one ought to have read,' Stella said.

'I don't know all that you've read.'

'Well, if I turn out to have read it, you'll have to choose again.' But she didn't have to. Stella chose *Madame Bovary* for Louise: 'I would have got it in French, but your French isn't much good,' she said, and Louise, whose French was almost non-existent although she had tried to conceal this from Stella, did not argue. After much agonising, she had chosen *Ariel* by André Maurois – a blue Penguin. She felt rather mean about this, because *Madame Bovary* cost two shillings, and *Ariel* only sixpence, but she knew that Stella would pour scorn on that kind of discrepancy. 'It's about Shelley,' she said and Stella replied, 'Oh, good! I don't know much about him.' They went home on the bus, deciding to inscribe the books when they got home, and inventing the awful things they thought other pairs of girls at the school would have given each other. 'Lipsticks, and *talc* powder and charms to put on their bracelets, and little notebooks to put people's birthdays in!' were some of the suggestions, until Louise, remembering Nora, said that they shouldn't be so superior.

'Why shouldn't we be? We are. It isn't saying much, after all. I mean – *look* at them!'

'You know, Stella, considering how democratic you are, you are extraordinarily arrogant!'

'I'm not. I'm simply being accurate. You're so undemocratic that you're used to people being inferior and think it's kinder to tell lies about them. I don't.'

'But there's a difference between people who've had opportunities and made nothing of them, and people who haven't.'

'Yes, there is. That's why I despise our schoolmates so much. They're nearly all far richer than we are, and expense can have been no object in their education, whereas most people – and certainly girls – don't get any opportunities to be properly educated at all. Look at your family! The boys all went to school where at least they are taught Greek and Latin, and you just having a governess!' Stella had been to St Paul's, one of the few places where education of girls was taken seriously, and Louise knew that if she wanted to go to a university she was clever enough and had certainly been prepared.

'Miss Milliment did her best. She was just too kind to us, and let us be lazy. Which I was.' She was beginning to find out all the things she didn't know, like the classics, languages, political economy, current events – the quantity appalled her.

Stella looked quickly at her, and said, '*You'll* be all right. You *want* to know things and, anyway, you know what you want to do. Lucky you!'

'My father,' she remarked later on when they were having a bath together before dressing for Peter's concert, 'says that girls should be educated absolutely as much as boys because then they are less likely to bore their husbands and children. Or, I suppose, if they don't have any of those, themselves.'

'It's funny. I thought your family would talk about politics all the time at meals. I was terrified.'

'They often do. It just wasn't a day for that. I think Pappy was anxious not to work Peter up before his concert.'

So they had a scene about Russian music instead, Louise thought, but she did not say so. It was new for her to observe things and have private views about them: at home she seemed to herself to have taken everything for granted. It was a sure sign that she was growing up – getting older and, surely, more interesting?

The family seemed to thrive on scenes. There was a scene between Stella and her mother about the dress Stella had decided to wear for the concert. In fact, it wasn't a dress: it was a scarlet jersey and a black and white check pleated skirt. Her mother said it was not formal enough for the occasion. Voices were so raised that Mr Rose emerged from another of the innumerable doors that lined the long passage and said that it was impossible to hear himself think with such a racket. He then joined the fray with gusto, disagreeing with his wife about the bottle-green velveteen being more suitable and insisting upon a cream tussore silk that Stella said was a hundred years old and too short for her. Peter's taste was quoted by both parents, although they did not agree on what it might be. Mrs Rose said that he would be ashamed of his sister turning up at his concert dressed as though she was going to play some *game*. Mr Rose said that Peter would detest her appearing in something so clearly meant to draw attention to herself as the bottle-green velvet. Stella said that if she wore the tussore silk Peter's friends would scream with laughter. Aunt Anna arrived and contributed a pink silk shirt to Stella's black and white skirt. This temporarily united the others – against *her* – and she leaned against the wall with little clucking cries of dismay. Mr Rose, although not exactly shouting, was speaking with that irritable clarity of enunciation that Louise associated with people trying to make an idiot – or a foreigner – understand. 'It is perfectly simple. You will wear the silk and do as you are told.' At this both Stella and her mother uttered cries of dismay; Stella burst into tears, her mother broke first into a cascade of sighs, disappeared into her bedroom and returned a moment later with a pale green woollen frock that she held against her daughter while tears slipped slowly down great tracts of her beautiful face. 'Otto! Otto? Would not this be the answer to the trick?'

He surveyed them both, his wife's suitably imploring expression, Stella's mutinous silence. That would have to do, he said at last. He was sick of the whole business. It was not, after all, of the slightest interest to him *what* his daughter wore; she was quite old enough to make a fool of herself if she pleased. He had no interest in the matter. He could not imagine why there had been such a fuss in the first place. He smiled with a weary, long-suffering kindness and shut his door, leaving Louise, and Stella holding the green woollen dress. Mrs Rose sighed again, and then went briskly down the passage, seemingly rejuvenated.

'Listen! What shall *I* wear?' Louise said anxiously to her friend.

'Oh, anything you like. They won't mind what *you* wear.'

Louise could hardly believe this to be true, but she had very little with her and, as she wished to save her best dress for the theatre, the alternative was a tweed pinafore dress with a cream silk shirt that Aunt Rach had given her for Christmas.

When she thought about Christmas she felt uneasy – sad. It had been spent, as it always had been, at Home Place, and although everybody had made efforts to make it seem the same, it hadn't been, although it was difficult to say that anything (which really mattered) was different. They had all had stockings – although there was no tangerine in the toe and Lydia had wept because she thought they had simply left hers out. No tangerines and no oranges – no lemons, so no lemon curd tartlets on Boxing Day, one of the Duchy's traditions – all details but they added up. But the house seemed colder, and there was hardly ever any hot water because the range took so much coke and the Duchy had changed all the light bulbs to a lower voltage to help the blackout, she said, and use less electricity. Peggy and Bertha, the housemaids, had gone off to join the WAAF, and Billy had gone to work in a factory. The garden looked different, the flower borders gone and McAlpine growing vegetables in them. He creaked about, very bad-tempered because his rheumatism was so much worse, and the Duchy had been trying to get a girl to help in the garden, but the first one left in a week – couldn't stand McAlpine, who refused to speak to her and complained of her incessantly behind her back. All the horses were gone except the two old ones so Wren, the groom, did odd jobs like chopping wood and stoking the boiler and painting bits of the greenhouse roof. He still wore his shiny leather gaiters and a nutmeg-coloured tweed cap that went, as Polly said, so very badly with his beetroot face, but he seemed shrunken and was often heard talking to himself in tones of great grievance. Dottie had been promoted to housemaid and Mrs Cripps had to make do with a much younger girl in the kitchen, who was worse than useless, she continually said. The Brig seemed much blinder than in the summer, and now made Aunt Rach take him to London three times a week when he went to his office and she was, as she said, making a joke of it, his very private secretary. Aunt Zoë was pregnant and being sick all the time, or lying with a green-white face on the sofa. Aunt Sybil – who at least had got thinner – seemed quite ratty, especially with Polly who said she spoiled Wills to death and worried Uncle Hugh by worrying so much about him. And *her mother*! Sometimes she thought that Villy actually *hated* her; she didn't seem to want to know anything about school, or her friend; she criticised Louise's appearance and the clothes that she chose to buy with her new dress allowance (forty pounds a year – for *everything*, her mother reiterated in the kind of voice that, to Louise, meant including STs). She disapproved of Louise growing her hair, which obviously if one was going to be an actress one needed to do in case one played a very old lady with a bun; she complained if she ever caught Louise doing anything that wasn't *useful*, like laying the table; she tried to send her to bed at a ridiculous hour, and spoke about her to other people – in front of her – as though she was some kind of petty criminal or idiot, saying that Louise couldn't be trusted to do *anything* she promised, that she was utterly wrapped up in herself, that she was so clumsy that she really wondered what would happen if Louise ever got on a stage. This last was the thing that hurt most, and things had come to a head when, on Boxing Day,

Louise had broken the Duchy's favourite china teapot: some scalding tea had spilled from the spout onto her left hand, the shock made her drop the pot, and tea-leaves and tea and bits of china were all over the floor. She had stood appalled, holding her scalded hand with the other one and staring at the floor, and before anyone else could say or do anything, her mother had said in her sarcastic voice, which was like a bad imitation of her friend Hermione Knebworth, 'Really, Louise, we shall have to start calling you Tony Lumpkin – or Bumpkin would be more appropriate!' There were strangers to tea; her face burned and, knowing she was going to cry, she rushed blindly from the room, knocking a book off a small table in her flight.

She was half-way up the stairs before her mother's icy voice stopped her. 'Where on earth do you think you are going? Go to the kitchen and get a cloth and a dustpan and brush and clear up the appalling mess you have made.'

She turned and got the things, and went back into the room, and picked the pieces of china off the floor, and swept up the tea-leaves, and mopped at the tea, until Eileen, who had been sent for to make more tea, came and helped her, while her mother expatiated on the variety of her clumsiness: 'The only girl who is staying at her domestic science school for three terms because she broke so many pudding basins during her first two.' There had been a feeling of unease in the room as nobody else seemed able to think of anything to say, and by the time she had finished the clearing up, her hand was hurting very much. When she had taken the dustpan et cetera back to Eileen she went to find the Duchy to apologise, but she didn't seem to be anywhere, although she did find Aunt Rach who was sewing name tapes on Neville's clothes for his new school. 'I don't know *where* she is, my duck. What's up? You look a bit under the weather.'

Louise burst into tears. Aunt Rach got up, shut the door, and led her to the sofa. 'You can tell your old aunt,' she said, and Louise did.

'She hates me! Really and truly, she *must* hate me – in front of all those people! She treated me as though I was a stupid little ten-year-old, and the way she goes on just makes me *more* clumsy than I would be if only she'd shut up.' There was a pause, and then she added, 'She never says anything *friendly* to me.' At this, Aunt Rach gave her hand an affectionate squeeze, but it was the bad hand. Aunt Rach looked at it, and then got the first-aid stuff; she lit the spirit lamp that the Duchy used for making tea, heated up the paraffin wax, waited and then coated the scald with it, which hurt very much at first, but by the time her hand was being bandaged, it had begun to feel better.

When all that was done, Aunt Rach said, 'Darling, of course she doesn't hate you. But you must remember, she's having a difficult time with your dad away. Married people are meant to be with each other, and when they can't be it is often harder for the woman because she is left at home and doesn't know what is happening to her husband. You must try and understand that. When people get as old as you, they do begin to realise that their parents are not just their parents, but people, with troubles of their own. But I expect you are noticing that.'

And Louise, who hadn't been at all, said yes, she did see. And she had tried to think about them like that, and now, as she fastened the cream silk shirt that Aunt Rach had *made* for her, she thought that it must be pretty rotten for her mother to have *her* mother practically going off her head and having to be taken to a nursing home. And living practically on her own at Lansdowne Road never knowing when Dad would get leave, which didn't seem to happen very often – her father was organising the defence of an aerodrome at Hendon. He had only spent two days with them at Christmas, which was better than Uncle Rupert, though, who hadn't got leave from the Navy at all.

She enjoyed the concert more than any she had ever been to. This was partly, she thought, because she *knew* the pianist (at least, she'd had lunch with him), and partly because, the Duke's hall being full of parents and relatives and friends of the performers, there was an unusual air of excitement and it was full.

There was an overture, and then a pause while the piano was moved into position and then the conductor returned with Peter, looking almost swamped by his tail coat. It was the third concerto of Rachmaninoff – the one with the amazingly long and mysterious opening melody. The moment he began to play, Peter seemed transformed. At lunch he really had not looked as though he had such powers – of technique, of rapt attention to the music as a whole. She felt slightly in awe of him after that.

∞ ∞ ∞

Next day they went shopping.

'Do you see your parents as people?' she asked Stella.

'Sometimes when they're with other people, I do. Not much when I'm alone with them, though. But that's

140

because they *like* being parents so much. They don't seem to notice my age, at all.'

'But don't you notice what they're like with each other?'

'Yes, but their relationship is playing mothers and fathers. That's what they do with each other all the time.'

'A pretty poor look-out for them when you and Peter are completely grown up.'

'It won't make the slightest difference. Even Aunt Anna concentrates now on being an aunt.'

'Has she always lived with you?'

'Good Lord, no. She came to stay one summer; her husband couldn't come with her for some reason – Uncle Louis is a lawyer in Munich – and then she got a telegram from him just saying, "Don't come back." And then she was going to all the same, but he rang up my father and after that my father said she must do as she was told.'

'So she's been here ever since last summer?'

'Since the summer before that. It's awful for her, because her daughter got married that year, and now she's had a baby, and Aunt Anna has never seen it.'

'But *why*?'

'My father knows why, but he won't talk about it. He's been trying to get Uncle Louis here, but so far no luck. She cooks for us because she hasn't got any money, and Father says it's good for her to have a lot to do.'

'It doesn't sound as though he's trying very hard to come here. Your uncle, I mean.'

Stella began to deny this, but then bit her lip and was silent.

'You don't want to talk about it?'

'How brilliant of you! I do not.'

'I don't mind.' She minded Stella's sarcasm very much.

They were on top of a bus, in front, on their way to Sloane Square and Peter Jones. Louise felt that the expedition was going to be spoiled if they didn't make it up before they got there. Just as she was thinking this, Stella laid a hand on her knee and said, 'Sorry! I didn't mean to be beastly. The main reason he doesn't come is that he has parents – awfully old – and a sister who looks after them. See? Now, what are we going to buy?'

And they reverted to a conversation that had been recurring for some weeks now. They could only buy one decent garment each and had been measuring themselves against the bedroom door at school all the term to see if they had stopped growing, and Stella had, but Louise had not.

'You could buy a skirt if it had a decent hem.'

'They don't nowadays.' Louise thought of clothes when she'd been a child, frocks with enormous hems, and even bodices that would let out for when you grew. 'I wouldn't mind a nice jacket that would go with everything.'

'We'll go over the whole shop first before we buy anything.'

They were so long in the shop that Stella had to ring home to explain that they would not be back to lunch. It was clear that she dreaded doing this, but luckily she got Aunt Anna. The conversation was conducted in German, so Louise did not know until afterwards that Stella had said they had met a school friend and her mother, who insisted on them going back to their house for lunch. 'So now we won't get any lunch unless we buy some,' Stella said when she had finished. They were both quite hungry, but neither wished to spend their precious allowance on food. 'And Pappy will give us a wonderful dinner,' Stella said. The shopping took so long because they could not make up their minds, and were scrupulously fair about letting whoever was trying on try on as much as they liked. In the end, Louise bought a light woollen dress the colour of pale green leaves, and Stella bought a blazer with brass buttons. And then Louise decided that, after all, she would buy the pair of deep terracotta linen trousers she had found earlier that were only two pounds as they were left over from the winter sale. 'They're Daks, from Simpson's,' Louise said proudly. She did look very nice in them, Stella thought enviously. *Her* father would have a fit if he saw them: he would not countenance any woman in trousers. When she said this, Louise said that her mother would think they were ridiculous too, but they were extremely suitable for someone who was going to be an actress. Stella then decided to buy the shoes she had seen that she longed for – scarlet sandals with huge cork wedges. '*They* won't go down well at home,' she said. By now extremely hungry, they bought half a pound of Rowntrees' Motoring Chocolate and ate it in the buses on the way home.

'What a heavenly outing. You're the best person in the world to go shopping with, Louise.'

Louise, flushed with pleasure at being so appreciated, answered, 'So are you.'

Going back to the flat was like entering a sort of foreign cave, Louise thought – it seemed so dark and mysterious, with its gilded mirrors and glinting pieces of coloured glass from the little Venetian chandeliers with small candle bulbs that spasmodically lit the long passage. Scents of cinnamon, sugar and vinegar, and Mrs Rose's scent had almost to be brushed aside by their movements; the airy, rocking sound of Schumann's *Papillon* came from the drawing room.

'Pappy is out!' Stella announced. Louise could not imagine how she knew this, but her glee and relief were evident. 'We have to show my mother what we have bought.'

'Everything?'

'As Pappy is out, I think everything. She adores clothes.'

Mrs Rose was lying on the sofa draped in a black silk shawl embroidered with brightly coloured unlikely flowers. It had an immensely long silk fringe that kept catching in everything – her long earrings, the kind that most people would only wear in the evenings, Louise thought, the rings on her fingers, the braid edging the sofa and even the spine of the book she was reading. She put her finger on her lips, and then said, very quietly, 'Your father is out.' There was the same kind of gleeful conspiracy in her voice as there had been in Stella's. 'And what did your friend give you for lunch?'

'Oh – some kind of fish pie – nothing wonderful. And bread and butter pudding.' She knelt by her mother, threw her arms round her, gave her several kisses and turned the book from her hands. 'Rilke again! You must know him by heart!'

Peter stopped playing. 'And we had hare and Aunt Anna's red cabbage. And then those pancakes with quince,' he said. 'Come on – let's see what you've bought.'

'We will have a dress show,' Mrs Rose said.

'We haven't bought all *that* much.'

'If your mother doesn't like you to wear trousers, they won't like me in them,' Louise said as she pulled the green woollen dress over her head.

144

'That's different. Anyway, it's my father who doesn't like that sort of thing. Mutti is far more broad-minded.'

'You go first.'

'No, you must – you're the guest.'

Afterwards Louise thought how extraordinarily different the Roses were from her family. The idea of parading in clothes after a shopping expedition in front of her family – and particularly her *mother* – made her want to laugh, only she didn't laugh. About the only person in the family with whom one could possibly do that would be Aunt Zoë, whom she knew was privately criticised for taking clothes and her appearance so seriously. Mrs Rose had both looked at and then examined each item: she had said, '*Very* pretty' about the green dress; she had admired Stella's jacket; she was enigmatic about the trousers. She said that she did not like Stella's red shoes, but that she would have bought them at Stella's age. Peter's contribution was to play snatches of what he clearly thought were wittily appropriate pieces of music: 'Greensleeves' and the 'Marche Militaire' for Louise, Chopin and Offenbach for his sister.

Then everybody dispersed for serious rests before dressing for the theatre, which, Louise discovered to her delight, was to be *Rebecca*, with Celia Johnson and Owen Nares. 'And supper at the Savoy afterwards,' Peter said. 'I hope you girls didn't have too much lunch.'

'Not too much,' Stella replied. When all was quiet, she sneaked off to the kitchen and got some gingernuts and milk for them. They lay and read the books they had given each other, and tried to make the biscuits last.

On her bed beside Stella she thought how lucky she was and how the war didn't seem to be spoiling anything. 'One of the things I like best about friendship,' she said, 'is just doing whatever you want to do with the other person there, but you don't have to talk to them.'

Stella didn't reply, and Louise saw that she was asleep. She put out her hand and touched the wonderfully soft dark hair. 'I love you,' she said but not aloud. It was wonderful to be free; to be able to leave her home, to start to find out about other people who were not her family. Anything could happen, she thought, *anything*! And I really want it to – whatever it is. I shan't marry – I'll just concentrate on being the best actress in the world. They'll all be amazed by me at home. I'll be the only famous Cazalet. Really, her family were extraordinarily *ordinary*. They weren't anything like as interesting as the Roses. They just seemed to muddle along with nothing much ever happening to them: they never went abroad – in fact, if it wasn't for them *she* might have been all over the place by now which would have given her useful experience. But no. All they did was get married, and go to the office, and have children. They weren't remotely interested in the arts, except, she had to admit, music, but when had her mother last read a Shakespeare play? Or any other play for that matter? And her father never read anything at all. It was amazing how he got through life so starved of any artistic nourishment. Perhaps she ought to try to rescue Polly and Clary from this bourgeois desert. She would, when they were old enough. The others were either still just children, or with her parents' lot, past saving. You couldn't possibly have a decent conversation about anything that really *mattered* – like the state of the theatre, or poetry, or even politics – look how much *Stella* knew compared to them! She bet they never thought about class structure or democracy or what would be fair to people. But if things turned out how

Stella seemed to think they would, they would be in for an awful shock. *No* servants! What on earth would they do without them? At least she knew how to cook now, which was more than could be said for any of them. If there was a social revolution, they would probably starve. She began to feel sorry for them in an angry kind of way; it was all their own fault, but still that didn't make it any better for them, as she well knew when things were her own fault. But, then, given the outstanding dullness of their lives, their senses were probably so blunted that they would not notice anything much: for instance, instead of being wildly, passionately in love like Juliet, or Cleopatra – who *was* old, after all, by the time she loved Antony – they were just fond of each other in a lukewarm unemotional way, so a giant social revolution would probably seem to them simply rather a nuisance. They seemed to have no experience of extremes, she thought, and that is what I am going to have. That's the point.

'It's only part of the point,' Stella said, as they dabbed Arrid under their arms after their bath. 'I mean, you can't live constantly at a pitch of joy or misery. The people you cite died anyway,' she added, 'and there's surely not much point in loving somebody so much you have to die.'

'That was just bad luck.'

'Tragedy is never just bad luck. Tragedy is not taking everything into account, usually one's own nature. I'm not going in for tragedy – not me.'

As usual she was silenced by Stella, who was, she felt, the most intelligent person she had ever met.

They all assembled in the drawing room for a glass of champagne and little pieces of salty fish on biscuits. Everybody looked extremely festive: Peter and Mr Rose in dinner jackets, Mrs Rose statuesque and romantic in yards of pleated black chiffon, Stella wearing her wine red taffeta, square-necked, with tight sleeves to her elbow, and Louise (profoundly grateful to Stella for making her bring an evening dress) in her old coral-pink satin that fitted like a glove to her hips and was drawn into a kind of bustle at the back.

'What beautiful ladies I am taking tonight!' exclaimed Mr Rose, with such enthusiasm that they all felt more beautiful. Peter was sent to fetch a cab, wraps and cloaks were put on, and the women got into the lift with Mr Rose; Peter was told to walk down. 'You smile,' Stella's father said in the lift to Louise. 'Why?'

'I'm so happy,' she answered without thinking.

'The best reason,' he said. In some ways he must be a very good father, she thought.

In the cab, Peter teased them about how they would be bound to fall in love with Owen Nares, who was playing de Winter.

'And why should we do that, pray?' Stella inquired, bristling.

'He's a matinée idol. All girls fall in love with him. And old ladies, of course. The ones with tea trays on their knees.'

'I shall have to be very careful then,' his mother said, whereupon her husband seized her hand and said, '"To me, fair friend, you never can be old—"'

'"For as you were, when first your eye I ey'd – so seems your beauty still—"' Louise continued.

'Go on.'

Louise looked at him and began to blush: '"Three winters cold . . ."' She went steadily on to the end.

There was a short acknowledging silence, and then

Mrs Rose put her fingers to her lips and laid them on Louise's hand. Mr Rose said: 'That is education. That is what I mean. Mark that, Stella. You could not have finished that.'

And Stella said, 'Of course not. Louise is wonderful. She practically knows him by heart.'

And Louise, slightly intoxicated by her success, said, 'I don't know anything else, much. Nothing like as much as Stella.'

But this only seemed to make the Roses approve of her more.

If anything was needed to fill her cup, it was discovery that they were in a box, something that had never happened to her before. Her family always chose the dress circle, although she had always had the secret wish to be in the front row of the stalls. But a box! It combined luxury and romance; she felt important just *being* there. She was settled in front with Mrs Rose and Stella and a programme was placed on the velvet shelf in front of her. Mrs Rose unbuttoned a small leather case to reveal a pretty pair of pink enamelled opera glasses which she offered as soon as Louise exclaimed at its prettiness. 'You can watch the people arrive. It is sometimes very amusing,' she said. The glasses were extremely good: she could see the expressions on people's faces as they wandered in, looking for their seats, seeing friends, laughing and talking . . . It was her *father*! Her father? It *was*! He had just bought a programme, had said something to the girl selling them, which made her smile, and then he had moved forward, put his arm round a lady who stood waiting for him. She wore a black dress, very bare – Louise could see the cleft between her breasts, and then her father's hand, which closed for a moment upon one of them. The lady said something, smiling, and he bent his head and kissed her quickly on her cheek. Then they moved down the gangway of the dress circle and went to seats in the third row. Everything blurred and she looked quickly away. There was a cold feeling at the back of her neck, and for a second she thought she was going to faint, but she must not. The desire to turn back and look again – it *couldn't* be her father – collided with a terror of his seeing *her*. It *was* him. She remembered her mother on the telephone: 'Daddy's away, he *never* seems to get any leave . . .' How could she prevent him from seeing her? People always looked at the people in boxes. At least he hadn't got opera glasses and he never used the ones you had to pay for because he said they were useless. She moved her head slowly back to look at them. Stella had taken the glasses, but she could see their heads bent together over the programme. She put her hand half over her face and turned towards the stage. In the interval she could say she wanted Peter to have a turn in front and she would be safe – or safer. But until then, she must just sit very still, with her hand over the left side of her face, and behave as though nothing was happening. Because the other hazard, she realised, was not letting the Roses know that anything was wrong . . .

'You're shivering. Are you cold?' Stella was asking.

'A bit. Could I borrow a wrap?'

Peter handed her his mother's shawl, which she pulled round her although she felt hot. 'Actually, I'm just longing for the play to start,' she said.

'Your wish is granted,' Mrs Rose murmured as the house lights began to dim.

The rest of the evening was like a frightful dream, only it seemed far longer than any dream. She tried, during

the first act, to pay attention to the play, but the knowledge that he was in the same theatre watching the same
thing beside the unknown lady with whom, she felt, he
must be in love (otherwise why would he lie to her mother
about not getting leave?) was suddenly too shocking to
be put aside for anything else at all. In the first interval, it
was proposed that they should stretch their legs, but
realising that this might mean going to the dress circle
bar, where she knew that they might be, she refused,
saying that she wanted to read her programme. They left
her, and she sat miserably in the back of the box discard-
ing wild notions of escape. She had no money with her,
so she could not leave a note and simply take a cab back
to the Roses' flat. Aunt Anna might not have any money
to pay the cab; she might not even *be* there. She could not
tell them that she felt ill, as that would mean at least one
of them taking her home, and she could not face spoiling
the evening with a lie. She *could not* tell them anything at
all. Her head ached, and she wanted to go to the lavatory,
but not knowing where it was and fear of encountering
him on his way back from the bar made her stay where
she was.

This was a mistake; throughout the second act, her
need became so urgent that she could not think of anything else, but they had insisted on her remaining in the
front of the box, and she was afraid of the commotion she
would cause by getting up and leaving which would
entail Mr Rose and Peter getting up to move their chairs
for her to open the door to the box. At the second interval,
she knew she had to risk it and Stella said she would
come too. There was a queue for the ladies'.

'A marvellous moment, when she comes down the
stairs dressed in Rebecca's dress,' Stella was saying. 'That

wicked Mrs Danvers is jolly good too, don't you think? Louise? What's up?'

'Nothing. I just desperately need—' She pointed at the lavatory door.

'Oh. I say, would you mind, awfully, but my friend's feeling ill. I think she's going to be sick.' The slightly resentful faces changed to a real fear, and Louise was allowed the next lavatory that was free. She remained there for some time because, with the eventual relief, she started silently crying. She found her tiny, inadequate handkerchief and mopped up the tears, and tried to blow her nose on some lavatory paper which was not of a kind to be much use for that.

When she came out, she found herself face to face with the unknown lady. For a fraction of a second they stared at one another: she had eyes the colour of blue hyacinths, and a small white lock that sprang surprisingly from the dark ram's horns into which her hair was fashionably set. Then the woman smiled – her lipstick was cyclamen on a long thin mouth – and pushed gently past her into the lavatory. The woman could not have recognised her, surely, but Louise had felt a flicker of something – surprise? interest? – come and go in those amazing eyes. Stella came out of the other lavatory, and Louise set about repairing her face.

'Better?'

'Much.' She did not want to talk to Stella until they were outside. Now she was afraid of finding her father lurking somewhere in the passage. 'You go first. I won't be a minute.' And because the cloakroom was so full of more people queuing, Stella complied.

Louise came out and looked in both directions, but he did not seem to be there. Stella was waiting for her.

'You were brilliant at getting me to the top of the queue,' she said.

'Wasn't I? I was waiting for you to make sick noises to back me up, but you didn't.'

This time she managed to insist on Peter having her seat in the front and Mrs Rose gave her an approving smile for her unselfishness, which it wasn't at all, she thought miserably.

And then, at the end of the play, she became terrified of meeting them outside the theatre where everybody would be trying to get cabs. Luckily the blackout helped all that: it was almost impossible to see anyone enough to identify them. But then she began to worry about the Savoy. Her father often went there after a theatre, she knew, because her mother enjoyed dancing. But she found that she could not bear to think about her mother, being lied to, believing him – or perhaps she didn't? Perhaps she knew and was unhappy, and that was what made her so difficult to get on with? She could not deal with thinking about it in front of all these people.

By the time they got to their table at the Savoy, and she had looked round the very full room and decided that they were not there, she thought she would feel better. She must pull herself together, put on a show of enjoying herself; anyone who knew about acting should know that that was possible. So she began chattering, and drank the glass of wine that was given her far too fast without thinking, but then she found she really did not want to eat anything. She settled for some cold chicken, as being the easiest thing to eat, and was teased by them for such a dull English choice. Once or twice during the evening she caught Mr Rose's eye upon her, a shrewd, appraising look that seemed momentarily to nullify her appearance of enjoying herself, but she persisted: if she smiled enough she could not be confronted. When she had left nearly all her chicken, she was offered an ice and managed to eat it. At last, the bill was paid, a taxi procured and they were trundling back through the dark streets.

'Thank you so much,' she said. 'I've had a wonderful time.'

'No, no,' Mr Rose answered, but whether he meant that she need not thank him, or that he knew it had not been wonderful, she did not know.

It wasn't until they were going back to school on the train that Stella tackled her.

'What's *up*?'

'Nothing's up, Stella, honestly.'

'Oh, well, if you're just going to tell me lies, I'll certainly shut up. And if you really don't want to tell me, that's all right too. I'll mind, of course, because I thought we told each other everything, but I would stop asking you. Well?'

'Something is. I can't tell you. I do partly want to,' she added, 'but it feels sort of disloyal.'

Stella was silent for a moment. Then she said, 'OK. If you're sure there's nothing I can do to help.'

'There's nothing anyone can do.'

'My parents were awfully worried about you. They really liked you. You're the first person I've brought home whom they've liked. Which is a good thing, otherwise they'd make a frightful fuss about my coming to stay with you in the holidays. I so long to see your house in the country and that great family clan.'

'How do you know your parents were worried about me?'

154

'They said so, of course. Anyhow, it was obvious, wasn't it? Even Peter knew *something* was wrong and he's not known for his perspicacity.'

'Oh.' It was disheartening to think that her acting had been such a failure.

'My mother just thought that you were taken ill, or getting the curse or something, but my father said nonsense – you had had some kind of shock.' The grey-green eyes were observing her intently.

Louise took refuge in anger. 'I've *said* I don't want to talk about it! Hell's bells and buckets of blood!'

That evening, she asked permission to ring up her mother in London.

'Darling! Are you all right? Is anything the matter?'

'Nothing. I just wondered how your weekend with Grania had gone.'

'It was rather awful, really. She didn't want to leave Aunt Jessica who was absolutely exhausted. She'd taken to getting up in the middle of the night and waking Jessica for breakfast. And then, when we finally got her packed and into the car, she thought she was going home. And at Tunbridge Wells she wouldn't get out of the car for ages. I practically had to *trick* her – say we were just going to have tea with some people. So *leaving* her there was ghastly.' Her voice tailed off, and Louise realised that she was trying not to cry.

'Oh, Mummy *darling*, how awful! I am so sorry.'

'It is very sweet of you to ring. They say she'll settle down – that people always do.'

'And what about you?'

'Oh, I'm all right. I came back and had a lovely extravagant bath – not one of the Duchy's four-inch jobs – and now I've had an enormous gin and I'm going to boil myself an egg. Did you have a nice weekend with your friend?'

'Lovely. We went to a concert – and to a play.' There was a pause, and then she said as casually as possible, 'Have you heard from Dad?'

'Not a word. They seem to work him dreadfully hard. He said that as he's head of the defence, he can hardly ever leave the aerodrome. Still, it's what he wants to do – the next best thing to joining the Navy like Uncle Rupe.'

'I see.'

'You must stop talking to me now, darling, or we'll all go broke. But thank you for ringing me up. It was most thoughtful.'

No, she didn't know. But whether this made things better or worse Louise could not imagine. All the usual emotions that she had about her mother had somehow got overrun by feeling terribly sorry for her. If her father was in the grip of some uncontrollable passion – which he jolly well ought *not* to be at his age – he might do anything! He might even divorce her mother and go off with that woman. She tried to think of anyone she knew of who had ever been divorced and eventually remembered Mummy's friend, Hermione Knebworth. Her divorce had been so unusual, and apparently so frightful, that people never talked about it; she had only been able to gather that Mummy didn't think it had been at all Hermione's fault. But Mummy wasn't like Hermione. She didn't have a dress shop, manage to be awfully good at business and also go about looking so glamorous all the time. If Dad divorced her – left her – she'd have absolutely nothing to worry about or do. And she was obviously far too old to start having a career. She suddenly saw her mother becoming like Grania after her husband

156

died – just sitting in a huge armchair refusing to enjoy anything and saying she wished she was dead. It would be all his fault. It *was* his fault already. She remembered Aunt Rach saying that people of her age started noticing that their parents were not just parents but people, and people were clearly far more nerve-racking than parents. Parents were simply people whom one reacted to; one didn't have to *do* anything about them – they were just there. That didn't mean that they couldn't make one miserable sometimes, but whatever they did, one wasn't *responsible* for them. I don't want to be responsible for my father: I hate him, she thought. Whenever she went back in her mind to that first sight of them in the theatre, she saw her father's hand closing for a moment round the woman's breast and was overwhelmed by the sick feeling of recognition of other things, other times, that she did not want ever to think about. And she knew that however much she tried to push it all down and out of sight or knowledge, that in fact she had hated him for ages, ever since that evening when poor Mummy had had her teeth out and she had been alone with him and he had felt *her* breasts. Mostly, she had avoided him; when he was there, she never met his eye; she snubbed any compliment; snapped at him, ignored him – or rather, tried to give the appearance of ignoring him; actually she was always horribly aware of his presence. Many of the rows with her mother had been about how rude she was to him – like that awful evening when they'd taken her out to see Ridgway's *Late Joys*, the wonderful Victorian music-hall show with Leonard Sachs being a witty and urbane chairman, and a strange young man called Peter Ustinov who was an opera singer explaining about a hitherto undiscovered fragment of a Schubert song 'Ziss Poor

Creature is Very Fond of Nymphs' and then suddenly breaking into the three bars of the fragment. That had all been lovely and they had laughed a great deal. But then they had gone to the Gargoyle Club, and her father had asked her to dance and she had refused, had said that she didn't like dancing and was never going to. Her father had been hurt, and her mother furious with her. In the end, *they* had danced, and she had sat and watched them miserably – she would have danced with *anyone* else in the world but him. The evening had been spoiled after that.

During the rest of that term, while she learned to make choux pastry, to bone a chicken, to clarify a clear soup, to interview a parlourmaid, while she and Stella read books, and she rehearsed her piece for her audition, and they washed each other's hair and invented a lot of silly jokes that made them almost speechless with laughter, and Stella told her many things about inflation in Germany and how unfair the treaty of Versailles had been, and why it was no good being a pacifist once you'd actually got a war ('It's preventive, you see,' she said, 'like alternative medicine; once someone's actually been shot in the leg, you have to get the bullet out') until Louise was dizzy with trying to follow the agility of her analogies – while, or in between these activities and this friendship, she reverted to what she called to herself the horrible secret, and had fantasies, daydreams of putting everything to rights. She would go to the woman and tell her that he was married and therefore could never marry *her*, that he was a liar and liars told lies to everyone so she would be the next victim. She would go to her father and tell him that she would tell her mother all about it unless he promised to give the woman up (these, with variations, were the main themes) – and *then* the best daydream of all, her parents coming to her with their arms round each other, smiling, happy, saying that they owed their happiness entirely to her – how could they ever thank her? – she was the most wonderful and *mature* child that anyone could ever have; her mother saying that she was also beautiful; her father saying what courage and understanding she had . . . These daydreams were like stale and stolen chocolates: afterwards she always felt faintly ashamed and sick.

All the same, by the time that last term was over, she had somehow become *used* to the situation, and the prospect of having Stella to stay at Home Place, and her audition at the acting school – now only three weeks away – went some way to making her feel that life was not too bad on the whole.

CLARY

May–June 1940

'She is rather *remote*, if not actually sulky, but I expect it is largely sexual frustration,' she wrote, and then looked at the fresh page adorned by this smooth and worldly sentence with satisfaction. She had come upon this phrase in a book and had been longing to use it. During the winter and ever in search of new subject matter, she had decided to write about all the things that she noticed people never *talked* about. She had made a list. Sex. Going to the lavatory. Menstruation. Blood generally. Death. Having babies. Being sick. Personal shortcomings that didn't sound romantic such as sulking, rather than being hot-tempered. Admitting to being frightened of things. Adultery, divorce – although it was going to be a bit difficult to write about them without any first-hand information. Still, quite a lot of good novels told you a bit about adultery. The after-life, or whether there was any. Jews and why people were against them. What was horrible about being a child (they only produced quaint or funny stories about their extreme youth). The possibility of losing the war and being slaves for the Germans. And so on. She kept the list and added to it from time to time but, disappointingly, it had not suggested a plot to her, and as Miss Milliment had rather unfairly stepped up the amount of homework that she and Polly were supposed to do – *and* given them quite arduous holiday tasks as well – she decided to write small portraits of anyone she knew who came to mind, just to keep her hand in. This one was about Zoë, who these days was pretty boring and therefore, from the literary point of view, something of a challenge. In the autumn, she had just come out of her gloom about the baby dying, and got pregnant again, and looked very pretty indeed, and then, when Dad said the Navy had accepted him and he was going off to a place called King Alfred's to be trained, all hell broke loose. She cried for days. Apparently, and according to Dad who got awfully upset by it, she had thought that men were not called up if their wives were pregnant. Or they *needn't* be, but where she had got this idea from, no one knew. It was daft. Even she – Clary – could see that the things had no bearing upon one another, but then Zoë had childish views – she was rather like an old sort of *worn out* child, Clary realised, and quickly put that down.

'Look after Zoë for me,' he had said the night before he went, which really was a funny way round. After all, who was the stepmother? But she couldn't imagine him saying, 'Look after Clary for me.' She rather doubted whether Zoë had ever been asked to look after anybody. It might be a good idea to give her an only medium-demanding animal like a rabbit for her next birthday to get her started on looking after something – or else her baby was in for a rather rotten time. (Of course, it was Ellen who really looked after all of them.) At Sports Day at his school, Neville had even pretended he hardly knew her. 'You've hurt her feelings, you fool,' Clary had hissed at Neville when they were meant to be getting plates of strawberries for the grown-ups in the tea tent. 'Well, she hurt mine wearing that silly fur fox round her neck. If you ask me, that's what feelings are for,' he added while he skilfully transferred some better strawberries to the plate he had chosen. He had grown a lot, but his front teeth looked far too large for him and he had spent a lot of the Christmas holidays up trees that Lydia was afraid to climb. He didn't seem to make any great friends at his school and he loathed games. His asthma was much better, but the night before Dad went, he quarrelled with everyone, drank what Emily said was the best part of her bottle of cooking sherry, unpacked his father's suitcase, threw everything into the bath and turned on both taps. Dad found him and they had a sort of fight but in the end he was crying so much that Dad just carried him off to his room and they spent a long time alone together. He had asthma all that night, and Ellen stayed up with him because Dad had to be with Zoë because she was so upset. 'Look after Nev, won't you,' he'd said to Clary next morning. 'He kept saying last night that now he'd have nobody, and I kept telling him he had you.' He'd looked so grey and tired, that she *couldn't* say how much *she* minded his going, couldn't say, 'And who do you think I'll have?' or anything selfish like that because she could see that some kinds of love simply wore him out, so she just made her face smile and said 'Yes, I will.' He smiled back at her and said, 'That's my Clary,' and asked her to come to the station with him. 'Zoë doesn't feel up to it,' he said. Neville had gone to school as usual, and Tonbridge had driven them to Battle; she'd waited on the platform with Dad with nothing left to say and the train coming in was a relief. 'Don't wear any of those wet vests,' she'd said as the most grown-up thing she could think of, at the end. 'No, no. I'll make His Majesty dry them for me personally,' he'd said, bent to kiss her and got onto the train. He waved until he was out of sight and she'd walked slowly back to the car where Tonbridge was waiting, and got into the back and sat stiffly upright. Once, she saw Tonbridge looking at her in the driving mirror, and in Battle he stopped and went into a shop and came out with a bar of milk chocolate which he gave her, and although she loathed milk chocolate, this was a considerable kindness. She started to thank him and then had to pretend that she had a bad cough. He drove her back to Home Place without talking, but when she got out of the car, he said, 'You're a little soldier, you are,' and smiled, so that she could see his black tooth next to his gold one.

Well – back to Zoë. She'd gone upstairs and Zoë was lying on the bed that still had Dad's pyjamas on it and Ellen was standing with a tray saying she'd feel better if she ate something, think of the baby. But that seemed to make Zoë cry more than ever.

Description of Zoë lying in bed. Dark silky hair, all tangled but somehow looking better than when she's done it; very white skin that has a kind of thick pearliness about it (creamy? satiny?); no colour in her cheeks, just a slightly darker cream; sooty eyelashes that look as though they have mascara on them even when they haven't; wide-apart eyes, not emerald – more like grass . . . well, exactly like Polly's last but one cat. Rather a short upper lip and then a longish mouth that turns up at the corners when she smiles, which makes a dimple in her left-hand cheek. What a horrible word dimple was. Shirley Temple has a dimple. If she was actually describing a heroine in a story, she'd never give them a dimple, but there it was, Zoë had one and this was meant to be a portrait. She couldn't write much about the rest of her because it had been under the bedclothes except for one arm that was just really a boring white arm with tremendously carefully manicured nails painted a shiny pale pink. This was being a failure. She suspected that one would need to be in love with Zoë to be interested in her appearance, and if one was in love with someone, how much did it matter what they looked like? She supposed that liking the looks of someone would be what made one get to know them better. The only person who'd ever seemed to like the look of *her* was Dad, that day when they'd been filling the bottles with spring water and he'd said she was beautiful – well, he'd said he was surrounded by beautiful women and she'd been one of them. The trouble about writing *anything* was that it made one think of something else. She felt she was a bottomless pit of memories, and she was only fifteen. What on earth must it be like when you reached the Duchy's age? You'd hardly be able to think at all for them; it would be like having so much furniture in a room that there was nowhere left to move.

Anyway, that day she'd sat on the side of the bed and tried to cheer Zoë up, saying all the things that *he*'d said about only being at King Alfred's for a matter of weeks, and then probably getting leave, and not being in the slightest danger, which nobody was as far as she could see, anyway, in the whole war, except in places like Finland and now Norway, although she knew that Polly did not agree with her at all about this. Then she had had to go and do lessons with Poll and Miss Milliment, and, extremely boringly, Lydia, because now that Neville had been sent to the prep school near Sedlescombe, they said Lydia couldn't do lessons by herself. She still had to do them partly by herself, because being merely nine, naturally Lydia couldn't understand most of what she and Polly did, but Miss Milliment was very patient and clever about dividing her time between them. The Babies' Hotel had gone back to London and they'd still been living in Pear Tree Cottage then, as the boys were home from school, but when term started, they'd all gone back to Home Place. Miss Milliment slept in the cottage over the garage and they had lessons in the little ground-floor sitting room. Mill Farm was let as a convalescent home for people – it had been meant for wounded soldiers only there weren't any, so it took people recovering from operations and things like that. In the weekdays Aunt Sybil and Aunt Villy went to London and Wills and Roland were left with Ellen. At the weekends Uncle Hugh came down with Aunt Sybil, but Aunt Villy came on her own – she didn't always come and Lydia minded. Sometimes they were taken to London to go to the dentist, or get clothes. Dad's house in London was shut up, so when she went it was with the others; she no longer had a London home, but she'd got all her valuable things, her books and the scrapbook with pictures of her mother when she was a child and a postcard from Cassis in France that her mother had written to her before she was even old enough to read – 'Darling Clary, Here is a picture of the place where Daddy and I are staying. We live in the little pink house on the right. Love from Mummy.' The house was marked with a cross in faded ink – for years afterwards she had lived on that love sent. Well, she was used to it now – to not having a mother – and Neville had always been used to it. But it made Dad pretty important to her. She'd had a good cry with Polly after lessons in the potting shed. Polly was awfully good to cry with because she cried as well, though not so much.

Dad had come back for a week at Christmas, but Uncle Edward only got two days. Louise went and spent a week

but Louise said this so feebly, that Clary could tell she didn't mean it.

'Well, I think you should tackle your mother about it.'

'Really, Nora, that's a ghastly idea. There's nothing to go on, it's nothing to do with me – and anyway, if that's how you feel, why don't you tackle *your* mother?'

'A, because it's your mother that is infatuated, B, because your father is away fighting the war, so it isn't fair on him, poor thing, and C, things *do* go on – your mother wore lipstick *every* day at Frensham, and if you ask me frightfully unsuitable clothes considering there's a war on, and it was she who thought of calling him Lorenzo which is obviously affected and—' she paused before what she clearly considered her trump card, 'it was obvious that his wife hated her even more than Mummy. Wives always know, you know—'

'Oh, do stop saying everything is obvious! Laurence, or whatever he's called, is married, Mercedes is a Catholic (*she* calls him Lorenzo, by the way, so it wasn't Mummy's idea) and *your* mother stopped doing her hair in that funny bun and made masses of puddings with Carnation milk because she knows he loves sweet things. It's six of one and half a dozen of the other, so there's nothing to stop you tackling your mother . . .'

'All right, supposing they're *both* in love with him. He looks quite foreign and unscrupulous enough to encourage that. Mummy said he was miserable with his wife because she was perpetually jealous of everybody. I've noticed they were pretty sharp with each other.'

'Who?'

'Jessica and Villy. I bet they're jealous of each other. I mean really, Louise, you must see that it can lead to no good.'

'Whatever I can see doesn't seem to be my business. And it seems to me utterly unfair that just when I'm trying to start my own life, I have to start worrying about them. And in a much *worse way*,' she added.

'How do you mean, *worse*?'

'Well, they've spent years simply worrying about things like have we cleaned our teeth, or done our homework, or stopped reading in bed when they've told us to. Now, according to you, we've got to worry about whether our mothers are flirting with someone who's married. Or worse. In some cases, much worse.'

'What cases?'

'Nothing.'

'You mean like them having an affair? Twerpy Lorenzo kissing them and things like that? You don't actually mean . . .'

But here, Nora's voice was lowered to such an extent that Clary could not hear what she said, and no longer being able to hear made her feel slightly guilty about what she *had* heard. But if one wanted to be a novelist, it was essential to grasp any opportunity to know what might be going on. Two sisters being in love with the same man was certainly a pretty strong idea, particularly if everyone concerned was already married. What baffled her was the way people's lives never seemed to reach any conclusion at *all*; after all, if these aunts, at their advanced stage in life, were going about falling in love with an unsuitable person (and come to that, who *could* be suitable? It was the general idea that was embarrassing, rather than *who* they might fall in love with), when could one ever say, well, *that* person has got their life arranged and all they have to do is go on with it. It made the whole idea of heroines being young and all that rather silly.

Supposing her dad fell in love with someone else while he was away? According to all that she had just heard, this was perfectly possible. The next thing she ought to do was to fall in love with someone, so that she would have a better idea of what it felt like. The trouble was that she didn't meet anyone, and the idea of mooning about being in love with Teddy or Christopher, the only boys remotely old enough, seemed hopeless: she didn't even like Teddy much, as he talked nowadays about nothing but aeroplanes and different kinds of gun and beating people at games. A much older man might be a better bet. She considered the older men that she knew, but either they were related, which she knew from dogs was bad for breeding, or – Tonbridge, Wren, McAlpine and Mr York each appeared to her, like 'Wanted' photographs in a police station – definitely not wanted by *her*, and that seemed to be that. Perhaps one could *practise* on a relative. But when she thought about the uncles, apart from them being too ordinary and well known to her for any serious romance, they weren't about enough any more. Dad was the only one who seemed to her worth it and she needed him as a father. The thought of Dad made her feel instantly homesick for him, and she decided to write to him instead of struggling on with Zoë's portrait.

Home Place
6 May 1940

Darling Dad [she wrote],
I really hope you are well and enjoying being in a destroyer. Before I tell you anything, I must point out that letters are now one and a half times as expensive as they were when I last wrote, twopence halfpenny in fact, and this brings me to the need to have a bit

more pocket money or you will have to have one and a half times fewer letters. Could you make it sixpence a week more bringing it to one and six every Saturday? I quite see that this is probably a detail to you, but my life seems to be composed of them [rather a good sentence, that]. It was awfully sad that you couldn't come home at all for Easter. Louise brought a friend from school – a fearfully intelligent person called Stella Rose, whose brother is going to be a famous pianist. Her father is a surgeon. Stella played the piano with the Duchy who said she was awfully good. According to Aunt Villy, they are thought to be Jewish, but I asked Louise and she didn't know and nobody else said anything about it. I hope you are better from being seasick. I do really sympathise with you about that – especially having to work as I can't do anything if I feel sick, but I suppose you just have to give people orders, you don't actually have to scrub decks or go up masts or anything like that. That's one good thing about being an officer even if you are the oldest sub-lieutenant in the RNVR. [She had got out his last postcard to copy this out, uncertain what it meant.] We had to do a short life of anyone we chose for our holiday task and I chose General Gordon. He was very religious and after a rather victorious time in China he got stuck up the Nile and besieged by enemies and we never sent reinforcements in time so he got murdered. You can see this bit in Madame Tussauds, but in spite of such a dramatic end, he didn't turn out to be as interesting as I'd hoped, and Polly had a much nicer time with Florence Nightingale. Polly is amazingly pretty; her face is thinner and she is growing her hair which is the

colour of a very good fox, don't you think? A pity
foxes don't have blue eyes. She is drawing animals
and did a very good fox which is what made me think
of that. I have written only one story and half a play
but I got stuck. The trouble is that not very much
happens here at all, except meals and lessons and
people fussing about the blackout and listening to the
news, which is rather boring. I don't want to make
any more things up, so I'm waiting for something
exciting to happen. Louise is supposed to be not
beautiful but striking, which I would personally hate
to be. She is quite grown up and going to her acting
school this term which has made her rather swanky
and distant – her character has definitely gone down
hill. [Then she remembered that he would want news
of Zoë and Neville.] Neville is quite well and he likes
being a weekly boarder so that is all right. He has a
horrible friend who wears spectacles and stammers
and does everything Neville tells him – called
Mervyn, wouldn't you know? Mervyn does all his
maths for him and Neville told the school that he
wasn't allowed to eat cabbage and they believed him!
Unbelievably naïve in my view. The worst thing that
he did last term was to put a frog down the lav, but
I'm glad to say he couldn't stand the remorse and he
told Ellen who told the Duchy and he got punished.
What do you think of Modigliani? Miss Milliment told
me about him when I was asking her about Jews,
because I couldn't understand how they could be
English as well, and she said because they hadn't got
anywhere proper to be of their own they'd had to live
in all kinds of countries where they had enriched the
culture – like Modigliani. His people are a bit like

people in dreams, I think. You know – you recognise them, but they're never anyone you've seen before. Do you think being instantly recognisable is a good thing? In painting and writing, I mean – and I suppose music but I'm distinctly unmusical so I don't care about that so much. But once you've seen a Modigliani you'd always recognise another one, wouldn't you? Well, is that a good thing or not? On the one hand, it might mean that whoever it was was doing the same thing again and again; on the other hand, they might just have made their own private language and the *things* aren't the same at all. As you're a painter, Dad, you should be able to answer that. I miss you [here she paused, and felt the familiar indigestion feeling in her chest] sometimes [she wrote carefully]. Please notice this stamp and remember about the beginning of this letter.

Love and hugs from Clary.

Now, what shall I do? she thought. She decided on a prowl about to see if she could find anyone doing something that she would want to do with them. It was pretty hopeless. Aunt Rach – the best bet – was in London with the Brig and wouldn't be back until six. She *could* do her homework – an essay on Queen Elizabeth's attitude towards religious toleration plus some algebra which she simply loathed – or she could do her weeding stint for the week – two hours spent however the Duchy or McAlpine dictated – or go to Watlington with Polly to get more khaki wool for the mufflers they were knitting (everybody was knitting; Zoë for her baby who now had millions too many clothes, Clary thought, and even Miss Milliment was struggling with a scarf but she was simply hopeless – it was full of holes from dropped stitches and not even straight at the sides, but she didn't seem to notice).

The prowl didn't yield much. Zoë was lying down, Ellen was ironing, the Duchy was in the greenhouse potting up tomato plants, and Wren was on a ladder outside whitewashing the panes in the roof and making the whistling sound between his teeth as though he was grooming a horse. You couldn't do anything with *him*: he talked all the time until anyone was there when he stopped saying a single word. The panes were all streaky because it wasn't his job. She wandered to the kitchen as lunch – macaroni cheese and stewed prunes – had been ages ago and she was hungry. Tonbridge was in the pantry cleaning out a decanter with shot and Mrs Cripps seemed to be helping him. A plate of flapjacks lay on the draining board looking completely delicious. She asked if she could possibly have one. Mrs Cripps pushed the plate towards her and then told her to run along. She went and sat on the stairs in the hall to eat it – very slowly – as though it would be her last meal on earth. War is boring, she thought, even Polly must be getting bored with it, which reminded her that she hadn't seen Polly since lunch.

In the end, she found her in the day nursery playing with Wills, patiently building card houses which he knocked down with one careless swipe. The nursery had their old gramophone in it and it was playing 'The Teddy Bears' Picnic'. Lydia, who was holding Roland under his arms in an effort to make him stand, said 'Look at Roly walking!' while his legs, clad in knitted boots, helplessly brushed the ground and he smiled with benign appreciation at every card crash. One side of his face was tomato-coloured, the other pale rose, and a heavy swag of dribble swung to and fro as he turned his head. Clary watched hopelessly. Soon Zoë would have one of these and she would be expected to love it.

'It's extraordinary how awful and unattractive they are,' she said to Polly after they had managed to escape on the lying grounds that they had to do something for the Duchy. Lydia, who had wanted to come with them as usual, had been placated by Ellen who promised to let her push the pram.

'I mean, puppies, and kittens, and foals, and even new little birds don't look so disgusting. I don't know why people have to start so fat and swampy. If I had one, I'd want to send it to kennels or a hospital or something until it got human. And they really only seem to like smashing things up, so it isn't even as though they have nice natures.'

'Well, you don't have to have one. You can simply not marry.'

'I could marry if I liked, and just not have one.'

'I don't think that's possible,' Polly answered consideringly. 'I suspect there's some kind of trap there. It's all or nothing.'

'Bet you're wrong. Look at Mrs Cripps.'

'The chances are she *isn't* Mrs Cripps. Cooks are often called Mrs just to please them. Also, we don't absolutely *know* she hasn't had children.'

Clary was silenced. They were walking up the fields to the shop at Watlington so that Clary could buy a stamp for her letter.

'I think,' Polly said, 'that people often get more boring as they grow older. I agree that human natures are inferior at any age. I mean, even man-eating tigers only do it because their poor teeth have given out or they have rheumatism and people are easier to catch. But Wills is very sweet. If he *could* build the card houses, that's what he'd be doing. As it is, he can only knock them down. I think it's a bit critical of you to be so against people.'

'I'm *not* – at all! You shouldn't say that! It's only babies I don't like.'

'You didn't want Lydia coming on our walk, and if I'd asked you why you would have said *she* was boring.'

'I should,' Clary replied, 'because she *would* have been!' She burst into tears. Either she was having to look after people, or she was being criticised, she sobbed. Nobody ever said *she* was sweet when she was a baby; they were all too busy telling her to make allowances for Neville because of his asthma. *Ellen* had frankly told her that she preferred boys. And Zoë had come and taken up so much of Dad's time that she felt she was just an appendage. And *now*, with him away for goodness knew how long, she was supposed to look after Zoë *and* Neville, neither of whom was in the least grateful. Neville had said that a boy at school had told him that there was a society for getting rid of girls or women except a few to be housemaids, like worker bees, and even though she could see that it would take them years as there were so many of them, it showed you how *against* women they were. She'd spent her whole *life* without a single person on her side . . .

'I'm on your side,' Polly said. They had stopped walking and Clary was sitting on the ground with her arms hunched round her knees. Polly knelt down beside her. 'You're my best friend,' she said. 'It's quite equal – we rely on each other. I'm sorry I criticised you.'

'Did you mean it?'

Polly hesitated. 'Yes, I did,' she said. 'But I know you have awfully high standards. I don't think most people could live up to them. All the time. In the same way, you can be critical and I still love you. I can't help noticing it, but it doesn't change my serious feelings.' She looked at Clary's anxious face and felt a surge of love for her. 'I really revere your honesty,' she said.

They got to their feet and finished the last field of Home Place land, climbed the gate onto the road at the top of the hill to walk the last quarter of a mile to the shop. Its front garden was full of aubretia and yellow tulips and forget-me-nots and two bushes of mauve lilac with the scent of pale honey, but inside it smelled as usual of tarred twine and bacon and oiled wool and Wright's Coal Tar soap. Mr Cramp stopped cutting coupons out of a ration book and went behind the counter at the post office end to serve Clary with her stamp, and Mrs Cramp finished measuring three yards of elastic before finding the wool for Polly.

'And how is Mrs Hugh keeping?' she asked Polly, as she detached two skeins from an enormous hank.

'She's very tired. She has something wrong with her back.'

'Like Miss Rachel. Those things runs in families,' Mrs Cramp replied comfortably as though two bad backs were more comforting than one.

'Have you heard from Peter?' Clary heard Polly asking politely. Peter was Mrs Cramp's son who'd worked in the local garage, but was now in the RAF.

'You could say we have and we haven't. He's not given to writing – well, he's never had any call for it – but he did give us a ring on the telephone two Sundays back – or was it three? Alfie! Was it the Sunday before last that Peter rang on the telephone or was it the Sunday before that?' But Mr Cramp couldn't rightly remember which it was.

'Heard from your dad, have you?' he enquired of Clary, and when she had said that she had, Mrs Cramp, lowering her voice to fit the subject, enquired after Mrs Rupert. Clary said fine, she was having the baby next month. 'Of course, she misses my father,' she added loyally.

Mrs Cramp looked gratified. 'She would do. Stands to reason. That'll be three and threepence for the wool, Miss.' She had put it into a weak paper bag, where, as there was not room for it, it seemed to take on a writhing life of its own. Polly paid for it and Mrs Cramp asked if they'd fancy a Chelsea bun. 'There'll be no more call for them today, and they won't be worth the eating tomorrow,' she said, as she popped two into another weak paper bag.

So on the way back, they sat on a bank by the wood and unwound their buns and ate them.

'It's funny, isn't it, how being in the country isn't a treat any more?'

'Oh, well. Nothing is, if it goes on long enough.'

This fired Clary, and she immediately thought of the things she would never get tired of. 'Being grown up for one thing.'

Polly didn't agree. 'But you don't just get grown up. Almost the moment you're that, you start getting old.'

'I don't think people notice that, as it's happening all the time, and is so slow, I don't think people realise what's going on until it's too late.'

'When they die, you mean? I should think they'd jolly well notice then. Tell me two good things about being grown up.'

'Going to bed just when you want to instead of when people tell you. Well, actually doing anything because *you*'ve decided instead of other people. I shan't ever get tired of any of that.'

'Well, I'm not tired of the country,' Polly said. 'When I'm grown up I shall have a little house with all my things in it and that will be in the country. I shall have a library and a swimming pool and plenty of animals and a wireless by my bed and a separate room to play games in. You can stay with me whenever you like.'

'Thanks.' She noticed that Polly didn't offer to have her to *live* there and it made her feel ungrateful. 'If we don't win the war you won't be able to.'

'Stupid! Of course I know that. And Dad says that if they don't get rid of Mr Chamberlain he thinks—'

'We won't?'

'He didn't *say* that. But I know he's worried. He absolutely *hates* Mummy being in London and she hates being away from Wills, but she won't leave him on his own – sometimes I notice them very nearly quarrelling!'

They got up and started to walk home, and while Clary was noticing how amazing the young oak leaves looked with the sunlight on them, Polly said in a rather shaky voice, 'Of course, there's always the possibility that we might get invaded during the week when they weren't here. I couldn't hide with Wills because he'd be bound to make a noise, and I don't see how I could escape to London—'

'Polly! Shut *up*! I'm not going to let you get into a state about that! You know perfectly well that if they thought that they'd be *here* – *or* they'd take you somewhere else. The Hebrides,' she added rather wildly. 'Honestly, if Hitler was going to come here, he'd have done it by now. It will probably all happen in France – like the last one. If it happens at all.'

'Yes, they would, wouldn't they?' The paper bag burst, and she undid the skeins and hung them round her neck. 'You're a great comfort, Clary. I honestly don't know what I'd do without you.'

Concealing the intense pleasure that this last remark caused her, Clary finished loftily, 'Just think of it as a pretending war, Poll – very boring, but nothing to worry about.'

That afternoon – the rest of that unremarkable day – was the last of its kind, she thought, although she didn't start to think it until the weekend, when the news said that Mr Churchill was now Prime Minister. Everyone seemed very pleased, and she could see, from the photograph in *The Times* next morning, that he had a more optimistic face than poor droopy old Chamberlain. The event was discussed at lessons the following Monday, and Miss Milliment explained about coalition governments and said that this meant that all the best people would be governing the country. She then suggested (but really told) her and Polly that they should start writing a journal of what was happening. It would help them to understand things, she said, and would be very interesting to read when they were older, 'Or even for your children,' she added. Lydia instantly said that she wanted to do it too, and before she or Polly could snub her, Miss Milliment said, of course, everybody should do it. Miss Milliment had an awful cold and kept blowing her nose on the same rather grey, sopping handkerchief that really only seemed to make her face damper, and Polly said that she thought Miss Milliment probably couldn't afford enough handkerchiefs. 'She hasn't had any new clothes since she came,' she said, 'excepting the cardigan Mummy bought her for Christmas.'

They thought about this. Then Polly said, 'Couldn't you give her some of your dad's?'

'I don't much *want* to.'

'Well, we can't afford to buy her any – they cost about threepence each. If you give people handkerchiefs, you have to give them at least six.'

In the end, they decided to apply to Aunt Rach, who always seemed to think of the right thing to do. 'Are we going to put *this* in our journals?' Polly asked.

'Good Lord, no. It's far too . . . *parochial*. You couldn't call Miss Milliment's cold a world event.'

She spent the afternoon wrestling with *The Times* and writing about people like Lord Halifax and Mr Attlee and someone with a lovely name, Lord Beaverbrook. They were to read the first bits of their journals later in the week.

Lydia hadn't got the hang of it at all.

This morning I got up and put on my blue dress, but I
couldn't find a blue hair ribbon to go with it.
Breakfast was horrible with soggy tomatoes and one
piece of bacon with an enormous band of fat. Ellen
was in a temper again because she'd been up all night
with Roly who is teething. I can't see what use one
single tooth will be to him, but I suppose he has to
make a start somewhere. There was a dear little rabbit
on the lawn but it annoyed the Duchy. Aunt Sybil is
staying down this week as she doesn't feel well. I

wish Mummy was not so well and stayed too. Neville was horrid at the weekend as usual; he has gone to the dogs in my view and looks like staying there. He threw fir cones down on me from a tree. I nearly cried and he said I was, which I wasn't. I hate him, but I don't wish he was actually dead as that would be wrong.

And so on.

She and Polly sat rolling their eyes with contempt and putting their hands over their mouths to stop them laughing aloud, but Miss Milliment said – you could hardly believe it – that Lydia had done very well. When everybody had read their bit, she talked for quite a long time about journals, and explained that they should not only contain events, but what the writer thought and felt about them, which made her see that hers – and Polly's – was actually rather dull. But it was annoying that Lydia seemed to have got it righter than they had when she was so much younger. 'A fluke,' she said to Polly, but Polly simply said think how nice it was for Lydia to be the best at something for once, and she felt humbled by Polly's niceness.

That week, Clary wrote her journal every day.

Tuesday, 14 May
On the news this evening, it said that Queen Wilhelmina had arrived as an exile from Holland which the Germans have reached. I suppose she's lucky to be able to leave, but all the same it must be awful for her. Miss Milliment said that the Dutch might open the dykes and flood everything which would make it impossible for the Germans to capture

the country, but there was nothing about this on the news. Perhaps they left it till too late, but Polly said it was probably more like car accidents – people always think it won't happen to *them* – so perhaps the Dutch thought the Germans wouldn't invade them at all. The Allies are going to join up with Belgium to stop the Germans which is more than poor Queen Wilhelmina had, so perhaps that will give them (the Germans) a nasty surprise. The thing is, it still all seems very unreal; life goes on just as though none of it was happening. We had horrible cauliflower cheese for lunch today and in spite of the Duchy saying how delicious and nourishing it was I noticed that Aunt Sybil didn't eat any of hers. She seems to get bad indigestion a lot of the time as well as her back, but Aunt Rach says it is because she worries so frightfully about Uncle Hugh, even though he rings up every night, which poor Dad can't do being in a ship. We aren't supposed to know where he is, but when Zoë showed Uncle Hugh one of his letters about coming back to that wonderful London air which Zoë couldn't understand, Uncle Hugh said he thought he was in the North Atlantic and going into Londonderry to get fuel and food and all the things they have to have. Zoë eats all the time – the Duchy makes her drink milk, and she gets extra eggs and the Brig gives her all his sweet ration, which personally I think is deeply unfair. She is much fatter than usual – I don't mean just her stomach which is vast, I mean all over – but she still stays madly glamorous. I've given up her portrait. I think it is impossible to write about a person at all well if you don't find them fascinating.

Zoë is the kind of person that I would quite like to
have a portrait – I mean a painting – of, rather than
have about in real life . . .

It was at this point that she began not to want to show
her journal to the others. This was another thing about
journals: if they were private, you somehow had more
chance to make them interesting. But she didn't really
want Miss Milliment to have the slightest idea of her
feelings – or the lack of them – for Zoë. In the end, she
kept two: the public one to be read at lessons, and the
serious private one that she read to herself – and quite
often to Polly, who didn't seem to have that problem at
all. 'I can't think of enough to say about people,' she said,
'and everyone has their good side.' Polly put drawings in
her journal – they weren't particularly apposite, as she
pointed out to her, just anything that came into her head
– at the moment the journal was full of moles because
she'd found a dead one on the tennis-court lawn and
learned how to draw it until it began to smell awful and
she buried it. Polly's moles were rather good: they had
the sort of expression that made you think *they* thought it
was quite all right to be blind. Miss Milliment admired
them very much and found her a book illustrated by
Archibald Thorburn which the Brig had in his study. But
he mostly painted birds and Polly wasn't so interested in
them.

Anyway, to get back to Zoë – no, I don't want to do
that, except that I will just say that if Dad hadn't
married her it would be me he would be writing to
. . . if he hadn't married someone else, that is.

But as all the old men she knew *were* married, this seemed probable. So she would still just be getting postscripts and the two letters of her own that he had sent.

'Lord Beaverbrook,' she wrote, 'has become Minister of Aircraft Production.' It was a wonderful name. She wondered if there was a Lady Beaverbrook. 'Clarissa Beaverbrook' she wrote on a separate piece of paper. It looked very grand. Although to people she knew well, she'd have to put 'Clary Beaverbrook'.

The news that week did not seem at all good. The Maginot Line, which Miss Milliment had made them trace onto their map, and which she had imagined as a huge kind of long mountain covered with guns and tanks with the soldiers living in tunnels underneath, didn't seem to count at all. The Germans simply went north round it, which as it hadn't got as far as the sea by a long chalk, anyway, was not really surprising, but it seemed to surprise the grown-ups.

Wednesday, 15 May
There was an awful air raid on a place called
Rotterdam yesterday. Thirty thousand civilian
casualties. No wonder Holland had to surrender. Now
everything seems to be pretty bad in Belgium. Polly
says it is all getting like the last war, with the
Germans fighting us and the French in France. She
says any minute now they will dig trenches and put
up masses of barbed wire and it will go on for years
just like last time. I must say it is a ghastly prospect.
What will become of Polly and me? We can't simply
go on having lessons with Miss Milliment for ever,
getting older and older and completely cut off from
the world. Polly says that ought to be the least of our

worries, but *one* can never be the least of one's
worries, can one? However selfish it is, there you are
with yourself day after day – a situation that cannot
be ignored, in my opinion. I feel boredom may
overwhelm me. Louise is so lucky having her acting
school to go to which means they let her be in
London. Of course she has a friend to be with. I
couldn't be at Brook Green by myself – or, anyway,
they would think I couldn't be . . .

She began to imagine herself in their house at Brook
Green on her own. She could have Grape Nuts for breakfast (no cooking) and then she would put on her coat and
go off and sit on the seats in buses near the door so that
she could watch everyone. In the afternoon she would go
to the cinema, and in the evening she would go home
and fry a chop – she had never actually done this but she
thought she could buy a few extra chops to start with
until she got it right. Money: she'd probably have to sell
things. The house was full of stuff in cupboards and in
the attic that nobody would notice. If she particularly
liked anyone – like a bus conductor or someone she sat
next to at the cinema – she would invite them back to
chops and a gin and it, which she knew how to mix from
Dad's drink cupboard. And if they were suitable, she
would fall in love with them. That would all be what
Aunt Villy called grist to the mill.

Because the other drawback I have to contend with is
that writing isn't a thing people seem to teach. You
can't go to a writing school like an art school or
Louise's school, and the word school seems to be the
key to grown-up approval. So they won't send me

anywhere unless I changed my profession to
something that they would count. And Polly, who
could probably get them to send her to an art school,
says she doesn't want to leave home at all while the
war is on. *And* I'm running out of books to read. This
place is becoming like a desert island, only not nearly
so exciting as any of them would be.

She stopped here, and began gloomily to review the
grown-ups round her. She couldn't think of *one* of them
that she would want to be. Not Aunt Rach – taking the
Brig to London on the train every day, and having to type
letters for him, although she'd never learned to type so
she kept making mistakes and did it very slowly. And
then getting back and being told about the six o'clock
news by the Duchy and Aunt Syb, and having a rest
before dinner because her back was hurting, and then
spending the evening knitting socks for seamen with foul-
smelling wool and listening to the nine o'clock news and
going to bed. Occasionally someone rang her up in the
evenings which always seemed to make her more animated, but it must always be a toll call, because she never
talked to them for long. 'God bless,' Clary sometimes
heard her say if she happened to be in the hall outside
the Brig's study where the telephone was. One couldn't
possibly want to be the Duchy because she was so very
old, at the end of her life almost, although that was a
tremendously sad thought, and she lived such a quiet one
that it might easily go on longer than most. Aunt Syb –
no definitely not. At the weekends she seemed more or
less how she'd always been – except for this last one
when Uncle Hugh had said after the six o'clock news that
he really wanted to shut their house in London because

anyway he needed to be on fire duty quite a lot of nights at the wharf. Aunt Syb had completely broken down, had burst into racking sobs and then rushed out of the drawing room, and Uncle Hugh had gone after her and not come down again for a long time, and then he *had* come down to get Aunt Rach, and when *she* got back she said that Aunt Syb had been rather sick because she'd eaten something that had disagreed with her, and that she would spend the week in the country, and they would discuss the house when she was better. She'd spent a lot of Monday in bed, and when she did reappear she looked rotten. She had asked Polly to buy her a bottle of aspirin at the shop, and she'd said please don't tell the Duchy who was known to disapprove of aspirin. Aunt Rach wanted Dr Carr to come and see her, but Aunt Syb got awfully worked up and said she wouldn't hear of it. The Duchy made her have arrowroot and Benger's Food and also tried to make her have Parrish's Food, but Aunt Syb put that down the wash basin in the bathroom. Polly said, and one couldn't blame her, it tasted like old iron railings. Neville had once drunk a whole bottle of it (you were meant to have about a dessertspoon in water) and gone about all red in the face and charged up for days – *he* hadn't been sick although everyone said he would be. Poor Aunt Syb! Her hair looked awfully dull – like unpolished old brown shoes – and her getting thinner had somehow made her more shapeless, sort of baggy, and she had quite deep marks on her forehead. There was something called change of life that neither she nor Polly had properly fathomed, but it got mentioned that week about the house – not to *them*, of course, but she heard Ellen and Eileen when they were changing the sheets. Change of life. Just what she wanted, she thought, but not, of course, if it meant you felt rotten. It sounded as though it could be the most marvellous thing, put just like that. No, she certainly wouldn't want to be Aunt Syb. And of *course* not Zoë, who now played clock patience all day, when she wasn't eating or sewing.

The following weekend Uncle Hugh had come down, of course, bringing Aunt Villy and Louise. Louise looked extremely glamorous: she wore terracotta linen trousers and an emerald-green Aertex shirt and a creamy cardigan slung over her shoulders and sandals. She had *green* eyeshadow and scarlet lipstick and very long hair, and she did exercises every morning that she said was writing the alphabet with her body – one wouldn't have known, Clary thought. Louise seemed quite prepared to spend time with her and Polly, largely, Clary immediately discovered, because she only wanted to talk about acting and her school, and the grown-ups talked about nothing much but how the war was going, which seemed to be worse and worse.

'I'm absolutely bloody fed *up* with war talk,' Louise declared. She took a very small packet of cigarettes out of her pocket and they watched, fascinated, as she proceeded to light one.

'When did you start doing that?' Polly asked.

'Weeks ago. Everybody smokes at school.' She blew the smoke out very quickly after each puff. 'They're only de Reszke Minors: I can't afford ordinary-sized cigarettes – none of us can. A lot of people smoke because they can't afford food,' she added. This was pounced upon.

'How much are de Minors or whatever they are?'

'Only sixpence for ten.'

'You can buy a chop for fourpence. And that would leave you twopence for vegetables and bread, et cetera.'

Louise looked cross. 'We haven't time for stupid things like *cooking*,' she said. 'If you are seriously trying to be an artist, you simply don't *do* that sort of thing. One person I know – a boy called Roy Prowse – just has mustard sandwiches for lunch. He's a brilliant actor – he did the most arresting Lear last week.'

'How old is he?'

'Much older than I am, nearly nineteen, but he's more like someone of twenty – he's frightfully sophisticated – he's working as a waiter and has been abroad on his own.'

'I should have thought he was a bit young for Lear.'

She turned on Clary. 'Honestly, how dim can you get? Do you seriously think there are old men of seventy at an acting school? Anyway, we have to do character parts – in make-up we learn all about how to put ageing lines all over the place on top of our five and nine.'

Clary deliberately didn't ask what five and nine was to pay her back for being called dim.

'Louise is insufferable!' she exclaimed to Polly when they were having their baths.

'She's certainly changed a lot. I think seventeen is probably a difficult age – you know, you're not quite one thing or the other.'

'I thought that that's what *we* were.'

'We are, but I think it gets steadily worse until – we're sort of . . . *finished*.'

'Mm. Personally, I think it's got something to do with her being so mad on acting. It is a pretty *affected* profession, don't you think? I mean, that friend of hers, Stella, wasn't at all like that. She wanted to know all about us, whereas Louise didn't ask a single thing. How *can* she say she's fed up with war talk? We're in a war, that's what we've got, her as well as us.'

'Well, if she comes down to dinner in trousers, the Duchy will be furious.'

But she didn't. Apparently she tried, but was sent back by Aunt Villy and returned rather sulky and subdued in her green woollen dress – too late for the glass of sherry that Uncle Hugh had poured for her.

Clary knew that the news must be particularly bad, because nobody talked about it at dinner. They kept to small things like the price of petrol having gone up: at one and elevenpence a gallon, the Duchy said they ought to lay up the big car and only use the small one. Uncle Hugh said how marvellous everyone was being at the wharf and Aunt Villy was actually quite funny about training to be an air-raid warden, after trying to get all sorts of war jobs and nobody wanting her. 'The language is all like filling in forms,' she said, 'so pedantic as to be almost incomprehensible. You never *start* anything, you commence. You don't *go*, you proceed, and so on.' And they talked about music because the Duchy always enjoyed that and Aunt Villy said she'd been to a marvellous concert that week, of baroque music that one hardly ever heard. Somebody asked who had been conducting, and she said, 'Oh – that friend of Jessica, Laurence Clutterworth. He really is most awfully good,' and she saw Louise suddenly look at her mother with an expression that was either wary, or hostile or frightened, or perhaps all three – she could not determine.

'You would have loved it, Duchy darling,' Villy was saying, 'and you, too, Syb. Next time he does a concert in London we must go. And I thought possibly, if he gets a bit of time off, he might come down here and we could have an impromptu concert?' She was back to the Duchy again, who said how nice that would be and, perhaps, if she got leave at any point, Sid could come too.

'She *gets* leave, but never with any warning!' Aunt Rach said. 'And last time she couldn't come because Evie had come up to London to collect her summer clothes and go to the doctor, and she insisted on Sid going with her.'

After dinner, however, they did listen to the news, and as Polly wanted to, she stayed. There had been a German attack, and the Belgian army had got cut off from the Allies. 'Bang goes gallant little Belgium,' Uncle Hugh said. He looked bitter. The news ended with something about someone called Trotsky being injured in his home in Mexico, but nobody seemed much concerned about that, and when she asked who he was, Uncle Hugh just said, 'A bloody little Red.' Then the telephone rang, and it was Uncle Edward. Villy had a long talk with him, and then came and fetched Uncle Hugh, who was also ages. When he came back, he said, 'It's time all the young were in bed.' Everybody concurred in this with such firmness that they simply had to go, and Louise, combining with them in resenting this treatment, became quite human, and they all played racing demon, turning up their cards in ones to make the game faster.

The next morning, however, it was clear that there had been major arguments. Uncle Edward and Uncle Hugh had decreed that Aunt Villy, Aunt Sybil and Louise were to remain in the country, although Louise fought for and obtained permission to go up to London each day to her school, provided she caught the four-twenty from Charing Cross like the Brig and Aunt Rach. But she would have to stop doing that if Uncle Hugh told her to. Any protests about all this died away during Sunday, as the Allies continued to retreat towards the coast, and in the evening they heard that the British forces were to withdraw to Britain. 'If they can,' Uncle Hugh said, and she saw the tic at the side of his forehead working away. 'Get me an aspirin, Poll,' he said. And Polly came back and said she couldn't find any. And then Aunt Syb said they were finished.

'But I bought you an enormous bottle on Monday!' Polly exclaimed which seemed to have been the worst thing she could have said all round. Uncle Hugh began asking questions, and Aunt Syb became tearful and cross, and Aunt Villy went and got some of her own aspirin for Uncle Hugh. There was an atmosphere of tension all over the house, she thought; it could be just that the war was going so badly, but it could be other things. What was so horrible was feeling that everything – every single thing – was or might be going wrong, and not only was there nothing she could do about it, but on some levels they didn't even *say* what was wrong. I have no *hand* in it, she thought angrily, although I'm just as much alive as everyone else. You bet the *consequences* will come my way.

Polly joined her when she was in bed, just starting to write to Dad. She looked miserable, and she got out of her clothes very quickly and left them all over the floor instead of putting them neatly on the back of a chair as she usually did.

'What's up?' Clary said.

'When I went to say goodnight to them, Mummy nearly shouted at me and said why didn't I knock. And then Dad snapped at her, and then they just went through the *motions* of kissing me, and then there was a kind of silence and I left.'

'What were they *doing* when you went in?' Her curiosity – always pretty bad – was thoroughly roused. Perhaps they had been in the middle of *sleeping* together. There seemed to be two kinds of that. But Polly said, nothing: Dad was standing by the window with his back to Mum who was just sitting on the bed taking off her stockings.

'I'm afraid they were having some sort of row,' she said. 'Which they *never* do normally.'

'It isn't normally any more.'

'No,' Polly said sadly. 'It isn't – at all.'

26 May

Darling Dad,
Actually it's the 27th, Monday morning, a
marvellously beautiful day – the kind that you like,
Dad, with little drops of dew sparkling on the grass
and interfering with spiders' webs, and no wind and a
sky like delphiniums without any of the pink bits. I'm
sitting in the comfortable apple tree that Polly and I
often use when we want to get away from things. The
orchard has buttercups and ladies' smocks in it; I
think it is rather a pre-Raphaelite scene, but actually
the things they painted are lovely, aren't they? It is the
soppy expressions on all the ladies wearing thin
nightdresses much too big for them that spoil it, if you
ask me. But the actual nature bits are frightfully good,
aren't they? I should be glad to know what you think
about this. Miss Milliment doesn't like them much –
she seems to like impressions of nature, but it is
probably because her eyesight is so bad, poor thing.

The news is bad, but I expect you know that. I
don't really understand what has gone wrong: one

193

minute the Allies seemed to be perfectly all right, and then in a few days they are surrounded by the Germans. It does seem extraordinary, when it is so peaceful here. Peaceful, my foot! About fifty aeroplanes went over just after I wrote that – the most enormous droning sound. I think they were bombers as they looked so huge, and they were going towards the sea. I do wonder where you are, Dad; at least you aren't trapped in France and ships can move about and escape, I should think. Uncle Hugh says Belgium will give in any minute, if they haven't already. [She stopped for a minute here, wondering whether to tell him about how odd people had seemed to be the previous evening. There was nothing he could *do* about it, she decided, and therefore it would only worry him. Instead, she wrote:] Mrs Cripps has taken to perming her hair. You know how it used to be, very straight and greasy – and she had those huge kirby grips that you said you were afraid of finding in the Christmas pudding? Well, now it's madly fluffy and stands out all over her head except when she goes to Battle once a week it comes out in the sort of waves you get on the sand after the tide's gone out, with little flat curls like snails at the ends. It is not an improvement, which is true, I suppose, of many changes, but that does not stop people from wanting them. Food has changed here. Mrs Cripps makes meat loaves – rightly named as they seem to have more breadcrumbs in them than anything else. And one day we had stuffed sheep's hearts that were absolutely disgusting. But I expect you are living on ship's biscuit and pemmican (what *is* that, Dad? It sounds like dried pelicans.) and condensed milk because I don't suppose they can get cows onto destroyers and just as well because feeling seasick with four stomachs would be no joke. We are keeping chickens now which makes McAlpine very cross, but the Duchy says extra eggs are essential for Zoë and Wills and Roly. Naturally I come into the band where I am not supposed to need them. The hens are called Flossie, Beryl, Queenie, Ruby and Brenda, the Duchy's least favourite names, which brings me to Zoë and the names for the baby. The latest are *Roberta* or *Dermot*. Honestly, Dad, you will have to put your foot down. Some smaller aeroplanes have just gone over. I wish I was in one of them, flying to you. I really miss you, Dad. [She crossed that out very thoroughly.] I regret your absence. This afternoon I am going to the dentist in Tunbridge Wells with Aunt Villy who is going to see her mother who is batty there. I very much hope I will go to see her too, as I have never met a mad person. You haven't answered about the pocket money, but I'll have to assume it will be all right or get Aunt Rach to lend me stamps. It is breakfast time – I heard the bell, so I'd better go and have it, although I hate Force and that's what we usually seem to have these days; the shop always seems short of Grape Nuts. Aunt Rach measured me against the dining-room door, and I have grown half an inch since last time which was just before Christmas. Do look after yourself, Dad. Don't get scurvy which I read is a real hazard for sailors; if you see anybody with it do tell me what they look like because although it is frequently mentioned in history, nobody says exactly what it *is*. Limes are supposed to be good for it, so all you have to do is to keep a bottle of

Rose's Lime Juice handy. But it is probably an
outdated disease, like the Plague.

Love from Clary.

Tuesday, 28 May
I couldn't write yesterday because of going to
Tunbridge Wells. We only drove to the station and
then took the train because of not using too much
petrol. They've taken all the names off the railway
stations which must be awful if you didn't know what
they were in the first place, but of course I can see it
would make things hopeless for the Germans. Only –
surely they won't be going about in *our* trains? I had
two stoppings and Mr Alabone said I must come back
in six months. Aunt Villy was very kind. She took me
to tea in a tea shop and we had scones and a rather
small piece of chocolate cake. Then we went to Forrest
Court which is where her mother, Lady Rydal, is kept.
We bought her a bunch of flowers, very pretty pink
and white striped tulips, and Aunt Villy bought her
some peppermint creams. I asked if I could see her
too, and Aunt Villy said no to begin with, but when I
said I'd really like to (I didn't say why) she said yes,
but I might find it distressing. 'She doesn't always
remember who people are,' she said. We waited in a
sort of sitting-waiting room on the ground floor, and
then the Matron came and said we could go and see
her now, and led us along a long passage that smelled
of floor polish and disinfectant. Aunt Villy asked how
she was, and Matron said much the same, it always
took old people time to settle down.

She was sitting in bed with a lot of pillows behind
her and wearing a bedjacket and her hair, which

always used to be done in a puffy bun, all straggling
down her back and the room smelled stuffy and a bit
of lavatories. She was talking when we came in, but
there was nobody else there. When she saw Aunt
Villy, she said, 'What has become of Bryant? You've
send Bryant away, haven't you? It is most unkind.'
Aunt Villy said she was on holiday, but Lady Rydal
retorted that she'd had Bryant for fifteen years and
she'd *never* had a holiday. We showed her the tulips,
but she didn't seem to like them at all, so Aunt Villy
unwrapped them and found a vase and got water
from the wash basin and arranged them, and Lady
Rydal, who kept picking at her bedclothes, stared at
me and said where was my mother? I didn't know
what to say, except that she was dead, but Aunt Villy
said quietly, 'I think she thinks you are Nora,' and
Lady Rydal burst out, 'You have no right to speak
unless you are spoken to! If only Jessica were here!
She would not allow me to continue in this disgraceful
place. I am no one's *dear*! The tea is Indian and they
have taken the silver. They keep Hubert away from
me. They answer back! They keep *all my friends* away.
I told them that I knew Lady Elgar was at the bottom
of this – they could think of no reply to *that*! That
woman has always disliked me – not content with
ruining poor Hubert's career, she has manoeuvred me
into this dreadful place and left me to rot! I write to
them – Lady Tadema, Lady Stanford, Lady Burne-
Jones – but they do not reply; not one of them has
replied and I cannot write to Jessica because she has
changed her name . . .' She went on, and she was
throwing herself about in bed so that the pillows fell
on the floor and Aunt Villy tried to put her arms

round her, but Lady Rydal seemed surprisingly strong and flung her off, crying, 'And I do not wish to use the commode! Oh! That anyone should speak to me of such things!' and then she began to cry – it was awful – a little high-pitched whiny cry, and this time Aunt Villy was able to comfort her, and she said, 'If you would be so kind as to give me a lift, not far, I live in St John's Wood, in Hamilton Terrace – the number escapes me but it has a blue front door and Bryant will give you a cup of tea in the kitchen and then we can telephone the police . . .' And then she looked at Aunt Villy for the first time and said, 'Do I know you?' And Aunt Villy said who she was; 'I've brought you some of your favourite peppermint creams,' she said. And Lady Rydal took them, and opened the box and looked at them, then she said, 'I have the most dreadful feeling that Hubert has died, and it is being kept from me. It is the only possible explanation for his not coming to my rescue.' And Aunt Villy said, 'Yes, he is dead, Mummy. That's why he hasn't come.' Then nothing happened for a moment and then Lady Rydal said, 'They do not understand! I must have Bryant back: Bryant gets me the numbers for the telephone. The telephone is useless without her! I ordered some cards to be made but I have no means of leaving them! People expect it. I cannot keep in touch! Some wicked person took me away and tricked me into this place and left me with nothing! A horrible dream that does not stop—' She broke off and then looked at Aunt Villy, and said in a quite different voice, low and fearful, 'Am I in *hell?* Is that what this is?' And Aunt Villy put her arms round her and said no, no, it wasn't that at all, and then there was a knock on the door and a nurse came in, and Aunt Villy told me to go back to the room where we were before so I don't know what happened after that.

In the cab going back to the station Aunt Villy smoked and didn't say very much, but when we were in the train she said she shouldn't have taken me, I must have found it very distressing, and I said it *was* but that that wasn't a reason for not taking me. I asked why, as she seemed so *very* unhappy there, Lady Rydal couldn't just come home with us and be in bed, and Aunt Villy said it was no good, she wouldn't stay there, and she needed a lot of nursing because of incontinence. I think that means you can't wait to go to the lavatory – an awful thought – but Aunt Villy said they had given her something to make her feel calmer, and they *said* that she would settle down in time. I wondered whether people go mad out of being bored with life, because Lady Rydal doesn't ever seem to have enjoyed anything very much, but I didn't like to ask Aunt Villy because she did look so upset. 'She probably loved the peppermint creams after we went,' I said, because it seemed awful to have spent your sweet ration on somebody who spurned the present, and Aunt Villy smiled and said she expected I was right. She asked me what Dad gave me for stoppings, and I said a shilling for each one, and she gave me two bob.

When we got back they said that King Leopold had told the Belgians to surrender – so of course they had. He doesn't seem to be coming to England like Queen Wilhelmina. The other thing that happened was that the Duchy was in a very agitated state about Aunt Syb, who she said had had such a bad pain that she

had sent for Dr Carr who thought she had an ulcer
and that she would have to go to hospital to have a
barium meal. What on earth can that be? If you have
to go to hospital to have it, it can't be very nice. When
Polly and I were doing our homework after supper,
Aunt Villy came into our room and asked how much
aspirin we had been buying for Aunt Syb. I thought
one bottle that week, but Polly said she'd bought a
second one. Aunt Villy said that explained it:
apparently Aunt Syb had been taking about ten or
twelve aspirin a *day* and that had given her an ulcer.
Polly was awfully relieved, and of course we said we
wouldn't get any more now that she'd seen Dr Carr,
but afterwards I wondered *why* Aunt Syb had wanted
so many in the first place. But this I did not mention
to Polly because what with the Fall of France and her
father in London, she has enough to worry about.

Wednesday, 29 May
It is so sunny and warm that Polly and I started to
unpack our summer clothes. They aren't up to much.
We've both grown so that our cotton frocks look silly
and there's nothing left to let down because Ellen let
them down last year. Also they don't fit us in other
places that I won't mention here – I've never liked the
idea of bulging anywhere, although Poll seemed quite
calm about it. 'It's a step on the way,' she said, 'it
happens to everybody.' I've never seen the point of
that: why, if it was the end of the world, would you
feel better because it was the end for everyone else
too? I do wish that Dad would write. It's well over
two weeks since even Zoë had a letter. She doesn't
seem to mind about that so much; she likes him to

ring up – I do, too, but when he does of course Zoë gets the lion's share.

Aeroplanes go over such a lot now that we hardly notice them. Aunt Syb and Zoë said they'd make us two new frocks each if Aunt Villy would get the material and she took us to Hastings in the car – what a treat! – and when we got out on the front to see the sea, we could hear a distant thundery rumbling and Aunt Villy said it was guns. There were quite a lot of people on the front, just leaning on railings and staring out. Of course you can't see France from there, and that made the guns feel worse. The sea was oily calm but we couldn't see any ships. Then Aunt Villy said, 'Well! It will all be the same a hundred years hence,' which was the only annoying thing she said that day, and we walked to the shop to get material. Aunt Villy said we could choose within reason, which meant, I suppose, that if we chose something she didn't approve of we wouldn't be allowed to have it. Polly said she wanted pink, because Aunt Syb always dressed her in blues and greens because of her hair. 'But I think pinks and reds are lovely together,' she said. She chose a piqué the colour of strawberry ice and a lilac-coloured Tootal cotton with tiny little flowers all over it, but I couldn't think what to choose because actually I don't care very much about clothes except I hate them to be at all frilly and girly-wirly. I asked Poll to choose for me because she really enjoys that sort of thing. She chose something called gingham – a sort of greeny-grey or greyish-green checked in thin white squares and a white and yellow striped stuff. Aunt Villy said they were good choices, and she got four yards of each. 'They may have to last

you a long time,' she said. Then we went to a chemist
and Aunt Villy bought charcoal biscuits for Aunt Syb
and a very nice torch for Miss Milliment to help her
see her way back to the cottage because she slipped
and fell last week and the blood all stuck to her
stocking but she hadn't noticed. Poll and I think this
means she doesn't take her stockings off *at night*,
which is unusual. *Then* we went to a bookshop and
kind Aunt Villy said one book each up to two bob and
I got ghost stories by M. R. James and Polly got—

Dad rang up! He spoke to me for a whole six
minutes! He said never mind if the pips go, I really
want to talk to you. He said he has almost stopped
feeling seasick, but that might be because he has been
at sea for quite a long time so he'd had a chance to get
used to it. He said there had been a whole bundle of
letters when he got in this time – even one from
Neville. I said it was difficult to write interesting
letters from a place where nothing happened, but he
said I wrote extremely good letters that interested *him*,
just keep doing it. He said quite all right about more
pocket money – tell Aunt Rach. I asked him when he
would get leave and he didn't know. He was off again
quite soon, but he'd ring up when he got back. I asked
him whether he knew if being bored helped people to
go mad and he didn't know and asked me why I
asked him, and I told him about Aunt Villy's mother,
and he said, oh, well, I might be right. Then he made
the noise that destroyers make when they're pleased
about something – a kind of honking whoop which
was very funny. I don't know what they make it with.
Me, of course, he said, and we both laughed all
through the pips. Then he asked me to look after Zoë,

as usual, and I said I was doing my best but he didn't seem to hear because he went on about her having the baby when he wasn't there and that was hard on her. I said she seemed placid and quite resigned to her fate which he seemed to find reassuring. I asked him how he thought the war was going, and he said he supposed not awfully well at the moment, but he was sure the tide would turn. It is quite frightening to think of the Germans as a tide, and I shan't tell Polly that. Then he said he thought he should speak to the Duchy, and I asked Polly to get her, and while she was doing that, he said, 'Remember I love you enormously,' and I said I did too. And then the Duchy came and he said, 'Sleep tight,' which was idiotic of him as it was only half past six. It's funny. I've wanted him to ring up or write for so long and now he has and it just makes me feel awfully sad – a bit frightened as well. I thought of a whole lot of things I hadn't told him and each of them seemed trivial considered separately, but I still wanted to have told him *all* of them, because as the weeks go by there are more and more things and in about a year he might hardly know me at all. It's different for him, because on the whole it seems to me that grown-ups don't change. If that is true, I wonder *when* people get sort of finished and stay like whatever they have become. And whether they can *choose* when it is.

I cried about Dad after he rang. I wasn't going to put that in, but I did, so I have. I just do miss him so much and hearing his voice, and then *not* hearing his voice is well nigh unbearable. I think probably that sex makes love less of a *strain*. So when it's a case of love, and sex is out of the question – not that I in the least want to *sleep* with Dad, but I can see that there might be something very tranquil about it if I did.

Here the thought that there must be more to sleeping with a person than *sleeping* with them recurred as it often had, but try as she might she could not think exactly *what*. And who the hell could she ask? Miss Milliment did not seem very interested in sex on the only occasions when she had tried some gentle pumping of her on the subject. She had tended to say rather vague things like it was only an aspect and one which, except from a biological point of view – and she did not teach biology – was better left to experience at the proper time than to discussion, which, she felt, would serve no useful purpose. Clary was back to having to find someone to fall in love *with* in order to find out about it. This made her stop wanting to write her journal properly for several days.

Friday, 31 May
The aunts have gone to Tunbridge Wells. Aunt Syb is to have her barium meal which apparently is thick chalky stuff that you have to drink down in one go and then they X-ray your stomach and can see if you have an ulcer. Also poor Aunt Villy is going to see her mother again. They have taken Miss Milliment as her eyes are needing better spectacles. Zoë has made me the yellow striped dress: I quite like it although I look a bit silly. Zoë said I should have white sandals, but I'm perfectly happy with sandshoes. It is quite hot and aeroplanes seem to go over all the time. I know this is an extraordinary week, but I can't think of anything to say about it. We go on having breakfast, lunch and supper and doing lessons and having free

time (ha, ha) in the afternoons. They always think of
something boring for us to do. Today it was carting
logs that Tonbridge and McAlpine have sawed to be
stacked in the garage. The logs have poor beetles and
woodlice in them, and Polly wastes an awful lot of
time getting them off and putting them somewhere
else although they might easily die a natural death
before the logs get used. They are getting people back
from France now, but there are thousands to collect
and quite a lot of them are wounded, which must
make it terribly difficult. They are clearing out the
people who are convalescent from Mill Farm in case
the beds are wanted for soldiers. M. R. James is rather
good: he writes as though he always wears a dark
suit. One cannot imagine him in shirtsleeves. The
stories frighten me just the right amount. Goodness, I
hate knitting! Poll likes it which, of course, makes her
much better at it than I am.

The trouble about a journal is the feeling that you
have to keep on keeping it. Polly has completely given
up hers; on the other hand, she's the one who reads
bits of *The Times* every day – in a way, if she *was*
writing her journal, she'd probably give a far better
account of what is going on – only about seventy
miles away she says – than I seem to do. She says she
can hear the guns sometimes, but she *listens* for them,
and it may be simply her imagination.

Here she stopped again, defeated. It was all very well
to say that we were living through history, a remark she
had overheard Tonbridge making to Mrs Cripps when
she went to fetch Miss Milliment's mid-morning glass of
hot water, but what, actually, was happening? And what

was it all *for*? If one didn't know these things, it was clearly impossible to have feelings about them interesting enough to put into a journal. The only feeling she knew was missing Dad and worrying about him getting torpedoed or shot or something. Perhaps everybody felt like that? Worried about the one thing they knew about and left the rest as a nasty mystery. She decided to do some investigating. She started with the servants because at least they stopped what they were doing and answered you. Dottie was turning down the beds and she only said that Mrs Cripps said that Hitler didn't know where to stop. When asked what she felt about it, she looked confounded: in fact, nobody had ever asked her in her life what she felt about anything. 'I don't know, I'm sure,' she said twitching off the counterpane, as Eileen had taught her to do, and catching the corners neatly together. Ellen, who was bathing Wills, said she was sure that all the soldiers would come back and that it was best to look on the bright side of things. Eileen said we had to remember that we had a navy and people like Hitler always went too far. It was better to be safe than sorry. Mrs Cripps said that Hitler didn't know where to stop and look at our air force – adding rather mysteriously that what went up must come down. The Brig told her not to worry her pretty little head about any of it. He was having his hair cut by Aunt Villy, jolly difficult as there wasn't a lot of it. Aunt Villy said that we must put our faith in Mr Churchill. Aunt Rach said it was all pretty awful, but don't you worry too much about your dad, my duck – and so it went on. It seemed as though none of them knew anything much, or were able or willing to tell her if they did. She gave up, having resolved to leave

Polly out of it in case of distressing her, but that evening when they were very slowly setting about going to bed, Polly suddenly said: 'What do you think it would actually be like if the Germans do invade us?'

As a matter of fact she had several times tried to imagine what it would be like and got . . . not nowhere – but rather, to a whole lot of different places that did not fit with each other. People being burned at the stake, little boys being sent up chimneys, like they were in Victorian times, Trafalgar Square being absolutely crammed with Germans in their tureen-shaped helmets, being a slave, sent to prison, Hitler living at Home Place with all of them washing his shirts and cooking and doing his housework, being spat at and made to learn German, living on black bread and water – these and many other random notions crammed her mind, sounding ghastly, of course, but sounding silly and pointless as well . . .

'What do you think?' she said.

'I find it so difficult to think about it at all. I suppose they could murder us all, and then send a lot of Germans to live here, and if they didn't actually kill us, I expect they would be very horrible to us, but it doesn't seem at all *real* to me. I mean, I can't see what *they* would get out of it.'

'Well, England and all the things in it – some of them pretty costly, like pictures in the National Gallery and the Crown jewels, and thousands of houses to live in. Oh, yes, and lots of beaches – they're pretty short of seaside resorts.'

'Not now they've got Holland and France and Norway and Belgium.'

'Well, I suppose, ruling the world. They'd get the

whole Empire as well – it wouldn't just be England. I mean, that's what dictators want, isn't it? Napoleon and all that.'

Polly sighed. 'I must say, I begin to see the point of being a conscientious objector, like Christopher was last year.'

'*I* don't. There's no point in that unless everybody was one, and it's obvious that that will never happen.'

'You know perfectly well that that is a stupid argument. All reforms are made by a few people who everybody laughs at, or martyrs.'

'Anyway,' Clary was stung by being called stupid, 'we have right on our side. Mr Churchill said that Hitler and all he stood for was evil.'

'Yes, but that's one of the things about good leaders: they always manage to make their side feel they're right. Hitler does that, you bet. And considering that nobody seems to know what's going on, let alone *why*, that's essential.'

Clary couldn't argue with that; it was what she had been discovering all day. Unless— 'You don't think that the uncles and so on *do* know, but they don't think they ought to tell us?'

'I asked Dad that last weekend. He said, "Polly, if I knew anything for certain, I'd tell you. You have as much right to know as anyone else."'

'But what does he *think*?'

Polly shrugged, but she looked uneasy. 'He just wouldn't say.'

They looked at each other; Clary had got into her nightdress – Polly was naked, and hunting for hers under her pillow. When she had found it and pulled it over her head, she said, 'Well, whatever happens, let's you and me stay together. You're my best friend, Clary, *anything* would be better with you. And anything would be worse without you.'

Tears rushed to Clary's eyes, and she was dumb, giddy, as joy like a rocket exploded in her heart and then subsided gracefully in separate stars of comfort and affection, when she was able to say, 'I feel just the same.'

Sunday, 2 June

Darling Dad,

I am writing again so soon because for once there is quite a lot to tell you. First of all: Uncle Edward has actually been to Dunkirk! He got two days' leave and went off in a yacht belonging to one of his friends at his club, and they sailed over and got to the beach, and then they had to anchor the yacht because it had a deep keel and Uncle Edward got the dinghy and rowed into the shore until it was shallow enough for people to get into the boat. He made three trips because the dinghy would only just hold four people including Uncle Edward. He got nine men on board, and then he went a fourth time and got one wounded person in but the dinghy got hit and capsized and he had to swim back to the boat holding up the wounded person which took him a long time, and then the yacht was so full that they thought they'd better just come back to England as quite a lot of bombs were dropping and German planes were trying to machine-gun them, but Uncle Edward said our air force was trying to stop that. Actually, Uncle Edward didn't tell me all this, he told Uncle Hugh on the telephone who told the rest of us. He said Uncle Edward got some shrapnel in his left shoulder, but he was OK all the same. The worst thing was that they didn't have enough to drink on the yacht – only one small tank of water and a bottle of brandy and tins of condensed milk but no tin opener; they had to break them open with a screwdriver. They made tea in a saucepan with the milk in it and Uncle Edward said it was horrible, so he nobly said he didn't want any. They ran out of petrol. By then they could see England, but there was very little wind so it took them ages to sail the last part. They sang songs – 'Roll Out The Barrel', and 'We're Going To Hang Out The Washing On The Siegfried Line', and 'Run Rabbit Run', and then 'It's A Long Way To Tipperary' – to please Uncle Edward. Some of them had gone to sleep, Uncle Edward said, and one of them was seasick *seven* times even though the water was so calm. Good thing *he* didn't join the Navy, Dad, don't you think? Oh, I forgot, Uncle Hugh said that Uncle Edward went up onto the beach to fetch the man who couldn't walk, and carried him to the dinghy, so it was specially bad luck it got hit then. Uncle Hugh said it was a splendid show and Uncle Edward deserved a medal and the whole family were most excited and we drank his health at dinner and he rang and had a conversation with Aunt Villy. Apparently he can't do it again, because his CO has told him to get back to the aerodrome pronto. That's a good word, isn't it, Dad? It sounds like the name for a rather sporting dog. Polly told me that she thought her father was a bit envious of Uncle Edward, but I suppose it would be more difficult to rescue people with one hand. He asked about you, Dad, but we couldn't tell him anything.

The next news isn't particularly good because it's

about Neville. He was not allowed home this weekend because guess what? Well, he has a garden with another boy – they all have gardens – and there was going to be a Judgement Day of them, and Neville put weed killer on all the other people's gardens so that he would win, but it was the kind of weed killer where everything grows up awfully well to begin with and that's what was happening on the Judgement Day, and he and Farquhar – the other boy – had moved all *their* plants round so much that they were all wilting and they came bottom and somebody sneaked anyway and they got found out, so it was snubs to him altogether. But the whole thing casts a rather bad light on Neville's character which has always been his weak point. The next step will be him giving weed killer to anyone who he thinks might be top in exams, in which case I should think he'll end up in prison as soon as he's old enough. Do you think people are capable of change, Dad? I think they must be, but only if *they* want to and the trouble with Neville is that he doesn't seem to realise his bad points, which considering how many there are is quite astonishing. However, I know we have to *assume* the best.

She read the bit about Neville again, as she had an uncomfortable feeling that Dad would say she was being too hard on him, but she decided that she had been perfectly truthful, and what more could he expect?

The third piece of news – that that morning, Zoë seemed to have started having her baby – was something that she felt uneasy about writing. It had been going on for hours now, with Aunt Villy and Aunt Rach helping

Dr Carr and the nurse; the nurse had arrived after lunch, and Dr Carr had called three times to see how things were progressing, but each time he had said it was too soon for him to stay. She would awfully have liked to watch as she had never seen a baby being born, but they had all said that of course she couldn't, and please keep away from that part of the house, but she and Polly had hung about outside Zoë's window and once they heard a muffled shriek which had intrigued and horrified them.

'Do you think it hurts a great deal?' she had asked Polly.

'I have a feeling it does – otherwise they wouldn't all be so sort of jolly and dismissive about it.'

'Very badly planned if it does, considering how many people have to do it to keep the human race going.'

'When Miss Boot's cat had her kittens they just seemed to pop out or come out quite smoothly like toothpaste from a tube. It didn't seem to hurt her in the least.' Polly had had the good fortune to see this at Easter, and Clary had missed it.

'You can't expect people to be like cats. Kittens have dear little squashy bodies – babies are much more difficult with their ears at the sides and toes and fingers and things sticking out.'

Neither of them was quite sure what actually happened, so they talked about it in a special rather offhand manner which each recognised as equating with alarm and ignorance, but they did not mention this.

'Besides,' Polly added, 'if it was as easy as kittens, people would have a nice lot at the same time to save trouble.'

Privately, Clary couldn't help wondering whether Zoë would die – after all *her* mother had – and she imagined

that Dad must therefore be more anxious than most
fathers. Better not write that news until more was known.

So, darling Dad, I don't think there is anything else to
tell you this evening. We had rabbit for lunch, because
Mr McAlpine's ferrets caught four yesterday. Rabbit
doesn't count as meat from the rationing point of
view. Oh, yes – Aunt Sybil went to Tunbridge Wells
to see if she had an ulcer and she had a barium meal
and she had. Zoë has made me a very pretty dress
and has cut out another. Aunt Syb is making two for
Polly. Aunt Villy bought a cardigan for Miss
Milliment but it wasn't big enough for her which was
rather embarrassing. It would have been nice because
her other cardigan smells quite a bit of warm cheese,
which is funny because with rationing we hardly ever
have cheese unless it's mixed with cauliflower – my
bottom meal – which we have once a week. Aunt Villy
said she would get another one when she goes to
London next week because they have Outsize there
which is actually what Miss Milliment is. I am reading
a frightening story called *The Turn of the Screw* by
Henry James. I haven't mentioned this to Miss
Milliment, because it has a governess in it who is, I
think, rather wicked and it might hurt her feelings.
She can do *The Times* crossword in twenty minutes.
She has agreed to teach us French as there is nobody
else to do it. She is frightfully good, although her
accent is nothing like as good as yours, Dad. Lucky
you, being a student in France. I don't suppose Polly
or I will ever get there until we are too old to learn
languages if ever. Anyway – *je t'aime*. You can say
that to a father, but if I was saying it to, say, Mr

Tonbridge, I'd have to say *je vous aime*, but naturally I
never would. He always looks as though he's meant
to be quite a different shape but somebody shrunk
him or something. He's nice, but I'd never *aime* him. I
do you, though. I'm hugging you in my mind. Clary.

It was nearly suppertime which was what the Duchy
called dinner on Sunday evenings. When she had addressed her letter, she realised that *again* she hadn't got a
stamp, and decided to pinch one out of the Brig's study
and pay him back on Monday. Dr Carr's car was in the
drive, and on the stairs she met Dottie carrying a pail of
hot water. Perhaps the baby was nearly born, but she was
keener on getting her stamp. She stood still; in the hall,
she could hear that the news was on in the drawing room,
which meant that most, or all of the grown-ups would be
listening to it. The glass dome had sky the colour of wild
violets; the front door was open, making a dark frame for
the piece of garden revealed; a bed of white tulips flushed
to ivory, the coppery wallflowers by which they were surrounded enhanced until they were like the back of bees
by the evening sun. Shafts of their delicious scent arrived
and were gone and came again. She had a moment of
such pure, perfect happiness, that she felt besieged by it –
unable to move. Imperceptibly, the moment was gone,
had slipped into the past and she was back to the dull
familiarity of anticipation; she was simply going to the
study to get the stamp.

The study was always darker than any other room,
chiefly because the Brig insisted upon his large pots of
geraniums on the window-sills, and they obliterated
much of the light. The room smelled of cigar smoke,
wood samples, the Lebanon cedar with which the many,

often open, drawers of his desk were lined and Bessie's basket – she was an aged dog with the marshy odours of one who plunged frequently into dark, silent ponds. Clary sat in the vast mahogany desk chair with its scratchy, horsehair seat and wondered where to look. Now she was actually doing it, pinching a stamp seemed rather more verging on petty crime than she had meant. Borrowing it, she reminded herself, but *asking* for it would mean getting caught up in some interminable story of the Brig's and, anyway, she would have to wait until the end of the news, and if she simply took one now, she could take her letter down the road and post it before supper and it would get to Dad sooner. She could buy another stamp tomorrow and simply put it back and not say anything, so no crime at all, really. She began rummaging in the drawers, and had just found a huge sheet of halfpenny stamps, when the telephone rang. It was the only telephone in the house and she knew if she didn't answer it someone would come and then they would find her. She pulled the telephone towards her, picked up the receiver and put it to her ear. An operator's voice said, 'Is that Watlington two one?' and she said yes, it was. 'I have Commander Pearson on the telephone for you,' the voice said, and then there was rather a lot of crackling, and then an unknown, but very tired-sounding man's voice said, 'Mrs Cazalet? Is that Mrs Rupert Cazalet?' and something made her say, 'Yes, Mrs Cazalet speaking.'

'Look here,' he said: 'I'm Rupert's CO. I don't know whether you have a telegram yet, but I just wanted to say how frightfully sorry I am. We were all so fond of Rupert – I say, are you there?'

She must have said yes, because he went on, 'But what I chiefly wanted to say to you was that you mustn't give up hope. He was on this shore party, you see, and helping to organise the shipment of the best part of a thousand men, but by the time it got light we had to push off. He did a spectacular job, and the chances are he'll turn up a prisoner. Rotten for you, I do know, but not the worst. But I didn't want you simply to get the telegram, because that will just say he is missing. I'm desperately sorry, Mrs Cazalet. I know it's a ghastly shock, but I sort of felt I must tell you myself and not just leave it to the telegram. We'll be sending his gear back to you, of course. I say – it's a terrible line – are you there?'

She managed to say she was, and thank you for telling me.

'I'm really sorry to have to tell you this. But don't lose heart. It may be a little while before you hear if he's a prisoner, but I should bet on that if I was you. We'll all keep our fingers crossed.'

She thanked him for that. She felt him searching for something else to say and then he said, 'Desperately sorry. Well – goodbye to you now,' and rang off.

She had pressed the receiver so hard against her ear that it ached when she hung up. She was so shocked that she felt quite calm – indeed, the trivial niggling thought came that if she had not pretended to be Zoë, the conversation might never have happened – that it was simply a kind of nursery justice meted out: she'd told a lie and serve her right. This was nonsense, but the other was not. Dad was . . . tears began to pour down her face. Dad was – might be – no – he *could not* be – but she, to whom the unthinkable, unbearable loss had already once occurred, could not disbelieve it happening again. Its awfulness made no difference at all.

She was still sitting in the chair, her tears as steady as

rain when, much later, Aunt Rach came to fetch something from the study. She was able, however, to recall everything that had been said – saying also merely that Commander Pearson had thought she was Zoë and by the time she could have told him that she wasn't, it was too late. Others arrived; the study filled up with people who tried to comfort her and she stared at each one in turn as though she could neither hear nor understand them. Eventually, she got stiffly off the chair to go and find Polly.

Zoë's baby – a daughter – was born later that evening, and the next morning the telegram did arrive, but they did not tell Zoë until she had recovered from the long labour. There was no further news when they told her.

POLLY

July 1940

The sky was a perfect blue with no cloud at all, but it was not empty.

'I can count seven,' Christopher said, and as he said that she could too: seven small pearly bubbles drifting down from the weight of the tiny rigid figures beneath them. Higher in the sky, apparently from nowhere, five bombers, black against the sun, appeared and above them, as frenetic as feeding swallows, the fighters wheeled and dived, banked sharply and climbed to regain height, inscribing the sky with thread-like tracks of white vapour, their wingtips glinting tinny in the strong light. It was impossible not to watch. A fighter, zooming down to attack a bomber, was hit by another fighter above and behind it; it changed direction, attempted to climb with the attacker on its tail when it was hit again, and, discharging black smoke, it went suddenly into a deadly vertical dive until it was out of sight. Before they could even feel, or think that they heard, its explosion, another fighter had reached the foremost bomber; for a second it looked as though there was to be a head-on collision; then the fighter veered away at the last moment, but the bomber was hit, and began rapidly to lose height. By now they could hear the uneven droning of its engines, and see that it, too, was emitting black smoke.

'It's going to crash,' Christopher said, as it became

obscured by the wood behind the field they were in. They waited, staring at the wood. The engine noise became much louder, then, suddenly, it reappeared above them – an enormous dull black ungainly monster with garish markings – almost grazing the tops of the large trees. It lurched away to the right of them and lumbered down the hill towards the house, belching black smoke and licked by scarlet flames.

'It's going to crash on the house!'

'No,' Christopher said, 'it won't do that. It'll probably get to the bottom of the hill. Come *on*!' And he began to run fast down the field. It's what Dad would do, Polly thought as she ran with him, but she was frightened: Christopher was not Dad.

Christopher tore through the gap in the hedge and jumped down the bank into the lane below and she scrabbled and slithered after him. 'Don't try and keep up with me,' he called and began really to sprint. She heard the plane crash. 'It's in York's near field,' Christopher shouted, as he turned left into the track to York's farm. She had been determined to keep up and did indeed arrive in time to see three men climbing out of the smoking wreck. Christopher ran towards them, but they, putting up their hands, also motioned him away, ran themselves and fell onto the ground just as there was a huge explosion from the crater in which the plane lay. Christopher had turned back to shout to her to lie face down just in time as something sharp and burning hot hit her on the leg. When she looked up she saw that mysteriously other men were in the field: Mr York, a man who worked for him, and Wren. Mr York had a shotgun, and Wren stood with a pitchfork towering beside him. The airmen got very slowly to their feet as the other men closed in towards them. Nobody said anything, but there was something very frightening about the silence. Christopher motioned to the airmen to put their hands over their heads. Then he walked up to them and took pistols from two of them; the third man had nothing. They looked dazed, and their faces were streaked with sweat. Two more farm hands had appeared as though from nowhere; there was another gun, Polly noticed; the other carried a billhook.

Christopher said very slowly and clearly: 'You are prisoners of war. Keep your hands up. Polly, go and ring up Colonel Forbes. Mr York, tell one of your men to lead the way. We'll take them into the church hall and guard them until they are collected.' There was another very minor explosion from the plane, which then subsided with its broken tail in the air. Christopher, uncertain for the first time, said, 'Were there more of you – in there?', but as one of the prisoners indicated that it was too late, Mr York spoke for the first time.

'A good few, I shouldn't wonder, but they're roasted, Mr Christopher – roasted to death, they are.' His tone expressed nothing but satisfaction at the good riddance.

Christopher turned on Polly. 'I *told* you to go!' he said; his face was white. 'Lead the way, Mr York, if you please.'

She turned and ran to the gate, and as she climbed it, looked back to see that they were following her – a single file with Christopher holding the two pistols. As she ran across the lane and up the drive she thought of the expression in Mr York's brandy-snap eyes: Christopher *had* been as good as Dad. It was lucky that he had gone out with Dad last weekend when the parachutes had come down in the hop field behind Mill Farm. Chris had told her that he had asked Dad how he knew they were

English parachutes and Dad had said that he didn't know, but that if they weren't, it was important for them to get there first. Feeling was running very high, he had said – particularly as Mrs Cramp's nephew had been shot down the week before. All the same, Christopher had been really brave and cool: he'd said things in just the right way – behaved with such authority that those farmers and even *Wren* had had to fall in with him. But, from being there, she knew now that they hadn't wanted to. They had wanted something quite different. She knew that Wren was a bit dotty; 'not himself' Mrs Cripps had been heard to say when it had been discovered that he had been pinching the kitchen knives which he sharpened to a murderous pitch in his hayloft. But the others were like that too.

The Brig's study was empty, and Dad had pasted the number on the pedestal of the telephone. It was really the headquarters of the local defence volunteers, but since this was in Colonel Forbes's house (his gun room had been turned into an office as it contained the only telephone in his establishment) it was always known as ringing Colonel Forbes. Somebody called Brigadier Anderson answered and Polly gave the message. 'Good show,' he said; 'we'll be along there right away. Watlington church hall, you said? Good show,' and he rang off. He sounds as though it's all good, clean outdoor *fun*, she thought. Since Christopher had arrived, supposedly for a short holiday and to come and help out with the greatly enlarged kitchen garden (but really, he had told her, because he had been having such awful rows with his father that he'd had to get away somewhere), they had had several serious conversations about war. The more she listened to him, the more torn she felt between the extremes of

221

there being absolutely no point in any of it and that being a conscientious objector was the only honourable course, and the opposite: that Hitler was a kind of evil devil who had to be destroyed at whatever cost. *Plus* there was the fact that the idea of being invaded, now that it was so much more likely, was something to be resisted in every way. That was what Mr Churchill said. It was said also that the King, who after all was entirely good, was practising with a rifle in the gardens of Buckingham Palace so that he could die fighting. He hadn't popped off to Canada like the Dutch royal family. It seemed dreadful not to be sure of what she thought, but she *wasn't* sure. She had tried asking Miss Milliment who, after listening to her carefully, had said that this kind of indecision could sometimes be a form of sincerity. She had added later, that principles could be very demanding, but that once adopted, one must be prepared to pay the price however high. There hadn't seemed to be any-one else to ask: Dad was working so hard that he looked permanently exhausted; Mummy spent all the time when she wasn't feeling rotten from her ulcer with Wills or writing letters to Simon at school. She had made two really pretty dresses for her, but she had been quite snappy to her when they were being tried on. It was ages since she'd had a conversation about anything with Mummy.

Christopher had been an unexpectedly welcome addition to her life. He worked with McAlpine every morn-ing and the Duchy approved of him, saying he was a natural gardener. But in the afternoons they had taken to going for walks, at first not talking very much, or even sometimes not at all, except that he would show her things – what he called a rabbit's main-line route through a hedge, or a nest where a cuckoo had deposited its egg earlier in the spring or elephant hawk moth caterpillars on the poplars the Brig had planted in Coronation year. But gradually, from asking him questions, he began to tell her other things, to show her his sketchbooks full of pencil drawings that she deeply admired. He could make the single claw of a bird interesting, or the fronds of different ferns that he found; whenever he found something that he liked, he sat down and drew it. For a long time she didn't tell him that she had been drawing things like that, because hers were so much less good, but in the end she showed him one of her best ones and he was really cheering about it. 'But you must keep doing it,' he said. 'It shouldn't be a treat, or a chore, or an unusual thing for you to do. It should be the most *usual* thing in your life.'

The only difficulty about this new friendship was Clary. Clary didn't want to go for walks; she spent hours in the apple tree reading books that were far too young for her like *Black Beauty* or *The Wide, Wide World*, and crying all the time she read. After the first, awful evening when the news about Uncle Rupert had come on the telephone when she had cried and talked and cried all night, she didn't talk about it at all. Only Polly noticed that she watched for the postman and always went through the letters before they were picked up from the hall table by their owners, and that every single time the telephone rang she became still – seemed to hold her breath. But so far, there had been no news about his being taken prisoner and it was nearly six weeks now. It was difficult to know what to do with her, or even what to talk about, but at the same time Clary had become wildly jealous of Christopher, jeered at her about him, and sulked after Polly came back from drawing afternoons. If Polly tried to include her, she was snubbed; if she tried to suggest something that she and Clary might do together, Clary said things like nothing would bore her more, or she was sure that Christopher would be much better at *that*. She was awful at lessons: poor Miss Milliment put up with sloppy homework or none done at all; she had stopped writing her journal because she said it was silly and pointless, and Miss Milliment, who never usually lost her temper, was brought very near it. Polly knew this because Miss Milliment would start talking more and more slowly and softly to Clary which actually seemed only to irritate Clary more, until only this week she had finally snapped at Clary, saying how dared she speak to anyone like that. There had been an awful silence while they stared at each other and Polly could see that Miss Milliment was really angry, her small grey eyes glaring behind her thick glasses. Then Clary had said, 'It doesn't matter. There's no one you could report me to, is there? No one who would really mind.' She had got up and walked out of the room, and Polly saw Miss Milliment's eyes fill with tears. The only person she wasn't spiky and nasty with was Zoë. She spent time every day with her, helping her with the baby, admiring its every little windy smile, helping to bath it and learning how to fold and pin its nappies, and fetching and carrying for Zoë with endless patience. The baby – named Juliet – seemed to keep both of them going and they talked of nothing else. And when Neville came home for the holidays and seemed to have a number of bad nights with asthma, she sat up with him, reading him Sherlock Holmes stories and making him clean his teeth again if he ate biscuits in bed. Polly knew these things, because she so often went in search of Clary to see if she was all right, and these were the only times when she was – or seemed to be.

She went now to find Clary to tell her about the prisoners. She was in her tree as usual, reading a fat red book that she recognised as being a Louisa Alcott. 'Beth has just died; it's awfully sad,' she said. 'Could you bring a dock leaf up with you? My hanky's soaked.'

Polly found the best one she could and, using the frayed old rope, she climbed into her position, slightly above Clary and opposite. 'It's so awful that they didn't know about TB,' Clary said, wiping her cheekbone with the back of her hand. 'Thousands of people must have died of it.'

'Did you see the bomber?'

'What bomber?'

'The one that nearly crashed on us.'

'Oh, that! Well, I heard a fairly loud noise. I didn't think of it *crashing* on us.'

'Well, it very nearly did. Christopher said it would try to avoid us. In fact, it crashed in Mr York's near field.' After a short silence, she said, 'Don't you want to know what happened?'

Clary put two fingers to mark where she'd got to on her page, and looked up. 'Well, what?'

'The plane blew up after it crashed just after three men got out. Mr York and people turned up like they do – from nowhere – but Christopher went up to the men and took their guns away and made them prisoner. Then he sent me to ring Colonel Forbes and marched the men off to the church hall! He did it all frightfully well.'

'Seems funny to me. A conscientious objector playing soldiers.'

'He was saving them! Saving their lives.'

'I don't see what you're so worked up about. They're *Germans*. Speaking for myself, I couldn't care less whether they're alive or dead.'

'You *must*!'

Polly was so shocked that she felt frightened. But Clary, whose face was not only tear-stained but had greyish green marks from the lichen on her hands, regarded her with a kind of steady defiance.

'They're human beings!' Polly said at last.

'I don't want to think about them like that. I just think about them as Them. A whole great mass of people who are ruining our lives. Everything is going to pot, if you ask me, and as there's absolutely nothing we can do about it, I don't see the point in having moral attitudes. The whole world is probably very slowly coming to an end, so you can't expect me to care about Germans I haven't even met.'

'Why do you mind about Beth dying, then? You haven't met her.'

'Beth? I've known her for years! And she's *not* coming to an end. I mean she dies, but she's still *there* whenever I want her. Generally speaking, I prefer books to people nowadays, and people *in* books to people anywhere else. On the whole,' she added after a painful pause during which Polly watched her struggle with the exception, recognising with a pang as she did so how often during the last weeks she had seen it before; how Clary would continue sulky, intransigent, snubbing, until something disturbed her preoccupation, hurtling her into the reflexes of curiosity – *where* was he? – until she was slap up against the awful question of was he indeed anywhere? – and then wearily back to the familiar anguish of at least

226

not knowing, all stuff that she had been through with Polly again and again during the first awful night after he had been reported missing. That first night they had eventually agreed that it might be better to accept the *idea* of him not coming back. 'You mean, being dead,' Clary had said unflinchingly. Then, Polly had pointed out it would be so wonderful when he did come back, and, if by any chance he didn't – 'Because he'd been killed,' Clary put in – then at least she – Clary – would have accustomed herself to the idea, up to a point. In the early hours after that sleepless night, this had seemed like an extremely sensible and even comforting solution, but, of course, it hadn't been at all, really. It had not been so bad at the beginning, when Clary had expected every tele-phone call to be her father, had watched the drive for telegrams, but as the days numbered themselves in weeks it became harder for her to accept anything of the kind; she clung more fiercely to the hope that was slowly becoming submerged by time and the silence.

'I see,' Polly said hopelessly.

'You see what?'

'What you mean about people in books.'

'Oh. Well, it's OK – you don't have to placate me.'

'I wasn't. I just said I see what you mean. I didn't say I agreed with you.'

'That's something.' But she said it nastily, Polly thought.

She made one more effort. 'I prefer you to anybody in a book,' she said.

Clary glared at her. 'That sounds to me like a really sucking-up remark.'

This was too much. Polly seized the rope and swung herself to the ground.

'What I mean is that if you read more you'd easily find someone preferable to me.'

Polly recognised that this, though mildly insulting, was intended as an olive branch. 'All I meant, you fool,' she said, 'was that I'm actually quite fond of you. You knew I meant that. Why can't you just take that sort of thing in your stride?'

'I never take anything in my stride,' Clary answered, but she said it sadly, as though it was a shortcoming.

'Don't forget tea, then,' Polly called as she left and Clary answered, 'I won't, but what can there possibly *be* for it?' There had been an accident with the butter that morning. (The accident had actually been Flossy, the kitchen cat, who had swiped what suited her and so besmirched the rest with her own hair and the juxtapositioning of an exceedingly dead shrew that she had turned out not to fancy that none of the pound packet could be used, and that was half the ration for the household for a week.)

'I don't know. Bread and dripping like Victorian winter teas.'

But actually, Mrs Cripps, on her mettle, had made drop scones and some kind of currant loaf and there was plenty of last year's raspberry jam. Everybody now had tea in the hall as the Duchy considered that there were not enough staff for separate teas. This cut both ways, Polly thought: it meant that conversation was no longer dominated by nursery manners – a string of clichés punctuated by the sort of silence where you could hear people drinking their milk, as Clary had once remarked; on the other hand, *if* you were hungry, you had formidable competition with the great-aunts whose capacity to eat enormous amounts of food while apparently hardly touching it was truly awe-inspiring. The virtuosity had been acquired through years of them trying to thwart one another: the last sandwich, the slice of cake with icing *and* a cherry, the most buttery piece of toast – these were things of which Flo wished to deprive Dolly, and equally, they were things that Dolly felt that Flo should not have. Like most Victorian ladies, they had been brought up to display no interest in food: their greed was surreptitious – hence the sleight of hand to mouth which meant that many people didn't get their share of anything to which you could help yourself.

The Duchy doled out the main courses at luncheon and dinner; it was tea and breakfast that provided the main battlegrounds. Now, because she wanted to keep things for Christopher, who was often late for meals, Polly made a plate for him with all the best things on it but when he eventually turned up, he wasn't hungry.

She went for a walk that evening with him, across two fields to the wood with a stream in it. The fields were rich with buttercups and ox-eye daisies and papery pop-pies, and grasshoppers kept springing aside from their knees. A cuckoo sounded from the wood, which stood fringed with foreshortened, dappled shadow. Christopher had been silent, and walked with long strides in a fast abstracted manner almost as though, she thought, if he was on his own, he would have been running. She had wanted to talk about the prisoners – to ask him what had happened in the church hall – to tell him about Clary but he seemed so preoccupied that she felt that anything she might say or ask would sound trivial. All the same, she had come for conversation rather than exercise, and once they were in the wood, she asked where they were going. He stopped and said, 'I don't know. Wherever you like.'

So she said she wanted to see the place where he and Simon had had their escaping camp last year. She had actually visited it with Clary in the Easter holidays when they had gone primrosing, but decided not to say this. Then she thought how odd it was that when one *wanted* everything to be good with somebody, one started not telling them everything. Like my parents, she thought, although it seems to have worked quite well with them. All the same, she didn't want to be that kind of person with Christopher, for whom she had great respect. So she mentioned that she thought she had been to the camp at Easter, but she was walking behind him and he seemed not to hear and, from the honesty point of view, at least she had *said* it.

When they got there, you would hardly have known that there had ever been a camp except for faint traces of charred sticks and ground left bare by ash from the fire. Christopher seemed uneasy there, and suggested that they walk on to the other side of the wood, 'Where there is a pond,' he said.

But when they finally arrived at the pond that gleamed in the evening sun like black treacle and exuded a swampy, faintly malicious odour, she found that it was just as difficult to start a conversation sitting on a bank as it had been walking. Christopher sat, with his long bony arms wrapped round his knees, staring at the water. She was still watching his rather convulsive Adam's apple and wondering if he'd mind being asked about the prisoners when he said, 'What I hate most is having to be *against* something all the time. But if you're in a minority, that's what you have to be. I can't be *for peace*; I have to be *against war* and then have to put up with people thinking I'm mad or a coward or something. And that's another thing!' he exclaimed as though she had just reminded him of it. 'The people who think war's a good thing—'

'They don't think that!'

'Well, *necessary* – can't be helped. Whatever it is, they are allowed to be moral about it – chock full of principles and integrity and all that. But people like me are supposed to be against war because we're afraid a bomb might drop on *us* or we can't stand the sight of blood—'

'I don't think everyone's like that . . .'

'Tell me somebody who isn't.'

'I'm not. I mean, I don't agree with you, but I accept—'

'Why *don't* you agree with me?'

'Because,' she said at last, after some furious thinking, 'because I don't see what else we could do. I don't know when this whole thing really started, but now it's here and we have to deal with it somehow. I mean, Hitler and all that. Nothing we can say will stop him going on with the war now. So it doesn't seem to me like the sort of clear choice you say it is. We have to make the best of two not very good choices.'

'Which are?'

Trying to ignore the hostility in his voice, she said, 'Well, having a war, as we are. Or letting Hitler just overrun everywhere.'

'You sound exactly like everybody else.'

Tears stung her eyes. 'You asked me.' She decided to go, but with dignity. 'I think I'd better get back to Wills,' she said. 'I promised Mummy I'd give him his supper and bath him tonight.'

When she was out of sight, she heard him call something and stopped to listen. It sounded like 'lollipop'.

'What?' she shouted.

'I said, I'm sorry, Poll.'

'Oh. OK.'

But really, she felt, although it might be OK in a sort of personal way the fact remained that she had failed to have a calm disagreeing conversation with two of the people she was most attached to, and she, who had often watched with contempt her parents and their peers saying things to one another that they did not mean found herself wondering uneasily whether concealment and deceit were a necessary part of human relationships. Because if they were, she was going to be pretty bad at them.

But when she got to Pear Tree Cottage, human relations seemed to be even worse. Lydia was having a row with her mother who seemed crosser, as Polly had noticed grown-ups often did, than whatever it was that they *said* they were cross about.

'I can't help it. You *asked* me! You said, wouldn't it be fun for me to have Judy to play with and it wouldn't be so I said it wouldn't.'

'You used to *love* playing with her.'

'No,' said Lydia consideringly. 'I never *loved* it. I put up with it.'

'I can't think why you're being so nasty about her.'

'Would you honestly *enjoy* spending your time with a copy-cattish goody-goody who is completely unfunny all the time and never stops boasting about awful friends with swimming pools and steals other people's eau-de-cologne to put on her spots? Her breath smells of drains,' she added. 'And if I've got to put up with bad breath I must say I'd prefer something more interesting – like a tiger.'

'Lydia, that will do! I don't want to hear another word about Judy.'

'Well, I don't either.' And so it went on.

Polly picked up Wills and hugged him. He fluttered his eyelids and a conspiratorial smile flitted across his face leaving it majestic and bland.

'Lydia! Leave the room! I mean it! At once!'

When she had gone, Aunt Villy said, 'Jessica could have come any other weekend! It doesn't make the slightest difference to Mummy *when* either of us visit her. She hardly knows who we are! No! She can't stand the idea of her friends coming here without her!'

Sybil, to whom these remarks had clearly been addressed, stopped ironing Wills's rompers and said, 'I suppose it *might* just be that it was a weekend that suited Raymond? If you are going to bath Wills, get on with it, Polly.'

When she was young, she would have gone reluctantly because this meant that the grown-ups were going to have a really *interesting* conversation. Now, however, she went with merely ostensible reluctance; it didn't do to let them think they could order one about, but on the other hand, she knew that the sort of conversation they were going to go on having was simply dull in a different way. It wasn't the *subject* matter that altered in private conversations, it was that they actually said what they *felt* about things, and their feelings, for some reason incomprehensible to her, were supposed to be concealed from children. It was quite a relief to be with Wills, even though he made it immediately clear that he did not wish to have a bath. He tore off his clothes and chucked them into the water, and then climbed onto the lavatory seat and pulled the plug. When, having cleared the bath of his tiny grey socks, his romper suit – the pockets of which proved to be full of fir cones and their mother's hair pins – his Aertex shirt and his stubby-toed sandals, she tried to lift him into the bath, he drew up his legs and wrapped his arms round her neck in a stranglehold. 'No water!' he shouted. 'Me dirt! Good dirty Wills!' His breath smelled of caramels. 'Not a bath,' he said more quietly in an explanatory sort of voice. In the end, she had to have it with him and they sat opposite each other; she washed bits of him surreptitiously, while he sat, apparently lost in thought, occasionally striking the water with the palm of his hand and nearly blinding her. He made her sing 'The Lambeth Walk' about eleven times while she was trying to dry him. By the time their mother arrived with his supper, Polly was worn out.

'Who *is* coming for the weekend, Mummy?'

'Some musician friends of Jessica and Villy. Clutter-worth. He's called Lorenzo, I *think*; I don't know her name.'

'He *can't* be called Lorenzo *Clutterworth*! It sounds like someone in a book!'

'It does rather, doesn't it? Or a bad play. Darling, when did you last wash your hair?'

'Why on earth do you want to know that?'

'Please don't answer back. I wanted to know because it doesn't look very clean to me.'

By the time she had finished that wrangle she badly needed Clary, but when she got back to Home Place she could hear what she recognised as Beethoven being played on the gramophone, which meant that Clary was having her music time with the Duchy. She would not be wanted there. Aunt Rach was not back from London yet. She could hear the wireless in the morning room, which meant that it was full of the great-aunts, who listened to every news bulletin and then argued with each other about what had been said. She certainly didn't want to get mixed up with them. She wandered upstairs, along the landing to the bedroom she shared with Clary. Clary was extremely untidy and somehow this made it much more *her* room, although Polly did make them have tremendous clear-ups from time to time. If only Oscar hadn't died! she thought. She seemed to be peculiarly unlucky with cats – in fact, she felt at the moment, not only with cats, but people, with absolutely everything. In between being frightening, the war made everything very boring. Here she was, simply getting older and older with nothing happening to her; she didn't even have a room of her own as she had had in London. If anyone had told her a year ago that she would be bored to tears living here, she would have laughed at them. Now, definitely not. The future yawned before her, like a huge incurious question mark. What was to become of her? What on earth was she to do with all the years that presumably lay ahead? All these years she'd simply been marking time – she hadn't acquired any sort of vocation, unlike Clary and Louise who had always seemed to know what they were for; all she had ever imagined was having her amazing house, which was going to be so full of things she had collected and made that it would be unlike any other house in the world. And then she had imagined that she would simply live in it with her cats. The thought *had* occurred to her that she might quite like to have Christopher in it: once, when they had been drawing together, she had thought he would be a good person to live with, and she had moved her house from Sussex to somewhere wilder, where there would be more animals.

But she hadn't mentioned it to him in case he said that he definitely wouldn't want to. And after this evening, 'You sound just like everyone else', it would be pointless to mention it. Usually, when she felt rotten and depressed like this, her house was a comfort: she could fly to it in her mind, and become engrossed in its decoration. This evening, when she transported herself through the shiny black door with its white pediment and pilasters into the small square hall that had black and white tiles laid chequerwork with a border on the floor (she had recently redone the floor) and admired her lemon and orange trees that lived in a pair of black and white tubs placed each side of the Russian stove, even before she reached the table she had made of marble mosaic with a border of shells on which stood the Victorian glass jug that had an ingenious way of keeping lemonade cool, picked up at a church bazaar last Christmas, this evening she was halted, struck suddenly by the dreariness of living quite alone (albeit with cats) for the rest of her life. Eventually the house would be finished, unable to hold another picture or table or rug or thing of any kind, and then what would she do? I was only going to live on sandwiches, she thought, because they wouldn't take long to make. And the cats were going to have lived on the *insides* of sandwiches. There would be hours and hours when she wouldn't have anything to do, because in spite of what Christopher had said about drawing, she really only wanted to draw enough pictures for the house – she hadn't wanted any drawings left over so to speak; the point of drawing would be over when she had enough. When Oscar died, Aunt Rach had brought her a tortoise from London, but he had soon got lost in the garden, so the very pretty shell-encrusted box she had designed for his hibernation would be useless. Children meant that you had to marry someone, and who on earth could she find to marry? Anyway, after bathing Wills, she wasn't absolutely sure that she would enjoy having children; she had noticed that her mother had become far more boring to talk to since she had had Wills – although it might just be having felt rotten for ages that made her so nagging in a watery kind of way. That, and worrying so much about Dad. Or perhaps it was what Louise had once said to her, that mothers didn't actually like daughters, but as the public expected them to, all their feelings got very twisted. She had asked rather anxiously whether fathers *actually* liked daughters, but Louise had got quite snappy then and said she hadn't the faintest idea.

Then Polly remembered that her mother's mother had died in India while she was at school in England. Perhaps if you had never, or hardly, known your own mother, you would find it difficult to be one? But Mummy made it plain that she adored Simon as well as Wills. From the daughter point of view, it was a good thing that she had Dad. Then she thought of poor Clary who was, in all probability, an orphan. She thought of the awful sign she had seen in London that ran the length of the building in letters about a foot high: 'Home for Female Orphans who have Lost Both Parents'. Think of having to live in a place that said that! Happiness, or rather*un*happiness, was clearly so relative, but this didn't make it any easier to be grateful for your lot if you weren't enjoying it. She decided to have two serious conversations, one each with Miss Milliment and Dad, about careers for an ungifted person. Cheered by this, she tidied the room, putting Clary's possessions in quite kind heaps, and then she washed her hair.

'Lorenzo!' Clary jeered. 'He sounds as though he'll be wearing white tights and a pointed beard and *ear*rings! It will be quite exciting to have someone so ghastly staying. What do you think his wife will be like?'

'Terrifically arty, I expect. You know, with homespun skirts and huge birds' mess necklaces slapping against her navel,' said Louise, whose school had finished its term. 'Mary Webbish,' she added.

The other two pretended not to have heard her as they both thought she showed off about what a lot she'd read: 'And it may not be all that much,' Clary had once said crossly, 'just different things from us.'

'Actually, his real name is Laurence,' Louise went on. She was painting her nails with dead white opaque nail varnish which Polly thought looked awful.

'Oh, yes, I remember now! That's just a name the aunts call him.'

'Who told you that?'

Clary blushed. 'I thought you did.'

Polly always knew when Clary was in a tight corner, so now she said, 'If he's really a conductor, I expect the Duchy will monopolise him. You know how she loves people to do with music.'

'I certainly do. She's in love with Toscanini.'

Louise turned on her. 'Don't be so ridiculous, Clary.'

'She is. "I'm in love with Toscanini," she said; she said it yesterday after we'd finished playing the *Pastoral* – that's the sixth symphony.'

'It was only a figure of speech,' Louise said snubbingly. She was really getting too old for them, Polly thought then, and said afterwards to Clary, as they were getting ready for supper.

'I know,' Clary said. 'She's always patronising or snubbing us.'

'I suppose she's bored. I am too, sometimes.'

'Strewth, Polly! I've always thought of you as being so
self-contained.'

'I've thought of me like that too. But it's beginning not
to work. The truth is, I feel pointless.' Without the
slightest warning, a tear slipped out of her eye. 'I mean –
I know it's not very important how *I* feel when there's a
war going on and all that, but I still *feel* it. I simply can't
think what I'm *for*. I feel as though I ought to face up to
what's the point of life, but it also feels quite dangerous
to think about it at all—'

'How do you mean – dangerous?'

'Well, as though there would be no turning back – as
though I might know something that I couldn't ever *un-*
know. I mean,' she added, trying to sound casual, 'supposing there *isn't* any point?'

'How do you mean exactly?'

'I mean, supposing *nothing* matters? Suppose the war
doesn't matter because we're just little objects that happen
to move and speak – like fairly clever little toys?'

'Made by God, do you mean?'

'*No!* Not even that! Not *made* by anybody. You see?
Now I *am* thinking about it, and I don't want to.'

'Well,' said Clary, breaking the teeth of her comb as
she dragged it through her hair, 'we can't be just that
because we have feelings. Could I borrow your vanishing
cream? Thanks. If you were just a clever toy you wouldn't
be feeling that it would be awful to be one. I grant you,
we can have pretty *bad* feelings, but it's not nothing.
Whether you like it or not you can think about things,

and feel and choose a lot of the time.' She rubbed her sunburned nose vigorously. 'I think it's just that you haven't made up your mind enough about what you want to do. What about your house? Doesn't that matter to you any more?'

'Not so much. Well, it *does*, but one day I'll have finished it.'

'So? Then you'll be able to start living in it.'

There was a silence. Then Polly said, 'I don't know if I want to do that. I mean, I don't feel it would be enough. By myself.'

'Oh – *that*! You mean you want someone to live *for*.' She sounded relieved. 'I'm sure you'll find them, Poll. You're so pretty and everything. Have you seen my indoor shoes?'

'One of them is just under your bed.'

'Oh, well. The other one'll be further under.' She lay on her stomach and fished it out. 'I think it's awfully difficult for people of our age. We need people to be in love with, and we're simply hemmed in by relatives and incest doesn't seem to go with modern life. We'll just have to wait.'

'You really think it's that? You can't wear that cardigan with that dress, Clary, it looks awful.'

'Does it? I'll have to – my other one's dirty.'

'You can borrow my pink.'

'Thanks. It's funny how I've got no taste in clothes.' She started to laugh. 'If I really *was* just a fairly clever toy, you could dress me in a little felt suit all sewn onto me and I'd never have to change.'

'No, I couldn't,' Polly answered, 'because I'd be a toy too.' The exchange left her feeling both comforted and misunderstood.

In the end, the famous weekend with Castles and Clutterworths was postponed. Everybody seemed to produce a different reason for this: Aunt Villy, who was palpably cross, said that there had been a muddle about dates; the Duchy said that Mrs Clutterworth was not well; Christopher said that his mother had told him that his father had made a scene in which he had refused to come and refused to be left alone at home. He had added that he was jolly *glad* they hadn't come, as he knew that his father would only have another go at him about what he was going to contribute to the war effort. He and Polly had become friends again, which was a relief to her although she still felt wary and no longer liked confiding in him to the extent that she had earlier wanted to do. She saw less of him as he worked all the mornings in the garden, and, as the dog fights continued above them, spent many afternoons watching for parachutes and bicycling off to rescue the airmen – none ever fell so near them as that first time. The Home Guard, as Colonel Forbes's and Brigadier Anderson's posse were now called, said he was a splendid chap – pity he was too young to join them. Christopher said they made him feel awful, as they all openly envied his youth and imminent chance to die for his country and he said he was too cowardly and bored by them to admit his true allegiance.

'Do you think part of believing something is that you *should* tell everybody?' he asked her one hot August evening.

'Not if you haven't the slightest chance of converting them,' Clary, who had overheard, chipped in before Polly could answer. This made Polly say that she didn't know how one could be *sure* that one wouldn't.

Christopher said that there wasn't an earthly chance of

changing Brigadier Anderson's mind about anything: 'He's one of those people who *always* thinks and *always* says and *always* does the same things,' he said.

'It would drive me insane if I was his wife,' Clary said. 'Do you think that was what Mr Rochester was like? I've never felt that the first Mrs Rochester's madness was properly accounted for.'

'There *you* go,' Christopher said at once. ' "Never" and "always" come to much the same thing.'

Clary shot him a half admiring, half resentful glance.

'I've never known a mad person,' Polly said pacifically.

'Yes, you have. Poor old Lady Rydal.'

She didn't want to pursue that. Clary had given her such a graphic description of her visit and, although Aunt Villy, when asked by the Duchy how her mother was, had recently said that she seemed much calmer and slept a good deal, she still dreaded the possibility of Lady Rydal getting the amount better that would mean she lived at Pear Tree Cottage and would have to be seen, and might at any moment go completely mad again. I could never be a nurse, Polly frequently thought. I'd be too sorry for the ill people to be any use. But she did not say this to anyone, since her two serious conversations – with Dad and with Miss Milliment – had both resulted in them suggesting that this could be a career for her. It was true to say that this had not been Miss Milliment's first choice. 'I have always rather *wondered*,' she said in her gentle, tentative voice, 'whether perhaps you and Clary might not benefit from university. It is the time when one can absorb most and I should like to think of you being exposed to really good minds, first-class teaching and the opportunity to meet many different kinds of people.' She looked enquiringly at Polly. 'It would mean, of course,

242

that you would both have to work very hard to prepare, as you would need to pass your school certificate and also your matriculation exams before you could apply. I had been meaning to suggest this little plan to Clary's father and your parents but circumstances have made that either difficult or impossible in dear Clary's case. But a university education could do so much to widen the possibilities of a useful and interesting career.' She peered at Polly through her tiny, thick steel-rimmed spectacles. 'I do not sense very much enthusiasm,' she said, 'but I should so much like you to think about it. In the case of Clary, I feel it would provide her with a goal, which at the moment could be most helpful to her. But perhaps you have set your heart upon an art school.'

'Oh no, Miss Milliment. I know that I couldn't be a painter. I'm just a kind of decorator really, and I really don't want to be anything more.' She noticed that Miss Milliment's long and distinctly odd piece of knitting had dropped from one knee and that stitches were slipping surreptitiously off the needle.

Miss Milliment clutched at the needle, but since she had her foot on the very end – or beginning – of her work, this simply precipitated all the remaining stitches into sly, diminishing loops. 'I think you are treading on it, Miss Milliment. Would you like me to pick up the stitches for you?'

'Thank you, Polly, I should. Although I have thought that it will require a second sort of courage for one of our brave soldiers to wear a muffler made by me. I seem quite unable to preserve the same number of stitches from row to row.'

'What I really wanted to know is what I should *do* with my life, I mean,' Polly said some time later when

243

she had tactfully unravelled enough of the muffler to get rid of the worst holes.

'I understand that. But there's time before you need make up your mind. And in the meantime, it is a good thing to consider how you may best prepare yourself.'

'I expect I'll have to do something about the war.'

Miss Milliment sighed. 'That is quite likely. I have always thought that you would make an excellent nurse, whereas I can see Clary joining some women's service as I think the adventure would appeal to her.'

'I'd be a *hopeless* nurse! I couldn't be objective enough! I'd be sorry for all the wounded people instead of helping them!'

'My dear Polly, I did not say that you *are* a nurse, I meant that you could become one. In any case, you will not be old enough to train for three years. But, of course, you would not be able to go to university for three years either. But it is possible that if you were a student any war service might be deferred until you had obtained your degree. I think perhaps we might discuss this with your father?'

But when Polly talked to him, he said that he didn't see any point in her going to university. 'A blue-stocking daughter!' he exclaimed. 'Quite soon I shouldn't know what to talk to you about. I'd far rather keep you safe at home.' Which was relieving, though not in the least helpful.

'I should think it would be quite exciting,' Clary remarked about the university idea.

'Well, Miss Milliment thought you ought to go too.'

'Did she? Has she got sick of teaching us, I wonder?'

'It can't be that, because she said we'd have to work extra hard for years and years.'

of the old cork bathroom mats and on it she marked the progress she imagined her father making, outlined – and more – by her in a serial told to Polly at night. Her experience of France was limited to *The Scarlet Pimpernel*, *A Tale of Two Cities* and an historical novel by Conan Doyle called *The Huguenots*. The Germans had become the Republicans, and the French, to a man or woman, the loyal underground that would assist an aristocrat to join his family in England. Uncle Rupe was being passed along the coast by these brave and loyal people. He had many narrow escapes but, in the end, that is what they always were, and occasionally he got holed up in some village for a week or two. This was happening more and more frequently, and Polly sensed that Clary did not want to get her father right to the west coast as then he would actually have to be got home. It was true that his French was very good as he had studied and painted in France before his first marriage, so he could *pass* as French easily, Clary thought. He had been planning to get a fishing boat to the Channel Islands but the Germans, of course, got there before him. He had been nearly burned to death in a barn where they had hidden him, had toiled for two days on an ancient bicycle with strings of onions on it (she had seen this in London), had been taken in a cart for a whole day hidden under sacks of fish manure ('They're all farmers and fishermen so they'd be bound to use old fishbones and heads and things like that') so that he smelled too awful for his hosts that evening and they took all his clothes to wash while he had supper wrapped in a blanket. Of course his uniform had gone long ago: he'd bought a complete outfit of French clothes with his gold watch. Sometimes he lived off the land: eating apples from orchards (Polly forebore

saying that they wouldn't be ripe), and even stealing eggs
from hens' nests. 'And he could milk the odd cow!' Polly
had once enthusiastically exclaimed, but Clary immediately said that he had never liked milk. Kind people often
gave him reviving swigs of brandy which they always
seemed to have about them, and Gauloises which luckily
were his favourite cigarette. He had got very ill swimming across the Seine at night where it was pretty wide,
but a kind old woman – a shepherdess – had nursed him
back to health; she had told Uncle Rupe that she was so
rude to the Germans that they dreaded coming to inspect
her farm.

Polly listened two or three nights a week to this saga
of triumphant adventure – the outcome of which was not
in question, according to the storyteller – but in which,
although she was frequently caught up in the tales told,
she could never believe. Privately, she thought, as the rest
of the family, that Rupert was dead, for if he had been
taken prisoner – a notion only the Duchy was known to
cling to – why had they not been told?

Even the news that four hundred were feared dead
when a French ship was torpedoed in the Channel did
not have the effect upon Clary that Polly both dreaded
and yet felt would be better for her. 'It just shows that
there *are* French ships about,' she said, 'and one day Dad
will be on one of them. Perfectly logical,' she added,
ignoring the possibility that he might have been on that
one.

The days crawled by. The dog fights continued, and
now Teddy and Simon were back from school and rushed
about the countryside on their bicycles hoping to capture
Germans. When this was discovered, they were forbid-
den, but Teddy got round it by haunting the Home Guard

headquarters where Colonel Forbes, who thoroughly approved of his attitude, gave him harmless and strenuous jobs to do. Simon, who was now as tall as his mother and very spotty, was excluded from this on account of his age, which hurt his feelings – much more, Polly knew, than he let on – and worse, left him at an unbearably loose end. Dad cleverly solved this by providing him with an extremely dilapidated wireless set about which he said, 'The moment you have got it working again, it shall be yours.' So in the end, *he* was all right, Polly thought rather resentfully. Where, metaphorically speaking, was her wireless set? Lydia and Neville, who were getting on better again, were patients for Aunt Villy's first-aid classes that she ran twice a week. They lay on trestle tables while anxious careful ladies from the village wound yards of crêpe bandage round assorted limbs. When they weren't doing that, they played for hours in what was called the very, very old car – one of the Brig's earliest vehicles that had been moved out of the garage when the Babies' Hotel had been evacuated and had sat ever since in a field beyond the orchard, where it was sinking slowly and majestically into the ground. All things that she would have enjoyed once, she thought sadly; she seemed either too old or too young for practically everything.

In August, her mother took her to London for the day to buy clothes for the winter as she had outgrown nearly everything from the previous year. Aunt Villy came with them as she was going to a National Gallery concert where the man who hadn't come for the weekend was playing. In the train Aunt Villy and Mummy took the corner seats facing the way they were going, so she sat opposite and pretended she didn't know them – had never seen them before. Aunt Villy looked quite smart in a grey flannel suit with a navy blue crêpe-de-Chine blouse, silk stockings and navy blue court shoes; her gloves and handbag all matched this outfit and her hat, perched on her wavy grey hair, had a white petersham ribbon bow at the back. She had make-up on as well: rouge on her cheekbones and rather dark cyclamen lipstick that made her mouth look a bit cruel. All the same, looking at her, you could see a bit what she must have looked like when she was young and had things in her life that excited her.

Mummy, on the other hand, wore no make-up and her gingery ash-coloured hair was in a straggly bun, with bits escaping and hairpins sticking out like the ends of paper clips. Her face was pale except for the small flurry of freckles on her nose and forehead, and already, from just standing on the sunny platform, shiny with perspiration. She wore a dress of green and black and white flowers and a cream linen coat that looked too large for her: it was already crumpled. Her stockings were too peachy; she had black shoes and white cotton gloves, which she was taking off as she settled in her seat. Her hands, white and smooth with small fingers adorned by her emerald engagement ring beside the gold one, were the smartest thing about her, Polly thought sadly. It was difficult to imagine how she had been when she was young; she looked now as though she had been born readymade middle-aged and had already been that for far too long. She was smiling at Aunt Villy now, fanning herself with a glove, saying yes, do open a window. The smile went out as suddenly as the sun from a swift cloud, leaving a kind of wan, but anxious neutrality behind.

'Galeries Lafayette do have some nice things for young

people,' Aunt Villy was saying. 'In fact, you could probably do everything in Regent Street, and then you'll be handy for the Café Royal and lunch with Hugh.'

'Oh, can't we go to Peter Jones?' Polly wanted to get her clothes at the same place as Louise, who said it was by far the best shop.

'No, darling, it's too much off the beaten track. I want to go to Liberty's anyway to get material for Wills as well as you.'

She subsided. It was supposed to be an outing for *her*, and she wasn't even allowed to choose where they would go. She wanted linen trousers like Louise had, but Mummy didn't approve of girls wearing trousers unless they were skiing or something.

At Robertsbridge a lot of people got on the train and by Tunbridge Wells it was absolutely full. An air-raid warning sounded there, but people went on reading their papers or staring out of the window without taking much notice. Then they heard planes right over their heads, and suddenly one seemed to be right on top of them and there was a burst of gunfire. A man next to Polly put his hand on her head and forced it down below the window. 'Machine-guns – what will they do next?' he said in tones of mild wonder.

But other people all looked out of the window and somebody said, 'They've got him!' and there was a sound of cheering all through the train. Polly straightened, cross to have missed seeing the plane shot down, and then amazed at herself for wanting to.

Mummy smiled at the man and told her to thank him. 'Thank you,' she said and glared. He gave her a humiliatingly comprehending smile and returned to his crossword.

Charing Cross station seemed to be full of men in uniform with huge canvas kitbags waiting for trains. Their necks looked raw from the chafing of their rough bomber jackets; their black boots were enormous.

Her mother wanted to walk up Regent Street, but Aunt Villy said that there was no point in her getting tired out before she'd started, and that they would all take a taxi; she'd drop them at Liberty's and take it on to her dentist.

The taxi was one of the very old yellow ones, with creaking seats and an ancient driver who took them slowly round Trafalgar Square and the huge buildings with sandbags piled against their windows round Piccadilly Circus, past Swan and Edgar, outside which people waited to meet somebody else, past Galeries Lafayette and Robinson and Cleaver – where Mummy said she ought to get more table napkins for the Duchy – and Hamley's, a shop all children were supposed to adore, but Polly had never cared for – toys, she thought, as they passed, had always seemed a dull substitute for the real thing – and finally, Liberty's, which looked like a gigantic Tudor house.

When they reached the floor that sold material, her mother – most surprisingly – said, 'Now, Polly. I want you to choose material for two woollen dresses, also one silk and one voile. I'll get the stuff for Wills while you are choosing, and then you can show them to me, and if I think they are suitable, you shall have them.'

This was unexpected and delightful, and she chose and chose, and changed her mind, and agonised, and in the end, actually *asked* her mother to be the final judge.

After Liberty's, they progressed down Regent Street. There was a slight altercation in Robinson and Cleaver, as Polly did not want to have vests bought for her – she had heard Louise say that they were bourgeois, something that Louise definitely thought it frightful to be, but her mother was adamant. At Galeries Lafayette Sybil bought her two skirts – a navy pleated one with a blazer to match, and an olive-green tweed – plus three shirts and two jerseys, a petticoat with lace round the hem and a beautiful nutmeg-brown winter coat with a mock fur collar. Then it was time to go to the Café Royal to meet Dad.

'Somebody's birthday, I see,' said the old lady who took all their parcels. 'Let me guess. You're too young to be getting married, so it must be your birthday,' and she blushed, because it did seem a tremendous lot, more than she had ever had in her life before.

'We'll get Daddy to take them home for us in the car,' Mummy said, when they were walking down the staircase.

'That won't be till the weekend!'

'Well, you'll just have to bear it, darling. We can't spend the afternoon carting all that around. There he is!'

Lunch was lovely. She had a glass of sherry and hors d'oeuvres and salmon with delicious mayonnaise and white ice cream with chocolate sauce – 'You can have whatever you like,' Dad said. 'It isn't often I have my two favourite women to lunch.' They all had salmon but she noticed that Mummy left most of hers. 'And what have you bought for yourself, my darling?' he said to her when they were choosing their puddings.

'I really don't need anything. I'll just have coffee,' she handed her menu back to the waiter. 'Honestly, darling, since I've happily lost some weight, I can wear all the things I had before Wills.'

'I don't think that's right, do you, Dad? Just having

things to wear isn't at all the same as having a lovely *new* thing.'

'Quite right. Mind you make her buy herself something really pretty and frightfully expensive this afternoon.'

'I promise.'

But, in fact, it turned out not to be possible. After lunch, and after Dad had put them in a taxi, Sybil said, 'Polly, I've got to go and see somebody quite near John Lewis where you can get your bras and the rest of your undies. Will that be all right?'

'Of course. But where are you going? Shall I meet you there?'

'No – there won't be time. When you've done your shopping, take a bus back to Charing Cross. I'll give you your train ticket, just in case. Oh – and yes – money to buy your things.' She fished about in her rather shabby bag and gave Polly some notes. 'Now, don't lose them. Here is the list of what I want you to get. And catch the four-twenty, even if I'm not there, which, of course, I will be. But if you think you are going to be late, take a taxi.' It was twenty-five pounds – more money than she had ever had in her life. 'Goodness! I won't need all this.'

'You can give me the change, but I want to be sure you have enough. Keep all the bills. And promise to catch that train.'

'Of course I will.' When the taxi had deposited her, she watched it drive off. She felt mystified and vaguely uneasy.

∞ ∞ ∞

Her mother did not catch the train. Polly waited at the barrier until the last possible moment, but there was no sign of Sybil, and she left getting onto the train so late that she got into the nearest carriage which turned out to be first class. Walking down the corridor as the train lumbered slowly over the river she saw something very odd: Aunt Villy in a first-class compartment. Sitting opposite her, leaning forward and holding one of her hands in both of his was a small man with a great deal of dark wavy hair whom she immediately guessed was Mr Clutterworth. They did not see her, and she hurried on, feeling uncomfortably certain that they would not have wished her to see them. Aunt Villy had said nothing about his coming to stay, but then her mother had said nothing about having an engagement in the afternoon. What *was* going on? She wished Clary was there as she would have thought of a dozen (interesting and amazing) reasons for both of these mysteries. Aunt Villy and (presumably) Mr Clutterworth had been gazing at each other, but he had been doing all the talking. It seemed extraordinary that Aunt Villy should have somebody in love with her, but that was what it had looked like, which led her to wonder whether her mother had slipped off to meet someone for the same reason. But she discarded this idea as her mother did not seem to have made the sort of efforts with her appearance that Aunt Villy had. And anyway, her mother adored Dad – she would never do anything behind his back. She tried to think about all her new clothes, but her thoughts kept veering back to her mother and what she could have been doing that made her miss the train.

When the train reached Battle and she got onto the platform, she saw Aunt Villy walking down it towards her – alone. This also seemed strange: where was Mr Clutterworth – if, indeed, it had been him?

'Where's Sybil?' Villy called as she came closer.

'She missed the train. She went off after lunch to see someone, and she told me to catch the train anyway, so I did.'

'Quite right.' Aunt Villy seemed unperturbed. Then Polly realised that Aunt Villy had known of the appointment. 'I'm sure she'll be on the next one. I expect Mr Carmichael kept her waiting. Those grand people often do.'

'Who is Mr Carmichael?'

'Didn't she tell you? He's a consultant. He knows all about people's insides. I probably shouldn't have told you. I know she didn't want to worry your father.' She glanced at Polly, and then said, 'It's nothing to worry about. Aunt Rach made her go – you know how she fusses about other people's health. It was just to be on the safe side. I expect she thought it would be easier for you not to say anything in front of your father if you didn't know. The best thing will be to say nothing about it. You won't, will you?'

Polly's mouth was suddenly dry. 'All right.'

'There's Tonbridge. Did you get some lovely things? You don't seem to have very much with you.'

'We gave most of them to Dad to bring down in the car on Friday.'

Aunt Villy gave her arm a little squeeze. 'I can't wait to see them.'

Polly smiled. Fear, like a splinter of ice, had pierced her and she dissolved it in a surge of white-hot, silent rage: insincerity, patronage, how she hated them both; how awful people were who said what they did not mean, who thought that little girls (she was sure she was thought of as a little girl) could be diverted by pretty

255

things, whose 'protection' was nothing more than their own ease . . . I could wipe the silly smile off her face if I asked her about the man on the train, she thought as she got into the front of the car with Tonbridge. All the way home, she hugged this piece of power to herself to blot out the rest.

∞ ∞ ∞

'God's teeth! It's extraordinary how devious they are!' Clary said. She had borrowed Zoë's tweezers, and was trying to pluck her eyebrows, which she felt were too bushy in the middle: 'If I don't do something about it, they might run into each other. Zoë said it would improve my appearance, but I really don't think anything will, do you?'

'Stick to the point,' Polly said crossly. She felt that her news about Aunt Villy deserved a more awestruck response. 'I thought you didn't care what you looked like, anyway,' she added.

'I don't *absolutely* not care.' She put down the tweezers. 'Well, what *I* think is that she probably is in love with Lorenzo, but obviously she wouldn't go about telling everybody. It isn't what you do if you are having an affair. I strongly suspect that part of the excitement is other people not knowing. And, of course, if Uncle Edward knew, he might easily kill Lorenzo and obviously she wouldn't like that. So it all seems fairly straight-forward to me.'

She could be extremely irritating, Polly thought. 'Don't you think she's a bit old for that kind of thing?' she said.

'Far too old in one way. But, on the other hand, that just makes it more pathetic. Mutton dressed as lamb,' she added rather wildly. 'One of *her* favourite expressions, come to think of it. But, of course, sleeping with people when you've got *grey hair* borders on the ridiculous in my opinion. When is this famous weekend going to happen?'

'I don't know. Some time in September, I think. Lorenzo has concerts and things so he's always travelling, I heard Aunt Villy say.'

'Well, when it does, we'll both have to keep a sharp look-out. "Mutton Dressed as Lamb" would be a jolly good title for a short story, don't you think?'

Seeing Clary's grin which somehow managed to be both cheery and rapt (lately she had been taking very seriously possible titles for works she would write), Polly felt, as she did sometimes, and always without warning, a kind of respectful and exasperated affection.

'If you lie on your back,' she said, 'I'll have a go at your eyebrows.'

In bed, much later, when they had cleaned their teeth, put out the light and opened the blackout because it was so hot, she reviewed the matter about which she had said nothing to Clary. Her mother had come back by the next train, had caught a cab from the station, had dropped in to Home Place to see her and apologised for not meeting her at the station. 'I had to go and see someone and they kept me waiting and everything took far longer than it should. Did you get the right bras?'

'Yes. Was it all right?'

'Was what all right?'

'Aunt Villy said you went to see a doctor.'

'Oh. Yes, I did. Yes, of course it was all right. I didn't tell you because I didn't want – to make a fuss with Daddy and spoil our lunch.'

So you made me worry more than ever, she thought.

'It was fun, wasn't it, darling? Quite an outing. The only thing I forgot to get you was a good mac, but I can do that next time I go up.'

'When are you going?' Sybil did not answer at once, so Polly said, 'Couldn't I come with you?'

And her mother answered immediately, lightly, 'No, darling, not this time. Now I really must fly. I've got to give Wills his supper.' And she went.

The main thing that emerged from this was that her mother *hadn't* asked her not to say anything to Dad, and this, she concluded, must be because there was nothing to conceal. All the same, she was glad that she hadn't told Clary, who had enough to worry about. This reminded her of something else she hadn't told.

'Are you awake?'

'Of course I am. I don't go to sleep like people in films – head touches the pillow, eyelashes flutter on the cheek once and *boom*!'

'We were machine-gunned in the train this morning. I forgot to tell you.'

There was a silence.

'Did you hear?'

'Of course I did.' There was another pause, and then Clary said resentfully, 'I must say, you have all the luck. You didn't tell me what you had for lunch either.'

'Hors d'oeuvres, salmon with mayonnaise, and ice cream. And sherry first.'

'H'm.'

'Clary, you could have come!'

'You know I hate shopping – especially for clothes. What did people do when they were machine-gunned?'

'Nothing much. It was all over in a second, anyway.

Then one of our fighters brought the plane down and everyone cheered.'

'Right. Well, now you've told me.' Polly could hear her humping the bedclothes round her in a sulky way. Then she said, 'But thanks for doing my eyebrows. Although I must say if it hurts as much as that, I'm never going to do it again.'

'You could put peroxide between them and have gleaming white fur in the middle.'

'Polly, you don't seem to understand. Not minding about my appearance is one thing, but turning me into a sort of mixture of King Lear and Groucho Marx would be quite another.'

Polly thought this was tremendously funny, and for a few minutes, choking with laughter, they vied with each other about what to do with Clary's eyebrows. 'I shall go about getting called middlebrow if I don't do something.'

'You could try cow's urine like Botticelli's ladies with their lovely smooth white foreheads – not a hair in sight.'

'Imagine trying to get a cow to put its urine into something portable! And, of course, if I *shaved* it I'd have five o'clock shadow, like Uncle Edward.'

'If you were a burglar it wouldn't matter – the mask would hide it,' and so on.

When silence finally fell between them again, Polly lay in the dark, listening to the distant drone of planes (the warning had gone hours ago as it usually did these days) and the occasional faint burst of anti-aircraft guns nearer the coast. She felt light with relief: that it had not been an Uncle Rupe in France night, that her mother was really quite all right, it had only been Aunt Rach fussing, and that at the weekend she would have all her lovely new clothes. It occurred to her how odd it was that she was in the middle of a war and could feel such simple things. Perhaps she had a shallow nature, but even that didn't seem to matter very much as at the moment after this idea came up, she fell asleep.

∞ ∞ ∞

Towards the end of the week, the war got much worse: the Germans kept on with bombing attacks all day all over the country. It was said that they were sending a thousand planes a day. 'We've shot down a hundred and forty-four of their aircraft!' Teddy announced with shining eyes.

'But we've lost twenty-seven,' Simon said.

'That's not much compared to a hundred and forty-four.'

'It depends how many planes we've got.'

But the next day, the losses and gains were more ominously even. Uncle Edward rang in the evening and had a long talk with Dad, as a result of which he said that he thought he should go back to London to the wharf on Sunday morning.

Simon had managed to make his wireless work, and he and Teddy spent hours listening to news and anything else they could raise from it. The reception was crackling, and often the announcers sounded as though they were under water, but Teddy and Simon seemed impervious to that.

Sunday was the day Dad went back to London. It was awful when he went: everybody was trying to be rather breezy and kept thinking of what seemed to her rather useless things to do.

'Their plan is to smash our air force and then invade,' Teddy said at breakfast. He seemed exhilarated by the prospect.

'How on earth do you know?' Clary asked in her most crushing voice.

'Colonel Forbes told me. He knows a lot about strategy. Anyway, we'll know if they do because all the church bells will ring.'

'Oh, good! That will make all the difference.'

'It will, as a matter of fact. It will give us all time to collect our arms. I've got the gun Dad lets me use to shoot rabbits with. And Simon's going to have Dad's swordstick. Just you remember what Mr Churchill said about fighting on the beaches and everywhere. But if you don't agree with that, at least it will give you time to commit suicide.'

'What with?'

'Oh, don't be feeble, Poll. There are hundreds of ways of doing it if you really want to.'

'Do you think we should commit suicide if the Germans come?' she asked Clary. They had been sent to pick all the greengages that grew on the walls of the kitchen garden.

'No. Teddy is just being silly. He can't see the point of girls. He's rather backward, if you ask me.'

'All the same,' Polly remarked, 'it does show how men actually *like* war, or at least get unduly excited by it.'

'We wouldn't have them if they didn't. And then they go off to have a nice fight, and leave all of us prey to wicked invaders.'

'Clary, I honestly don't think that's fair.'

'It isn't. I've just said it wasn't. I mean – look at us. A whole lot of women and children—'

261

'There are men here—'

'The Brig is almost completely blind. McAlpine's got such awful rheumatism that he can hardly dig for victory let alone do anything else for it. Tonbridge is so weedy that if a German sneezed on him he'd probably fall over. And Wren is practically always over anyway and mad to boot.' She had been ticking them off her fingers, and now finished with, 'And your precious Christopher doesn't believe in war, so he'd probably simply sit back and watch us being raped or whatever it is they do. And if what stands between us and all that is simply Teddy with his rabbit gun and Simon with a swordstick, we don't have an earthly.'

She was sitting on top of the small steps they were using to reach the higher greengages. Now, having chosen two particularly ripe ones, she handed one down to Polly, and biting into her own she said, 'What I find peculiarly irritating is that nobody will say what rape actually *is*. If there's a danger of it, I really do think we ought to have some idea of what we're in for. But they simply won't say. It's all part of this family's determination not to talk about anything that they think is at all unpleasant. I think we should talk about everything that *is*. But when I ask any of *them*, I get nowhere. Aunt Rach said I shouldn't have such morbid curiosity, but it doesn't seem like that to me. It's just curiosity. I want to know *everything*!' She handed down the small trug she'd filled with fruit for Polly to put into the huge one perched on the wheelbarrow. 'But you don't, do you, Poll?'

'Want to know everything? I wouldn't have time for everything. In any case, nobody knows *everything*. The trouble is that, when you know things, you have to do something about it.'

'No, you don't. You just know it, store it up in case it comes in useful.'

'I can see it might for writing books,' Polly said. She began to feel sad, as she often did these days when confronted with her lack of vocation. 'Did you ask Miss Milliment? She's usually quite good about information.'

'Miss Milliment doesn't know the first thing about rape,' Clary said contemptuously. 'I asked her, and I could tell at once.'

'How? She's so old, I bet she does. How could you tell?'

'You know how her face is that very pale lemony grey? Well, it started going the colour of dead leaves.'

'Embarrassment,' Polly said promptly. 'I should have thought that showed she *did* know, but didn't want to tell you.'

'No. She knew it was something awful, of course, but she didn't want to discuss it. *And* she didn't really know. Of course that must be embarrassing for an older person.'

'Look it up in the dictionary.'

'Good idea, Poll!'

The conversation came to an end then, because Clary picked a plum with a wasp in it and got stung.

As Polly wheeled the barrow back to the house to hand over the greengages to Mrs Cripps (Clary had gone back to the house to put vinegar onto her wasp sting), she thought how odd it was that ordinary things had started to feel unreal. This must be because what she *didn't* know – that hung over them, that they almost seemed to be waiting for – had begun to seem . . . not only bizarre and melodramatic, but *more* real than what was actually going on. It's all this waiting, she thought, to grow up, for the war to get worse or better, or be over.

263

The next morning, Teddy said that a German bomber had dropped bombs over London. 'It got shot down, though,' he added. He and Simon had made a notice-board in the hall on which they pinned the latest bulletins. Dad rang up Home Place and had a long talk with the Duchy, at the end of which she said that it had been decided that everybody in Pear Tree Cottage should move into Home Place. This turned out to be partly because Emily, the cook at Pear Tree Cottage, had decided to go back to Northumberland to live with her sisters, but it was also, the Duchy said, because it was thought better for everybody to be in one place. Feelings about this were mixed.

'We've got to *move*!' Clary cried. 'We've got to give up our nice friendly room we've always had and move into that horrible little room with the jiggly wallpaper.'

'Really?'

'Really. They're going to turn our room into the night nursery for Roland and Wills. I can't see why they couldn't have the smaller room: *they're* smaller and they're too young to care about wallpaper.'

But during lunch, Aunt Rach reminded the Duchy that Villy had said that Edward had said that Louise must stop staying with her friend in London and come home. 'So you may stay in your room and Louise will join you.'

'We'd much rather move into the little room,' Clary said at once.

'I'm afraid you can't. Neville and Lydia will be having that room.'

There was nothing to be done but grumble. 'She'll keep us up all night, painting her nails and talking about acting,' Clary said despairingly, as they shifted their beds to make room for a third and an extra chest of drawers.

'It's worse for me,' Neville said. He had very quietly stood on his head to surprise them in the doorway. 'I have to sleep with a *girl*!' he went on as his face slowly became scarlet. 'I've marked the room in half with blackboard chalk and I'm going to *charge* her if she enters my territory.'

'Neville, it is extremely rude to listen to other people's private conversations.'

He eyed Clary unblinkingly. 'I *am* extremely rude,' he said.

She pushed him, and he collapsed easily on the landing against Lydia, who had just arrived from trudging upstairs with an armful of her possessions. This made a terrible mess, and Lydia cried as boxes of chalks, weak envelopes filled with beads that she strung into endless necklaces as presents for everyone, her shell collection, two bears and the skin of a grass snake pinned to a piece of balsa wood tumbled and rolled all over the place. Clary scolded Neville, who instantly disappeared, and Polly started to help her collect her things. 'Put all the beads in my hat,' she said, as she retrieved the snakeskin, hoping that Lydia wouldn't notice that it was damaged but, of course, she did. 'My most unusual thing!' she wailed. 'It might take me the whole of my life to find another one!'

'It isn't too bad, but I bet you Christopher could find you another.'

'I want to find it myself! I don't want anyone else's findings.'

'If you sit still, I'll put some lipstick on you.'

That worked. Lydia sat on the floor holding up her face, rapt, as Polly dabbed her moist cherry mouth with the hard dry Tangee she hadn't used for ages.

'What's unfair,' said Lydia, 'is that they make all of *us* share with whoever *they* like – they even said that if ghastly Judy comes to stay they'll put her in the room with Neville and me – but *they* don't share. I mean, they could easily put Uncle Hugh in with Mummy when Aunt Syb goes for her exploration.'

'What are you talking about?'

'She's going for an operation so that they can explore her. I heard Mummy talking to her about it, and then when they saw me they said that French remark that means they don't want you to know what they are talking about.'

'... *Poll*! For the *third* time! Do you want the bed by the window or not?'

'I don't mind,' she said, lurched to her feet, and went blindly in search of her mother.

THE FAMILY

Autumn–Winter 1940

'Of course I'll drive you,' Edward said, 'don't be silly. But we ought to get a move on if you're to catch your train.'

She smiled bravely at him: she'd done her make-up in the bathroom while he was dressing, and one looked terrible if one's mascara ran.

'I'll pop down and pay the bill,' he said. 'Give me your case.'

He stood in front of her, a case in each hand and his hat tucked under one arm.

'I wish I'd seen you without your uniform,' she said without meaning to.

'Darling, you have. I couldn't have been more without it last night. I'll meet you at the car.' The reception desk had embarrassed her so much when they had checked in – Squadron Leader and Mrs Johnson-Smythe – that he didn't want to repeat the experience. 'Don't be long,' he said and went.

She looked round the room. Last night, it had seemed so romantic: the large double bed, the little pink silk bedside lights, the heavy silky curtains drawn and the dressing table with three mirrors and a brocade-covered stool in front of it. Now, it looked desolate – untidy, even squalid. The bedclothes pulled back from the dented pillows, the wreck of their breakfast tray on the end of the bed – all crumbs and greasy plates and coffee rings on the tray cloth – the powder she had spilled on the dressing table and the wet bath towels, one on the floor – Edward's – and hers on the stool. The curtains were drawn to show a clear but uninviting view of the car park, and she could see that the thick carpet she had enjoyed walking upon with bare feet last night, was not, in fact, very clean. She knew he was married: he had been frightfully honest about that. She thought he was the most honest man she had ever met in her life; his blue eyes looked at one so seriously when he said things, even when he found some of them – like being married – difficult to say. Just the thought of him looking at her made her shiver. '*Sure* you want to do this?' he'd said as they drove to the hotel after dinner. Of course she had wanted to. She hadn't told him that she'd never done it before: she'd always thought she wouldn't do it until she was married – that the first time would be her wedding night; she would wait for what the other girls in her company called Squadron Leader Right. Now she could see that all she'd been waiting for was to be in love – nothing else really mattered. He'd been a bit shattered when he found it was her first time: 'Oh, darling, I don't want to hurt you,' he had said, but he had. She had loved him kissing her, and his touching her breasts had been really exciting, but the rest of it had been quite different from what she had imagined. The third time it hadn't hurt in the same way. She could see that in the end it wouldn't hurt at all. It was being wanted that was so amazingly exciting – or, at least, being wanted by someone as attractive as Edward.

She had been standing by the window with her compact mirror, trying to make a hard line of her mouth with lipstick, but she was so sore from his moustache that it was all red round her mouth and that made the lipstick look blurred. She smeared round her upper lip and chin with the very white powder she used. That was the best she could do. Now, leave the room, go down in the lift, walk firmly across the reception hall – no need to look at anybody – and out to the car. She twitched her tie, put on her cap, hung her bag over her shoulder and walked stiffly out of the room.

He was putting their cases in the back of the car when she reached it.

'Well done, sweetie,' he said, and she thought how sensitive he was to realise that leaving the hotel was an ordeal for her.

'Now, ma'am. Where to?'

'Paddington.'

'Paddington it is.'

In the car, she thought fleetingly how lovely it would be if her weekend leave was going to be spent with him, instead of with her parents in Bath where there would be nothing whatever to do as all her friends were away at the war one way or another, with Mummy criticising her make-up and Daddy giving her patronisingly weak gin and limes.

On the Great West Road on their way into London, they got caught behind an immensely long army convoy and she lit them both cigarettes when he asked for one. 'Happy?' he asked her as she handed him his. She knew he wanted her to say yes she was, so she did, but really she was struggling with panic at the thought of parting and the anti-climactic hours to follow until they met at Hendon on Monday.

'Have you just got the weekend, like me?'

'That's it. We just have to make the most of it.'

She wanted to ask him if he was going home, but there was no point because of course he would be. He had four children, she knew that, but when she had asked him their ages, the nearest she dared get to her curiosity about his wife, he'd smiled and said, awfully old – except for the youngest. 'I'm old enough to be your father, you know,' he said. That was another thing she admired about him: a great many men might have pretended they were younger than they were, but not Edward. In fact, when they reached Paddington, and he put her on the train, he said to the aged guard, 'Look after my favourite daughter, won't you, George?' and the guard had smiled approvingly, and said of course he would. Edward put her in a corner seat. 'Have you got anything to read?' but she hadn't, so he went away and came back with *Lilliput*, *The Times* (which she'd never read in her life) and *Country Life*. 'That'll keep you busy,' he said; then he stooped down and whispered in her ear, 'It was fun, wasn't it, darling? The greatest possible fun?'

She felt her eyes grow hot with tears, and before she could even blink them back, he'd handed her his wonderful silk hanky that smelled so extraordinarily delicious. That was another thing she loved about him: his thoughtfulness, as well as his generosity.

'I'll give it back to you on Monday,' she said, still trying not to cry.

'You keep it, darling. There's plenty more where that came from.' He took off her cap and kissed her mouth – one quick kiss. 'Bye, sweetheart, have a lovely leave.' And he was gone. She dabbed her eyes and tried to open the window so that she could see him walking away down the platform, but by the time she got it open, she couldn't see him. She settled back in her corner; it was really thoughtful of him to go quickly like that. She blew her nose repressively, and soon after the train started, she fell asleep.

∞ ∞ ∞

'Poor Mummy!'

'Yes, indeed. Poor Mummy!'

'I must say, it makes me see the point of voluntary euthanasia.'

'Except that in Mummy's case she's not *compos* enough to make that sort of decision.'

Recognising the logic that all her life had irritated her about her sister, Villy remained silent.

They were sitting in a tea shop, drinking grey coffee with a plate of Marie biscuits, untouched, between them. There had been an urgent summons from the nursing home, as Matron had thought that Lady Rydal was possibly on the way out, as she had put it on the telephone to Villy yesterday (Thursday) evening. But when they had arrived at the nursing home that morning – Jessica from Frensham, Villy from Sussex – Matron had met them with the, as it turned out rather distressing, news that Lady Rydal seemed a little better. 'She's holding her own,' she had said, rustling down the passage before them. 'Of course, she has a very strong heart, but I can't hold out *too* many hopes.'

They had spent a miserable hour with their mother, who lay flushed and somewhat shrunken on her pillows, her restlessness reduced to moth-like movements of her spectral fingers onto which the large diamond rings had been taped with Elastoplast. 'She won't be without them,' Matron had said, 'and they keep slipping off and getting lost in the bedclothes. Lady Rydal? Here are your daughters come to see you!' But her cheery tones of one announcing a great treat were unheeded. She had not seemed to know them, or to care who they might be. Only once during the hour, when they had been conversing quietly and pointlessly to each other, she had suddenly said quite clearly, 'After the fall, when my horse had refused, they came and cut my laces – and oh! the exquisite relief! But, of course, one needs the support, and quite soon my back began to ache.'

'When was that, Mummy darling?' But she had taken no notice of the question.

Jessica sipped her coffee and made a face. 'I suppose soon there won't be any coffee at all. That will be particularly awful for you because you love it so much.'

This was an olive branch – or rather, twig; it had only been a minor irritation, and Villy was glad to take it. 'You'll come back with me, won't you? I mean, it seems to me that anything might happen, and it's such a long journey for you.'

'Thank you, darling. Well, just for the weekend, anyway. Then I must go back to shut Frensham up. Store everything, and see if I can find a tenant.'

'Really? What does Raymond say?'

'He doesn't seem to mind which is surprising, but he's actually got this job at Blenheim and he's so thrilled that he can't think of anything else.'

'Jess! How wonderful! What's he doing?'

'He says it's terribly hush-hush and he can't say. That friend of his mother's – old Lord Carradine who was always nice to him when he was young – mentioned his name and, of course, being disabled, a desk job's just right for him. He didn't want me to tell anyone until he'd had his interview, which apparently he sailed through. It's just so *wonderful* that he's found a niche.'

'So what will you do?'

'Well. I was wondering whether Judy could join your lot with Miss Milliment. I don't like her going to a boarding school and she does love being with Lydia.'

Remembering Lydia's remarks about Judy, Villy replied, 'It's a lovely idea, but of course I'd have to talk to the Duchy. And Miss Milliment too, I suppose.'

'*She* won't mind. She was worrying in the summer about not being useful enough.'

'*Was* she? When was that?'

'When we came over at the beginning of the holidays. She said she felt she ought to take herself off for a few weeks, but she didn't know where to go. I couldn't offer to have her because Raymond finds her difficult.'

'What will you do? Do you want to join the clan?'

'It's awfully sweet of you, darling, but I rather thought I'd perhaps take over Mummy's house in London. We can't just leave it closed down with everything in it.'

'Bryant's still there, isn't she?'

'Yes, but we ought to do something about that. I mean, with the nursing home, I don't think Mummy can afford to go on paying wages to servants whom she's never going to need any more. I know it's awful,' she added as she saw Villy's face, 'but I thought we ought to agree what kind of settlement we could make, with Bryant particularly, who has been jolly faithful and is really too old to get another job.'

'Yes, we should. But why London for you especially?'

Jessica answered vaguely that she was thinking of getting some job or other, 'some kind of war work, even if it's only cooking in a canteen', but after that, there was constraint between them. Jessica knew, and Villy suspected, that war work was not the only reason. To change the subject Jessica said, 'Any news of Edward?'

'He's coming tomorrow. He was coming tonight, but then he rang to say he couldn't get leave until tomorrow.'

'I suppose one must be grateful for small mercies.'

'Oh, one must. Otherwise there would be nothing to be grateful for.' Her tone was almost dramatically bitter, and Jessica decided not to reply.

In the car, when Jessica was driving them back, Villy said, 'Isn't it a bit unwise to set up in London just now? Won't Raymond want you to be safer – to find somewhere near him? Oxford?'

'Oh, no! He's delighted to be away on his own. And I think it's good for him to be with entirely new people, who don't know a thing about the chicken farming or dog kennels or any of those things that didn't work out. And, quite frankly, I'm glad to get him away from Frensham, because it proved to be in the most awful state – Aunt Lena had done nothing to it for years, and he was in a fair way to spending every penny we'd got repairing it. If I'm in London, it will be easy for him to pop up when he's free . . .' There was another silence while both of them thought about the same, quite different thing.

'And how's Sybil doing?' Jessica asked with a kind of bright concern.

'She'll be home in about a week.'

'Did she have to have—?'

'Everything out? Yes, she did, poor dear. She'll need a longish convalescence. But they said it was the only thing to do. Of course, we all thought she'd got cancer – including her. She was frightfully brave – just desperate that Hugh shouldn't know.'

'He didn't?'

Villy shook her head. 'It never seemed to occur to him, thank goodness. But he's got so much on his plate with Edward away and having to live in his club and fire-watching at night as well as working all day that I don't think he's had the energy or time to do any more than accept what he's told. I think he's just profoundly relieved that they found out what was wrong and did something about it.'

For the rest of the journey they compared notes on how similarly and differently difficult Angela and Louise were being.

It was funny how like their mother Villy was about other people's misfortunes, Jessica thought: she behaved almost as though they had been sent personally to try *her*.

And Villy reflected wryly how when Jessica really wanted to do something, she would make out that it would be better for other people that she did it. Just like Mummy used to be about the summer holidays when they were children. She would say that it was essential for Papa to get away and have a rest from his composing, when all he wanted to do was to be left in London in peace to get on with it. Generally, these adverse percep-tions that they had about each other did not, on the whole, diminish affection, but this afternoon, because they were both withholding what most occupied their thoughts, there was an edge to them, and they were both formally commiserating and carefully comforting each other about their difficult daughters as recompense. 'At least she's got a good and useful job at the BBC' (Angela) and 'I'm sure she's very talented – after all, she must inherit some of it from you' (Louise).

Jessica looked her haggard, but these days more

elegant, self with a long chiffon scarf of the palest turquoise wound round her long throat, making a contrast
of muted bravado with her yellow-green dress. Even her
hands, which last year had looked so ravaged by housework, had become white and smooth, decorated on their
backs by veins that matched her scarf, and a large silver
Amy Sandheim ring set with turquoise. Of course, having
more money had effected all this, Villy thought, and that
idea made her feel some of the old, compassionate affection that she had for her sister. 'The scarf's awfully good
on you,' she said.

'It hides my awful neck, which is beginning to "go" as
Mummy would say.'

'Darling, you'll always be fearfully attractive.'

'I shan't wear as well as you do.'

Later, Villy remembered that she'd left her car at the
station in Battle. 'I'm afraid we'll have to go there for me
to retrieve it.'

This they did, and then drove in tandem the two and
a half miles to Home Place.

On her own, Villy reflected that by taking their
mother's house in St John's Wood, Jessica would be able
to see Laurence any time as he and his wife lived quite
near in a flat in Maida Vale. Of course, that's why she
wants to go there, she thought, and I'll be stuck in the
country. She began to wonder whether there was any
way in which she could persuade Edward to reopen *their*
house in Lansdowne Road. She had not seen Laurence
since his concert at the National Gallery and they had
had that wonderful afternoon together, walking along
the Embankment, when he had poured out to her the
agonies of living with his insanely jealous wife who did
nothing but mope when he was away, locking herself in

276

her bedroom with French novels and migraines, and emerging on his return to make terrible scenes. His work meant that he had to travel all over the country, and she always imagined him in the arms of every violinist or singer he accompanied, when what he longed for was a quiet domestic life with somebody who understood that music came first. When she thought of his dark eyes burning into hers, she shivered with a kind of romantic excitement that she had never felt before in her life. They had had tea at the Charing Cross Hotel, and he had held her hand and told her again and again how lucky he felt to have met her. When she had said that she must catch her train, he had said, 'I'll catch it with you.' Enchanted by this gesture, she had explained that her sister-in-law and her daughter would also be on the train . . . 'We'll go first class, as first-class people should,' he had returned grandly. In the end she had made him curtail his journey at Tunbridge Wells, but that hour had been one of the most charming in her life. She had told him about her early dancing with the Russian Ballet; how Cecchetti had said what an extraordinary talent she had for dancing – he had not been able to believe at first that she had not started until she was sixteen – and how marriage had put a stop to all that. He had a gift for sympathy that she had never met before in a man and she was not able to recognise that the life she had led for the last twenty odd years had precluded her having much or any experience of men to whom she was not related one way or another. He was a very good listener, he asked the right questions, he seemed almost to know in advance what she wanted to tell him. When he left, he kissed her hand, and she looked at the place as a young girl might – indeed, she felt like Karsavina in *Spectre de*

la Rose. Since then, he had sent her two letters – or rather
two postcards enclosed in envelopes: one from Man-
chester and one from Maida Vale. 'I think so often of our
lovely talk in the train – and indeed elsewhere,' he had
written in the first. In the second he had referred to 'our
oasis in the desert of our lives'. To each of these communications she had replied with four- and five-page letters in which she had poured out her frustration about
the futility of her life. When she had first used that word,
he had stroked the side of her face with one finger and
said, 'You have a Russian soul, you want constantly to
go to Moscow. Moscow is your dream – your great
retreat.' After that they had made tragi-comical Napo-
leonic jokes about the great retreat *to* Moscow, and she
felt that, at last, someone was entering into the tragedy
of her life. So the letters enlarged upon this game – she
needed him to see that she was gallant, and employed
her lightest touch. Of course she did not send them –
there was nowhere safe to send them to. To believe that
he understood her enabled her to admire *his* fortitude,
his patient endurance of the yoke of jealousy. She sensed
that he had not gone as far in his profession as he had
wished – he had several times said things which implied
that: 'That was when I had just won the scholarship to
the college,' and 'That was when Professor Tovey actually asked to be introduced to me after a concert, when I
won the gold medal for—' It was amazing how much
ground they had covered in that one afternoon. Before
that, she had practically not seen him alone. But since he
had been conducting an amateur orchestra and choir for
a spring season in Guildford, Jessica, who had, of course,
joined the choir, had seen him a good deal.

She looked in her driving mirror: Jessica was close behind her as she turned into the drive.

∞ ∞ ∞

'All the same, I don't really like the idea of you being in London.'

'Darling, it's perfectly all right. They've got a whacking great air-raid shelter in the basement, and we all get popped safely into it if there's the slightest danger.' She put out her hand, and Hugh took it. 'You're such an old worrier.'

'Well, with any luck, I'll have you home far sooner than you think. I'm seeing the Great White Chief before I leave here, and I know that if you have a good nurse he'll let you go.'

'That's very grand of you. How did you manage that?'

'I arranged it last week. He told me that this was his day here and that he'll be free when he's finished operating. If I get him to agree, the hospital can't keep you.'

He smiled down at her, and she realised how exhausted he was. If it made him feel better to have her in the country, of course she would go . . . although, at the moment, even the thought of getting out of bed made her feel shaky and tearful from weakness. And with everybody moved into Home Place, she could not imagine where a nurse could sleep, even supposing they were able to get one. He was saying that he thought he'd better go, he did not want to miss seeing Mr Heatherington-Bute, and although in one way she didn't want him to go, seeing *anyone* for more than half an hour made her desperate with fatigue.

'Goodbye, my darling girl,' he said. 'Mind you eat that smoked salmon; it will build you up. I'll give your best love to Polly and Simon and Wills,' he added, anticipating her. 'And I'll ring tomorrow.'

Then he was gone, and she was left with the litter of gifts he had brought: not only the smoked salmon, but two novels, although she did not feel up to reading, the pink roses that she must ring for a nurse to put in water, the large bunch of black grapes – he never came empty-handed. I'll call the nurse in a minute, she thought wearily, turned her face away from the door and fell asleep.

∞ ∞ ∞

Half an hour later, he let himself out of the huge black door and walked down the steps from the hospital, and then across the road to his car. His mind was curiously blank, as though it had temporarily absented itself from his body, which none the less knew how to put one foot before another, how to open the car door and lever itself into it.

When he was sitting, fragments of what the man had said to him occurred but in no coherent order: 'Your wife is doing very well – as well as can be expected.' 'I'm afraid I have to tell you that of the two tumours we removed, one was not benign.' 'Operation itself a complete success, so all should be well.' 'Felt you should be put in the picture.' Then he had stopped talking and offered him a cigarette. 'But she'll get better, won't she? A complete success, you said.' That seemed unanswerable, but it wasn't. Every time he screwed himself up to ask a direct question, the man answered in such a way that he felt none the wiser – neither terrified, nor reassured. There

280

was every chance that she would show a steady improvement. He could see no reason to be unduly worried. The only point on which he seemed unequivocal was discussion with the patient herself. 'Oh, no, no, no,' he had said, his rather heavy, plum-coloured jowls shifting uneasily from side to side, and this *did* relieve him: above all else, he did not want her to be worried, and Mr Heatherington-Bute had enthusiastically concurred. Nothing was more injurious to patients – particularly *women* – than anxiety.

On this note, he had found himself leaving: Mr Heatherington-Bute had risen, had extended a white, fastidiously shaped hand, a series of ever-widening smiles – like the ripples on a pool – were regularly disturbing his face, and he was imploring Hugh to get in touch with him whenever he felt inclined.

Hugh realised that he had not asked when he might take her home which had been the question at the top of his list, and the inclination to get in touch with Mr H. B. there and then occurred, but he quenched it. Obviously, she wasn't up to coming home *now*, and he could talk to Matron on Monday about dates. He had realised when he had been talking to her that she was actually feeling pretty done up. Her skin had that translucent, milky quality that had been coloured only by the small bruising marks of fatigue, minute fronds of viridian veins lacing her eyelids, which if she had been well would have been invisible, and the dusty shadows under her eyes, her hair still done in two plaits for the operations and still not loosened, and her mouth still blistered from the fever she had had for a couple of days afterwards. Thinking of her mouth – and the still irresistible way in which she drew in her upper lip with her teeth when she was thinking hard – he remembered with a pang that he had not kissed

281

her when he had left. Would she have minded – would she have noticed even? Suddenly he was overcome by a longing for her – to hold her in his arms, to watch her breathing, to hear her small soft voice, to reminisce, to chat, to gossip with her of nothing important, except that it had been shared, that their knowledge was equal, their responses sometimes delightfully different . . .

No, to go back and see her now might worry her. She might think that he had had an awkward time with Mr Heatherington-Bute – that there had been some bad, or difficult news. When, in reality, it hadn't been at all like that: he was very pleased with her, she was making jolly good progress, the operation had been a complete success . . . In rehearsing how he would tell her what had been said, he began to feel relief himself – naturally these professional chaps had to cover themselves, would never stick their necks out a hundred per cent . . . It was quite right *not* to go back again to see her – never mind how much he wanted to – it would do him good to think of others for a change. He lit a cigarette and started the engine. It seemed very odd to be driving to Sussex, *away* from her, when always it had been the other way round and Fridays had been the best day of the week, but he'd soon have her home. He'd talk to Rachel about finding a really good nurse, because then she could come home sooner.

∞ ∞ ∞

'F U C,' she wrote laboriously, 'fuss?'
    'Fuck. It's got a k at the end.'
    'Oh, well, you didn't say that.'

'You write so slowly,' he complained. 'The next one's easy. Bugger. B U G G E R.'

Lydia licked her pencil and went on writing.

'Ready?' Neville said. 'Balls.'

'Balls? I really can't see anything rude about them. This is getting a bit boring, if you ask me.'

'Shut up! Shit! Spew – gloomy blood! *Soixante dix*!'

'How on earth do you spell that? It sounds foreign to me.'

'It is. It is a foreign position – probably the rudest in the world.'

'Get into it, Nev – let me see!'

But he was not to be caught out. 'Have you written the others down?'

'Not yet.'

'Well, get on with it, or you'll forget them.'

'I won't. What was the first one?'

He told her. As a long-term plan for getting rid of her in what he decided had become *his* bedroom, it was proving laborious. She simply forgot the words – on the other hand she never failed to ask him awkward questions about what they meant. And it was going to be difficult to get her to launch into a proper display of rudeness in front of everyone at mealtimes, if she had no idea what she was talking about. Sometimes, he had to admit, *he* didn't know, since it was the fashion at school to pretend to know everything anyway, which cut down everyone's chances of acquiring new information. *Soixante dix*, for instance: for the life of him, he couldn't think of *any* rude English position at all let alone a foreign one. What he was trying to be was what they called a bad influence – so bad that they would remove her from the bedroom. He'd get a wigging for it, but it would be worthwhile: they might even move him in with Teddy and Simon! If horrible Judy came, which had been mentioned as a possibility, then they easily might, and poor old Lyd would be left with the goody-goody. But if Teddy and Simon refused point blank to have him, he might end up alone, and what he found about being alone was that although he often thought he would like it, it usually made him sad. At school you were never alone – even the lavatories didn't have walls from the floor to the ceiling so that other people could hear everything. The other worrying thing about being alone for him was when he had an asthma attack. If nobody was there, and he couldn't find his sniffer, he could feel pretty awful. Lydia had always been decent about that: she sat up and read to him until he felt better and she shut up about it the next day. Also, when he was alone, he could not help thinking about things generally, and they all seemed to be bad. The war *wasn't* turning out at all like he had thought it would; far from being exciting, it seemed simply to make things that used to be exciting either impossible or dull, and dull things duller. Then there was the question of Dad which he found he couldn't think about at *all*. How *could* Dad go off like that and leave him and Clary with nothing? Because he certainly wasn't counting Zoë and that horrible baby she'd deliberately had. There had been too much death in the family for its own good, he thought. His mother becoming dead at the beginning of his life; and now Dad, just disappearing without warning – Ellen would be the next to go, he shouldn't wonder. He felt the need to be alone coming over him now, and watching Lydia's head bent over her exercise book, he wished he hadn't started the whole thing; he couldn't see a particularly good end to it whatever happened.

'... gloomy blood just sounds disgusting,' she was saying. 'I can *spell* it, but I don't think I'll bother. I'm really only interested if it's breathtakingly rude.'

'Naturally, I know a lot of far ruder things but you're not old enough for them.' He was becoming bored with the whole thing.

'I'm catching up with you nearly. I'll be nine in November.'

'But the fact remains that you're only eight now. *And* a girl.' Escaping from her meant leaping out of the very, very old car on the stinging nettle side, but he was so bored it was worth it. He ran, with smarting legs until her wails of dismay had become merely funny. In the orchard, he found dock leaves and rubbed his legs until they were streaked with green. Then he lay in the long grass and wondered what to do with his life. Do a bad deed, if he could think of one. He and Hawkins at school had made a pact about seeing who could collect the most bad deeds throughout the holidays, and the person who won would get half the other person's pocket money for the term. In order that there should be no argument, they had constructed an elaborate points system. A small bad deed would just mean that people got cross and told you not to do it again: one point. A better bad deed would mean that you got a punishment: two points. The best of all was if you did something that *had not been done before* and for which you were punished: three points. This last was surprisingly difficult, but the best of all was doing something really bad that had not been done before *and* was not found out. You got five for that. 'How will each other know that we did it?' he had asked, and Hawkins said that there was such a thing as honour, and that if real friends betrayed one another they would go to hell. 'That's just a matter of fact,' he had said. He was six months older with bright ginger hair and in summer the freckles all ran into each other over his nose so that it looked yellow. He had been bitten by a snake and had not died and had been to the Chamber of Horrors at Madame Tussauds in London where he said he had seen some terrible things, in fact the only boring thing about him was his conjuring tricks that you could always see how they were done, but he kept on practising on anyone who would watch and, of course, as Hawkins's best friend Neville had had to do more than his share of that. Otherwise he was wizard fun. A bad deed popped into his mind and he went off to do it.

∞ ∞ ∞

'He gave me ever such a fright,' Eileen said, holding her side to show she meant it. 'I went in, because I thought I'd left my dusters in there, and there he was, without a stitch on, doing the Lambeth Walk on the billiard table with Mr Hugh's golf club. *I* don't know,' she finished, as she took the restorative cup of tea proffered by Mrs Cripps. 'All the curtains drawn as well, and the table lights on – it gave me ever such a turn. I couldn't find Ellen, so I had to get Miss Rachel. He didn't ought to take his clothes off – a big boy like that.'

'Whatever next, I wonder?' Mrs Cripps had returned to sieving breadcrumbs. 'Of course he misses his father, poor little mite.' There was a hush in the kitchen, and Edie, who stopped washing up out of respect, dropped a pie dish on the floor where it broke – it came to pieces in her hand; she wept as Mrs Cripps scolded her.

∞ ∞ ∞

'It was really so killing, I had the greatest difficulty in not laughing,' Rachel said to the Duchy. 'He hadn't cut or damaged the cloth, thank goodness. But what makes him *think* of such things?'

'He wants attention,' the Duchy said calmly. 'He misses his father. Zoë has never been much use to him, and Clary is too old in some ways and too young in others to comfort him about that.'

They looked at each other with many of much the same thoughts. 'A little treat on his own?' Rachel ventured.

'Certainly, but not today. He mustn't think that dancing on billiard tables reaps a reward. In fact, I think Hugh had better give him a good talking-to this evening when he gets home.'

∞ ∞ ∞

Zoë could hear Juliet crying as she walked up the drive, and by the time the house came in sight, she was running. This quickly made her out of breath. She had known at Mill Farm she was late, because her breasts had begun to feel too heavy and full, but it had been impossible to leave the poor chap she had been reading to until the nurse came to relieve her. Supposing Ellen was not with Juliet; suppose she had fallen out of her basket and hurt herself; she caught her cardigan on the latch of the garden gate in her hurry, and turning impatiently to free it, she tore the pocket. In the hall, she almost collided with Eileen carrying a tray with the silver to lay the dinner. By the time she had got to the top of the stairs she had a stitch in her side but she still ran along the passage to her room. Ellen was walking up and down with Juliet who was scarlet and pumping out little regular screams of rage. 'She's only hungry,' Ellen said. 'She's a regular little madam when she wants her food.'

Zoë sat in the high-backed nursing chair, unbuttoned her shirt and unhooked her bra, removing the sodden pads. Ellen handed her the baby who was stiff and sweating with rage, settled her in the crook of her arm. The baby made a few apparently random, almost blind movements of her head and found the breast, whereupon her body instantly softened, and on her face an expression of (stern) rapture instantly occurred. 'Don't let her have it too fast,' Ellen advised, but she said it with a proper adoration and Zoë could tear her eyes for a moment from her baby to smile.

'I won't.' Ellen handed her a Harrington square for her other breast which leaked in sympathy and limped from the room – she had rheumatism that had made her painfully lame.

Zoë stroked the damp wisps of hair with her fingers and the baby's eyes, fixed upon hers now with that look of considering trust that she never tired of, flickered at the interruption, then returned to their steady gaze. Her complexion was now a delicious rose colour; her tiny bare feet curling with pleasure made Zoë want to seize one and kiss it – an interruption that she knew would not be popular. 'You have a widow's peak,' she said, going through her inventory of perfections which were so many. The silky, touchingly defined eyebrows, the amazing wide-apart eyes, still the colour of wet slate but likely, she had been told, to change, the dear little nose and the charming mouth the colour of red cherry skin, and her head with the reddish gold hair, such a perfect shape – like a hazelnut, she thought . . . It was time to wind her. She lifted her up and placed Juliet over her shoulder, stroking the small of her back. The baby made a few small creaking sounds and then burped – she was the perfect baby.

It was the Duchy who had suggested that she should go and help at the nursing home at Mill Farm in the afternoons, and almost frightened by the completeness of her absorption in Juliet, she had agreed. The Duchy had been unfailingly kind to her and Zoë cared very much for her good opinion. It had been the Duchy who had told her about Rupert – not until two days after Juliet was born and her milk had come in. She had cried – easy, weak tears – but the news had a kind of unreality, a distance about it that made her unable to feel what clearly they all expected her to feel – anguish, hope at first, now ebbing away as the weeks went by. She could not *absorb* the idea that he might be dead and she would never see him again – would not or could not think of it. The Duchy, whether she realised this or not, had never pressed her for responses. She had told her the truth and then left her to refer to it if she had wanted to. But she hadn't. There had been one time with Clary, when there had been a second's awful, unimaginable reality, but she had fled from it, retreated into the existence, the possession of Juliet. 'I can't,' she had said to Clary. 'I can't think about it now. I can't.' And Clary had said, 'That's all right. Just don't think he's dead because he *isn't*.' And she never talked about it again. For nearly three months now her whole existence had been Juliet: feeding her, bathing her, changing her nappies, playing with her, taking her for walks in the old Cazalet family pram. At night, she slept dreamlessly, but in some magic way, she always woke a minute or two before Juliet for her early morning feed – her favourite time when there seemed to be nobody in the world but the two of them. The war receded for her: she did not listen to the news on the wireless, nor read newspapers. She spent hours making intricate, pretty dresses for Juliet to wear when she was a little older, fine lawn dresses, with pin tucks and drawn threadwork and edged sometimes with a narrow hand-made lace that the Duchy gave her. Sybil had become her friend in an amiable, undemanding way: she had a proper admiration for Juliet and was quite happy to talk about babies in a knowledgeable and reassuring manner, and she had crocheted three matinée jackets, had shown her how to cut Juliet's nails to stop her scratching her face. But two weeks ago the Duchy had suggested that she might like to help at Mill Farm which contained a number of young airmen who had suffered frightful wounds – mostly burns – and were rested up there between oper-ations. 'They need visiting,' she had said. 'I've talked to Matron, and they are a long way from their families who can't see them often, and I think you should get out more.' It had not been exactly a command, but Zoë had known that she was meant to comply. So it was arranged that she should go three afternoons a week. It was Villy who had warned her that 'burns can make people look very strange', but even then she had been unprepared for what she found at Mill Farm.

'It is very good of you to come and help us, Mrs Cazalet,' Matron had said the first time she went. 'We're such a small unit, but they all need a lot of nursing and I'm kept short of staff – only four nurses, and one of them on nights.'

'I don't know anything about nursing,' Zoë had said, alarmed.

'Oh, we shan't be expecting *that* of you. No, no, it's company they need – a new face; some of them like to be read to. I thought I'd start you off with Roddy – he wants a letter written for him, and then you can give him his tea.' She was leading Zoë along the passage to the small room that one of the children had had when Villy had been there, which was now filled by the high hospital bed, a bedside cabinet with a drawer and cupboard below, and a chair for visitors. 'Here's Mrs Cazalet come to see you, Pilot-Officer Bateson,' Matron said, her tone both cheerful and quiet, 'and there's plenty of time for her to write your letter before tea. Dear me, those pillows do slip, don't they? I'll give you something to rest your feet against,' and she went away.

Pilot-Officer Bateson, who was propped upright, turned his head slowly towards Zoë, and she saw that the right-hand side of his face was covered by intolerably taut, glistening mulberry-coloured skin that dragged up the side of his mouth into a lopsided smile. He had no eye on that side of his face, and the other side of it was not smiling. His arms were in splints to the elbow and heavily bandaged. They lay on two pillows each side of him.

'Hallo,' Zoë said, and then could think of no more to say.

'There's a chair there,' he said. She sat down. The silence was broken by Matron's return with a bolster. She lifted his sheet and blanket up from the bottom of the bed and Zoë saw that one leg was in a splint. 'Oh, yes,' she said, seeing Zoë looking at the splint, 'Pilot-Officer Bateson has really been in the wars.'

'One was enough, Matron.' He looked at Zoë and she thought he was trying to wink.

'Now then,' Matron was saying, as though he hadn't spoken, 'you can push your good leg against that, and it will help to keep you in your place.'

'I don't think there's much chance of me getting out of it, Matron.'

She finished arranging his bedclothes and straightened up. 'I wouldn't put it past you,' she said; she managed to sound matter-of-fact and affectionate. 'His writing-pad's in the drawer, Mrs Cazalet,' and she went away again. Her absence induced panic in Zoë: she did not know whether to look at him or not look at him, but he solved that for her by telling her, 'Bit of a sight, aren't I?'

She looked at him then and said, 'I can see you've had a bad time,' and felt him relax against his pillows. She got up and took the pad of paper, which lay beside a fountain pen, out of his drawer. 'Shall we do your letter?'

'OK. It's to my mum. I'm not much of a one for letters, I'm afraid.'

'Dear Mum.' There was a long pause, and then the sight of her with the pen poised drove him on. 'Well, how are you? It is a nice place here. I'll be staying a few weeks until they send me back to Godalming for the next op. They say I am doing very well. The food is good and they look after us very well.' There was a long silence, and then he said rapidly, 'I hope Dad is enjoying the Home Guard and your work in the canteen isn't too tiring for your back. Please thank Millie for her card.'

'Hang on,' Zoë said, 'you're going too fast for me.'

'Sorry.'

'It's all right. I've just got to Aunt Millie.'

'She's not my aunt, she's the dog,' he said. Then he said, 'Do you think that's enough? I can't think of any more.'

'It isn't quite a page.'

'Oh. Oh, yes. Please would you ring Ruth and tell her not to come. You could tell her we're not allowed visitors only I don't want her to come. Well, I hope this finds you—' He stopped. 'That won't do, will it?' She realised that he was trying to smile and felt her eyes prick with tears. 'Just put, your loving son Roddy,' he said.

By the time she had found an envelope and addressed it, read the letter to him and packed it up, a nurse arrived with a tray on which there was a plate of sandwiches and two cups of tea. 'Matron said you were giving him his tea. There's a straw for his drink,' she said. 'Are you quite comfortable?'

'I'm fine, Nurse. How are you?'

'Mustn't complain,' she answered. She had put the tray on his bedside cabinet and attended to his pillows, the ones behind his head, and one which supported his left arm. 'No more dressings?' he said, and Zoë caught a note of barely concealed apprehension.

'Not tonight,' she said. 'We're letting you off tonight. I'll be back for the tray. Call if you want anything.'

She would have to feed him, Zoë thought, and began to feel anxious about how it should be done. She put the straw in his tea cup.

'It'll be too hot,' he said. 'I can't drink it hot.'

The sandwiches were quite thin with the crusts cut off. She drew up her chair nearer the bed, picked one up and held it to his mouth. He tried to take a bite, but she realised that he could hardly open his mouth and that it hurt him, so she broke off a small piece and pushed it in. 'Bit of a crock, aren't I?' he said.

'An awful crock.'

'When you smile you remind me of someone. A film actress.' He seemed just to have held the food in his mouth, but now he swallowed – she saw the movement in his smooth bony throat. 'Live near here, do you?'

'Yes. Just up the road.'

'I see you're married.'

'Yes.' There was a pause, then she said, 'He was in the Navy.'

A heavy splinted arm came clumsily down against hers. 'Rough luck,' he said, and she could see the left side of his face blushing. ''Fraid I can't lift my arm,' he said. She put down the sandwich and lifted it carefully back onto its pillow. While she fed him the rest of the sandwich, she told him about Juliet, and he was courteous, but not really interested. She asked him if he had brothers and sisters, and he said, no, he was the only one. He'd had a younger brother, but he'd died of diphtheria when he was eight. He asked her to eat some of the sandwiches because he wasn't up to more than one and they kept on at him about eating. She gave him his tea, holding the cup while he sucked from the straw. 'I like a nice cup of tea,' he said.

When he'd finished, she said, 'I suppose you can't read with your arms like that.'

'I couldn't, anyway. My eye's not much cop for reading.'

'I could bring you a book and read it, if you like?'

'I would,' he said. 'Something light.'

'It's very kind of you,' he said stiffly when it was time

for her to go. He said it almost grudgingly and as though he did not like her. But when she was at the door and smiling in farewell, he said, 'Vivien Leigh! That's who you remind me of! You know. *Waterloo Bridge*. I saw it three times. Could you ask the nurse to come, please?'

Gradually, after that first time, she learned more about him, but chiefly from Matron. He'd got his plane back on one engine, but there'd been a fire in the cockpit and he'd broken his leg getting out. 'He got a DFC for it,' she said: he'd shot down three planes that day. He had terrible nightmares. He was twenty and he'd only been flying a month apart from his training. When she asked whether they would be able to patch up his face any more, Matron had said that they probably would, but his arms and especially his hands were so terribly burned that they weren't sure what was going to happen about them. Then she had looked at Zoë and said, 'He's not the worst. He's not even the worst here. And we don't *get* the *very* worst cases. They keep them at Godalming.' She had given Zoë a quick little pat on the shoulder, and said, 'You're doing a good job with him. Just remember he's still in shock. Apart from his crash, the shock element from burns is one of the worst things he has to contend with. How's the baby?' She always asked after Juliet, and one afternoon, when it was Ellen's day off, Zoë took her down to Mill Farm to show to Matron and the nurses, and a lot of very satisfactory baby worship went on, with everybody wanting to hold her and saying how lovely she was. But when they suggested she take Juliet up to show her to Pilot-Officer Bateson she said she didn't think it would be a good idea and they did not press her, although what she actually did turned out to be worse. She left Juliet with Matron, who said she was writing

person to kiss me – since—' and tears began to slide out of his eye, slowly at first and then more and more. She found her handkerchief and mopped him up, held it for him to try to blow his nose. That was when he told her about Ruth – his girl; they hadn't known each other very long – met in a dance hall; she was a lovely dancer and had hair like Ginger Rogers. They met twice a week, once for the cinema, and once to go dancing. 'Used to,' he said wearily. She had written him a letter saying she wanted to come and see him when he was at Godalming, but he hadn't answered it. 'I don't want her to see me,' he said. And Zoë, who had learned some things during these weeks, had not argued with him, just listened to the lot.

Then she went back to her chair, picking up the monkey, and said very casually that Matron had said they thought they would do more to his face. 'And anyway,' she finished, 'people don't love people just for their faces – or at least it's awful if they do.'

'What makes you say that?'

'I've been that sort of person. It makes you feel rotten in the end. You know. Like being loved just because you've got a lot of money.'

He thought about it. 'All the same,' he said, 'that's how it starts, isn't it? You like the look of someone.'

'And then you like other things about them. If there are things to like.'

'A lot of men are after Ruth, though,' he said. 'She loves a good time – dancing and that. She's only eighteen – much younger than me.' After that, Zoë spent at least as much time talking to him as reading aloud, which she recognised had been more a way of her dealing with their mutual shyness and embarrassment than anything else . . .

Juliet was finished. She had fallen asleep on the second breast; it seemed a shame to wake her, but she had to be winded and then held over her pot, but as Ellen was not there she decided to spare Juliet the pot.

Outside, she could hear car doors slamming, and went to see who had arrived. Two cars, one with Villy and one with her sister. Since going down to Mill Farm she had been getting on better with Villy, but Sybil was really her favourite, and she thought then that when she came home, she would help look after her. There was a knock on the door, and Clary came in to borrow a skirt.

'The thing is I seem to have got ink on that dress you made me. My beastly fountain pen which has leaked.'

'I'll just put Juliet down.'

'Why don't you call her Jules? You know – like Juliet's nurse. "Thou wilt fall backwards when thou hast more wit," although why falling back should be witty I can't think. I think Jules is a lovely name. *Jules*,' she said lovingly, bending over the cot. The baby opened her eyes and gave her a fleeting smile. 'You see? *She* likes it. Where did you get that sweet little monkey?'

'One of the patients at Mill Farm got a nurse to buy it and gave it to me for her.'

'Gosh! He must love you. Look at your monkey, Jules!'

'She's nearly asleep, Clary – better leave her. Let's see what I can find you.'

Clary had grown a great deal in the last year and had pitifully few clothes. I ought to do what Sybil did for Polly, she thought, as she rummaged through her wardrobe. Meanwhile, she had several things she could no longer get into – her waist was a good two inches larger. She pulled out a dark grey hopsack skirt cut in six gores that had used to fit round her hips like a glove.

'Try that on.'

Clary got out of her shorts – they were torn, Zoë noticed, were pinned together at the waist with a safety pin – and stood in her faded yellow Aertex shirt and dark blue knickers. 'Better take my sandals off,' she said. 'One of them's got a bit of tar on it that won't come off except onto things.'

The skirt fitted her perfectly, although it was rather long. 'I'll take up the hem for you,' she said, but Clary cried, 'Oh no! I like it long.'

'You need a nice shirt to go with it.'

'This'll do, won't it?'

'I don't want it just to do, Clary, I want you to look beautiful.'

And Clary smiled, but she answered, 'I'm afraid it's rather an uphill wish.'

However, by the time Zoë had found a scarlet shirt, and brushed Clary's hair and held it back from her forehead with two combs – she was still growing out her fringe – she really looked striking, 'like a photograph of a grown-up,' she said, unexpectedly and unusually delighted with her appearance.

'My shoes won't fit you. What have you got?'

'Only sandshoes, and lace-ups and these sandals. And wellingtons, of course. Couldn't I just be in bare feet – like a romantic oil painting?'

'You know the Duchy wouldn't let you. It'll have to be your sandals. But I promise you we'll go shopping soon and get you some nice shoes. Look – you'd better have these skirts as well. They're exactly the same pattern and I can't get into any of them.'

'But you will when you've stopped feeding Jules, won't you? You'll get thin again all over, won't you? I really think you should, Zoë. Thinness suited you. You could do what Aunt Villy calls banting whatever that may mean.'

'I don't know if I want to bother. Why does it matter to you, anyway?'

'It doesn't exactly matter to *me*,' Clary began, and then stopped: they had reached that brink beyond which Rupert lay dead – or alive – and both retreated from it.

'Polly plucked my eyebrows,' Clary said quickly. 'It hurt awfully, I must say.'

When Clary had gone, having gathered up her old and new clothes, thanking her more effusively than suited her natural manner, Zoë looked critically at herself in the mirror for the first time since Juliet's birth. She had clearly, as her mother would have said, 'let herself go'. Not only her waist and hips had spread, but her stomach – she could feel it with her hands – was still like chamois leather. She stepped nearer the mirror to examine her face. She still had her creamy skin, but the lower half had filled out so that she could see – almost – the beginnings of a double chin. She was twenty-five, an age that, until she reached it, had seemed over the top; she must start doing exercises and stop eating snacks between meals. Vivien Leigh, Roddy had said, but Zoë wore clothes that concealed her shape, and, anyway, she was sure he had meant her face. When he had said that he went dancing with his girl once a week, and how she loved a good time and had a lot of men after her, she had fleetingly remembered how much she had used to love dancing and men wanting her, how it had all seemed like the most delicious game where she chose what happened, she dispensed the favours, she accepted the sexual homage . . . Until Philip, when it had suddenly stopped being a game at all. And then the baby that was not Rupert's and had not lived. But even its death had not diminished her guilt, since that fed upon the continuous deception – chiefly with Rupert but also with the whole family – that she was unhappy because their child had died and she was the only one who knew that this was a black lie. And then, last autumn, after the war had begun, when they were in London packing up her mother's flat in Earl's Court (she had been invited to lodge with her friend in the Isle of Wight for the duration of the war), she had not wanted Rupert to help her, but he had insisted ('It's too much for you on your own'). He had ordered tea chests into which they put the smaller objects that it was thought her mother would want to keep – the furniture was to go into store, and the things to be thrown out or sold were piled on the sitting-room floor. The flat, as places do that have been deserted for some time, had the air of being only one resentful step from actual squalor: the net curtains that hung at all the windows were so dirty that it looked as though there was a fog outside. Rupert tied some of them back to admit more light, but this only disclosed the shabbiness of the fumed oak furniture and pink damask upholstered sofa, the indeterminate, shadowy stains on the pink fitted carpets, the broken elements in the gas fires, the gnarled, discoloured parchment shades to the sconces, the dust that lay evenly on every surface – upon every photograph frame and ornament. She had packed her mother's clothes into cases that could be dispatched to her while Rupert dealt with the kitchen. He had to keep asking her whether things were to be kept or not – battered old aluminium saucepans, an attenuated set of Susie Cooper china, fish knives with yellowing bone handles, a teapot in the shape of a thatched cottage and an embroidered linen bag that was full of crocheted egg cosies and paper cutlet frills. 'Extraordinary mixture!' he had remarked while he was still trying to be cheerful. When he said things like that, she had snubbed him, had defended her mother: there was nowhere for her to keep things – that sort of defence – until he had said, 'Darling, I'm not getting at your poor mum: I mean – going through *anybody's* things must be a bit like this.'

She hadn't replied. She had not been back to the flat – not once – since the night she had spent in it with Philip, and this had been comparatively easy, since her mother had hardly been there either. It seemed now in small and piercing ways to be exactly as she had left it that morning. Even the same small and cracked piece of Morny lavender soap lay in its dusty declivity in the bathroom and the kitchen contained the remains of a packet of coffee that she had used. She had not thought she would return, and coming there with Rupert added another dimension to her discomfort.

'Poor little Zoë: you had to sleep on this,' he had said when they arrived and he sat on the sofa to read through the list her mother had sent of the things she wished packed off to her.

For a mad second she imagined herself saying calmly, 'I was raped on it actually.' Unable to stay in the room with him, she said that she would pack the clothes, and that he had better do the kitchen. 'We don't want to spend all day here.' She almost snatched the list from him as she added that there was no point in his reading it. In the bedroom, she collapsed on the slippery pink counterpane decorated with machined chain stitch, suffused with guilt and irritation at herself for being horrid to him and for agreeing to let him come to the flat at all. Alone, she felt, she might have gone back over the whole affair one last time, have exorcised or written off the whole Philip episode – might have been able to rationalise her further deception of Rupert (as long as she didn't *tell* him, she had to continue lying) as simply evidence of loving him, of not wanting to hurt him. If only she hadn't been pregnant, *had* the baby, she thought, she might have been able to confess the rest of it. He would be hurt and angry, but when she told him how desperately sorry she was, she felt he would forgive her. But not the child. After years of refusing to have his child, how could he bear her to have been what must look like wilfully careless that one night? As though she'd *wanted* this other man's baby?

'The jar of flour has got extraordinary little flies in it! Are you all right, darling?'

'Just trying to think about where to begin. Perfectly all right. Chuck out all the food things.'

It did not take long to pack her mother's clothes. Moths fluttered out of her grey squirrel coat, which she had had ever since Zoë could remember, but apart from the moths it was terribly worn – it had better go.

It would be nice to give her a new one, she thought, but she had no money excepting what Rupert gave her and Neville's school fees had more or less eaten up the small difference in salary that working for the firm had made (the Brig did not believe in paying his sons a penny more than they were worth, and Rupert would be paid even less in the Navy).

When she had finished in the bedroom, she found Rupert in the sitting room looking at an old photograph album that had been lying on the desk.

'Couldn't we keep this?' he said. 'It's almost entirely pictures of you from birth upwards. I could write to your mother and ask if I might have it?'

'You've got pictures of me: Mummy gave you some.'

'Not these. I should hate these to get lost.'

'I should have thought from today that you could see that Mummy didn't throw things away much.'

The rest of the time in the flat had been like that: she had been filthy to him – everything that he had done or said provoked her; and everything that she found there seemed to compound her guilt, which by then had extended to her mother. Her mother's diary, an expensive and belyingly gay scarlet leather one that was almost blank – 'get hair done' would be the only entry for a week; or, 'take winter coat to cleaners'. Regularly, every month, there was 'bridge with Blenkinsops (here)' or, on alternate months, '(with them)'. Hardly anything else. The loneliness shrieked at her. And the possessions! The sitting room was full of objects that succeeded in being unnecessary and undesirable – the kind of things that would be given by someone who neither knew well nor cared for the recipient: things made of pottery, raffia, sealing wax, dolls dressed in ethnic costumes, fans, wax flowers and endless photograph frames, made of silver, leather, brass, shells, passe-partout, and practically every one except for two of her father contained pictures of herself. In the bottom drawer of the rickety little bureau, she came across a box that was full of her baby and childhood clothes. It was ridiculous that her mother had kept them all these years. She said something of the kind to Rupert and then immediately wished she had not, because of course she knew very well why they had been kept. But Rupert only said, 'It's because she loves you, darling.' He was kneeling on the floor wrapping the frames in newspaper and putting them into a tea chest. He had stopped commenting on the photographs, and sounded weary.

When they had finished, he said that they were going to a pub – he needed a drink.

The pub had only just opened and was almost empty. 'Gin and It?'

She nodded.

It was one of those cavernous pubs with a lot of mahogany panelling and frosted glass, a coal fire and all the chairs covered with mock red leather. She chose a table in a corner, and waited, feeling dirty and dispirited, for her drink.

'He let me have a packet of fags.' He put the glasses on the table. 'I got us doubles.'

'I was wondering', he said when he had lit a Goldflake from the packet of ten, 'whether you'd like to have your mother to stay for a bit at Home Place. I'm sure the Duchy would make room for her...' He looked at her face and then added, 'Or you could go to the Isle of Wight for a week or two, if you like.'

'She wouldn't want to come to Sussex, and I can't stay with her – her friend wouldn't want me.'

'You don't want to see her?'

'It isn't that.'

'But you feel so guilty about her, Zoë. Don't you want to do something about it?'

'I don't! I don't feel guilty. I do feel sorry for her.'

'That's not much use to her, though, is it?'

'What do you mean?'

'I didn't realise, until today, how much her life is

bound up in you. Suppose I should have – you are her only child. And you've been grumpy and defensive all day, so I know damn well you feel guilty.'

There was an angry silence. Then he reached out and took one of her resisting hands. 'Darling. It's not wicked to feel guilt, it's just sad and useless. I found that out when Isobel died. The only thing that stops it is admitting to yourself what you can't do, and doing what you can.'

She stared at him frightened: he had almost never spoken of Isobel since before their marriage.

'What could you do about *her*? After she was dead?'

'Look after our children, for her as well as for myself. You know about that. You've started to do it with Clary.'

'*She* started it,' she said, her voice uneven.

He gave her hand a small squeeze, and put it back on the table.

'You *connived*,' he said. 'I'm going to get us another drink.'

Watching him walk away from her to the bar, she was suddenly flooded with every ingredient of love, some familiar, some quite new to her: she felt tender, fortunate, and unworthy, and filled with a longing to do anything to make him happy.

They went back to Hugh's house where they were staying the night, had dinner with Hugh at Ciccio's in Church Street. (Rupert had said earlier that he hoped she wouldn't mind as Hugh had to spend so many evenings by himself, and she *had* minded when he said it – had taken it as a slight – but by the time it happened she didn't mind at all and in fact it was a lovely evening.)

'If you two want to go to dance somewhere, don't mind me. I'm ready for bed,' Hugh had said when they had finished their coffee and Strega. Rupert had looked

306

at her, and she realised how often he had let her choose, and started to blush as she said she didn't mind which they did. So they all went home, and that was when Juliet began. She had conceived her for Rupert – had had no idea of the intense joy their child would bring her. But he had been away when she was born . . . might never know anything about her.

Sitting in the chair by Juliet's cot and remembering all this, she began to acknowledge his absence, began to mourn it for the first time – to allow the terrible fever of hope that it was only absence to infect her as she wept and begged silently for his life.

∞ ∞ ∞

'Bet you didn't know that, Miss Milliment.'

'Indeed no. I had always thought plane trees occurred in this country far later than Chaucer.'

She had been reading over the Brig's latest chapter of his book about trees in Britain, a task she had taken over from Rachel who had had to go to London for the weekend.

'Most people seem to think that they were brought here about the time of the East India Company. Utterly wrong, as you can see.'

'John Evelyn has rather a good account of Xerxes and a plane tree.'

'Does he now? Amazing feller. Find it and read it to me, would you?'

Miss Milliment obediently hoisted herself to her feet and pattered over to the large glass-fronted bookcase. Finding a book in it was a great trial to her, as the bookcase stood in a dark corner of the study, and the books were not arranged in apparent order. Rachel, of course, would have known where it was. She hunted, but she could only read the spines of the books by taking each one out. 'I'm afraid I may be some time finding it,' she said apologetically, but the Brig did not seem to notice: he was in full spate about the tremendous size of plane trees he had known at Mottisfont, some rectory in Sussex, and the avenue at Cowdray Park, and at the same time feeling for his whisky decanter with purple gnarled old hands . . . 'Find me a glass, would you, Miss Milliment?'

She stopped looking for the book and searched for one of his immensely heavy cut-glass tumblers. The room was so full of furniture, papers and books that her passage through it was difficult.

'There's that piece of Pliny's somewhere, about eighteen fellers eating inside a hollow tree. Just read that to me, would you? It might be suitable.'

Pliny she *could* find, because he was lying on the desk, but finding the piece that he wanted was another matter. Fortunately for her, a car arrived which the Brig identified as belonging to Hugh; she was asked to find another glass, the monologue on the girth of plane trees ceased, and he became fidgety in his desire to hail Hugh at exactly the right moment so as to entrap him. 'Is that you, Hugh? *Hugh?* Is that you? Ah! The very feller I wanted to see. Have a drink, old boy. Thanks, Miss Milliment. She's been reading to me because Rachel went to London to sort the books at Chester Terrace. Should do the same with my cellar. Do you remember when you came on leave and all I'd got was three bottles of what I thought was undrinkable claret? Bought it for one and nine a bottle in an auction – twelve cases; I'd taken to giving it as wedding presents it was so bloody awful – and we got those three bottles up and they were absolutely superb! Remember that?'

Hugh said that that had been Edward's leave. Miss Milliment put the second glass by the decanter and retired. As she left, she heard the Brig saying that in that case, Hugh would not know the story: he thought it had been a Mouton-Rothschild 1904, but it might have been '05 – anyway, whenever he tried it, it had never seemed to come round . . .

Miss Milliment trotted across to the cottage over the garage that was still called Tonbridge's cottage, although he and his family had only occupied it for a few weeks two years ago. Her room, one of the two upstairs, was small, but it looked onto the pine wood at the back of the house which smelled lovely after rain. For a while she had been at Pear Tree Cottage, but now that everybody had moved back into Home Place she was here again, and although it was a very bare little room, she liked it. Dear Viola – so thoughtful – had come to inspect it, had felt the blankets on the bed – only two and an eiderdown – and had said that she needed at least two more, which was true as the ones on the bed managed to be both thin and felty. She had also offered the wonderful luxury of a bedside lamp, and got her a small table at which she could write letters. Most thoughtful, but unfortunately there was nobody really for her to write to. She *had* had to write to her landlady in London to say that she was giving up her room there, and *then* she had had to make the journey to London to collect the remainder of her things. It had been rather unpleasant as well as extremely tiring. She had burned her boats where that lodging was concerned. And then she had suddenly felt, as she returned in the expensive taxi from Stoke Newington to Charing Cross station, that now she was homeless. The thought caused her moments of such overwhelming panic that she had had to speak quite severely to herself: 'Now, Eleanor, you must cross that bridge *when* you come to it,' But this had been succeeded by her wondering whether at some point one became too old to cross *any* bridge. She had tried, in the train, to read – she had come across a second-hand copy of minor eighteenth-century poets for a penny at the church bazaar last Christmas. But the panic, though it had subsided to anxiety, had not gone, and kept washing over her in irregular surging waves. She told herself that it was because the landlady had been rather unpleasant about everything: 'It's all right for *some*,' she kept saying. No doubt she was upset at losing a long-term lodger, but it seemed sad that she had stayed so long there and ended by being so resented. Perhaps it had always been so, and she had stupidly not noticed. She had tried not to be a nuisance but, of course, that did not guarantee that she had succeeded. She had had no extras: no coffee for breakfast like Mrs Fast; no laundry done like Mr Marcus. All that was behind her, she told herself with repeated firmness. But what lay ahead? There would come a day when dear Polly and Clary and Lydia would not need her any more, and Roland and Wills would still be too young. *She*, on the other hand, might find that teaching anyone was beyond her. Her eyesight had become much worse: she knew that she needed new spectacles, but was so afraid that this would not make the difference that it used to do, that she had not made the effort to go to Hastings or Tunbridge Wells to procure any. Her knees had become painful: in the early mornings, if she stayed in one position for too long, if she was on her feet for more than a few minutes; in fact, nearly all the time. 'Really, Eleanor, I am getting rather tired of your troubles. What was that song? "Pack up your troubles in your old kit bag and smile, smile, smile."' She tried to smile, and tears came to her eyes. She wiped them carefully with a handkerchief that rather needed to be washed, and went back to her poetry.

But when she arrived at Battle, and found dear Viola there to meet her, instead of having to take a cab or an uneasy drive with Tonbridge, she was overcome again. Miss Milliment sat in the front of Viola's car while she and the porter stowed her suitcases in the boot, trying to quench this awful desire to break down.

'There. All safely stowed.' Viola got into the driving seat. 'We'll soon be home. Miss Milliment!' For she had not been able to stop herself after all. It had all poured out. Her fear of becoming useless, of not knowing how to get through the remainder of her life. Of being a nuisance – she really didn't want to be a nuisance, she kept saying as the tears ran down into the folds of her chins. And Viola's kindness (she was so *very* kind!) seemed stupidly to make her cry more. Explanations, apologies, even excuses of which, in her ordinary frame of mind, she would deeply have disapproved, streamed out . . . She needed to feel *useful*; she had been useful to dear Papa, and by the time he died she had found teaching was the only thing she could do that fulfilled that need. She was afraid that she might be getting too old to be much more use. She did not want charity – to feel that people had to put up with her when she could do nothing. She was afraid that she was a little tired: the cab driver had refused to go upstairs in her lodging house to fetch the suitcases, and her landlady would not help. One of them had slipped from her hand on the staircase and fallen right to the bottom where it had burst open, and it had been very difficult to repack – so this was only the consequence of fatigue and Viola should not take it seriously. She had saved some money, of course, but she did not really know where she could go that would make it last. This last made her blush from her hot forehead downwards and she was instantly ashamed to have mentioned that part of the subject at all. And Viola listened, with an arm round her heaving shoulders, and gave her a handkerchief and actually said, 'Dear Miss Milliment, you will never be abandoned. I promise you. We owe you so much.' Blessed words! Comfort, affection, the restoration of some kind of dignity! Then Viola had asked her whether she would like to have a cup of tea at the Gateway Tea Rooms, an offer which, as she had not felt like the pastry she had bought on Charing Cross Station, that when opened, looked as though it was filled with a dead mouse, she most gratefully accepted. They had had tea and scones and Viola had said that of course she didn't know exactly what the future held – clearly they would not stay in Sussex when the war was over – but that whatever they did, Miss Milliment must find a home with them. This last had endangered her equilibrium all over again; Viola had quickly stopped talking about it. Instead, she reminded her most delightfully of old times – when Sir Hubert had been alive and she had gone to Albert Place to teach dear Viola and Jessica, and how they always knew that it was nearly lunchtime because the housemaid came into the schoolroom to change the lace curtains, which, fresh that morning, would be grey with soot by noon – particularly in winter when there were the pea soup fogs.

'Those fogs! Do you remember, Miss Milliment? We

312

hardly ever have a fog like those were, do we?' And so on. It was pleasant and soothing. Then she had got hiccups which was most embarrassing in a public place, but Viola had laughed and made her repeat the old saw: 'Hiccup – ticcup – three drops in a teacup – stops hiccups,' which she had taught both Viola and her sister all those years ago.

'My aunt May taught me that,' she said. 'Oh dear! I'm afraid I shall have to do it all over again.'

'It is very agreeable to talk about old times,' she said as they went back to the car. 'Oh dear! I am so sorry!' One of the handles on her extremely battered and ancient handbag had broken, and as it was too full to shut properly, pencils, a leather purse that was held shut by a paper clip, spectacle case, a number of hairpins and an unspeakable comb fell onto the pavement. As Villy bent to retrieve these things, she resolved to buy her a new bag, but knew better than to say so.

In the car they talked about her present pupils, beginning with Lydia, whose concentration, Miss Milliment admitted, left something to be desired, but who had showed distinct improvement during the summer term. 'I do try not to *loom* over them during the holidays,' she added. 'It must be most tiresome to have a governess who never goes away.'

'I was wondering,' she added a few moments later, 'whether you would object to my teaching Lydia on her own in the afternoons. She could join the older girls in the mornings for our reading aloud, but I fear it is discouraging to do everything with the great girls, who naturally are far ahead of her in other subjects.'

Villy said that she thought this was a good idea.

When they reached Home Place, she carted Miss

313

Milliment's frighteningly heavy suitcases up the narrow stairs to her room and kissed the soft wrinkled cheek which was another extraordinarily pleasant (and unusual) experience for Miss Milliment.

Tonight, being a Friday, she would be dining with the family, which she did twice a week. The other evenings she ate early with Lydia and Neville. She had suggested this arrangement, as it released Ellen from having to preside over the children's supper just when she was needed to bath Wills and Roly. As she struggled into her mustard and brown outfit, still described by her to herself as her best, she reflected that she had not bought any new clothes for about two years – had felt that she ought to save as much as possible against the rainy days. But since that most comforting talk with dear Viola, she had no excuse, and if they brought in clothes rationing, she would be rather in the soup, she thought, as she hunted through the pile of odd stockings to pick out the two shades of buff that most nearly matched. She would have to go to Hastings on the bus, and *then* find a shop that sold things for larger people, but she could hardly ask anyone to accompany her, as one could not buy things like underwear excepting by oneself. She had never been any good with her needle, and almost everything had by now got past mending, anyway: there were huge ladders in her lock-knit bloomers, holes of varying sizes in her two cardigans, and she often had to fasten things round her with safety pins, which occasionally burst open causing the most disagreeable sensations of pricking – not to mention the anticipation of worse embarrassment. 'You must pull yourself together, Eleanor, and refurbish your wardrobe.'

It took her a long time to dress, partly because she kept stopping to look out of the window to see what the fading light was doing to the tops of the trees in the wood. The pines became smoky, and the oaks more livid in their watery bronze – she could not describe their hues; sere was a very useful word for poets, she thought, romantic and non-committal, but if one was painting the trees it would not do at all. And then below the wood was a steep grassy bank, in spring richly decorated with primroses and later, more delicate still, with wild strawberries and the dark purple vetch, stitchwort, scarlet pimpernel, all flowers she had grown up with in her youth. Now only the ferns and grass remained, but it had a different beauty – a natural dense border above which the trees rose with majestic grace. The courtyard in the foreground was full of warm, domestic colour: cobblestones, the slaty blocks so often laid outside stables (easy to wash down and how beautiful when they were wet – now, alas, only from rain!) and a mellow brick path that ran unaccountably across it and ended by the kitchen garden wall where once there had been a door, blocked off. The narrow rosy bricks were tufted with moss and weeds, but this simply added to their charm. She had spent what must have amounted to hours surveying this scene, originally in the hope that thereafter she would only have to shut her eyes to recall it, now simply from pleasurable habit. She had once – only once – unearthed her aunt May's ancient box of water-colours and attempted to paint what she saw, but she was hampered by the state of the paints, all dry and cracked and unwilling to yield their colours, and the single paint-brush in the small black box had lost most of its hairs and was intent upon losing what remained. It had been absurd even to try, but in spite of her failure the attempt had absorbed and excited her to such an extent that Polly had been sent over to fetch her for supper.

Rachel sat on the shrouded unmade bed in her room at Chester Terrace looking at a photograph of herself with her brothers, taken soon after the first war when they were all together again. Edward was still in uniform, very debonair, smiling, with an arm round her shoulder. Hugh stood a little apart: his arm was in a sling, his Norfolk jacket hung loosely on him and he looked as though the sun hurt his eyes. Rupert, in an open-necked shirt and looking incredibly young, had just finished laughing at something. The photograph had been taken on the croquet lawn at the house they had had in Totteridge, before they all moved to London. The Brig had taken it: he had been an eager, not to say interminable photographer in those days and had, of course, taken five or six pictures on that occasion. This was the best, and it had sat, framed on her dressing table, for years. Now, like everything else in the room, it had been put away in the wardrobe wrapped in tissue paper. She wanted it for Clary. She shut up the wardrobe, which still contained a row of evening dresses and her ermine wrap given her by the Brig when she was twenty-one. There seemed to be no point in moving *them* to Sussex. The cupboard smelled of camphor, her dressing table was bare and dusty.

She started to descend the flights of stairs – her bedroom was on the sixth floor – stopping at the drawing room to make sure that the furniture was still entirely covered with dust sheets, the smaller carpets rolled up, the very large one covered by an immense drugget, the shutters properly fastened. The chandelier hung safely in its huge linen bag like a gigantic pear waiting to ripen. The room, indeed the whole house, had the heavy, dull air characteristic of fully furnished houses that are uninhabited. She wondered if they would ever live there again. On the ground floor in the hall were the packing cases now full of books that she had been sent to London by the Brig to collect. Tonbridge would superintend their loading onto one of the firm's lorries next week. She was tired, and longed for a cup of tea, but the water and gas were turned off and in any case there was no milk.

She decided to walk across the park to Baker Street and catch a bus that would take her nearly to Maida Vale, although there would be another walk after that to reach Sid's house. A taxi would be extravagant, although she knew that Sid would scold her for not taking one . . .

∞ ∞ ∞

'You *walked?*'

'I took a bus part of the way.'

'My dear one, you're incorrigible! I've put on the immersion heater. Would a hot bath be the ticket?'

'A hot cup of tea is what I crave more than anything in the world.'

'A cup of tea you shall have.'

She followed Sid down the dark little flight of stairs that led to the semi-basement where there was a kitchen, a larder, a pantry, a wine cellar and a WC. Everything was very clean, but there were great cracks in the kitchen walls, the green paint on them had split and was peeling, and the linoleum was worn through to the flagstones in places. Sid switched on the light, essential in this room whose heavily barred windows were further barricaded by a black brick wall. It was a Victorian kitchen uneasily adapted to modern life.

Rachel said, 'I must go to your lav.'

'The one down here *is* working: I had it mended last week. Do you want any toast or anything like that?'

'Just tea.'

And then a bath, Sid thought, as she filled the kettle. She thought of Rachel in a bath with the kind of tender anguish that had become so familiar and yet still astonished her. And if she'd taken a cab we would have had another hour together, she also thought, as she warmed the pot. But considering that they had a whole weekend – until Sunday evening when she would be on duty again – and Rachel had consented to take the plunge of staying in London with her instead of going back to Sussex . . .

'Did you find out what was on at the Academy?'

'*La Femme du Boulanger.*'

'Oh! Let's go!'

'You're really not too tired?'

'Heavens, no! This is our treat. We could have supper out.'

'That would be wise. You know my cooking. Let's drink this upstairs: it's more cosy.'

'I'll carry the tray.'

'You will not! You may turn off the light for me.'

They went upstairs to the little sitting room, which was crowded by the old Bechstein grand, and sat in the two armchairs with pieces of old flowered linen on the arms to hide the threadbare upholstery. Sid poured out the tea and produced Rachel's favourite brand of Egyptian cigarettes.

'You are clever! Where did you get them from?'

'Found them in a shop in Soho.' She did not mention the exhaustive search this had entailed.

'Wonderful. I must say I miss them. Passing Clouds are not at all the same.'

319

They smoked and looked at each other with small, excited smiles, and exchanged desultory pieces of news of a kind that did not interfere with their intense happiness at being together – and alone. Sid produced a half-bottle of gin and the dregs of a bottle of Dubonnet that had been in the house for years, and they drank. Rachel told Sid about the photograph which of course Sid immediately wanted to see. She gazed a long time at the ravishing picture of Rachel – her hair piled on top of her head, her white high-necked blouse and neatly belted long dark skirt and face that looked out with an expression both so innocent and so frank that she had to resort to a kind of levity to conceal how much it moved her.

'My word, you were a tearing beauty!' she said.

'Nonsense!'

'Of course, still are.' But this did not go down well either. Rachel's utter lack of vanity and unselfconsciousness about her appearance became disturbed by any reference to it. Like her mother, Sid thought, their beauty had to remain silently in the eye of the beholder. Now she had gone faintly pink and was screwing up her eyes with little frowns of disapproval and embarrassment.

'Darling, I don't love you for your appearance,' she said now, 'although I might be forgiven if I did.'

Rachel was wrapping up the picture again.

Sid said, 'I suppose I couldn't have a copy?'

'I'm sure the negative is lost. The Brig took so many, and the Duchy cleared out a lot of stuff like that when we moved to London. I got it for poor little Clary. She is so deeply unhappy about her father.'

'No news at all?'

'None. Honestly, Sid, I've given up hope. I think even the Duchy has, at last.'

'But Clary hasn't?'

'I don't think so. She doesn't talk about him so much, but she never talks about him as though – as though . . .' Her words trailed away and there was a silence. Then, her voice high and trembling, she said, 'It must be happening to so many people! So *much* grief and shock and agonised patience and dying hopes! Sometimes I think we are *mad*! What good will it all do?'

'What evil may it avert?'

'Oh, *Sid*! I find that hard to believe. That it could all possibly be much worse!'

'I know you do. It's easier for me to believe that.'

'Why is it?'

Sid said steadily, 'I don't have anything to lose. *You* will not have to go to war. So. I don't have anything to lose.'

But she realised that Rachel did not, or did not want to, understand her and dropped the subject.

They drove, in Sid's dirty old Morris, to Oxford Street and saw their film and then dined at McWhirter's, a basement restaurant of a block of flats in Abbey Road – tomato soup and poached cod – and Sid told Rachel about the ambulance station (she was now a driver). Rachel, an excellent listener, loved hearing about the people who worked there: '. . . an ex-chiropodist – well, I suppose everyone is ex really, excepting our taxi driver with flat feet. He's invaluable, but of course he hardly has to use his "knowledge", as he calls it, because we only operate in one district. Then there's a gym teacher who terrifies the nurses she drives because she so enjoys going

321

through red lights and driving on the wrong side of the road—'

'How do you know he has flat feet?'

'He tells everybody. He wanted to join up and they wouldn't have him. He never stops complaining about it. Then we have a pacifist who gets drunk, God knows what on, and tells us all the ghastly things he'd like to do to "warmongers" which, we feel, includes all of us. This is during the interminable evenings when we all drink tea – well, all of us excepting him.'

'It all sounds rather fun,' Rachel said; there was an element of wistfulness in her voice. She had never learned to drive or had a real job.

'Most of the time it is extremely boring. Nothing happens. Of course, we do have the odd case of appendicitis or strokes or heart attacks, but the regular lot see to most of that. We're sort of emergency extra, and so far, there hasn't been an emergency.'

'Thank God.'

'I know. Shall we go home? I can make a much better coffee than they'll give us here.'

As she pushed in her latchkey to open the front door, she thought this was how it ought always to be. She and Rachel going home together. When they had shut the door, she felt for the light switch, then changed her mind, and put her arms round Rachel, who returned her embrace. They kissed. Rachel said, 'It was a lovely evening.'

'*Wasn't* it! Exactly the right kind of film. I wonder why films as touching and funny and charming as that are always French?'

'I always enjoy everything I do with you.'

A little nugget to store away, Sid thought, as she turned on the light.

She made the coffee and they drank it sitting on the battered chairs in front of the ancient gas fire that Sid lit. Then she remembered that there was a little cherry brandy left, which had been given to Evie as a present, but it had not agreed with her, 'So we may finish it with impunity.'

They had said all that needed to be said about Evie earlier on: she was away, working for a pianist of international renown and seemed to enjoy her position. It was wonderful, Sid said, not to have to worry about her. Much later, and having finished the cherry brandy (there was more there than Sid had thought), they began their favourite conversation about what they would do after the war: a long holiday – but where? Sid was in favour of Italy, if it was practicable; Rachel inclined towards Scotland where she had never been. It was midnight before they retired.

When Sid had installed Rachel in Evie's room, which was actually far the nicest of the two bedrooms, and had left her to unpack and bath, she went down to make her a hot-water bottle. She was aware of a faint tension that had sprung up between them – almost occurring on the climb upstairs. She knew why *she* felt tense: she had stayed many times now at Home Place, and occasionally even in Rachel's room – in separate beds – if the house was full, and they had fallen into the habit of her lying in bed with Rachel for a short, sweet, and usually agonising time, when, with Rachel settled in the crook of her arm, she was unable not to imagine further intimate delight. But this was the first time that they had spent a night in a house alone together, where they need not think of other people. This should have made for greater ease, but did not: it simply highlighted the disparity of feeling between them. To Sid, it somehow implied a dishonesty in Rachel; if, in the other circumstances, Rachel had always worried about other people and what they might feel or think, what could she say now, when there were no people? But, of course, she also knew that that was not the point at all. Rachel had (unwittingly) made it painfully clear that any kind of sexual intimacy revolted her. It is I who am dishonest, she thought; how often, how many thousands of times had she told herself that she had conquered those feelings, that they were useless and possibly worse, since if divulged they would almost certainly drive Rachel away, and then she would have nothing? But tonight, the first opportunity that had ever arisen in their lives together, she knew that she had not overcome anything at all. When Rachel was absent, she could simply long for her presence; when she was present, she longed for her responsive body.

She struggled with this hopeless dilemma as she went upstairs again, but when she arrived at Rachel's room, could not resist saying: 'As you will not have your love to keep you warm, here is a hot-water bottle.'

'Sid!' She had undressed and stood in her petticoat, sponge bag in hand. '*Sid!* What's the matter?'

'Nothing at all. Let me get you a dressing gown – you'll be cold.'

'That would be angelic: there wasn't room in this case for mine.' She followed Sid to her far smaller bedroom and received the old plaid man's dressing gown, thrust tenderly round her shoulders. The bath was running and thin clouds of steam had reached the passage.

324

Rachel said, 'What's the matter? Aren't you going to come and talk to me in bed?'

'You have your bath. Of course I am.'

Rachel fell asleep quite soon after her bath, relaxed, her head upon Sid's shoulder.

'. . . wouldn't it, my darling?' Sid was saying, and then, looking down, she saw that there would be no reply. She lay, hopelessly awake until the luminous dial on Rachel's travelling clock said half past two, and then, knowing that if she had no sleep she would spoil the next day, she gently disentangled herself and went to her own bed where sleep continued to elude her.

∞ ∞ ∞

On the Saturday afternoon there was to be a tennis tournament in which all the children, down to Neville and Lydia, were allowed to take part. It had been organised by Edward and Hugh. Lots had been drawn for partners and each match was the best of three games. They had been playing since two o'clock, beginning with a children's match. 'The little beggars just get stoked up by food,' Edward had said, and Neville, playing with Simon, had been beaten by Clary and Polly. 'I loathe tennis, anyway,' he had said, scarlet with distress, 'and if I hadn't had to play with Simon who kept hitting all the balls out, I would probably have won.'

'You would not,' Simon said, whose disappointment was if anything more intense. 'You didn't hit the balls at all. You simply missed them. I can't think why you entered the tournament.'

'You must learn to lose politely,' Clary scolded Neville.

'Why should I? I'm not going to spend my life losing

things. Either I shall win everything I go in for, or I shan't do the thing.'

'*Someone* has to lose, Neville,' Lydia said maddeningly.

'There are lots of people to do that. I'm just not going to be one of them.'

'Well, you two can be ball boys.'

'Oh, thanks *very much*.'

'That will do, Simon,' Villy said sharply.

'In any case, all teams are to get two chances,' Edward said. 'It was pretty bad luck on Simon drawing Neville,' he added to Villy.

'Anyway, nobody is to spoil a lovely afternoon,' somebody else said, and the next match began.

It was an exceptionally beautiful afternoon: mellow, balmy and sunlit, the sky above a pale but piercing blue, the sun just hot enough for the spectators to watch in comfort, but not too hot for the players. Zoë brought Juliet in her pram, and Hugh had Wills struggling off and on his knee. The Duchy came and went with her trugful of dead heads; only the Brig was absent, working in his study with Miss Milliment. Jessica, who was a poor player, was teamed with Christopher: they lost their first match. By four o'clock everyone was very thirsty, and the Duchy had tea brought out to the terrace above the tennis court.

'We really should have lemonade,' she said. 'Such a pity there are no lemons.'

'Wills and Roly and Juliet won't know what a lemon is, will they?' Lydia remarked; she very much enjoyed not being in the youngest echelon. ' "The answer is a lemon" won't mean anything to them, will it?'

'It will mean more,' Neville said. 'Because it will mean nothing.' There were cucumber sandwiches and flapjacks for tea; Simon counted the flapjacks and worked out that he'd be lucky if he got two. At the appropriate moment, he started going round asking people very gently if they were going to want their flapjack. This paid off, because Zoë didn't want hers; on the other hand, his aunt had given a piece to Wills, who having tried it, was now busily burying it in a flower bed – a ghastly waste. Babies were so stupid sometimes that he was ashamed of ever having been one, although he was sure he'd never been as idiotic as that. Polly lay on the lawn beside her father. 'What *are* piles?' she was asking. 'They're things Ellen keeps on saying you have to be careful not to get, but she won't say what they are.'

'They're rude – that's why,' Neville said at once. When nobody denied this, he improvised, 'They're little pointed lumps you get on your bottom so that when you sit down they dig into you. They *may* have ants inside them. Yes. Kind of ant heaps in people.' He turned to Lydia. 'You know all about bottoms. Tell them.'

'I don't.' Lydia wriggled uncomfortably.

'You do. I told you.'

There was a short silence. Then Lydia, unable to resist being appealed to for information, said, 'B U G G E R. You mean that?'

'I don't think we want to hear anything about that, Lydia,' Villy said as severely as she could manage. She resolved to discover what went on in the blue room in the evenings: perhaps Neville was getting a bit old to share a room with a girl.

Another match finished. 'Your backhand's got much better, Teddy,' his father said, and Teddy glowed and looked casual.

'Has it?' he said, as though this had happened unknown to him.

'White chrysanths,' the Duchy said, 'a lovely early variety. I do adore them.'

'They smell of bonfires, foreign bonfires,' Clary said after sniffing them.

'I think they smell of frightened mice,' Neville said to crush her.

'He's missing his father,' Villy murmured to Jessica.

The air-raid warning sounded, but nobody took much notice. The players just coming off the court wanted tea, and there was no hot water left.

'Come on, Poll,' Hugh said, getting to his feet. 'Let's you and I go and get it.'

Almost before they reached the house, they heard the droning of planes – it sounded like a great many of them.

Polly said, 'I expect they're ours?' but her father did not seem to have heard her. Coming out of the house again with the jugs of hot water, they saw the planes, wave upon wave of them, flying very high, and glinting in the sun, all heading purposefully in the same direction. Polly, watching her father watch them, said, 'Are they Germans?'

And Hugh, without taking his eyes off them, said: 'Bombers.'

'Well, they're not going to bomb *us*, are they?'

'No, not here.'

The noise had increased – the whole sky seemed to be vibrating – but the planes were so high that it was a distant, rather than a deafening sound.

Hugh said, 'You take the water, Poll,' and went into the house.

She met Uncle Edward on her way back to the terrace.

'Where's your father?'

'He went back into the house.'

When she reached the others she heard Teddy saying, 'Well, if they *are* heading for London, I should think they'll flatten the whole place – there must be thousands of them.'

'Not thousands, Teddy.'

'Oh, well, Mum, you know what I mean. There's still more coming over. A wizard number. Where's Dad gone? He's got the list of who's to play next.'

Villy said a trifle wearily, 'He's probably gone to telephone Hendon to see if they want him back.'

He had, of course, but they said, no, no need, it didn't look as though they were the target. But Hugh, desperately trying to reach the hospital, simply could not get through.

∞ ∞ ∞

The day had been an extraordinary mixture – certainly a day of the kind that neither of them had ever spent before. It had begun with an affectionate quarrel about Sid using her entire bacon ration for their breakfast – two rashers each – but she won, and they had tomatoes and fried bread as well.

'I should have brought my ration book,' Rachel said as they lit their first cigarettes of the day.

'Nonsense! I mostly eat at the canteen anyway. I'd never be bothered to do bacon for myself.' She felt her tiredness from lack of sleep dissolving from the pure happiness at the prospect of their day together. 'The great question. What would you like to do?'

'National Gallery concert?'

'I'm afraid they don't have them on Saturdays.'

'Well, I have to do some shopping. I need a warm suit

– tweed or something. And I wanted to buy you your birthday shirt. And I ought to go and see Sybil. She doesn't have Hugh at weekends.'

That was the first – then – very small cloud. She said, 'I don't have you in the week *or* at weekends. This is our time, isn't it?'

'Yes. Let's go out to lunch somewhere posh after shopping and it is going to be *my* lunch after eating all your bacon. Then we can see what we feel like.'

Unsure whether this meant that the visit to Sybil was off, or at the least, unlikely, she dropped the subject.

Ordinarily she hated shopping, but not with Rachel. The pleasure of helping her choose, of sitting on a small gilt chair at Debenham and Freebody while Rachel paraded in various suits was intense. Eventually with a blue-grey Donegal tweed long jacket and box-pleated skirt packed in a beautiful box, they returned to the car and drove to Jermyn Street and Rachel chose her shirt to give Sid – brown and coffee-coloured striped silk – and then Rachel found the perfect tobacco silk tie to go with it.

'Darling, it's a very expensive place. I don't think you should give me a tie as well.'

'Of course I shall. The Brig gives me such a generous dress allowance, and I haven't spent any money for ages.'

The thought that it was the Brig who was indirectly responsible for these things was faintly depressing. Ideas like 'They pay her to stay at home. They've made her utterly dependent' occurred. She dismissed them quickly as unfair and nonsense. Of *course* Rachel had to have some money: nobody could exist without any at all; she was unreasonable to have such a qualm. 'Let's buy you things now,' she said. But getting Rachel to spend money on herself, beyond the most extreme necessities, proved almost impossible. Rachel refused to buy herself a shirt: she really did not need one, she said. She agreed to get a jumper to go with the suit, and they walked up Burlington Arcade for that. Then she would not buy a cashmere, 'Oh, no, darling, I've never had one of those – they're fearfully expensive,' and chose instead a lambswool twinset, jumper and cardigan, in a clear forget-me-not blue. 'Do you think it will go with my suit?'

'Sure to.' It matched her eyes, Sid thought.

Rachel also wanted some new bedroom slippers: 'My old ones are exactly the shape of very old broad beans.'

When it came to lunch, Rachel said that one of Edward's favourite places was Bentley's, which was within walking distance, and they both liked fish, so they went there. Rachel made Sid have lobster as she knew it was her favourite thing and she had a plain grilled sole; they drank half a bottle of hock and were utterly happy. Sid had to help Rachel about tipping, and it was then that she realised that Rachel had never taken anyone out to a restaurant meal before in her life. 'I'm awfully bad at sums,' she said, 'so although it must be very bad form, I shall have to tell you the bill.' They were the only two women lunching; there were the usual pairs of people, and men on their own, but no other ones or twos of women, and Sid noticed that people looked at them – talked about them – smiled to each other, and then studiously *avoided* looking at them, but she did not think that Rachel noticed this at all. Her attention was so happily fixed upon Sid that she did not even finish her sole, 'It was enormous', and once, when Sid said how much she was enjoying the treat, Rachel reached out and took her hand (it was then that Sid became uncomfortably aware of people eyeing them), but she would not reject any gesture of affection from her love and clasped the hand held out to her with conscious bravado. It was another small cloud, but she kept it to herself.

The trouble began when, walking back to the car, Rachel asked Sid to drop her at Sybil's hospital. 'And if we see a flower shop, I'll just nip in and buy something to take.'

'What will you do then?'

'Oh, I'll get a bus and join you at home.'

'I'll wait for you.'

'Don't. It'll worry me thinking of you hanging about.'

'Have you told her you're coming?'

'No. I wasn't sure whether I could.'

'And now you are?'

'Well, there's no reason not to. We haven't anything special to do.'

'Couldn't you go tomorrow? Early evening – before you catch your train? I have to be on duty at six.'

'No, I promised them I'd catch an afternoon train and be back in time to read to the Brig before dinner.'

'You never told me that.'

'I'm sure I did. I said I had to get back on Sunday.'

She simply did not understand, Sid thought. No, she did not. Listen to her now.

'Poor Syb has had such an awful time. It is a very small thing to pay her a visit. It would be horribly selfish not to. Surely you can see that?'

'And it would also be selfish *not* to read to the Brig for once – just once, in order that we could have more time together?'

Rachel looked at her, her forehead puckering. 'Of course it would.'

Sid burst out, 'Well, I wish to God it would be unselfish to see *me*. But I suppose it will never be that until your parents are dead!'

There was a dead silence. Then Rachel, her voice distant and trembling, said, 'What a really awful thing to say.'

Resisting wildly the desire to apologise, to sweep it all away with remorse, Sid said, 'But you only want to do things that you feel you ought to do – for other people. You never do anything for yourself.'

Still distant, Rachel answered, 'Why should I? I have a wonderful life. And I happen to love my parents very much.'

They did not speak after that – all the way up Regent Street to Portland Place and thence down New Cavendish Street to the hospital. There was a small flower stall outside the main door. Rachel got out. 'I'll be back about five,' she said.

Sid watched her choose a bunch of roses and walk through the large entrance. She drove a few yards further on, and then she stopped the car, turned off the engine and wept.

It was nearly two hours before Rachel emerged. During that time Sid had finished crying, had smoked eight cigarettes, had told herself that she had been quite right, that she was able to confront things and that Rachel was the coward – the dependant – the one who would risk nothing. She told herself that Rachel was *naturally* loving and unselfish. She told herself that it was *she* who was spoiling their short time together – by jealousy, by being possessive, by getting at poor Rachel about what she clearly conceived to be her duty . . . She remembered Rachel saying, 'I always enjoy everything I do with you.' It was not that Rachel did not love her: 'I'd rather be with you than with anyone in the world,' she had once said, an old bone that Sid kept safely buried, but could always dig up for comfort. It was she who failed abysmally to make the best of what she had got; she was greedy and bad-tempered and possessive. By the time Rachel reappeared, she was entirely the villain of the piece.

'You shouldn't have waited!'

'I wanted to. Forgive me for being such a beast.'

'You weren't a beast. It's all right, really.'

She took Rachel's hand and kissed it. 'I'm so sorry. It's wonderful to have you at all.'

And Rachel smiled, and screwed up her eyes and leaned over and kissed her, and said, 'Sorry I sulked.'

'No, no – it was *all* me. All of it.'

'I was thinking. Why don't we go to a theatre tonight?'

'Lovely idea. We'll get an *Evening Standard* at Baker Street.'

Then they talked about Sybil, about whom she asked with all the concern that she would, in any other circumstances, always have displayed.

'She's still very weak, poor darling, and *longing* to come home. But she doesn't want to be a nuisance. And she thinks Hugh wants her to stay in the hospital longer, but is trying to get her out because he thinks she wants to.'

'It does sound complicated.'

'I know. But married people always have their jungle paths. *They* know them, but they always sound funny to outsiders.'

'I suppose they do.' She thought how wonderfully secret and safe it would be to have a jungle path or two herself.

'You know, in spite of that huge lunch, I'd love a cup of tea.'

'As soon as we get home, you shall have one. It is tea-time after all.'

Rachel looked at her watch. 'Nearly a quarter to five. It certainly is.'

They parked outside the house and carried their shopping in just as the air-raid warning sounded.

'Oh dear.'

'We're always having them; nothing much happens.'

But shortly after that they could hear the faint popping sounds of anti-aircraft guns.

'Do they ever hit anything?' Rachel asked, as they went down to the kitchen to make tea.

'They must occasionally, but mostly I think it's simply to keep the planes too high to be accurate about their targets.'

When they had had tea and chosen a theatre, Rachel remarked, 'If we can hear the ack-ack, there must be an air raid somewhere.'

'If there is, it's a long way off. Let's play a spot of Brahms.'

'Oh, Sid, I'm rotten! Nothing like up to your standards.'

'To hell with that. I love playing with you.'

So Rachel struggled through the sonata in G major and Sid was wonderfully patient with her mistakes. Then they decided to have a drink, and Rachel said she wanted to see Sid's garden. 'There's nothing to see; it's a wilderness, I'm afraid.' But Rachel opened the French windows and started to go down the little flight of wrought-iron steps when she called, 'Sid! Come and look!'

And Sid shut her violin case and joined her. There was a gigantic cloud of smoke in the distance, rising slowly in the sky as they watched, like some vast balloon.

'Where do you think?'

'Well, that's due east, so it might be the docks – the East End at any rate.'

The sun was setting and, as they watched, the blue-violet sky round the smoke balloon seemed to be tinged with pink. The ack-ack sounded more distinct out of doors – a pedantic little yapping sound. They both watched and listened for a few minutes and then Rachel said that she could see the garden from there so she wouldn't go into it, after all.

'I'm going to mend your dressing gown for you,' she said.

'Oh, would you, darling? If you do that, I shall pay you in *gin*.'

'What about our theatre?' Sid said when she had been sent and returned with some primitive sewing things.

'Well, I sort of feel that perhaps it would be nice if we stayed in after all,' Rachel replied as she put the torn sleeve inside out to get at the seam.

Sid was delighted. She lit the fire and got drinks.

'Dinner,' she announced, 'could be toasted cheese or a vintage tin of sardines. Or both, of course.'

'Oh, *one* will be quite enough. I can't see any more, darling. Could you do the blackout?'

Sid fastened the front shutters, and then went to the French windows to draw the curtains. She could no longer see the balloon of smoke, but the sky from there was an unearthly orange red. There was no sound of gunfire.

Rachel sensed that there was something odd, since Sid was so still. She got up and joined her. Together they watched.

'It's as though the sky was bleeding to death,' Rachel said. 'It must have been a very bad raid.'

'The All Clear hasn't sounded. It isn't over yet.'

As though to confirm this, they heard the guns opening up again.

'It may be us this time,' Sid said. 'There's an air-raid shelter in the next street. I think we should make some sandwiches and a Thermos in case we have to go to it.'

But they didn't have to. An hour later, when they turned off the lights in order to look out of the windows, the sky was still flaming, but against it, or within it, were not one, but several great plumes of dark smoke.

'Let's turn on the news.'

'My wireless is bust. I keep meaning to take it to be mended, but I haven't. I'm sorry.'

They ate the sandwiches and drank the Thermos of coffee. 'We mustn't waste it,' Rachel said. 'I hate to think of you in London,' she added.

'I'm all right. I have a nice, safe, dull job.'

They played piquet, and Sid, who usually won, lost each game. The old adage rose to her lips, but she did not say it. By mutual consent, after one more awestruck look at the sky, they went to bed.

The telephone woke Sid after she had gone to her own room, and even after she had fallen asleep. It was her ambulance station calling her out. 'There simply aren't enough ambulances, or bloody well anything else come to that, so we'd like you to report at once,' the voice ended.

It was half past four. She got into her boiler suit with a jersey underneath it. Then she went to tell Rachel.

∞ ∞ ∞

The family were just finishing a late dinner, which had been put back because everybody wanted baths after the tournament, when the telephone rang. Hugh leapt to his feet. 'It'll be Sybil,' he said. He had been trying to get through to the hospital ever since the first wave of bombers had flown over them.

'I do hope that it is,' observed the Duchy. 'He has been worrying so much, in spite of the news.' They had earlier heard that there had been an attack on London, and various anxieties had ensued: apart from Hugh, Villy worried about Louise, who had rung to say she wasn't coming down until Sunday as there was a play she simply *had* to see, the Duchy had fretted about Rachel, and Edward had privately worried about Diana with whom he had spent the previous night, and who had announced her intention of staying on in London in order to shop that day.

Hugh returned; he did not look relieved. 'They've hit the wharves,' he said. 'A big raid on the East End and the docks.'

'Which wharf?' the Brig asked sharply.

'All three of them, I'm afraid. The sawmills went up like a powder keg. All the sawdust. It was old George. He said he thought another attack was starting while he was speaking to me. It wasn't his night for duty, but he went to see. He was ringing from a box and he ran out of money, so that's all we know.'

There was a silence. Then Teddy said, 'Does that mean we're ruined?'

'Quite possibly,' his father said. 'Hugh, we'd better go to London.'

'No point tonight,' the Brig said. 'There's nothing you'll be able to do tonight. Go tomorrow morning, first thing.'

Polly burst into tears. 'Think of all the poor people!

Having their houses smashed up and being bombed to death!'

'Poll darling,' Hugh said, sitting by her, 'we'll hope it isn't as bad as that.'

But the next morning she discovered that it was, of course. Four hundred people had been killed outright; over fifteen hundred had been seriously injured, and thousands of people had found their homes reduced to ruins of rubble and broken glass.

LOUISE

Autumn–Winter 1940

It was her very first really grown-up dinner party – not a family affair, which automatically relegated one to the shaky status of being only conditionally grown up, but a party which, with the exception of Mummy's friend Hermione Knebworth who had invited her, was full of strangers, all older than herself, treating her as an equal. Hermione – goodness she was kind! – had invited her out of the blue, and more than that, had persuaded Mummy that she should come to London and stay the night. What she had actually said to Villy was, 'Darling, I need one young girl madly – everyone else is as old as the hills and so *attached*, and it is time that Louise met some decent people instead of all that greenery-yallery crowd at her acting place.' But Louise did not know this. Her mother had simply said that Hermione wanted to speak to her.

'Hermione? I don't know anyone called Hermione – excepting Leontes' wife, of course.'

'Hermione Knebworth. Of course you know her.' Villy had to shout because Louise had only got as far as the landing at the top of the stairs, and she was in the Brig's study. '*Louise!* Will you please come at once. It's a toll call.'

Louise had taken to doing everything (nearly) that her mother told her to but very, very slowly. Now as she wandered down the stairs, she was the picture of wounded dignity. '"Since what I am to say must be but that which contradicts my accusation,"' she murmured, '"and the testimony on my part no other but what comes from myself—"'

'*Louise!*'

Anyway, it had turned out to be an exciting invitation. Anything, in any case, was better than mouldering away at Home Place. The acting school had closed because of the Blitz, and although she had tried to get a job in various repertory companies nobody seemed to want her. She had had a brief row with Mummy about what she should wear; she didn't really have a decent frock, and she wanted Mummy to lend her one, but of course she *wouldn't* – said they would be too old for her, so she was reduced to her old coral-pink satin that she was absolutely sick of and that anyway was a bit too short for her.

But when she reached Hermione's luxurious flat in Mayfair, almost the first thing Hermione said was, 'I expect you'd like to borrow something exciting to wear,' and took her to the shop – only five minutes' away – and found her a heavenly blue chiffon with plaited chiffon shoulder straps so she couldn't wear a bra, in itself a dashing prospect. And Hermione *gave* her a box in which was a pair of french knickers and a petticoat – pale blue satin with creamy lace and a beautiful pair of pure silk stockings.

And now eight people were seated in Hermione's midnight-blue dining room – pitch dark in the day, but she never ate lunch at home – with candles on the table, having an amazing dinner that Hermione had had brought in from a neighbouring hotel: caviar, which she had never had before, and roast partridge and a chocolate mousse and pink champagne, and then a delicious savoury of mushrooms and tiny pieces of fried bacon. She ate everything, but she didn't talk much because the whole atmosphere was so new to her, and everyone was miles older and she didn't want to say the wrong thing. There were two couples, the men in army uniform, and their wives in evening dress, of course; one man who was not so old, but was extremely quiet and seemed devoted to Hermione, although she took very little notice of him, and another not so old man in naval uniform, who sat next to Hermione and opposite Louise. He wasn't as old as the couples, but he was *old*, at least thirty, she thought. She sat between the army officers who were very nice to her in dull and courteous ways, asking her where she lived and what she did, and Hermione interrupted, saying, 'Malcolm, she's Edward Cazalet's daughter – you remember Edward?'

'Oh, yes. Yes, of course I do,' And Louise noticed that his wife looked at her with renewed interest.

Now they were all teasing Hermione about her conjuring up such a delicious dinner. 'She could do it if we were all on a desert island.'

'I am deeply grateful that we aren't.'

'I don't know. A bit quieter at nights, don't you think?'

'I sleep at the War Office mostly. Underground, you know. Don't hear a thing.'

'Poor Marion can't do that.'

'Poor Marion spends most nights gambling wildly at an ARP post.'

'That's not true! We have incident after incident, now they've turned their attention to the West End.'

'And Hermione,' he went on disregarding her, 'Hermione simply makes *frocks*.'

The silent man came to life. 'That's quite untrue,' he

exclaimed. 'Hermione gets up at five every morning and works in a munitions factory.'

The other, less old man looked up from his partridge. 'Really? Hermione – in all those hours we've spent together, you never told me that.'

'She wouldn't.'

'Anyway, I shall probably have to give it up,' Hermione said as though she didn't want to talk about that any more.

But the silent man was now not to be silenced.

'Do you know why? She found a way of doing her part of the job so much faster than anyone else, that she upset the whole line. Brought the factory practically to a halt.'

'John darling, don't go *on* about it! Offhand, I can't think of a more boring subject.' But she smiled at him with her clever grey eyes and asked him to light her a cigarette and he subsided again into an amiable and total silence.

They didn't actually talk about the war, but there was some gossip about personalities. General de Gaulle: 'Awkward chap – very stiff, and none of that famous French tact,' the man who slept at the War Office said; and General Ismay who, it turned out, had been a prefect at the school the other chap had been to: 'Charming feller – gets on with everybody.' Everyone seemed pleased about President Roosevelt's re-election. 'We stand a far better chance of help, tacit or otherwise with *him* than we would with a Republican.' The conversation became rather dully technical then with the men talking about a deal Churchill had made for fifty American destroyers. The women were talking about their children: 'Would you believe it, Jonathan *cried* because we didn't have fireworks on Guy Fawkes night!' and Louise was beginning to feel disappointed when the man opposite her leaned over the table and said, so softly she could barely hear him, 'You – are – *lovely*!' and then held her eye with a look of such beguiling admiration that she felt herself beginning to blush, and was quite unable to think of a reply.

He smiled then, and said, 'I could see that destroyers are not your subject.'

'Oh *no*! How could they be anybody's?'

'Well, here I must tell you that they have to be mine because I'm in one.'

'Oh!' What traps there were when you knew nothing about the person! 'I'm sorry,' she said.

'Tell me *your* subject.'

'Well, I'm learning to be an actress. At least I was – but the school closed down because of the Blitz,' And after that it was easy: she told him all about how she had auditioned for repertory companies, but without success; how the school *might* be going to evacuate to the country somewhere where there was a free theatre and continue as a student rep; how she had always wanted to play the men's parts in Shakespeare; and how her family were against all this, and felt she should do something useful for the war. By now they had reached the chocolate mousse.

'Don't you want your pudding? It's absolutely delicious.'

'I don't really care for puddings,' she said untruthfully, but it sounded grown up not to care about them.

'Don't you? I adore them. The stodgier the better. My favourite was suet roll with treacle at school.'

She was rather taken aback by this. 'Well, I do like

some. It's just that I've eaten rather a lot of everything else.'

'Well, you are probably very wise.'

Somebody claimed him then, and she ate a few spoonfuls of the chocolate mousse not to seem rude. She looked up and Hermione gave her a marvellously reassuring smile. She had earlier introduced Louise saying, 'This is my new daughter.' I wish she *was* my mother, Louise thought. She'd be perfect as a mother. She looked unbelievably glamorous in a scarlet silk dress that clung everywhere to her with a long slit up the side so that she could walk, and red satin shoes that matched. She smelled of gardenias. Louise only knew this because she had asked. The whole flat had this faint perfume, as though she only had to walk through a room to scent it. 'It's Caron's Bellodgia,' she had said. This had been before people arrived, when she had walked round the dining-room table, putting knives and forks completely straight, twitching napkins, tweaking the roses in the middle of the table, telling the waiter to change the claret glasses. Everything seemed to be made perfect by her in a few moments, and Louise had noticed that the waiters did not seem to mind her drawling, imperious voice telling them how wrong something was at all. 'I really cannot bear glass butter dishes,' she had said, 'do change them. White china is what I said I wanted. And not a speck of parsley in sight, please.' And they all said, yes, m'lady, and rushed off to do what she wanted.

After dinner, they repaired to Hermione's drawing room, which had fat chairs with gilded arms – reminding her of Stella's home a bit – and there was coffee with the proper coloured sugar to put into it. The man who had admired her sat himself down next to her – she remembered that he was called Michael something, but she felt shy about asking him what else he was called because she'd been told when they were introduced and hadn't remembered.

But then, Marion said, 'What about the famous picture? Is it finished? May we see it?'

And the man said, 'I left it in the hall. It's Hermione's picture.'

'I'd adore you to see it. Do bring it in, Michael.'

It was a full-length portrait of Hermione in a dark grey satin dress standing by a white marble fireplace with one arm lying on its shelf. Behind her on the other side of the fireplace, was a very dark, rather dirtyish yellow velvet curtain. It was tremendously well painted, Louise thought: you would know immediately that it was Hermione, because her hair, her features, all seemed to be right, but at the same time it didn't give you much idea of what Hermione was actually *like*. The satin of the dress, the heavy folds of the velvet curtain, the white veined marble were immaculately painted. It seemed to her a brilliant picture, but somehow not really a good portrait of *her*. She didn't have to say anything about it, because everybody else was exclaiming, 'Fabulous! *So like* you! Jolly good! I was afraid it was going to be one of those modern jobs when you don't know what's going on, let alone whether it's meant to be any particular person.'

Hermione said, 'It flatters me, but I expect I should have been cross if it hadn't.'

People ran out of things to say about it quite quickly, but she noticed that Michael went on looking at it in a serious way, almost as though it was new to him.

Soon after that, a night club was proposed. 'There's been a warning,' someone said, and somebody else

346

retorted, 'There's always a warning. I don't intend to have my night life disturbed by Herr Goering.'

Marion said, 'I honestly think I'll opt out. I'm on duty tomorrow night, and I'm frightfully short of sleep. But do go, Frank, if you want to.'

'No. I'll take you home, and then I'll repair to the old bunker. I may be chairborne, but there's a hell of a lot of work at the moment.'

In the end, it was just four of them: Hermione, the silent John, Michael and herself who went to the Astor in Berkeley Street in John's car.

The place seemed very dark when they went into it, but Louise found that one soon got used to that. It was fairly full, but they knew Hermione and a table was quickly found for them. Champagne was ordered and Michael said that he would like some soda water as well. Hermione asked Michael to dance with her and, slightly disappointed, Louise was left with John, who also seemed disappointed.

'Shall we?' was all he said.

But he was easy to dance with: the small floor was very crowded and he was skilful at avoiding other dancers.

'Did you like the portrait?' she ventured, to break the silence.

'Don't know anything about pictures,' he answered. 'But I should think *anyone* could make a good picture of Hermione.'

'She's the most glamorous person I've ever met.'

This animated him. '*Isn't* she? Tremendously bright with it, too. In fact, she's the most amazing person I've ever met in my life. Have you known her long?'

'Well, she's a very old friend of my mother's. So, in a

sort of way, I have. Although, you know, you don't ever *know* your parents' friends.'

'I suppose not.' After a while, he said, 'Do you know Michael?'

'Never met him before. What's his other name?'

'You don't know that?' For some reason this pleased him. 'He's supposed to be famous. A famous portrait painter. His pictures cost the earth. Hermione would never have afforded to be painted by him. Someone gave it to her, but she won't say who.' He was depressed again.

'How did he paint it if he's in the Navy – he said in a destroyer?'

'He's been on sick leave. Got appendicitis. Ship's doctor had to take it out. Made a bit of a hash of it, so he's been on leave for about six weeks.' At this point, the dance came to an end, and they went back to their table.

When it became her turn to dance with Michael she discovered that he was an almost frighteningly good dancer. It was a quickstep, and he whirled her into all kinds of elaborate decorations. She became tense with the effort to keep up with him.

'Just relax and follow me,' he said, but these directions seemed incompatible to her.

'Sorry. I'm not good enough for you.'

'Nonsense! I've just had more practice. I used to go to the Hammersmith Palais every week. See? When I turn your shoulder, you just go the only way you *can* go.'

But it didn't seem to be like that at all for her.

'The others are dancing,' he said. 'Let's go back and talk. My subject is only beginning to be destroyers. What it has been up till now is faces. And you have the most extraordinarily beautiful face. I can't wait to draw it. Lots of people think my paintings are rather vulgar, and I expect they are right, but I draw rather well. When can I draw you?'

'I don't know.' She was overwhelmed by his description of her face and longed to go away and look at it to see how it had changed. 'I'm only up for one night. My parents are sticky about me staying in London.'

'I'm sure they're right. Well, perhaps you could—'

But at that moment something so extraordinary happened that it seemed as though everything stopped. There was a dull, very loud explosion, and the next second it felt as though the whole room lurched, as though the walls were stumbling to stay upright; the large dimmed chandeliers shook with an uneven chinking sound, the little red-shaded lamps on each table quivered, and their champagne swayed in the glasses. There was a gasp in the room and she heard one woman cry out, '*Oh!*' in an unnaturally high voice, but all this seemed to happen at once. Then, very slowly, a small piece of plaster fell from the ceiling on to their table beside their glasses. Through it, she had sat bolt upright, motionless.

Michael took her hand. 'What a brave girl,' he said. 'I had been going to say, come down to Wiltshire for a weekend, my mother would like to meet you. Now I am sure that she would.'

'A bomb?' she said.

'A bomb fairly near, I should think.'

Hermione and John returned to the table at this point.

'They really are the *limit*!' Hermione drawled. 'One can't even have a little innocent exercise and fun without them trying to spoil it. Let's have another bottle of delicious champagne to cheer us up.'

When the waiter came for the order, he said that *they said* the church in Piccadilly had been hit. Some people were leaving, but Hermione said they should stay. 'It isn't as though they're *raining* down on us.' She looked at Louise. 'Are you all right, my pet?'

Louise nodded. Now, after being called brave, she was feeling rather shaky.

A long time later, when she and Hermione had been deposited at Hermione's flat and were taking off their wraps in the hall, Hermione remarked, 'You were a great hit with Michael Hadleigh. Did you have a good time?'

'Oh, it was a wonderful evening. It was terribly kind of you to ask me.'

Louise kissed her sculptured, scented face; Hermione gave her a little pat, and said, 'I warn you, he's a great breaker of hearts. I'm sure you'll be seeing him again, but don't get *too* taken with him, will you, darling?'

'No, I won't.' She said that because she felt it was expected of her, but privately she wondered whether he could, or would break her heart.

Hermione eyed her, looked as though she was going to say something, and changed her mind.

Then, when Louise had undressed and was brushing her teeth, she knocked softly on the door. 'Forgot to tell you, darling, I'll be off early in the morning, so I shan't see you.'

'Are you going to your factory?'

'I'm off to my very own factory. Yes. You sleep as late as you like, and ring for Yvonne when you want your breakfast. And be a good girl and catch your train back to Sussex before lunch, or your mother will never let me have you again. *Compris*?' And she was gone.

As she got into bed, the All Clear went. It was twenty past four. It would hardly be worth poor Hermione going to bed, she thought, as her head touched the pillow and sleep overcame her.

The next morning she was awoken by Yvonne who said there was a gentleman on the telephone.

'This is Michael,' he said, 'Michael Hadleigh.'

'Hallo.'

'Have I woken you up?'

She looked at her watch: it said ten. 'Not really.'

'I've rung my mother, and she says it would be lovely if you came down next weekend.'

'Well – I don't think—' She had planned to see Stella then.

'The thing is that it is my last weekend before I rejoin my ship. So it is rather then, or heaven knows when. *Do* come; I shall be unspeakably sad if you don't.'

So, she said that she would see if she could rearrange her plans and, of course, she could.

'Michael Hadleigh? The one who paints those Academy-type portraits? Why on earth do you want to see him?' This was Stella at her most spiky. 'I know,' she added. 'I bet he told you you were unbearably beautiful and you couldn't resist the bait.'

She could be maddening as well. 'And his mother's the daughter of an earl. It'll all be frightfully grand.'

'How do you *know* all that?'

'Mutti reads all the sort of papers that tell you that kind of thing. She's always hoping to spot someone eligible for me – at least, that's her ostensible reason when we tease her about it, but actually she's a straightforward snob. She loves reading about high life.'

'Well, come and stay with us the weekend after, and I'll tell you all about it.'

'All right, I'll come, but *not* because I want to hear all about *that*. And, Louise, for goodness sake don't fall for him because it'll ruin your life. You're far too young to get all tied up with anybody.'

The being far too young rankled. Stella could be very bossy. *She* wouldn't think *she* was too young for anything, and nineteen was not that much older; it was a bit much having one's best friend treat one as a child.

'I have no intention of getting tied up with anybody,' she said as loftily as she could manage.

∞ ∞ ∞

'Spend a *weekend* with Michael Hadleigh? The portrait painter? Certainly not!'

'Mummy, it's not just with him. It's with his parents. They have a house in Wiltshire. He's on leave; he's going back to his ship after that.'

That was better, but it still didn't do the trick. Her mother rang Hermione who gave her Lady Zinnia's telephone number in the country, and Mummy rang *her* – it was all most humiliating, but it also had made her really want to go. So when her mother finally said that she might go and began fussing about things like her not wearing trousers, Louise sulked and was offhand about the whole thing.

It wasn't until she was sitting in the train to London, a headscarf over her newly washed hair, wearing clothes that she would have died to let her friends at the acting school see – an olive-green tweed coat and skirt, *stockings* and proper shoes (socks and sandals were the mode at school) and with a handbag (people used canvas fishing tackle satchels in which they could conceal their gas

352

masks) and her mother's rather expensive Revelation suitcase on the rack above her, that she began to feel both nervous and excited about the prospect ahead. She had told herself all kinds of things about it: that an actress should get as much experience about as many different kinds of people as possible, that the pangs of homesickness from which she still occasionally suffered could only be vanquished by frequent efforts, that he probably hadn't meant a word that he had said about her – and, after all, it wasn't much – but then she would remember him saying it: 'You – are – lovely.' It was like a double brandy on an empty stomach. Her family did not mention, let alone discuss, people's appearance, with the exception of her mother who criticised it. She knew that she was clumsy: movement classes at her school had made that clear to her, apart from her mother's devastating remarks. But nobody had ever said that she was OK to look at, let alone *lovely*. Perhaps he is the only person in the world who would think that, she thought. She knew that painters had some funny tastes about people's appearance, liking sometimes quite fat and sloppy people, or people whose faces could in no way be described as conventionally beautiful. It was quite likely that he was one of them. Why did it matter to her so very much? She did not know, only vaguely supposing that people loved you starting from that, and if they didn't have that to start with they would not bother to love the rest. And it seemed to her that, apart from becoming a great actress, she wanted someone to feel that she was the most special person on earth. She was not exactly hunting, but she had begun to want to be hunted.

He met her at Pewsey station in the late afternoon wearing a polo-necked jersey and very old grey flannel bags, a stocky, rather square figure – but I do not feel like Lydia or Kitty Bennet about uniforms, she thought. How useful Jane Austen often was, because otherwise she would have caught herself thinking how much more glamorous he looked in naval dress.

'Your train was hardly late at all,' he said, 'although, of course, the "hardly" seemed a long time.' He took her suitcase from her. 'It's wonderful that you could come. Mummy is longing to meet you.'

A fiery sun was setting, leaving a cold, darkening, translucent sky. They drove along a valley with large fields of stubble – like golden stumpwork – and beyond gentle shoulders of chalky downs, moth-coloured in the dying light. It was far less crowded country than the kind she was used to: there were fewer trees and those there were were gracefully windswept by the prevailing wind. He drove fast through the narrow, winding roads that climbed up out of the valley, through one or two dark little hamlets, whose only signs of life were the occasional wisps of smoke from chimneys, until they reached a wood, and in the middle of it a drive.

'Here we are,' he said. The wood thinned out to single trees and she could see railings on either side of the drive and then the dark mass of the house before them. They had not talked in the car much: she had asked him who would be there, and he had said, just the parents. He stopped the car, and she got out and waited, shivering slightly while he collected her suitcase from the boot.

There were two doors, the second made mostly of glass, and then they were in an immense hall, at the end of which was a double staircase rising to a gallery. A very old manservant appeared and said that they would be having tea in the library.

'Right. This is Miss Cazalet's case. Get Margaret to take it up, would you?' He turned to her, untied her headscarf and gave her a reassuring smile, 'There, my beauty,' took her hand and led her through a vast oak door, along a passage to another oak door which opened into a square room that seemed to be entirely lined with books, except for the huge stone fireplace, where a log fire burned, on each side and in front of which were three sofas. On one of them lay a fragile-looking woman with white hair who was embroidering something in a round frame.

'Mummy, this is Louise.'

When Louise got near to take the hand held out to her, she realised that she was not as old as the white hair had made her think from the doorway. She wore a blue Chinese silk padded jacket embroidered with birds and flowers over a long thick white woollen skirt, and silver earrings, which looked like some kind of fish, dangled from her large, but elegant ears.

'Louise,' she said. Her eyes were as pale as they were blue and looked now at her with a kind of shrewd brilliance, as though, Louise felt, she was transparent. 'Welcome, Louise,' she said, and then, turning to her son, who bent to kiss her, added, 'You were quite right, Mikey. She is a little beauty,' but somehow there was a touch of impersonal patronage about the way in which she said it that made Louise feel simply uncomfortable.

'Where's the tea?'

'I rang for it, darling, when I heard your car.'

'Where's the Judge?'

'In his den, as usual, working. Come and sit down, Louise, and tell me about yourself.'

But this invitation increased her unease, and she heard

herself being very dull in her answers to the questions put to her while she ate hot scones and bramble jelly and cherry cake.

'My favourite cake!' Michael exclaimed when he saw it, and Louise saw a small complacent smile flit for an instant across his mother's face.

'Really, darling? How very lucky for you!'

'Well, you must act for us this evening,' she added to Louise as she delicately licked bramble jelly off a finger and rubbed it with a large, very fine white handkerchief. God, no! Louise thought.

After tea, Michael got out his Senior Service and offered her one. When she had taken it and he had lit it for her, Lady Zinnia said, 'You smoke? It used to be fashionable when I was young, but my mother always said that it was common for girls to smoke.'

'Oh, Mummy, according to you, she thought everything girls did was common. Times have changed. But if you'd rather we didn't smoke in here—'

'Darling, I wouldn't dream of telling you what, or what not, to do. I was only considering that if Louise wishes to become an actress, she should look after her voice . . .'

At last, Michael said come and see his studio, and took her upstairs and along what seemed like miles of sombre passages to one end of the house where there was a very large room with skylights along one side of the ceiling.

'Hang on a minute while I do the blackout,' he said pulling down a series of roller blinds. Then he switched on the lights and the room was blazing. The floors were bare wood, and it smelled pleasantly of paint. He went to open the wood stove at one end, sat her in a large armchair and offered her another cigarette. Then he said:

'Don't be overwhelmed by Mummy. She hates people to be afraid of her, but she does rather tease new ones to see if they will be. Stand up to her. She'll appreciate that. She has trouble with her heart, and as she's always been an extremely active person, it is hard for her. And, of course, she worries about me far too much, although naturally she would never say so.'

He seemed to be saying two things at once, Louise thought. She felt it was rather difficult for a stranger to stand up to someone who had a bad heart and was suffering from anxiety. All she said now was, 'Don't let her make me *act* anything. I'd be speechless with terror. Honestly, I can't think of *anything* that would frighten me more.'

'Darling Louise, we shall *all* be acting this evening: people are coming to dinner, and Mummy loves us to play charades. So it won't just be you. Although I expect you'll knock spots off the rest of us – being a pro and all that.'

'Oh. Are a lot of people coming?'

'A neighbouring family, the Elmhursts. Now, tell me more about you. I want to know every single thing.'

Because he seemed really interested – not merely curious, as she felt his mother had been – she was able to launch into what he seemed to find an entertaining description of her family; and she found that when she was telling him about the great-aunts, for example, she could imitate them perfectly and make him laugh. She told him about Uncle Rupe, and he said how awful that must be, and then about doing lessons with Polly and Clary, 'Until, of course, I got too old,' and then about the cooking school and her great friend Stella and then back to her burning desire to join the student rep when it relocated to the country if only her parents would let her. 'Although I think they want me to learn typing so that I can get some boring war job,' she finished. 'But they might let me have this one year.'

'Until you're eighteen?'

'How did you know my age?'

'I asked Hermione. She said you were just seventeen.'

'I'm seventeen and a half,' she said, feeling that her actual age was undermining her.

'You are a remarkable seventeen and a half,' he said.

She asked to see some of the pictures that were stacked against the walls.

'You won't like them. They're not modern or adventurous or anything. I simply have a kind of deadly facility and most people are reassured by it and pay me lots of money for them.'

The ones of women were all rather like the one she had seen of Hermione: wearing evening dress, and, in many cases, jewels, sitting in large gilded armchairs, or lounging gracefully on sofas – not quite smiling, looking more as though they had been, and got tired of it. She did not know what to say about them. There were two that were different and although they were leaning face outwards against a wall, he did not actually show them to her. One was of a very beautiful girl in riding clothes, and one of a young man in an open-necked blue check shirt – strikingly handsome in a poetic faun-like manner. She was not sure what was different about these pictures, except that, apart from them being idealistically beautiful, the girl looked as though she might also be stupid, and the boy petulant. Brought up by Miss Milliment at least to look at pictures that she considered to be good, but by painters who were, by and large, dead, she realised that she had never looked at contemporary work at all, let alone by someone she knew. Excepting Uncle Rupe, of course, but she realised now that she had taken his painting, like his being her uncle, uncritically and for granted.

'I didn't think you'd like them,' he said. 'They're rather cheap and vulgar, aren't they really – like me.'

'You don't really *mean* that!'

'But I *do*. I'm second rate. Mark you, that's not *bad*. Most people would be extremely glad to be that.'

'Aren't you most people?'

'Of course not. I'm just as unusual as you are.'

She looked at him to see if he was laughing at her, and was not sure.

'Darling Louise, I'm *not* laughing at you – you amaze me too much for that. Knowing Shakespeare practically by heart, and being so brave about bombs – and – oh, I don't know – everything! I kind of knew – the moment I saw you – that you were special, and by golly, you are!'

Before she had to say anything to this, a bell sounded from below, and he got up.

'Dressing time,' he said. 'I'd better show you your room.'

He led her back along the passage, past the head of the staircase to the passage the other side of it.

'Bathroom's at the end,' he said. 'There's time for a bath if you want one. I'll come and fetch you in half an hour.'

During that weekend, he made two drawings of her, took her riding (he turned out to be a brilliant horseman: there was a row of cups he had won for jumping in shows, including ones at Olympia and Richmond), acted in charades with her – he wasn't particularly good, but he was uninhibited and clearly enjoyed it; played the piano – which he did by ear – and sang songs like 'Don't Put Your Daughter On The Stage, Mrs Worthington'. Through it all, he never failed to *admire* almost everything she said and did. On Monday morning, he put her on a train at Pewsey, kissed her face, and asked her to write to him.

'But what,' said Stella, the following weekend after she had listened to much of this, 'was he *like*?'

'I've *told* you!'

'You haven't at all. You've simply told me things you did. You seem so bowled over by the grand house and dressing bells and being unpacked for, that you haven't noticed anything interesting at *all*. What does he look like?'

Louise thought for a moment. 'It's funny. If I described his appearance you'd just think he was dull, but he isn't. He has terrific *charm*.'

'Go on.'

'Well, light brown hair – not an awful lot of it, as a matter of fact. I should think he'd go bald fairly young. Of course, he's not *young* now: he's thirty-two. Pale blue eyes – sort of greyish blue – but they look very hard at – at everything . . . Quite a large forehead.' She stopped there; he had the suspicion of a double chin, and somehow she didn't want to mention this to Stella. 'A small nose,' she added.

'I can see him as if he was in front of me,' Stella scoffed.

'He has a lovely voice. I think that's possibly the most outstanding thing about him.'

There was a silence. Then Louise said defensively, 'You think I mind far too much about appearances, don't you?'

'No. Everybody ought to mind about what they see. It's *what* you see that matters. Tell me about the parents.'

Louise was on her mettle now. She related her first impressions of the fragile creature on the sofa, and how they proved to be more and more wrong during the weekend. 'She's actually very powerful, I think. She designs and makes jewellery, but she's done lots of other things. She used to make pots, and plates, but Michael said since her heart trouble she'd had to stop that. She *adores* Michael. I had the feeling that he was the most important person in her life . . .'

'What about her husband?'

'She was perfectly *nice* to him, and he obviously adores *her*, but he was working most of the weekend; I only saw him at meals. He was extremely kind to me. He's the sort of person who finds out what you are interested in, and then talks about it, and, of course, he *knew* all about everything. And it wasn't just with me. When a whole lot of people came to dinner, he took a lot of trouble about two of the girls who were pretty frightened of Zee.'

'What?'

'That's what she's called. But all the young men simply loved her: she had them all round her.'

'It sounds as though she doesn't like women,' Stella remarked.

'Oh. No, no, I don't think she does.'

'In which case, watch out.'

'She asked me to come again.'

'That's probably because Michael wants you to. It doesn't mean she *likes* you.'

'I don't suppose she does.' She sounded so disconsolate that Stella laughed and threw an arm round her shoulder. 'Cheer up! None of all that is anything like as important as being a world-famous actress, is it?'

'Shut up! I'm not even going to be allowed to be that! They'll make me do some dreary typing job until it'll be too late! I feel as though I've been marking time all my life, and now, just when it might *begin*, this beastly war will spoil it all.'

'Most people can't do what they like in a war.'

'I bet they do. My father *loved* organising the defence of an aerodrome. He didn't at all want to go back to sorting out the mess at our wharves after the bombing. And I bet that there are lots of people who *like* fighting. I know you think I'm selfish and I agree with you. All I mean is that so are a lot of other people, but it doesn't show so much because they happen to want to do the things that are popular.'

The more she talked like this, the worse she felt. In a minute, she knew, Stella would point out to her that the thousands of people who'd been bombed out of their homes could hardly be said to be liking it, so she added quickly, 'Of course I know I'm very lucky compared to most people, but I don't find that that makes one feel much better, just rather guilty for feeling awful at all.'

'All right,' Stella said equably. 'Let's go back to Mozart.'

'Only the slow movement, then. You know I can't manage the other ones.'

They had spent a morning playing two pianos. Neither of them performed very well, but they enjoyed it. Stella was a better sight reader than Louise, and was prepared to tackle works she had not practised, and Louise had not practised anything for months now, but they forgave each other, stopped and started again until even they got too cold to continue – the log fire in the drawing room smouldered all day and sent its serious heat up the chimney (the Duchy always played in mittens).

Stella loved staying *chez* Cazalet. She said it was like living in a village instead of a box, which was how she rather unfairly described her parents' flat. What she really enjoyed was the lack of curiosity displayed by the family about what each other was doing and thinking. There were no cross-examinations, no post-mortems of the kind that she and Peter had to endure about almost everything they could be seen or sometimes imagined to have done. She longed to have a flat of her own and had pointed out to Louise that if she joined her at Pitman's, they might be allowed to share a place, and might then go on to get jobs in the same institution: the Ministry of Information, the BBC or the like. But Louise clung to the idea of having one year in which to make it as an actress, in the same way that Stella had been implored to do her first year at university which she had refused; she did not want, she had said again and again, to be cut off in that kind of way from what was really going on. 'I want to be *in* the war,' she had said. Her father had finally given in – not because she was right, he had said, but because she had to start learning from her own mistakes. She had told Louise about all this, and Louise had said that all parents were difficult the moment one had a mind of one's own. 'Considering what opposite things we want, it's a pity we can't swap parents,' she said, and this had had the unexpected (to her) result of Stella's eyes filling with tears and being given a hug of unusually emotional proportion. Having Stella to stay was one of the best things in her life, she thought, because, although she had thought she would miss Michael, her time with him had very quickly

'Honestly, Stella. A, I'm not thinking of marrying anybody for years and years, and B, Michael is not in the least like Karenina or Monsieur Bovary.'

'He doesn't sound much like Heathcliff or Romeo either,' Stella retorted. 'In fact, he sounds as though he might turn out to be quite dull.'

It was getting very near to being a quarrel. 'I'm going to sleep,' Louise said with offhand dignity. 'I don't want to discuss the matter any more.'

The next day, Stella apologised, 'Not because I think the things I said were wrong, but because I don't say them in the right way,' which didn't feel much like an apology to Louise. All the same, it was duller than ever at Home Place when Stella went, and she was overjoyed when a letter finally arrived addressed to her mother from Mr Mulloney (one of the teachers from the acting school) saying that he had now found a theatre in Devonshire and a large house three miles away where the students could live, and he had also procured a Mrs Noel Carstairs to be Matron of the establishment. Louise was to be offered a scholarship which meant that she would only have to pay two pounds ten a week for her keep. After much persuasion her mother said she might go.

There were a few more minor rows about her packing, as Louise insisted on taking every single garment that she possessed on the grounds that if they did modern plays they would be expected to dress themselves. Polly and Clary were suitably envious. 'I do hope we will be allowed to come and see you performing,' Polly said. 'You are so lucky knowing what you want to do.'

'And stopping being educated so young,' Clary added.

Aunt Rach took her to Tunbridge Wells and bought her a warm dressing gown. The Brig gave her five shillings.

Her mother gave her two months of her allowance – seven pounds, plus money for her railway ticket – and said she was to ring up when she arrived. Aunt Syb had knitted her a warm jersey, 'It was to be for your Christmas present, but I expect you'll need it before that,' and Aunt Zoë gave her a pot of Elizabeth Arden Eight Hour Cream. 'Put it on your mouth at night,' she said. 'It's wonderful for stopping chapped lips.' Lydia gave her a diary that turned out to be last year's, but she said it didn't make any difference. 'You simply move on a day, and you can choose whether you want it to be the right date or the right day of the week,' she said. 'I worked it out before I gave it to you.' She had put 'For my sister Louise from her loving sister Lydia' in red ink on two pages at the beginning. 'We've had those days, so it doesn't matter,' she said.

Louise thanked her and felt touched. Everybody was being far nicer to her now that she was going away, and on her last evening she did fleetingly wonder whether it would all prove so frightening and awful that she would want to come home, but quenched the idea as quickly as possible.

Stella met her at Charing Cross as a surprise, and went with her to Paddington station where they bought very horrible sandwiches – a choice of meat paste or beetroot; they got one of each.

'Where can we eat them?'

The station was crowded and there was nowhere to sit.

'On the platform,' Stella said. 'I'll get a platform ticket.'

They sat on Louise's suitcases, which they'd lugged from the taxi to the platform to save a porter so that Louise could buy a packet of de Reszke Minors.

'I'm going to miss you awfully.'

'I you as well.'

'But not so much. You're going *to* something.'

'Yes, I know. I really *shall* miss you. Mind you write.'

A lot of the glass had fallen out of the station roof and water dripped on them.

'Aunt Anna made you these. I nearly forgot.' She rummaged in her shoulder bag and produced a little cardboard box. 'Her special cinnamon cakes. She cooks and cooks because she's so unhappy.'

'Oh, thank you! Thank her.'

'*Write* and thank her. She never gets any letters any more.'

'I will. Oh! I *do wish* you were coming too.'

Then they couldn't think of anything much to say, and both were relieved when the long, drab train came slowly into the station.

'Right. Let's find you a good seat. Would you like the rest of my sandwich? I don't really want it.'

'No, thanks.'

They lugged the suitcases onto the train, and found Louise a corner seat.

'I'm going to go now,' Stella said. 'I'm not very good at seeing people off.'

'OK.'

They hugged, and then she went. Louise watched her through the open window, but she didn't turn back. She pretended for a bit that she had just said a final farewell to the only man whom she could ever love, and from whom she was being separated because she had to go back to Devon to nurse a brother who was dying slowly of some incurable disease. Tears were soon running down her face at the sadness of this heroic sacrifice, quelled only by the appearance of an elderly couple. She quickly sneezed a lot and blew her nose, and the couple looked at each other, and then took their cases off the rack and left the compartment. Just as she was imagining telling the others in the company how to keep people out of your compartment in a train, two middle-aged ladies arrived; she started sneezing to see if it really worked, but it didn't. They looked at her with distaste, but settled down in the seats furthest from her. Now she wondered whether she would have to keep up the sneezing for the whole journey. She decided that she wouldn't, and if they asked her, she'd say that it was the station air that had given her hay fever.

The train started. It was not a fast train and stopped a lot, at stations and sometimes outside them. By four o'clock it was dark, and the blinds on the windows were drawn by an old guard and Louise began to worry that she wouldn't know which was her station, as all the names were blacked out, but the guard said that they called out the names of the stations when the train stopped at them, and that she was due at Stow Halt at ten to six. The middle-aged ladies had eaten an enormous picnic which ended with tea out of a Thermos, the sight of which made her feel very thirsty. She opened Aunt Anna's box of cinnamon cakes and tried to eat them very slowly while she read her Stanislavsky *An Actor Prepares*, slightly hoping that one of the ladies would ask her if she was interested in the theatre, so that she could talk about it. At one station a large number of sailors boarded the train. They filled up the carriage, and a lot of them stood in the corridors, smoking. Their uniforms looked so new that it was almost as though they were wearing fancy dress; their boots, which made their feet look enormous, and their large canvas bags made going to the lavatory very difficult. She was aware of a surge of muttered jokes as she edged her way through them. When she got back to her seat, she gave up Stanislavsky and read *The House of the Arrow* instead, which was exciting with a rather conceited detective called Hanaud in it. The sailors all got off at Exeter, and by the time she reached her station she was alone, and struggled to pull the window down behind the blackout blind in order that she could open the door. It was pitch dark, and very cold. She stood, shivering, a suitcase each side of her. They were too heavy for her to carry both of them at once. Then a man with a torch came towards her saying, 'Are you for Stow House?'

'Yes.'

'This your luggage? Right. You follow me.'

She got gratefully into the battered old cab, which smelled, she thought, of damp prayerbooks.

'I've two others to collect,' he said, when he had stowed her cases.

The other two turned out to be a boy called Reuben who had been a second-year student when she joined, and a girl who was new called Matilda. They sat, almost silent, crammed on the back seat for the short drive, unable to think of anything arresting enough to say to one another.

Chris Mulloney was waiting for them full of theatrical hospitality in a dark mosaic-paved hall. He wore, as usual, his shapeless tweed trousers, dirty white tennis shoes, and grey polo-necked sweater, which because of the shortness of his neck embraced quite a lot of his ears. Above it, his domed bald head was adorned by a woolly cap. His merry brown eyes gleamed beneath the tundra of his tufted eyebrows, and he had a nose that people said someone had hit a long time ago.

'My darlings!' he said. 'Welcome to Exford, my darlings!'

Louise, pressed momentarily against his rotund but rather surprisingly firm stomach, smiled uneasily. The last time she had seen him, he had reduced her to tears as he had made her repeat the same line again and again with him telling her how much worse it was each time. He had been regarded with awe in London, as he certainly got results. He had two weapons, artificial rage and real, profound sentiment, and used them both to the hilt.

'Matron,' he now said in a rather jokey voice (inverted commas round the title), 'will show you to your rooms. Matron!'

Sharp on cue, the lady appeared at the head of the stairs above them. 'This is Louise, Reuben and . . .'

'Matilda,' Matilda said.

'Matilda. Mrs Noel Carstairs.' He said it as though she was famous, or at least they should know who she was. She was a tiny little bird-like woman with peroxide blonde hair in much need of attention. She wore a sort of dressing gown of pale blue satin, the neck edged with ruffles of rather dirty lace, and held a piece of paper in her hand at which she peered hopelessly. 'Darlings,' she said – she had a foreign accent – while she searched for their names. 'Ah, yes. Louise! You are to share with Griselda. Come!'

The room was small, with two beds, two chests of drawers and one cupboard. 'In the daytime you will look on the sea. That is OK?' Her faded and wistful eyes looked out below enormous blue false eyelashes that seemed almost too heavy for her. Her face was otherwise shiny and devoid of make-up. 'Today I rest my skin,' she said. Her high-heeled slippers, which had no backs to them, clacked away across floorboards stained the colour of black treacle.

Griselda must have arrived: one of the chests had bottles and pots on it, and a photograph of two middle-aged people in tennis clothes. The bed furthest from the window was clearly Griselda's: her gas mask and a woolly dressing gown lay upon it. The room was icy cold, and there was only one light, which hung from the middle of the ceiling shrouded in an ageing parchment shade. No reading in bed, Louise thought. She felt cold and depressed. She unpacked a warmer jersey and went in search of a bathroom.

The house seemed to ramble interminably, with dark passages going off in about three directions. Eventually she saw an open door to a large bedroom that contained three girls.

'I was looking for a bathroom.'

'*The* bathroom. And nearly *the* lav. There's another rather murky one at the back of the kitchen, but the plug is bloody difficult to pull. I'll show you.'

'I'm Betty Farrell,' she said as she led the way. 'The kitchen's mildly warm because of the range. It'll be supper quite soon. I should go down there and introduce yourself.' She was small and cheerful, with freckles and a turned-up nose.

The bathroom was small: a bath that had been painted cream inside for some reason, a small rusty geyser, a kitchen sink and a lavatory with a wooden seat. The sash window would not shut properly, and someone had stuffed pieces of newspaper in the crack, but not effectively.

The kitchen was huge, seemed to be full of people, and was distinctly warmer. Chris introduced her to everyone, ending with a drab, thin girl who looked much younger than anyone else and wore her long hair in an untidy pigtail. 'And this is my invaluable daughter Poppy who keeps the whole household together.'

Poppy smiled shyly, but did not say anything. She was lifting an enormous saucepan off the range and now staggered to the sink with it, and tipped the contents into two colanders. The steamy smell of hot greens rose in the air. A long kitchen table was laid with knives and forks.

'Sit ye down, my darlings, and dinner will shortly be served. Annie? Annie, go and help your sister, do.'

An even younger girl, a child with long fair hair hanging down her back, removed three fingers from her mouth, went to the range and lifted another large saucepan full of boiled potatoes and lurched, in a heavy uneven trot, to the table. As soon as she had deposited the potatoes, she returned the fingers to her mouth. At the same time, and at the far end of the room, a thin, fair boy had been telling some story, interrupted by shrieks of laughter from several girls round him. Now, as he moved to the table, one of them said, 'But do, *do* tell the parrot story – go on, Jay!'

'Go on, while Chris is carving.'

He looked round the table. Everybody had sat down excepting Poppy who was now carting an immense grey joint of meat which she put in front of her father and Annie was collecting serving spoons with her left hand.

'The parrot story? Right: the parrot story.' He had a slightly pedantic drawling voice which seemed particularly suited to story-telling. He described an old lady's parrot, reputed to have remarkable intelligence and

372

encouraged by its proud owner to walk across a clothes line which had been slung across the room for that purpose. He became the parrot, precariously putting one claw on the line, almost losing its balance, and then proceeding with the other claw. Then as narrator he described one oldish lady giving a titter of nerves and excitement at the spectacle. He was the parrot again, looking up from the line on which he wobbled and saying in a parrot voice: 'Ludicrous, no doubt, but *fucking* diffi-cult.'

People laughed, and Louise joined sycophantically with the others, but privately she was confounded. She had never heard anyone use that word, and was unclear what it meant, but she knew that it was what her mother would have described as unspeakably rude. She glanced at Chris, but he was intent upon carving. Annie, who had now sat down, was staring at the meat, and Poppy was making gravy at the range. Then she caught Jay looking at her; he did not say anything, but he smiled, a small knowing smile, as though he knew exactly what she was thinking, and this made her blush. She bent her head over the steaming plate in front of her, so that people would think it was the food that had made her hot.

During supper, everybody talked about acting. Appar-ently, they were to start by doing some scenes from Shakespeare which they would perform to local schools, but Chris refused to discuss the casting. After supper, two people washed up, and the others drifted away. Griselda turned out to be a striking girl with blue-black hair, high cheekbones and long, narrow, slanting eyes – very fascinating, Louise thought, as they trudged upstairs together.

'What happens in the morning?'

'Oh. Breakfast. You can't have toast, because the toaster's broken, but bread and marge and some sort of jam and tea. Then we go into Exford – three miles, and most of us hitch to save bus money.'

'What's the theatre like?'

'Pretty dingy and it reeks of gas. The dressing rooms are freezing, and a lot of the seats in the auditorium are broken. Still, it'll be *our* theatre.'

'What happens to the rest of us while some of us are rehearsing?'

'Well, Lilli gives us voice lessons.'

'Who's Lilli?'

'Mrs Noel Carstairs. She's Romanian actually. She was *the* musical comedy star in Romania. Then she came here and married Noel Carstairs – you know, the impresario? – but he left her for someone far younger and she's miserable.'

'Is that why she didn't come to dinner?'

'Oh no. It was one of her raw-food days. She's always doing things to make herself healthier. She makes fearful little plates of grated carrot and cabbage and eats them in her room. She walks backwards on the sands for hours because she says it's good for the figure. She has a huge picture of the Queen of Romania in her room – all signed in a spidery hand – you can't read it. She's quite mad, actually, but awfully sweet.'

In the morning she could see that the house was on the front of a wide estuary: the tide was out; there was an expanse of glittering sand and a row of little houses on the opposite shore. It was a fine, clear day with heavy frost. She woke full of excitement to find Griselda already dressed in trousers and a jersey.

'The bathroom might still be free if you want it,' she said. 'I get up early otherwise there's a frightful queue.'

Washed and dressed in Aunt Syb's new red jersey and her – also new – dark blue corduroy trousers, she joined Griselda in the kitchen. Poppy was there, preparing a breakfast tray for her father. The kitchen was not very warm: 'The range was nearly out,' Poppy said apologetically, 'and could I have your ration book?'

A large black cat sat in the middle of the kitchen table watching Annie cut scraps of last night's joint and put them in a saucer. Griselda and Louise ate bread and marge and jam while they waited for the big black kettle to boil.

'I'll take you in today on the bus,' Griselda offered. 'Then you'll know your way around.'

'How long have you been here?'

'Less than a week. I came early because our house was bombed and my mother didn't want me staying in Bristol.'

This took her aback, as she realised that since leaving home, she had not thought about the war at *all*, that nobody had mentioned it the previous evening, and that things like ration books and gas masks had become so much a part of life that she had almost forgotten the reasons for them.

'I'm sorry,' she said. 'It must have been awful for you.'

Griselda shrugged. 'I simply hate talking about the war,' she said, 'don't you?'

The rest of the day was wildly exciting. The condition of the theatre didn't matter to Louise at all. It was a *theatre*, with a dark red curtain trimmed with dirty yellow braid. Stepping onto the dusty stage for the first time was a delight – an arrival, the beginning of her career. The odours of gas, old flats and the musty, cold, sweaty smell of the battered old seats in the auditorium thrilled her; the dressing rooms with their concrete floors, faint odour of old greasepaint and rows of bare electric light bulbs round the spotted mirrors were all that she could wish for. When they were ranged on hard wooden chairs on the stage lit by working lights and the curtain was up and they were given their scenes to rehearse and the casting was announced, she felt dizzy with joy. She was to play Katherina in the first courting scene from *The Taming of the Shrew*, and also Anne in two scenes from *Richard of Bordeaux*. The only sadness was that as the company consisted of ten girls and only four boys, the girls were having to double, which meant that they would only play every other performance, while the fortunate boys were not only in nearly every scene but would get to play all the time. Griselda was cast as Lady Macbeth, to do the murder scene with Roy, who from the read-through was easily, Louise thought, the best actor there. He was also doing Petruchio with her. She had Jay to play opposite her as Richard.

At lunch-time, they went to a café facing the river, and she shared a fried egg and chips with Griselda – dividing the egg with scrupulous care and counting the chips. They were both very hungry.

∞ ∞ ∞

In the weeks that followed she learned much – and not only about acting. Her letters home were carefully considered: she was terrified of being taken away if she sent any information that might alarm them. When she wrote asking for an additional allowance for bus fares and lunches, she did not, for example, explain that otherwise the nightly joint, boiled greens and potatoes (the only thing that Poppy knew how to cook) was the one meal of the day (they frequently went without breakfast, as the range constantly went out which meant no water could be boiled, and the marge and jam got used up before rations enabled Poppy to buy any more). She also did not mention that most mornings they hitch-hiked into Exford to save the bus fare (and buy cigarettes); and she particularly withheld the method some of them employed – that of lying down in the middle of the road and pretending to have fainted or to be feeling ill which invariably procured a lift. She said that they all had very interesting conversations after supper in the evenings, reciting poetry aloud, and had they heard of Dylan Thomas and T. S. Eliot who were both simply marvellous poets. She did not mention someone's birthday party when there was a competition for who could wear least, and that she had won it with two pieces of stamp edge and a powder puff. She did not, of course, mention the swearing that was immensely fashionable: people said fuck nearly all the time. She did not say that one night they got drunk on a wicked yellow-green sticky drink called Strega which some Dutch people who lived on a boat in the estuary gave them. She did not mention the rather awful weeks when Annie was discovered to have hair that was literally stiff with louse eggs, and that the whole company by then had caught them. Exford ran out of fine-tooth combs, and they had to keep washing their hair at the sink with frightful smelling stuff. She did not say that 'Matron' was really a little tired old actress with no domestic or nursing skills at all, and that

nobody present had ever been one, and only one person knew one, so I didn't learn much. People being virgins is rather frowned upon – I *think* – at least it is by the oldest girl here who is called Ernestine and is supposed to be twenty-five, but she looks miles older. I am learning a lot about life as well as acting. A very interesting actor here, called Jay Coren, is amazed at how little I've read, and he gave me a novel by Ernest Hemingway who he says is the greatest novelist in the world. It is called *A Farewell to Arms* and is nearly all about sex – but the people are in love – and she has a baby and she dies. You must read it. Something amazing. Chris has hired the most wonderful costumes for us for the Shakespeare, etc. I have the actual dress that Gwen Ffrangcon-Davies wore for *Richard of Bordeaux* when she played with Gielgud! It is yellow with a marvellous headdress. And for Katherina I have a terrific red velvet dress embroidered with pearls. It is awfully hot, though, and it smells rather. We get *free* seats for the cinema which fortunately is almost next to the theatre so one can nip in and see a bit of film when not wanted for rehearsals. I had to go to *The Private Lives of Henry VIII* nine times to see all of the film. But rather grand, don't you think?

Lilli gives us voice lessons; we each get two a week. Also we spend quite a lot of time cueing each other. The days go very fast, and our first night is next week! I do so *wish* you could come to it. But think of me at eight o'clock next Friday – we start with *The Shrew*. Poor Roy has awful boils on his neck, and when he tried on his ruff it made them much worse . . .

She thought for a bit. It was much easier to write to Stella than to her mother, but she'd used up all her news. Oh!

> You needn't worry about me and Michael Hadleigh. He hasn't written, so I should think he's forgotten all about me.

And the very next day she got a letter from him forwarded from home. She knew it must be he, because the envelope had 'Received from HM Ships' where a stamp would have been. She took it into the broken-down old greenhouse in the back garden of Stow House so that she could read it in comfortable privacy.

> Darling Louise,
> I had quite decided *not* to write to you because I was afraid you might not want me to, but I couldn't go through with it. But if you don't want me to write, then just drop me a line and say so, but I hope you won't feel that. It's lateish at night and I am Officer of the Day and I keep getting interrupted to go on 'rounds' and do various other routine jobs, and as I'm the only officer in the ship at the moment I don't get much peace.
> This is an awfully difficult letter to write. Inhibitions . . . the censor, and also because it is the first letter I've written to you. But all these weeks when we've been at sea, I've kept seeing you sitting with such a beautiful dignity in the nightclub when the bomb fell – and you so young! I think I am a little afraid of your youth, as well. Oh, Louise, whatever you do, don't take me seriously, because it would

need only that to make me take myself seriously, and that would be laughable.

But we did have fun that weekend, didn't we? You were marvellous in the charades – Mummy was *most* impressed. Those drawings I did of you don't do you justice. But I've got one with me now, and it does at least serve to *remind* me of small, important things, like the way your mouth turns up at the corners, and the way your eyebrows tilt suddenly in the middle – not triangular, but interestingly angled – no, that's wrong, I mean that they are more like gentle little pitched roofs than the usual curve.

I wonder whether your repertory company is going to happen. Whether it does or not, I have no doubt that you will be a tremendous actress. And if you refuse to know me, in later years, I shall haunt the West End theatre where you will be playing the lead, and tell people that I knew you when you were young . . . Darling Louise, I've got to go and sort out a mooring line that seems to have come adrift. Goodnight.

Yours ever, Mike

She read it very quickly – gulped it – and then again very slowly. My first love letter, she thought, and then wondered if indeed it could be said to be that. She examined it again, trying to be calm. He said 'Darling Louise' but, then, people here called each other darling all the time, even when they were saying quite catty things – it didn't mean a thing. But then the bit about not taking him seriously – that might be because he didn't *want* her to take him seriously – but the bits about her face, her beautiful dignity and her mouth and eyebrows . . . Well, you could like things about a person without being in love with them, and he *was* terrifically sophisticated and old and must have met hundreds of girls. He was flattering her but nobody else had ever done that. One had to admit that it was exciting; she tried to say this aloud and very calmly, but her hand, holding the letter, was trembling. It was rather – *adult* (a word much in use at Stow House) to get a letter like that. She read it carefully once more, and then folded it up and returned it to its envelope. She would keep it in her bag in case she wanted to read it again.

The dress rehearsal on Thursday went on from ten in the morning until half past eleven in the evening. This was partly because everything had to be done twice, so that all the girls went through it. Chris sent some of them to get fish and chips for everybody in the evening, and Lilli made quarts of tea in one of the dressing rooms. Louise felt a complete flop. She did not actually forget her lines, but was flat, whereas Roy preserved a uniform, it seemed to her, very professional standard. Chris, and a lady who had mysteriously appeared a few days previously, sat in the stalls, and she took his notes on each scene. The notes devastated her. 'You're supposed to be sexually attracted to the man – right from the start,' he stormed, 'and you might as well be talking to the postman who'd delivered your letters late. Come *on*, girl, you know what I'm talking about.' The trouble was that she didn't, really. She had not the least idea how one behaved towards a stranger to whom one was sexually attracted, but she would have died rather than admit *that*. She smiled with complicit weakness, and, self-conscious and wooden, went through it all again. After it, he gave her the practical notes: when she was moving late on lines, when she had lost pace on the first waspish exchange by not picking up her cues fast enough, the point at which she upstaged Roy during a speech, 'You can't expect the attention of the audience to be on you *all* the time,' and so on. Afterwards in the dressing room, as she was getting out of the red velvet dress, she started crying, and people were very nice to her: Lilli said she must not spoil her make-up, and the other Katherina, Jane Mayhew, fetched her yet another cup of tea, before she climbed into the dress to do her scene. Then she was alone for a few minutes. She mopped her eyes carefully, and stared into the brilliantly lit mirror. Perhaps I'm no good after all, she thought. One of the things Chris had said to her was that she moved clumsily: what Mummy kept saying. Of course it was true. Not much 'beautiful dignity' about her now! she thought, looking at her smudged eyes and the tracks her tears had made in carefully applied five and nine. Her black tin box of make-up – her most treasured possession – sat before her, hardly used. It looked far too new. Some of the others had deliberately made theirs look dirty and much used, but she had thought this cheating; this would be her precious box all of her life and she wanted its dilapidation to be genuine.

There was a knock on the door: it was Jay, with a packet of cigarettes.

'He did put you through it,' he said, seating himself on the dressing table beside her. 'That must mean he thinks you're good.'

'What on earth makes you say that?'

'I've noticed. With some people, he just tells them when they've got a line wrong – the words, I mean – and then tells them it was jolly good.'

'Perhaps they were.'

'Nope.'

'Perhaps *he* thought they were.'

He shook his head. 'He's a bloody fool in many ways, but he doesn't get that sort of thing wrong. What do you think of his girlfriend?'

'Is she?'

'You bet. She's living in Exford. For the moment. My bet is that she'll move in quite soon. Under some pretext like helping the poor benighted Poppy.' He looked at her. 'Are you cold? You're shivering.' Suddenly he leaned forward, and put his hand under the old silky kimono her mother had let her have, felt for and found her breast. 'Just as big as my hand,' he said with surprising gentleness. When he kissed her mouth, a lock of his yellow hair fell forward and tickled her neck.

'There.' He straightened up; he was smiling at her in a watchful sort of way. 'I rather go for you,' he said. 'Now I must don my fucking white tights.'

He had left the cigarettes. On the packet, he had written, 'For Anne of Bohemia' and in brackets underneath '(Mrs Queenie Plantagenet)'.

She felt suddenly much better. Then Lilli came back and showed her how to use her brand new hot black on her eyelashes.

When she went out into the auditorium to watch Jane and Roy do the *Shrew* scene, she looked covertly at Chris's girlfriend. She was quite old, with long dark hair cut in a fringe and a muffler round her neck. In the dark, that was all she could notice. She turned her attention to the acting. Jane was small and red-haired with a surprisingly powerful voice and an air of great assurance. The unhappiness that Louise felt lay beneath Katherina's shrewishness was not apparent. She was almost *pretending* to be bad-tempered and she was making up to Roy like anything. Roy seemed to her to give exactly the same performance. It had not shifted at all since the read-through. She felt that there must be something wrong in this, but could not think what. She noticed at the end that Chris gave Jane only perfunctory notes, and none to Roy at all, and wondered whether Jay had been right. He seemed much *older* than the others and she decided that she liked older men. I can say that now, she thought, because I know two of them. His kissing her, his hand on her breast, had seemed at the time to happen so fleetingly that it had felt unreal; there had been no warning of it and no conclusion, but now it touched her – there was something light and daring but unmomentous about it that was entirely new to her.

She came to from this reverie to hear Chris announcing a ten-minute break before they started on *Macbeth*.

'Griselda has been sick,' someone said as she went back to the dressing room to find the poor girl hunched over a bucket, her face, under her pallid Lady Macbeth make-up, the colour of a duck's egg. 'I can't remember my lines!' she moaned. 'I start, and then I just peter out. Oh, God! It's no good. I can't go on. Helen will have to do it instead.'

In the end they sent for Chris who marched in saying, 'So you've been throwing up, have you? That's a good thing. You've sicked up your nerves, and now you'll be ready to go. Just say your opening lines to me and then we'll carry on.' He was squatting in front of her, and now took both her hands. 'Now. Screw your courage to the sticking point, girl, and you'll not fail.'

She stared at him, and then started falteringly, ' "They met me in the day of my success—"'

'You see?' he interrupted her. 'You know it. *I* know you know it, and *you* know you know it. You can take the letter quite slowly – I don't suppose Macbeth's handwriting was all that good.'

She was smiling at him now. He rose to his feet, still holding one of her hands, and led her out of the dressing room.

'I thought you were marvellous!' Louise exclaimed later as they sat with a large carton of Trex between them carefully smoothing it over their unnatural complexions. (It was the smart thing to use Trex: somebody had been round to rather a well-known actress's dressing room in a London theatre and that was what *she* had been using, so they looked down on the poor novices who painstakingly bought cold cream.)

'So were you. Especially Anne. You play far better with Jay than Helen did.'

'What do you think of Jay?' Louise asked very casually.

'Well, he's very intelligent and all that, but he's got a rather cruel mouth, don't you think?'

Privately, Louise thought that this sounded a bit silly: what on earth was a cruel mouth? What was different about one from a kind mouth? But Griselda went on: 'You know. It's sort of rather large, and curving, but *hard*. And he's got cold eyes as well. I don't think I'd trust him.'

There she went again. 'Cold eyes.' Eyes, as they had been told, could change utterly, depending upon what the person was feeling. In the theatre, your eyes were your most important feature. Hers were sore now from her efforts to remove the hot black sticking in blobs to her eyelashes. She would have to ask Lilli about how to get it off.

'He's very good as Richard,' Griselda said. 'And he tells wonderful stories. God, I'm hungry! I could eat absolutely anything!'

'Will there be anything when we get back?'

'I don't know.'

They had to share three cabs home because it was so late. Poppy had left two plates of thick sandwiches filled with a choice of cheese and bloater paste, but Tsar Alexander had interfered with the latter and nobody wanted the stodgy remnants he had left.

'Annie should have taken him up to bed,' Chris said; he was ravenous.

'She did, but I'm afraid he came down again. It's my fault, I should have left them in the larder, but I was afraid you might be even later and I'd be in bed and you wouldn't see them or know they were there.'

'You could have left a note, Poppy. Never mind, girl. No tears, please – I've had enough of emotion for the day. Bring me up a little something in bed, there's an angel.'

In the end, most of them decided that they were more exhausted than hungry and dispersed, leaving Poppy trailing round the kitchen with a tin of corned beef and some water biscuits. 'I can't use the bread or there won't be enough for breakfast.' She looked as tired as they did.

'She doesn't have a very nice life,' Louise said while they were undressing quickly because of the cold.

'No, and it's rather unfair because she wants to be an actress too.'

'Does she really? She doesn't look as though she could act.'

'Well, it's an acting family. Her mother was apparently awfully good.'

'What happened to her?'

'She died in a car accident some time ago. Not sure when. Lilli told me when she gave me a manicure.' Griselda was trying not to bite her nails because Lilli, who was shocked by this, had said that she must learn to care for them.

'Perhaps I ought to help her. I've been taught cooking.'

'I shouldn't, if I was you. If you let them know you can, Chris'll have you doing it all the time.'

This prospect was so awful that Louise resolved on selfish silence.

The day of the first night everybody slept late and they had an indeterminate meal in the middle of the day. In the afternoon, Louise got back into bed – the warmest place – and settled down to write her letter to Michael.

'Dear Mike – Darling Mike – dear Mike,' she began, and then stopped. 'Dear Mike' looked cold, but on the other hand 'Darling Mike' looked copy-cattish, for certainly she would never have dreamed of calling him darling at all if he had not done so first. In the end, she took a fresh piece of paper and left that part of it blank to be put in at the end when she could see what sort of letter it turned out to be. 'Thank you for your letter. It was sent on from home because the repertory company *has* happened; in fact, tonight is our first First Night and we are all very nervous. We are doing scenes from Shakespeare and two scenes from a play by Gordon Daviot who is actually a woman.' She went on in that vein, telling him about the dress rehearsal and how bad she felt she'd been, but ending 'Anyway, if one has wanted to do something all one's life and now at long last is doing it what more can one want? We live in a rather cold, bare house with not much to eat, but none of us minds because everybody is totally *dedicated* to their art and if you are that, material things are of no account, don't you think?' (She thought that bit was rather good, but was afraid that he might find all the theatre part a bit dull.) 'Yes, it was fun at the weekend. I loved our ride and the charades and nobody has ever drawn me before. And your mother was very kind,' she wrote carefully, because she couldn't think of anything else to call her. 'I did write her a Collins – that's what we call thank you letters for visits in our family because of Mr Collins.' Then she wondered if he had read *Pride and Prejudice* and added 'Austen' in brackets.

Then she put, 'But of course you would know all that' so that he wouldn't be hurt at her thinking he didn't know things. Then she read the letter through. It seemed to her very dull. 'I'm afraid this isn't a very interesting letter. I see what you mean about writing to somebody for the first time. You don't quite know how well you know them on paper.

'I can't really imagine life in a battleship. Uncle Rupert used to feel seasick for the first two days. It must be awful to have to fight feeling seasick, but I remember my governess saying that Nelson often felt like that, although I cannot imagine why that should be a comfort to you. But I hope it's not too bad. Anyway, love from Louise.' Then she thought again and wrote underneath: 'P.S. I wasn't really brave when the bomb fell. I just sat still because I didn't know what else to do. Of course I'm glad you like my appearance.' Then she put 'Dear Mike'. The Mike made 'dear' OK, she thought. She wrote his name, and the name of his ship, c/o GPO. It seemed a funny address, but that is what he had put on the paper, so it must be all right.

The First Night came – and went. Stella sent her a telegram which was lovely of her, because all the others got telegrams from their family except for her. 'The house' as she had learned to call it, was only half full, but that didn't matter to her; they were a real live audience who had paid to come, and that was the point. Jay kissed her again in the wings while she was waiting to go on. 'There, my honey,' he said, 'a stirrup cup of affection or lust – take your choice.' Roy was beautifully reliable and some of the time she pretended he was Jay which made him feel more interesting. She remembered what she'd thought about Jane's performance as Katherina, and put the sadness in a bit. It was lovely curtsying in the sweeping red velvet when she took her curtain call. Afterwards Chris came round and gave her a smacking kiss on each cheek and pressed her to his hard, round tummy and said, 'That's my girl! You did well, Louise. You'll do better, but you did well.'

They all went home on the last bus, and then sat round the kitchen table going over all the details of their performances, and finally fell into their beds. The next morning, Louise found brownish greasepaint on her pillow which made her wonder whether Trex was the best thing.

They played four evenings and four matinées to schools – the latter were rather a noisy audience, but at least they filled up the house – whereas the evenings, for the general public, were not very well attended. The local paper reviewed the scenes, and every single person in them was mentioned. The piece was not signed, and although it was clear that Chris knew who had written it, he refused to tell them anything except that it had not been him. Still, to read 'Louise Cazalet gave us two well-contrasted performances as Katherina and Anne' was rather exciting. She bought two copies, one to send home and one to keep in a scrapbook together with the programme.

As soon as the Shakespeare week was over, the next two plays were announced by Chris. They were to do *Hay Fever* and *Night Must Fall*. The reason that he announced both plays was that even with the girls doubling on the female parts there were not enough parts for all of them to be in both plays. Louise, to her disappointment, was cast as Sorrel in *Hay Fever*, the ingénue and, she thought, the dullest part, and not cast at all in *Night Must Fall. Hay Fever* was to be performed at Christmas and, after it, Chris said that she might go home for a couple of weeks if she liked. She did not want to go, had a fear that they might not let her come back if she did. But then she got another letter from Mike – his third – saying that he was getting a week's leave while his ship was undergoing a refit and was there the slightest possibility that she could spend at least some of it with him? If not, he would try to get down for a night to Devon to see her.

Because communications are so difficult [he wrote], I am brazenly proposing that you should meet me at Markham Square on Friday, 10 January. I have looked up trains from Exford, and find that you could arrive with luck about three. If you can't make it, write to me, and then when I get to London, I'll ring you up to see whether any other plan is possible. Do try, darling little Louise – I so long to see you. You would be the best antidote to my present life that I can think of. The High Seas are extraordinarily *wet*; I feel amazingly privileged when at last there is time to fall upon my

bunk, and only have the condensation dripping
quietly onto my nose. However, we make the odd
killing . . . No more of that. One of my jobs is to
censor the men's letters, so I am becoming quite an
authority on domestic and marital situations. I
sometimes wonder whether you have fallen madly in
love with some handsome young actor, and cannot
help hoping that you haven't . . .

She wrote back saying that she would come to Markham Square on that Friday and that she could be away
for a week. The bit about his wondering whether she
was in love she did not answer, because she didn't know
what she felt – either about him, or about Jay, who had
taken to coming into their room when Griselda was not
there, lying on the bed beside her and reading poetry to
her. She enjoyed this and when the poetry subsided into
his kissing her and stroking and kissing her breasts she
discovered a sort of enjoyment in that too, but not of the
kind that she had expected. She had thought that by the
time somebody kissed you, you were certainly, surely,
in love with them. But the blissful rhapsody that she
had so often read about escaped her. She liked Jay – was
a little afraid of him, of his soft, satirical voice, his
sophisticated vocabulary, his pale, appraising eyes. But
he could be very gentle with her, and when she was not
afraid, the bottom of her spine seemed to unfurl as
though it was not rigid at all; it seemed to have small,
hitherto unknown fronds attached to it. But her body did
not seem to connect with any of the rest of her. She
could shut her eyes and Jay became anybody, any fingers, hands, mouth. 'Do you love me, then?' she asked
one evening.

There was a pause. She was lying on her back, and he propped himself on his elbows to look down on her. 'That, my dear girl, is a ridiculous question. How would you like it if I asked you that?'

'I shouldn't mind.'

'No,' he said, 'you wouldn't. At least you don't pretend. You're not full of all that romantic sentimental nonsense. I find you attractive, which I expect you've noticed by now. If you weren't such a confirmed and utter little virgin I'd have you.'

'*Have* me?'

'Fuck you. But I have a feeling,' he added after waiting for a reply, 'that this would either horrify you, or produce a sonorous response that wouldn't suit me. So I don't try.' He picked up Geoffrey Grigson's *New Verse* and continued to read:

> *Annie MacDougall went to milk, caught her feet in the*
> *   heather,*
> *Woke to hear a dance record playing of Old Vienna.*
> *It's no go your maidenheads, it's no go your culture,*
> *All we want is a Dunlop tyre and the devil mend the*
> *   puncture.*

and so on until the last verse:

> *It's no go, my honey love, it's no go, my poppet,*
> *Work your hands from day to day, the wind will blow*
> *   the profit.*
> *The glass is falling hour by hour, the glass will fall for*
> *   ever,*
> *But if you break the bloody glass, you won't hold up*
> *   the weather.*

393

Without saying anything, he riffled through the book and went on:

> *I have a handsome profile*
> *I've been to a great public school*
> *I've a little money invested*
> *Then why do I feel such a fool*
> *As if I owned a world that had had its day?*
>
> *You certainly have good reason*
> *For feeling as you do*
> *No wonder you are anxious*
> *Because it's perfectly true*
> *You own a world that has had its day.*

He shut the book and looked at her again.

'You see? If you want to know what's going *on* in the world, read the contemporary poets. *They* know.'

'Were those poems by the same person?'

'No. The first was by Louis MacNeice, and the second by W. H. Auden. Both people you should have heard of, but I don't suppose you have.'

She shook her head, so disconsolately that he stroked it.

'Cheer up. Here's something to cheer you up.'

Then he read in a voice rather like the one he had used for the parrot story:

> *Miss Twye was soaping her breasts in the bath*
> *When behind her she heard a meaning laugh*
> *And to her amazement she discovered*
> *A wicked man in the bathroom cupboard.*

'Do *you* soap your pretty breasts in the bath? Your pretty dukkys, as Henry VIII used to call them?'

'It wouldn't matter if I did,' she said. 'There isn't room in this bathroom for a cupboard.' The things that he knew fascinated her. 'I wish I knew more,' she said. 'The world seems to be full of things I don't know.'

'I'll make you a list of poets if you like. That would make a respectable start.'

He did. But sometimes she didn't see him alone for days. This was partly because he spent time with Ernestine, the oldest girl there, whom none of the other girls liked but whom everyone was slightly afraid of. Ernestine had a room to herself on the ground floor. It had a fireplace in which she had a coal fire which meant she had the only warm room. She possessed a wardrobe of glamorous clothes, and painted her long fingernails with white varnish. She was small, with beautiful legs and a good figure, but her face looked much older than the twenty-five that she claimed to be. She wore her long dark brown hair in a kind of sausage fringe across her forehead, and the rest of it hanging down her back, and her long thin mouth was always painted with a cyclamen lipstick. She had a loud, grating voice which was largely used to jeer at things: society, the class system, the English – she said she was half French – the rich, anybody whose work did not involve the arts, virginity which she described variously as prissy and craven. She had lived in Chelsea before, and said it was the only civilised haven in the great inhibited, class-ridden tract that made up the rest of London. She had very little talent, but was convinced of her potential greatness. Chris allowed her a lot of leeway; some people thought he actually sucked up to her, and certainly he gave her privileges, like the room, which the others did not get. She was always talking about her lovers – notably one Torsten, a Norwegian, whom she said was the best she had ever had. People listened politely when they had to, chiefly at meals, but avoided her when possible. It was thought that she was paying more than anyone else to be there, and that Chris needed the money. She had clearly decided that Jay was the only man there worth her attention, and made it plain to Louise that she resented her. Somehow she had got wind of the letters from HM Ships – being on the ground floor she could always go through the letters before anyone else – and sneered a good deal at Louise about her sailor man. 'They say all the nice girls love a sailor, but all I can say is that I'm not a nice girl, thank God. Louise must be a *very* nice girl, don't you think?' this to Jay.

'Absolutely charming,' he answered promptly with such a straight face that Louise felt he was on her side.

The evening before Louise was to go, Ernestine suddenly invited her to her room. She had learned that Louise was going away for a week. 'I might have something for you.'

Unable to think of any decent way of getting out of this, Louise joined her after the customary roast meat and cabbage.

Ernestine offered her one of her black Balkan Sobranies and a glass of wine. Louise was seated on the end of her orange divan, while Ernestine found glasses and a corkscrew.

'Are you going home to your family?' she asked, when she had poured a glass and handed it over.

'No.' Louise found it difficult to lie, and also a part of her wanted to assert herself before Ernestine who thought the rest of them such a pack of children. 'As a matter of fact, I'm going to see my sailor, as you call him. He's got a week's leave and it happens to fit in.'

'Good for *you*!' She seemed genuinely admiring. 'I rather thought that that might be what you were up to.' She raised her glass. 'Here's to you both!' When she wasn't jeering, her husky low voice was rather pleasant. 'He's not a sailor all the time, is he?'

'Oh no. He's a painter.'

'An art student. Oh my!'

'Not a student. A proper painter. He does portraits.'

'What's his name?'

'Michael Hadleigh.'

'Michael *Hadleigh*? So you have a *famous* lover!'

'He's not exactly my *lover*.' She felt herself beginning to blush and took a large swig of the wine. 'I mean, I just *know* him – that's all.'

Ernestine leaned towards her and filled up her glass. 'Well, it sounds as though he wants to know *you* better. You don't expect to spend a week with him holding hands, do you?'

'N-no.' That sounded idiotic to her. 'Of course not.'

'Well, then, my dear, perhaps you need a little advice.' She got up and went to a chest of drawers, returning with what looked like a tube of toothpaste. 'A precaution,' she said, handing it to her.

Louise looked at it. 'Volpar Gel,' she read. 'What's it for?'

Ernestine rolled her eyes. 'My God! I can't *believe* it! To stop you getting pregnant, you poor little innocent. Of course, later on, you'll be needing a Dutch cap.'

Louise had a sudden vision of herself wearing one of those little white caps with stiff wings on them that occurred in Dutch pictures, and spooning jelly straight from the tube into her mouth. It seemed fantastic and silly and how on earth it would stop one having a baby she couldn't imagine. She finished her second glass of wine while she considered this.

'I am certainly not thinking of having a baby,' she said. She said it as though she had considered the matter and decided – calmly, of course – against. I should like to go now, she thought, but Ernestine, as though she had divined this, lit two cigarettes and handed her one. The gold tip was smudged with cyclamen lipstick, and Louise did not want it, but she felt it would be rude to refuse.

'Of course you aren't. I'm only trying to help. I don't suppose "Mummy" has told you much, has she? Anyway, you just go to any chemist and ask for a tube, and you'll get it. The other thing I wondered was whether you would like to borrow some less schoolgirly underwear. Torsten gave me a couple of nightdresses that he said gave him a kick. I'll show you.'

One was black chiffon, and the other of fuchsia-coloured satin trimmed with black lace.

She really meant to be kind, Louise thought, and decided that the easiest thing to do would be to accept one of them. She need never wear it, and Ernestine wouldn't know.

'It's awfully kind of you—' she began.

'Balls! Always come to Auntie Ernestine when you want any advice about sex. You'd better take the tube as well. I don't see you getting up the nerve to go into a chemist to ask for it.'

Soon after this Louise made her escape. She felt uncomfortably that although she didn't really like Ernestine much, she seemed to have meant well. She had also opened up vistas of what the week before her might hold that made her almost – but not quite – wish that she had never agreed to it.

∞ ∞ ∞

The Week . . . It seemed wonderfully long – the opposite of what she had imagined a marvellous time to be. She had thought that when she was really enjoying herself the time would go in a flash, but these seven days spun themselves out, so that after about two of them, she felt as though she had been living like that for years. The first day she felt very nervous. He was wearing his uniform as he had been the first night that she had met him. He put his arms round her and gave her a hug, kissing her face in a brotherly manner. He had made plans. They were to go to a revue, *New Faces*, at the Comedy Theatre. 'I got seats for the early performance,' he said, 'so that we can have some supper before we drive down to Hatton. I know it's not highbrow enough for you, but it's supposed to be awfully good. Is that all right?'

She said it sounded lovely.

'There's plenty of time for you to change and have a bath.' He led her upstairs; the house seemed very quiet.

'The servants are all in Wiltshire,' he said. 'My stepfather is going to shut the house and live in his club, or take a small service flat. He doesn't want Mummy to be in London.'

'Your stepfather?'

'Yes. Did you think he was my father?'

'I did. But nobody said his name. I mean, the servants called him Sir Peter, and you and your mother called him Peter, so how could I know?'

'You couldn't. Don't look so anxious. My father died in the last war. I can hardly remember him.' He showed her to the spare room and the bathroom a few steps down on a half landing. 'I'm going to have a bath too. My quarters are up top. Don't be long, I don't want to waste you.'

The revue was wonderful; the most memorable bit, she thought, was the lovely Judy Campbell singing 'A Nightingale Sang In Berkeley Square'.

Afterwards, he took her to Prunier's and she had her first oysters. Then he told her more about his father. 'He was a bit of a hero, so I feel I have a lot to live up to.'

She fell asleep in the car driving to the country, and he woke her by gently ruffling her hair. At the door of her bedroom, he kissed her again in the same way that he had greeted her in London, and said, 'Sleep well. See you at breakfast.'

It wasn't at all how Ernestine had envisaged.

One or two curious things happened during the week. His mother, Zee, had announced that Rowena was coming to luncheon the following day. Michael had seemed upset by this.

'Oh, Mummy! Why?'

'Darling, she wanted so much to see you on your leave. I hadn't the heart to refuse her.'

Rowena turned out to be the beautiful girl in the painting. She arrived impeccably dressed as a country lady: tweed skirt, cashmere to match, well-polished shoes, and a velveteen jacket that suited the ensemble. Louise, in trousers and a Viyella shirt, felt uncouth beside her. Her natural pale blonde hair hung in a simple bob, she wore no make-up, and her face was colourless, so that her large, wide-apart pale eyes dominated it. She looked unhappy. Lunch was rather a tense affair; Zee made

Michael talk about his ship – which, Louise noticed, he seemed very much to enjoy. His mother seemed to know a great deal about his naval life: when he mentioned Oerlikon guns, she immediately knew what they were. She and Rowena sat more or less in silence throughout the meal. After it, Zee suggested that Michael should show Rowena the stables, and settled herself with Louise in the library.

'Poor little Rowena,' she said as she matched some wool. 'She is *so* in love with Michael. But really, it simply isn't *on*.' She looked up from her sewing at Louise, silent and pinned to the spot. 'But I think she understands that now. Michael is a great breaker of hearts. I do hope you won't let him break yours.'

After about an hour, they returned. Louise noticed that Rowena had been crying. She thanked Zee for the lunch, and said that she must be going.

'I'm sure that Michael will see you to your car.'

As they left the room, after polite goodbyes, Louise caught Zee observing her. She smiled, and Louise found herself unable to return it.

Later, when they were up in the studio, and Michael was pinning paper to his board to make another drawing, she said, 'The portrait you did of Rowena is awfully good.'

'Yes,' he answered absently, 'one of my better ones. Now, you sit in that chair – there.' He drew up a small, low stool and sat, so that he was slightly below her. 'Now, turn your head a little to the right, and look at me. A little more – more, now stop. That's perfect. Sorry. Relax, I've got to sharpen my pencil.'

But she felt she couldn't leave it there. 'Your mother said that she was very much in love with you.'

'I'm afraid she is. Poor little Rowena. We did have a bit of a fling. She's perfectly lovely, of course, and she has a remarkably sweet nature, but, as Mummy said, she isn't the brightest. I'm afraid I should have got fearfully *bored*.'

'You mean, if you'd married her?'

'If I'd married her, yes.' He was sharpening the pencil with a penknife very carefully, scraping the lead to a point. Then he said, 'She realised when she saw you. So you don't have to be jealous.'

'I'm not jealous!' She really meant it, she wasn't; she was shocked. She imagined Rowena preserving her dignity in the face of what seemed to her almost vulgar humiliation, getting into her car and driving far enough down the drive before she broke down . . .

'Darling Louise! You are looking quite fierce. But Mummy was quite right. It was high time I told her, and she said she knew the moment she walked into the room and saw you. Now, let's get you back into position. Head to the right, no, that's too far, that's better. That's perfect.'

Somehow or other, he soothed and charmed her into not thinking any more about it at the time, and indeed as the week continued, found herself so basking in the general approval that emanated from his mother and stepfather that she did not think about it at all. She was treated as though she was a precocious little genius, one of *them* – privileged, gifted, lucky in every imaginable way – and because of her youth, petted, admired, encouraged to entertain. Sir Peter shared her passion for Shakespeare and this time easily persuaded her to play some of the great set pieces to him: Viola, Juliet, Queen Katherine from Henry VIII and Ophelia, and talked to her about the plays, taking her opinions seriously and with a courteous approval. 'Don't you think that Katherine and Wolsey

were the only two parts he wrote of that play?' Why did
she think that? Because their parts were written in iambic
pentameter, whereas Henry and the others were not, and
so on. When they played acting games in the evening, she
was sufficiently encouraged by their admiration to shine,
discovered, in fact, her talent for comedy. At home,
nobody had been anything like so interested in what she
did and who she was and these benign expectations went
to her head. They were compounded also by the fact that
the family seemed to consort so much with the great and
famous. There seemed to be nobody whom they did not
know, and usually intimately. She noticed this most with
Zee, as she now confidently called her. It was impossible
to mention a politician, a playwright, a conductor whom
she had not known or knew now. The visitor's book was
full of their names, together with actors, musicians, writ-
ers, painters and dancers of renown. They were predom-
inantly men. Books in the library were inscribed by their
authors in varying tones of homage and affection to her,
and Louise concluded that someone who had clearly been
– and still was – so much loved must be a very wonderful
and unusual person. One day at tea-time a telegram
arrived for her, and Louise noticed that at once Peter, as
she now called him, moved across the room to be near
her while she opened it. She read it and handed it to him
with a smile: 'Winston,' she said. 'I sent *him* one telling
him how well I thought he was doing.'

It was all a far cry from Stow House – or even from
her own family. They asked her about her family and she
described them as interestingly as she could: her mother
dancing with the Ballets Russes, her father's distinguished
war record, the way they all lived together under her
grandfather's patriarchal roof. On Friday, her mother

rang up, and she went to the small study called the telephone room.

'I had no idea that you were not at Stow House,' her mother began; she sounded very displeased.

'Well, they didn't want me for a week, and Michael asked me to stay here as he had a week's leave.'

'You should have rung to tell me your plans. You know that perfectly well.'

'Sorry, Mummy. I would have if I'd been going anywhere new. It's only a week, anyway.'

'That isn't the point. Daddy had a couple of days off, and he wanted us to go down to Devon to see you. We might have gone all that way, and then found that you were not there. We very nearly did, as a matter of fact. Daddy wanted it to be a surprise.'

'Gosh! I *am* sorry. Well, I'm not *in* the play they're doing at the moment, and I honestly didn't think about you coming or anything.'

'You are *with* the family, aren't you?'

'Oh, yes. They're terribly kind to me. Michael's mother used to go to parties with Diaghilev and people like that. She says she must have seen you dance.'

'Really? Well, I hope you are not being a nuisance. And having a nice time.' she added doubtfully, as though the two things were unlikely to go together.

'Lovely. I've got to go back to Stow on Monday. Will you be able to come to my next play?'

'I doubt it. Your father hardly ever gets a weekend off. Ring me up when you get back. Please don't forget to do that.'

She said she wouldn't. She asked after her grandmother, and was told that she was not very well. It was a relief when Villy said she must ring off now as it was a long-distance call. It had not felt like a very friendly conversation.

She discovered on Saturday that it was the last day, as Michael had to report back at noon on the Monday. His mother was coming up to London with him to spend his last evening with him there. 'You do understand, don't you?' he said. 'She wants to have me to herself because the Lord knows when I'll get any more leave.'

'Of course I do,' she answered mechanically, not thinking about it very much. He took her face in his hands and kissed her. This time he pressed his mouth to her lips, a warm and soothing kiss. 'Oh, Louise,' he said, 'sometimes I selfishly wish that you were a little older.'

'Now what are you going to do?' he asked later in the morning. She hadn't thought. Trains were looked up and it was found that she could not get to Devon on a Sunday – she would have to spend the Sunday evening in London. She rang up Stella, whose mother answered, saying that Stella was in Oxford with friends until Monday evening. She was afraid to ask whether she might stay at the Roses' without Stella, so she said it didn't matter, she would write to her. Then she remembered that Lansdowne Road, though more or less shut up, was still used by her parents for the odd night. She rang home, and asked whether she might go there, and how she could procure a key. Her mother went away to ask her father, and then he came on the telephone and said what a lovely idea, but he wouldn't dream of her spending a night in London on her own, would come up and meet her at Paddington and take her out to dinner, what time was she arriving? This conversation took place in front of Michael who could hear her father's loud and cheerful voice, and he instantly gave her the time, which, in a daze, she repeated. 'Good-oh. See you then,' her father said, and rang off.

'That's wonderful,' Michael said. 'Now I shan't worry about you.'

She said nothing. It wasn't wonderful; she realised that she was actually dreading it, but she could see no way out.

She had avoided being alone with her father for so long now that the reasons for doing so had become faded and blurred. Her skilful wariness had been successful and therefore the terror had resolved into a kind of distaste; it was like not thinking of something that made her feel sick – she could will herself never to think about it. Now she felt trapped and fear started to simmer inside her and could not be quenched.

The day went. At tea-time, his mother demanded that he bring down his drawings of Louise 'so that we can see which is the best. And how you want them framed, darling.'

There were four drawings, two in pencil, and two in ink, one sepia and one black. The best was to go into his next show that his mother was organising for him. The compliments, the pleasure at being the centre of attention, was now alloyed; still she wanted to cling to them, to hold the day up for ever, to tell them to keep her safely, indulgently with them . . .

'I *think* the black ink,' his mother was saying consideringly.

'They're none of them quite right. I'll do better next time,' Michael said.

'When will the next time be?' she cried suddenly, and they all looked at her, and she realised from his mother's face that she had said the wrong thing.

'Not long, I expect,' Michael said easily, and she realised that he was speaking to his mother.

The last evening – just the four of them for dinner – was a special meal with all Michael's favourite dishes. 'It's like going back to school!' he exclaimed when the treacle tart appeared, and his mother said, 'Oh, darling! I wish you were!' and for the first time Louise understood that she was afraid of Michael being killed which seemed to her both a horrible and an impossible idea, for did not this family live a charmed life where nothing bad happened? Afterwards, they sat in the library and there were coffee and Charbonnel and Walker chocolates, and he bit into one and said, 'Oh no! Marzipan!' and his mother said, 'Give it to me then.' They asked her to do Juliet and Ophelia for them once more, and she did and her own Ophelia made her weep which they seemed to think made it even better.

When they went upstairs to bed, Michael said very quietly, 'May I come and say good night to you?' and she nodded. She undressed, and wondered whether she ought to put on Ernestine's nightdress, but when she looked at it, it seemed worse than ever, so she changed back into her old Viyella. She cleaned her teeth and brushed her hair and then sat on her bed and waited, beginning to feel nervous. But when he came, and sat on the bed beside her, he simply put his arms round her for a long time without saying anything. Then he held her a little away from him. 'You're so young, you stop me in my tracks.'

She stared back at him, disagreeing with this and wondering what was going to happen.

'I just wanted to say goodbye to you. Tomorrow my mother and your father will be there. I should like to *kiss* you goodbye.'

She gave a little nod and he put his arms round her again and kissed her – this time trying to open her mouth and, not liking that but wanting to please him, she did not resist.

After what seemed quite a long time, he gave a little groan and let her go. 'I must leave you,' he said. 'This is getting a bit dangerous. Sleep well. Write to me. Thank you for making it such a lovely leave.'

Lying awake in the dark, she felt deeply confused. Being in love seemed to involve rituals that she did not in the least understand; the very little that she had gleaned had been so obliquely and implicitly collected – mostly, she supposed, from her mother, and had been largely composed of what one should *not* do or say. The only injunction that came to her mind now was her mother telling her that she must not 'be a strain on men' – this had been on the beach at home, when she had taken off her shirt and sat in her bra in the sun for a few minutes. It had been incomprehensible to her at the time; she had only recognised her mother's hostility and even there she had not been sure whether it had been directed at her particularly, or towards men in general. The implication, though, was that men felt differently from women, but there was also something else that was more frightening, because although she was certain that it existed, she did not know what it was. If people never talked about sex – women, at least – it must be because there was something pretty awful about it (little snatches of conversation between her mother and Aunt Jessica recurred, and the general message was that one's body was rather disgusting and the less said about it the better). Perhaps being in love with someone simply meant that you were so fond of them that you could bear what they did to you. She had begun to think that she loved Michael, but now she felt that this couldn't be true because she had started to mind his tongue the moment it came into her mouth . . . she had begun to feel frightened which must be wrong. There must be something wrong with *me*, she thought. Perhaps I am just what Stella said – vain and keen on being admired, which has nothing to do with loving someone. It must be my fault. This made her feel very sad.

The next day, Margaret packing for her, signing the visitor's book (on the same page as Myra Hess and Anthony Eden) and, after lunch, Peter tucking Zee into the back of the car with a fur rug with Michael beside her, she was put in front with the chauffeur; the first-class carriage to Paddington, and there, at the end of the platform, she could see her father waiting. His greeting her and her introducing *her* friends, and her father taking off his hat to Zee and saying, 'I do hope my daughter has been behaving herself,' and Zee answering, 'Quite beautifully,' and tucking her arm in his she led him down the platform, talking to him as though he was an old friend, which left her and Michael to follow together. 'Darling Mummy,' he said, 'the epitome of tact.'

Her father offered to give them a lift, but Zee said she and Michael were happy to take a taxi. She watched them get into one and be whirled away, with Michael waving to her from the open window. She felt a moment's anguish, followed at once by desolation, a terrible flatness: she was going to her own home with her father, but this felt familiar without being reassuring.

Her father tucked her arm in his and walked her to his car.

'Well, my sweetie, it's a very long time indeed since I had you to myself. Did you have a lovely time?'

'Lovely.'

'What a charming woman Lady Zinnia is!' he exclaimed, as he put her luggage in the boot. 'I must say she doesn't look as though she could have a son as old as that.'

'Michael is thirty-two.'

'That's what I mean.'

'Now,' he said, 'it being Sunday night, there's not much we can do in the way of amusement. So I thought I'd take you out to a slap-up dinner. I've booked a table at the Savoy Grill for eight o'clock. Mummy said I wasn't to keep you up too late because of your train tomorrow. But you've plenty of time to get changed.'

The dinner went all right. She got through it by asking news of everyone in the family she could think of. Mummy was very tired, because she felt she should visit Grania rather a lot as she was so miserable and, on top of that, Aunt Syb was not really recovered, so she had to look after Wills as well as Roly quite a lot. What about Ellen? Ellen was getting very rheumaticky, and with Zoë's baby there was a hell of a lot of laundry, all of which she did. And what about him? *He* was all right, longing to get back to the RAF, but Uncle Hugh had taken Syb away for a holiday in Scotland – damn cold in this weather, he should have thought, but she wanted to go there – so he had the business on his shoulders, and what with organising the fire-watching at the wharves, he didn't get home for many weekends. Teddy had won the squash tournament at his school, and was learning to box. His report otherwise had not been too good. Neville had run away from school but, luckily, he had told an old lady on the London train he had taken that he was an orphan on his way to Ireland and she had smelled a rat. His luggage had consisted of two pairs of socks, a bag of bull's eyes and a white mouse that he had stolen from another boy. Anyway, the old lady had invited him to tea in her house in London, and had most intelligently looked up his surname in the London telephone directory. 'I got a call at the office,' her father said, 'and went and fetched the little beggar, and Rach took him back to Home Place.'

'Why do you think he ran away?'

'He said he was bored with school, and he didn't think anyone would mind. Clary was furious with him. Now, what about an ice for your pud?'

On the way home, he said, 'You're not, you know, too taken with that bloke, are you?'

'He's just a friend. Why?'

'Dunno. You're still a bit young for that sort of thing.' He put a hand on her knee, and squeezed it. 'Don't want to lose you yet.'

The sirens went just as they got back to the house, which had felt very odd when they'd first gone there: shrouded, quiet, cold, and not very clean. She said she was very tired, and thought she would go straight to bed. All right, he replied, though he seemed disappointed. 'I'll just have a nightcap, and then I'll join you.'

What did he *mean*? she thought, as she undressed as quickly as possible (her room was *freezing*) and pulled the Viyella nightdress over her head. What *did* he mean? Then she thought, Don't be idiotic, he meant he was going to go to bed too. She looked through her old chest of drawers to see if she could find any socks; there were planes overhead and anti-aircraft guns began firing. Her drawers were full of old things – clothes she had outgrown, and objects that she no longer liked: a black china dog, and her gym-khana cups, and old, greasy, twisted hair ribbons.

She did not hear him coming upstairs, because bombs were dropping, and their distant but shattering sound excluded smaller noises. He opened the door without knocking, a glass of whisky in his hand.

'Just came in in case you were frightened,' he said. 'Get into bed, you look cold.'

'I'm not frightened in the least.'

'Good for you. Get in, and I'll tuck you up.'

He sat on the bed and put his whisky on the table beside it.

'I know you're growing up,' he said. 'I can hardly believe it. It seems only yesterday that you were my little girl. And look at you now!' He began to pull the sheets round her, and then slipped his hand under them, bending over her as he took hold of her breast. His breath smelled of whisky – a horrible, hot, rubbery smell.

'Very grown up,' he said and suddenly put his mouth on hers, his tongue, like a horrible hard worm trying to squirm in.

Terror – like a sudden high tide – travelled up her body at an unearthly speed; if it reached her throat she would be engulfed and paralysed, but she would not be so drowned . . . The moment she could recognise choice, rage rescued her. She drew up her knees, put her hands on his neck and pushed him, with a jolt, away from her. In the sudden second of silence, before either of them could move or speak, a bomb fell very much nearer, the house seemed to shiver, and some glass fell, with a seeming reluctance, from her bedroom window.

'I'm sorry,' he said; he looked both hurt and bemused.

She sat up in bed, her arms wrapped round her knees.

'I wouldn't have hurt you,' he said. He looked sullenly self-righteous, she thought. But that was not enough.

'I saw you at a theatre,' she said. 'You seem to be hooked on people's breasts; you had your hand on hers. I saw you from a box.'

His face flushed, and she saw his eyes become hard and wary. 'You can't have! It must have been someone else.'

'I had opera glasses. It *was* you. The lady had dark hair with a white streak in it and violet eyes. I saw her in the ladies' in the interval afterwards. And, of *course*, a very low-cut dress,' she added; the shafts were going home and there could not be too many.

'She's an old friend,' he said at last. His flush was subsiding, but his eyes were cold as blue glass.

'Of yours and Mummy's?'

'Mummy has met her – yes.'

'But she doesn't know that you go to the theatre with her – or anything else? She doesn't know about the weekends?'

That went home. Now he looked really stricken. 'How on earth—' he began, and then changed his tune. 'Darling, you're not old enough to understand—'

'Stop treating me like a child when it suits you – and like a – like a tart when it doesn't! I hate you! You're horrible – and you—' Her voice broke and now she was furious with herself for wanting to cry so badly.

'You tell lies,' she finished inaudibly.

'Listen, Louise. I do occasionally, but that's only because I don't want to hurt Mummy's feelings. And you don't want to either, do you? Telling her any of that would only make her awfully unhappy. I can't explain why things are as they are – you'll just have to trust me.'

He saw her face, and said, 'I mean, you'll just have to accept that.'

There was a silence during which two more, more distant, bombs fell.

'I really only came in because I thought you might be frightened of the raid,' he said. 'I was going to tell you that we could go to an air-raid shelter if you liked. I'm sorry that – that I got carried away. It won't happen again.' He picked up his glass and finished the whisky.

'No,' she said; she longed for him to go away.

He got up and stood with the empty glass in his hand staring at the blacked-out window. 'Well – your bed's not near the glass, anyway,' he said. When she looked up from staring at the bedclothes round her knees, he was gazing at her, uncertain – abject.

'I'll say good night then,' he said, awkwardly. He walked to the door as though his legs were stiff. 'I'll knock on your door at half past seven in case you're not awake.'

'All right.' It felt as though saying that sealed some tacit, uneasy pact.

She waited, rigid, until she heard his door shut and then put her face into her hands to weep. It should have felt like a victory – a triumph – but all it felt like was a dead loss.

At the station in the morning, after he had tipped the porter to find her a good seat, had bought her *The Times* and *Lilliput* and *Country Life* to read in the train, had found the guard and asked him to look after her and given her a pound to have lunch, he stood for a moment in the compartment. Discomfort had settled like scum between them; he said he thought he'd better get onto the platform. He gave her shoulder a little pat, then a quick,

414

clumsy kiss on the top of her head. When he reappeared at her window which was half open, he said, 'I think I'd better be off.' Then, suddenly, with his left hand, he wrote with his finger on the grimy glass: 'Sorry, do love you. Darling!' in his best looking-glass writing – one of his tricks when she'd been a child was to take two pens and write in different directions – one looking-glass, one straight. He turned to her when he'd done it, tried to wink, and a tear fell out of that eye. Then he raised his hand in a salute and walked away without looking back.

CLARY

Winter–Spring 1941

28 March

It was Polly's birthday yesterday and rather a flop,
but as I pointed out, sixteen is better than fifteen – at
least it's another year of this awful in-between no
man's land that we both feel we are in. Polly says that
the war makes it worse, and I started by disagreeing
with her, but when I think about – well – everything,
Dad and everything, I have to agree with her. My
point really is that it would have been a no man's
land anyway and, as I told Polly, you can perfectly
well have two reasons for something when one would
have been quite enough. Uncle Edward says that
morale is high, but that doesn't necessarily have much
to do with what happens. Miss Milliment disagreed
with me about this, and when I said look at the
Charge of the Light Brigade, she immediately pointed
out that however mad and silly it was to make the
charge, it did succeed in spiking the Russian batteries.
My morale isn't high, but that's another thing you
can't mention unless it is. Anyway – Polly's birthday:
Mrs Cripps made her a cake – coffee which is my
favourite, but she likes lemon and you can't get them
– and Zoë made her a lovely bright blue jumper, and
Lydia gave her a lavender bag she made, but she used
last year's lavender so it is rather prickly and doesn't

416

smell much. She got a pound from the Brig, and the
Duchy gave her a little silver chain, and Miss
Milliment gave her *Great Expectations* and I gave her
an amazing glass case full of *huge* unlikely butterflies
– extremely rare and valuable, I should think – for her
house – I got it in Hastings. Aunt Syb and Uncle
Hugh gave her a silver wristwatch with her initials on
the back. Neville tried to give her that wretched white
mouse he ran away with – at least, he said it wasn't
the same mouse, it was one of its children. Mice have
gone out of fashion at his school so he didn't have to
pay for it or anything. I call that a really thoughtless
present and I told him. So he let it out in the garden
and gave her the magnifying glass that Dad gave him
for a birthday once, and I told him she would treasure
it because of Dad but he said it was him she should
treasure it because of. I am quoting Neville here,
naturally – I know that one does not end a sentence
with a preposition if one can possibly help it. Still, it
was ultimately kind of Neville. Aunt Villy gave her a
beautiful handbag of real leather and Louise sent her
a book of poetry called *New Verse* which I honestly
don't think she'll read because she said I could
borrow it for as long as I liked. I think mine was the
best present. Bully and Cracks – or perhaps in a
journal I should say the great-aunts – gave her an
evening purse made of brown and gold beads which I
cannot see her ever using in a *war*, and a nightdress
case embroidered with hollyhocks by them. She is
hoping it will get worn out before she gets her house
because it won't go with anything else, it is so
horrible. Wills gave her a bunch of colt's foot daisies
and two stones. My present cost five bob but of course

417

I didn't tell her; it's easily the most expensive present
I've ever given. After supper we played Head, Body
and Legs, and Consequences. Head, Body and Legs
reminds me awfully of Dad because he drew such
lovely funny ones and it must have reminded the
others but nobody said anything. They've stopped
talking about him and now I have too because when I
do they get all kind and embarrassed and it only
makes me know that they think he is dead. But I think
now that he may well be not trying to get home
because he is working as a spy against the Germans in
France. I told Polly this, and she said it sounded like a
possible idea. Then I told the Duchy after we'd played
the ninth symphony – the one with voices – and she
said she thought I might be right but I wasn't sure if
she really believed me, but when I'd put the records
away she said, 'Come here, my treasure,' and gave me
a terrific hug and I said, 'Don't you believe me?' and
she said, 'I believe that *you* believe it and I can't tell
you how much I admire you for it.' I must say that
was rather pridening.

Teddy was very excited because there's been a big
naval battle in the Mediterranean and we sank seven
Italian warships and most of the Italians lost their
lives. He is rather a bloodthirsty boy and can't wait to
be eighteen and fighting the war.

What are my views on war by now after a year
and a half of it? I feel divided between wanting to be
against the whole thing, and feeling that if there has
to be a war, women should be allowed to fight as well
as men – I mean really *fight*, not just be secretarial or
domestic in uniform. After all, women are getting
killed by bombing when they can't retaliate at all, so

it's no use men saying any more that war is men's business. But on the third hand (if you can have one), there are some things in a war that I should absolutely hate to do, like be in a submarine, or stick bayonets into people – although Polly says she thinks there is less of that nowadays. And I wouldn't at all like to be in a tank. Polly says that this is like the submarine and connected to claustrophobia, but I've never shown any signs of that. But then she asked me whether I'd like to be a miner, and I wouldn't, and then she reminded me about the scene I made (when extremely *young*) in the caves at Hastings, felt sick and cried and nearly fainted and had to be carried out. So I must be. Of course, if you're not *in* the war, it is simply boring. Nastier food, and the bath water is seldom hot and being rather stuck because of not much petrol – all petty inconveniences, I agree, but petty things are still *there*; they don't go away by being small. Our room was so icy this winter, that I invented a way of dressing entirely in bed.

I'm not going to write this every day or it will get like Lydia: 'Got up, had breakfast, went to lessons. We did geography and sums . . .' Oh! it makes me yawn even to write *that* much.

17 April
There was a really awful raid on London last night all night. St Paul's is still standing with rubble all round it. Uncle Hugh rang in the morning so that Aunt Syb wouldn't be too worried, but she is – all the time. She looks ill from worry. He said that there were five hundred planes that dropped thousands and thousands of bombs. Uncle Edward is back in the RAF

so Uncle Hugh has to do all the family business by himself. The Brig doesn't go to London much now, because he can't do anything if he does, but Aunt Rach goes up for three nights a week to help in the office and she stays with a friend, but she has dinner with Uncle Hugh one evening a week because he is rather lonely.

Aunt Jessica comes down here for weekends sometimes, but she has her mother's house in London as poor Lady Rydal will never occupy it again. One of the worst things about being so old must be all the last times you do things. It must be sad for her to know she won't ever go back to her own home, but Aunt Villy says she is past noticing that kind of thing. I don't see how she can know that; I should think there must be some extremely sad, clear times, when Grania *knows* what is happening to her, but I think other people prefer to imagine that she is dotty all the time. It's the same thing as not talking about anything difficult or awful. Hypocrisy is rife, if you ask me.

4 May

There is something going on about *Angela*. Aunt Jessica came down and she and Aunt Villy had a long, private talk and emerged with that face they both have when things aren't all right. I was passing the door (I really was – like people in books) and I heard 'a most unsuitable entanglement'. That means, I suppose, that Angela knows someone whom her mother disapproves of, but how on earth could she go through life only knowing the ones who would meet with parental approval?

Anyway, Aunt Villy is going to London with Aunt

J. tomorrow, and guess what? They are bringing the
famous Lorenzo and his wife down with them for the
weekend! That will certainly be interesting. We do get
rather short of human nature here, by which I
suppose I mean people to observe whose behaviour
might be unpredictable. Miss Milliment is getting
more and more fussy about my writing what I *mean*,
but at least she doesn't seem to baulk at anything I
want to mean – like the rest of the family.

The Duchy is worried because now Christopher
has gone home, McAlpine can't manage the whole
garden and priority has to be given to vegetables. She
interviewed a *girl* gardener last week who wears
breeches and very thick oatmeal stockings and is
called Heather. If she comes, she will sleep in
Tonbridge's cottage with Miss Milliment, but it is
betted that she won't stay because McAlpine will be
so horrible to her. Jules is nearly out of nappies and is
trying to walk. Ellen says she is very forward for her
age – not quite one – and not having to air nappies for
her all the time, which stops any heat from the
nursery fire reaching people, will be a mercy. I must
say she is a very sweet baby – awfully pretty with
curly dark hair – whereas Roly still looks a bit like Mr
Churchill – an endless face and tiny features.

I asked Neville why he ran away and he said he
was sick of doing the same things every day and
being educated, which he says just means being told a
whole lot of things that won't be any use to him in
later life. Also he is bored of Mervyn who he says is
soppy and never has a single idea of anything
interesting to do in their spare time, and also Neville
despises him for not running away as well. In Ireland

he was going to live by the sea with a donkey and
fish. I said what about when Dad comes back? This
was a mistake: he tried to kick me and said, 'I hate
you for going on about Dad. I really hate and loathe
and dislike you for being so silly and horrible talking
about him just whenever I'm not remembering him.
That's why I wanted to go to Ireland. To get away
from everything.' So then I realised how awfully he
minds. I said I was sorry and I really hoped he
wouldn't go away because I'd miss him, and when I
said it, I realised that it was true: I would. But both
those things – being sorry and missing him – sounded
feeble and I could see he thought so too. 'Well, please
don't go yet,' I said, 'I might come with you if you'd
wait a bit.' Not a satisfactory talk at all; I'm actually
quite afraid he *will* run away again, and have decided
to talk to Aunt Rach about it as she is the most
sensible of the aunts.

18 May

The Lorenzo weekend has got put off, because this
evening Lady Rydal died. They rang in the middle of
dinner; Aunt Rach answered the telephone, and came
back and said that Matron would like to speak to Mrs
Cazalet or Mrs Castle, so they both went to talk to
her. When they came back, Aunt J. said she thought it
was really a merciful release. I can't see anything very
merciful about it; mercy would have been her not
having to go through all that miserable time in the
nursing home in the first place. Anyway, they said
there would be a lot to do – arranging the funeral, and
putting it in *The Times*. Then they both wanted to ring
up Lorenzo to put him off, and in the end, Aunt

Jessica won (there is definitely something funny going on about all that – what a pity there isn't going to be the chance to find out what) and she came back after rather a long time, and said he sent his love and was frightfully sorry. They are going to Tunbridge Wells tomorrow, and Aunt J. rang up Uncle Raymond, but she couldn't get him, and Aunt Villy tried to ring Uncle Edward, but *she* couldn't get *him* and I could see the Duchy worrying about the extravagance of all these toll calls. She was only sixty-nine, but if you'd told me she was eighty, I would have thought it more likely. I do wonder what it is like to die. Whether you know you are, or whether it just happens, like the lights fusing, and whether it is actually rather exciting. I suppose it depends very much on what you believe happens to you, if anything. Polly and I had a long talk about it. Polly thinks we may have other lives, which is what Hindus believe. Miss Milliment says that all the great religions take what happens to you after death very seriously, although, of course, they don't agree. But I don't have a great religion and nor does Polly. We spent a bit of time trying to think what we would like to have happen, and I thought being a sort of interested ghost might be good. Then she said that she supposed that what happened to you might be whatever you *did* believe. And since Lady Rydal was a very Victorian Christian, her heaven would be a harp-playing-long-white-clothes-wearing affair, we both think. And, of course, being reunited with her husband. Well, she never seemed very happy when she was alive, so perhaps being dead will be more enjoyable for her. I wished I'd been there when she died, because I've never seen a dead person, and I feel

I need the experience. Still, at least they might let me go to the funeral.

When Lydia was told in the morning about her grandmother, she burst into racking sobs which Polly and I thought was rather affected as she never seemed to like Grania very much. When we confronted her with this, she said, 'I know, but you *ought* to cry when people die – they like it.' I said how on earth did she know that, and she said that if *she* died, she'd want everyone who knew her to cry like mad. 'To show how sad they are that I'm not there,' she said. This was at the beginning of lessons, and Miss Milliment said there was something in what she said. She's *always* sticking up for Lydia and making excuses for her because of her being younger than we are. Nobody ever stuck up for me when I was Lydia's age. Except for Dad – he did.

The funeral is to be in Tunbridge Wells. Uncle Raymond is coming, and Nora from her hospital, but Christopher can't, and I'm not sure about Angela. Judy is coming from her boarding school where, thank God, she is all through terms. We are allowed to go as well, although it isn't our grandmother. It is to be a cremation, but I don't think you actually *see* that.

22 May

We went yesterday and it was horrible. A horrible little chapel with Grania on a kind of table at the end, and someone played an organ and the clergyman got her names wrong. She is Agatha Mary, and he called her Agartha Marie, and suddenly some curtains beyond the table opened and poor Grania simply slid away to be burned to smithereens. Then we all stood outside for a bit, and then we came home. The only person who wasn't family was someone called Mr Tunnicliffe who was Grania's lawyer. Apparently you go back and collect the ashes and strew them somewhere that you think the person would like. But I don't imagine anyone asked her where she would like her ashes strewn – it isn't an easy question to ask people, because I suppose it sounds a bit as though you might be looking forward to them being dead. But it *did* feel sad to think that someone who talked and was about the place is suddenly turned into ashes. I keep remembering her in the nursing home, all wild and muddled and unhappy, but still alive, and it has made me feel extremely sorry for her.

3 June

It is exactly a year since Commander Pearson rang up and told me about Dad. Three hundred and sixty-five days, eight thousand seven hundred and sixty hours, five hundred and twenty-seven thousand six hundred minutes since I have ceased to know where he is. But he is somewhere – he must be. I'd know, I'd feel, if he wasn't. If he is working as a spy, someone must know it. The English might not, but I've suddenly thought of General de Gaulle. He's the head of the French; I bet, even if he doesn't actually know offhand, he could find out. So I've decided to write and ask him. I've also decided not to tell anybody, except possibly Poll, because I don't want them trying to stop me. I feel very excited to have thought of such a good thing to do, but as it is going to be a very important letter, I'll practise it, and only put the final version in this journal. It's a pity I can't write it in French, but I'm afraid I'd make too many mistakes, and General de Gaulle must have learned a good deal of English by now, and anyway, he'd have lots of secretaries and people who could translate it for him. I'll write a very polite, businesslike letter, and not at all long, because I feel that Generals probably don't like reading much.

Clothes coupons came in yesterday. Polly is lucky, because Aunt Syb bought her a lot of clothes last year, and masses of material to make things. Luckily I don't mind about clothes much, but I have been growing a lot, so the trouble is I soon won't be able to wear a lot of things, although there is nothing wrong with them except for size. Oh well, I can't see this family letting me go about naked, so there's no need to worry.

My letter (I think).

Dear General de Gaulle,

My father, Lieutenant Rupert Cazalet, got left behind at St Valéry when he was organising troops to be evacuated onto his destroyer last June. He has not been reported as a prisoner of the foul Germans, so I think it very likely that he is working with the Free French as a spy on our side. He is a painter, and he lived in France quite a bit when he was young, so his French is so good that the Germans might easily think he was French. Possibly some kind French people are hiding him, but he is awfully patriotic, and he would be more likely to be working than just hiding. As you must have an unrivalled knowledge of the Free French, etc., I wonder whether you could find out if that is what he is doing? He might be pretending to be French, but I expect the people he is working with would know that he was secretly English and his name. If you do know, or could find out for me, I should be profoundly grateful, as naturally I have been worried. He wouldn't be able to write letters, you see, but I just want to know that he is all right and not dead.

Yours sincerely, Clarissa Cazalet.

Of course I didn't do what I said; when it came to the point, I wanted to practise the letter in my journal. I think I should put '*My* dear General de Gaulle' or just 'My dear General – like 'My dear Manager' when you write to the Bank, according to Aunt Villy. And perhaps I should put yours faithfully, as I should think the General must be keener on faithfulness than sincerity in his position.

Then I had to find out where to send it to, but I did, by asking a few casual questions of Miss Milliment, and there is a Free French headquarters in London. I put private and personal on the envelope and I read the letter to Polly, who thought I shouldn't say 'foul Germans' but that is just Polly not wanting to be horrible to anybody so I didn't change it. He must loathe them just as much as he loathes Field Marshal Pétain who is doing awful things – particularly to Jews – in France. He handed over a thousand of them in Paris to the Germans and, according to Aunt Rach, who seems to know this kind of thing, he's arrested many thousands more. I really do think it is filthy to go for people because of their race.

Louise's repertory company has come to an end.

They've run out of money, and two of the boys in the
company have been called up, so they're stuck
without enough actors. Aunt Villy is very pleased,
and says that perhaps now she will get down to doing
some sensible war work. Polly and I don't think she
will at all. We agree with Aunt Villy about her being
completely selfish, but Polly says that she thinks
artists are supposed to be. Miss Milliment said it
wasn't that; it was simply that serious artists tended
to put their work first and a lot of the time this was
inconvenient for them, but other people only noticed
when it got in *their* way. I must say, Miss Milliment is
far broader-minded than our family; as Polly said,
she's altogether broad – we fell about laughing until
Polly said how horrible it was of her to refer to Miss
Milliment's physical bulk. Then I remembered Dad
talking about a charwoman he had before he was
married. Whenever Dad wanted her to do anything
serious, like scrubbing a floor, she said she was bulky
but frail, and then he felt he couldn't ask her to do it.

July
I think it's about the 4th. I still haven't had a reply to
my letter. Polly says think how long it takes us to
write our thank-you letters at Christmas, and General
de Gaulle must get letters on a scale that we can
hardly imagine. I can't see why he would. His own
friends and family in France couldn't write to him,
and I shouldn't think there are many people in my
position.

Louise is back. She has stopped wearing quite so
much make-up so she looks better, but she's remote
from us somehow. She spends hours writing letters to

get a job in a theatre, and also to some man in the Navy she met. She's also writing a play that has a rather good idea. It's about a girl who has to choose between marrying someone and going on with her career as a dancer. That's the first act. In the second act we see what would happen if she went on with her career, and in the third act what happens when she marries the man. She's calling it *Outrageous Fortune* which personally I think is rather pretentious. But I do think it's a good idea. She reads bits of it to us, but she only wants us to say how good it is. She told me one thing of great interest. Angela has fallen in love with a married man about twenty years older than she is. He works in the BBC with her and he's called Brian Prentice and she wants to marry him, but of course she can't as he is already. I said how sad, but that was that, but Louise said no it wasn't because Angela has started to have a baby and the aunts J. and V. are awfully worried about it. Louise saw her in London at poor Lady Rydal's old house because each of the grandchildren (the girls) had to choose a piece of Grania's jewellery. They chose in order of age, so Angela got Grania's pearls, and Nora had the huge long crystal necklace, and as the aunts were keeping the diamond rings, there was only some gold filigree earrings left for Louise. I don't know what Judy or Lydia got – they weren't even given the chance to choose. But that was when Louise saw Angela, who she said looked awfully pale and was completely silent. What can happen, I wonder? I suppose she must have gone to bed with him – obviously a bad thing to do – it must be terrifically enjoyable if that's what happens. She might not have known that he was

married, in which case it must be entirely Brian
Prentice's fault. But, as Polly says, faults don't make
things nicer for people, or change them. Louise says
there is something called Volpar Gel that means you
don't have babies. And even Dutch caps help, she
said, but when I asked what they were and what you
do with them, she simply wouldn't tell me. 'You're
too young,' she said. There must, thank God, be a
diminishing number of things I'm too young for, but
then, I suppose, before you can turn round there start
to be an increasing number of things you are too *old*
for. You can't win. I'm looking forward to being
thirty, which I should think would be the brief
interval between those horns of dilemma.

Why doesn't General de Gaulle *answer* my letter? I
think it's really thoughtless of him, and actually quite
rude. The Duchy says you should answer letters by
return of post.

Poor Aunt Rach has spent an awful morning
cutting the great-aunts' toe nails. I heard her saying
that they were like the talons of old sea birds – all
curving and frightfully tough. Apparently that's one
of the first things you can't do when you are really
old because you can't reach them. I warned Polly
about this, because it really means she'd better not
live in her house entirely alone. She said what did
hermits do, because they were nearly always old and
had to be alone. I should think they end up with claws
like parrots.

For lunch today we had rissoles from the butcher
made to a new formula that means they have hardly
any meat in them. Neville said they were like a field
mouse after a car accident; they were actually just

extremely boring to eat, but the Duchy said they were only eightpence a pound, and we should be grateful. I don't think anyone was.

One interesting thing. A friend of Dad's is coming to stay! He is on sick leave from the Army; he was at the Slade with Dad, and they went to France as students together. He's called Archie Lestrange and I do vaguely remember him, but before the war he was mostly in France so Dad didn't see him much. It will be nice having a friend of Dad's to stay because, not being family, he might talk about him a bit. I hope he really does come, unlike the Clutterworths who never seem to get here. Now I'm going to bath Jules, because it's Zoë's day – or one of them – at the nursing home and Ellen has a tummy upset – rissoles, I shouldn't wonder. I bath her, and I give her her bottle and put her on her pot and then into her bed and I read to her from *Peter Rabbit*. She keeps interrupting but she minds if I stop.

I got interrupted then and a good thing too – re-reading the above has made me yawn with boredom. Why is it that so much of ordinary life is crammed with trivial routine? Does it have to be? Is it the war that makes everything so deeply grey? What on earth will change it? Polly thinks that being grown up will make all the difference, but I honestly think she is wrong: it seems to me that the grown-ups have, if possible, even greyer lives. I am sure if I had a more interesting mind I should be less bored, and had a talk with Miss Milliment about that, as she has been in charge of my mind for some time now, so she must be partly responsible. She did at least listen to me which is more than most people do, and then she didn't say anything for a bit and then she said, 'I wonder why you've stopped writing?' and I said I was writing this journal, but it was pretty boring, and she said, 'No, I mean the kind of writing you were doing a year ago. You were writing stories. Now you only do whatever homework I set you, which isn't at all the same thing.' I hadn't thought about that, but it's perfectly true. I haven't written a single story – since Dad went away. I said I hadn't felt like it, and she answered quite sharply that she hadn't thought I wanted to be an amateur, but a real writer. 'Professionals do their work whatever they are feeling,' she said. 'I am not surprised that you are bored if you are idle with a gift. You are boring yourself and that is a dreary state of affairs. Doing the least you can do *is* extremely boring.' But her small grey eyes were quite kind when she said this. I said I didn't see how one could write if one couldn't think of anything to write about and she replied that I would think of something if I disposed myself to do so. She ended by saying that if I hadn't thought of anything within a month, she would start teaching me Greek, which would at least be a new exercise for my mind.

It's funny. The moment I began to think about writing, I didn't feel bored at all. I simply felt how difficult it would be to find the time. I made a list of all the things I am expected to do in a day. For instance, not only are we supposed to tidy our rooms, which we've always been supposed to do, we have to make our own *beds* because there aren't enough housemaids to do it any more. *And* we have to iron our clothes sometimes because Ellen gets too tired to do it all. Polly is a beautiful ironer, but then she minds

432

about her clothes; I loathe ironing and I wouldn't
actually mind if my clothes weren't ironed at all. Then
we have to help clear the table after meals. *Then* we
have to do some outdoor job in the afternoons –
whatever Heather or McAlpine or the Duchy says,
and believe me, between them they think of pretty
dull things. We have to collect water in bottles from
the spring at Watlington (I like that unless it's pouring
with rain). Then we have to *mend* our beastly clothes
with Bully or Cracks or Aunt Syb or Zoë seeing that
we do it properly. One of us is supposed to go round
every single window in the house in the evenings
making sure that the blackout is properly done. We
take turns. We have to do *all these things* on top of
lessons every morning and homework after tea. There
is some time after homework and after supper, but
I've decided to tidy up my share of our room and
that's going to take several days, because I haven't
really done that for years: I mean shelves and
cupboards and things since I got my stuff from
London. It might take weeks. Polly says I'll love it
when it's done, but that sounds to me like what
people say about cold baths. Starting writing again is
a bit like that as well or perhaps that's more like
swimming in the sea – awful getting in and lovely
when you are. Anyway, apart from doing all these
things, I have to try and think what to write, but
when it comes to writing I find I can't think at *all* – it's
only when I'm apparently not thinking about
anything, that any sliver of an idea slips into my
mind, and even then I don't seem able to *think* about
it. It seems to be a mixture of remembering things and
feeling – sometimes just remembering a feeling, and

that often happens when I'm doing something quite unconnected. All the same, even not thinking about it seems to make it easier not to think about the other thing. What I do now is have a think about Dad every morning when I wake up. I just wish him a good, safe day and send him my love, and then I stop. It is a tremendous relief arranging it like that. Of course I worry about the General not answering my letter, but that is somehow a different-*sized* worry. Polly got very worked up about my having to face the fact that he might write something about there being no trace of Dad and that meaning that there was no hope. She doesn't understand: it wouldn't be that. Either the General will know something about him, or he won't. But his not knowing only means *he* doesn't know. It won't mean that Dad is dead. It simply will not mean that.

POLLY

July–October 1941

'It's too far for you; even if you got there, you'd be too tired to come back.'

'No, I wouldn't.' She looked angrily at Simon, who was, she felt, simply echoing Teddy in the most irritating way. 'But if you want to be on your own—' she said.

'It's not that,' Teddy said quickly: it was against family law deliberately to exclude anyone from an outing. 'It's just that I can't see you bicycling nearly forty miles.'

'Camber's not twenty miles!'

'Jolly nearly. And we've got three-speed bikes.'

'OK. I can see you don't want me.'

'They don't want me either,' Neville said, 'which is much more serious.'

'I tell you what,' he said to Polly when the boys had made an uneasy escape. 'When they're old and wrinkly and *beg* me to take them out in my racing car, I simply shan't. Or my aeroplane, which I'll probably have for long journeys. I shall just tell them they're too old for anything nice – silly old farts.'

'I don't think you should call them that.'

'It's what they are or jolly soon will be. Stupid chaps are farts and stupid girls are tarts. A boy at school told me. Farts and tarts, you see?'

He watched her, hoping she would be shocked. He had grown so much in the last year that his shorts were inches above his bony knees, but his hair still stood up in tufts from his double crown and his chicken neck made him look in some way vulnerable. Nothing of him seemed of a piece: his second teeth looked too large for his mouth, his feet, encased in dirty sandals, seemed enormous, his ears stuck out, his thin, egg-brown torso with its tidemark of ribs looked fragile and went very ill with his huge leather belt and sheath knife attached to it. He was heavily marked by trivial wounds – scrapes, cuts, blisters, hangnails, even a burn on his right hand from an experiment with his magnifying glass. His habitual expression was both challenging and anxious. She suddenly wondered what it was like to be him, and knew immediately that she would never know.

'I was thinking of bicycling to Bodiam,' she said. 'Like to come?'

She could see that pretending to consider this gave him pleasure. Then in a voice that was a remarkable rendering of Colonel Chinstrap from ITMA, he said, 'I don't mind if I do.'

The gesture turned out to be costly. She got her usual, first-day stomach cramps on the ride there and the rest of the time – their picnic, exploring the castle, stopping him having a swim in the moat, talking him down from the terrifying height he achieved in an oak tree – was discoloured by her terror of starting to bleed with nothing to staunch it, and frightening and revolting him therefore. She could hardly bear the ride back, said she was tired and would have to go slowly and he could go on if he liked, but he didn't. He kept riding ahead, turning round and coming back to her. 'It's a good thing you didn't try to go to Camber,' he said cheerfully. 'You would have had to stop and sleep the night in a field or a church or something.'

Later, he said encouragingly, 'It's not your fault, though. You can't help being a girl. They do tire easily – I think it's something to do with their hair.'

When they got back, she asked him if he'd put her bicycle away for her and he said of course he would.

She staggered upstairs, had a bath and lay on her bed. Her head ached, her stomach ached and she felt rotten; she did not even want to read. But *he* had enjoyed himself, it had been worth it. Thereafter she decided that she would do one thing every week for someone else and made a list of the people so that she could note the appropriate good deed against each name.

Some, like the Brig (reading aloud to him from the *Timber Trades Journal, crashingly* dull), were easy; some, like her mother and Miss Milliment, were not. In the end, she decided to knit Miss Milliment a cardigan – a huge enterprise and it would take her months, but it could be a Christmas present on a scale that she would not ordinarily have given. Her mother was nice about that idea, and offered to find a pattern that would be likely to encompass Miss Milliment's frame. 'It will have to be a man's one,' she said, 'which means that you will have to remember to make the buttonholes on the left side. Do you really think you'll stick to it? Otherwise it's a waste of an awful lot of wool.'

She promised she would, and she and Clary went to the Watlington shop to choose the wool, but Mrs Cramp turned out only to have baby wools or khaki or navy blues. 'There's no call, these days, for much else,' she said. In the end, Aunt Villy kindly got some in London after an anxious discussion about which colour would suit Miss Milliment best. The trouble was that every time a colour was suggested, it seemed to be the worst colour: wine wouldn't go with her lemony skin, bottle green would make her hair look like seaweed, grey was too boring, red would make her look like a London bus and so on. A misty, heathery blue was the final choice. Well, that was Miss Milliment, and since it had to be knitted entirely when she was not present, it did not get on very fast. Her mother was a great problem. 'The only thing she would really like would be for Dad to stop being in London, and I can't do anything about that.' Polly complained to Clary. Then one day, she went into her mother's bedroom and found her unpinning her hair at her dressing table.

'I really must wash my hair,' she said. 'You couldn't possibly help me, could you? It's so difficult to get all the soap out, and leaning over a basin for ages makes me feel rather queasy.'

After that, she washed her mother's hair once a week, on Fridays before Dad came home for the weekend, and she even devised a brilliant method whereby, on the right chair, her mother could sit with her back to the basin with her hair hanging over it, so she didn't feel sick at all.

Dad was another problem. She saw so much less of him these days and when she did she could see how awfully tired he was. The tic at the side of his forehead was almost always throbbing when he arrived at Home Place on Friday evenings looking grey with fatigue. Also, she hardly ever saw him alone: there were so many people in the house, and as she now had dinner with the grown-ups, he did not come up to say good night to her. At dinner there was usually a lot of war talk: Hitler had invaded Russia so now Russia was on *their* side which *she* thought simply meant that it would go on for longer.

Then, one Saturday, he asked her to come to Hastings with him: 'Just you, Poll, because I don't see enough of you.'

They went in his car because he said he got an extra allowance for business, and it was quite a relief to be off, because so many other people had wanted to come too. 'You're *sure* you don't mind?' she had said anxiously to Clary.

'Course I don't!'

But she knew this wasn't true, and said, 'I so want to have Dad to myself for a bit.'

And Clary had given her that unexpected lovely smile and said, 'Of course you do. I perfectly understand *that*.'

Teddy and Simon had clamoured to be included, but Dad had dealt with them. 'This is for Polly and me,' he said. 'Be off with you!' as they tugged the door handles. Polly had put on her pink dress and whited her tennis shoes, but they were still damp and got whiter as they dried on the way to Hastings.

'Have you got any special plans?' she asked, as the shouts of 'Unfair!' faded.

'We're going to try and find a present for Mummy. Who knows? We might find other things. I might see something suitable as a post-birthday present for you.'

'You gave me my lovely watch.' It was a bit sloppy on her wrist, and she moved it.

'We chose that together in Edinburgh at the end of our last holiday – I mean, the holiday we last had.'

She glanced at him, wondering why he was being so pedantic.

'What?' He'd caught her glance.

439

'I was wondering why you were being so pedantic.'

'Can't think. What do you think of the Russians joining up with us? Better than having them against us, wouldn't you say?'

'It just seems to make the whole thing more universal to me,' she said. 'If only it was *America* on our side.'

'They're not exactly *against* us. Mr Roosevelt's doing his best for us. In fact, we'd have been up a gum tree without him.'

'But it's not the same as them actually joining up with us and helping to fight the Germans. After all, they did come in last time.'

'They may yet. But think, darling Poll, how much you are against war, and then imagine being an American. How would you like it if *they* were having a war and *we* all had to leave this country and go thousands of miles to fight for them? All the men, that is,' he added; he did not approve of women going into the services. 'You might very well feel that it's their war, and they should get on with it.'

'Dad, do you know, I've never met an American?'

'That's a bit what I mean.'

'On the other hand, if Hitler wins over here, he will probably set about other bits of the world which might be them and then they would be sorry.'

'I think he may have bitten off rather more than he can chew with Russia. Hitler's not going to win,' he added.

'How long will it all be, then?'

'I've absolutely no idea. Not for a while yet. But things are better than they were last year.'

'What do you mean? All the frightful air raids, and rationing and the Fall of France and all those other countries. It seems to me much *worse*.'

'This time last year we were damn nearly invaded. That would have been worse. And we only just won the Battle of Britain. I can tell you now, Poll, that I used to have nightmares about that happening, and me being stuck in London and unable to get to you all.'

'Oh, Dad! *Poor* you! I see what you mean about it being better.' She felt very pleased that he was telling her important things like his nightmares. 'I didn't know grown-ups had them,' she said.

'Oh, darling! All kinds of things are much the same when you are grown up. On a lighter note, I think we'll visit Mr Cracknell first. And there is quite a good jewellery shop we can try thereabouts too.'

When they were nearly in Hastings he asked, 'How are they all at home, then?'

'All right, I suppose. Who especially?'

'Well – your aunts – and your mother for a start.'

'Aunt Rach has an awful back.'

'I know,' he said quickly. 'She says a lot of the time she is like an old deckchair that has got stuck. I make her go to that very good man in London, though. And I think she likes working in the office.'

'Aunt Rach loves to be *needed*,' she said. 'More than most people.'

'Quite right, she does. And?'

'And what? Oh – the others. Well, I think Aunt Villy is bored. I think she'd really like to be doing some terrific war job. Doing Red Cross work and teaching people first aid and working in the nursing home at Mill Farm isn't enough for her.'

'My word, Polly, you are perspicacious.'

'But Aunt Zoë, on the other hand, is actually quite happy. She looks after two people now in the nursing home – reading to them, and writing letters for them – things like that – and, of course, she absolutely adores Juliet.'

Hugh smiled, his tender, approving smile that was largely reserved for babies. 'Of course she does.'

'What about Mummy?' he said after a silence. 'How is she, do you think?'

Polly thought. 'I don't know. The trouble is, I don't think she feels very well a good deal of the time. She loved her holiday with you, but it seemed to make her even tireder. She went to bed for two whole days when she got back.'

'Did she?'

'Don't tell her I told you that. I shouldn't have. She didn't want you to know.'

'I won't.'

'I got awfully worried when she had to have an operation. But it all turned out OK, didn't it?'

'Oh, yes,' he said heartily. 'Very OK. But people sometimes take a long time really to get over that kind of thing, you know. Here we are! Hastings, here we come!'

Mr Cracknell's shop was rather dark, and everything in it seemed dusty, but it contained some fascinating things. Furniture, of course: Dad bought two chairs that had ears of wheat carved up their backs. 'I can't resist them,' he said. But there were also a number of wooden boxes, some inlaid with mother-of-pearl, some with brass. Inside they had ruched satin or velvet in crimson or dark, bright blue; some had little cut-glass bottles and pots with silver lids. Some were sewing boxes, with tiny little spools – again made of mother-of-pearl, round which strands of rich and faded silk were wound. Pairs of steel scissors and books of steel needles, and a sharp, pointed tool for making holes in things were arranged on the top layer inside, and some of the boxes had a secret drawer at the bottom that sprang open when you pressed a button. She was entranced by them, and explored each one carefully, imagining which she would like most. Then she found a plain rosewood box that, open, proved to be a little writing desk: 'It was for travelling,' her father said. 'Ladies took them on visits.'

When open the box made a gentle slope that was covered with thin dark green leather. Underneath the slope there was a place to keep papers. 'Clary would love this,' she said. 'Dad, do you think it might be not more than twenty-five shillings? Because that's all I've got.' It seemed a lot to her, but she knew that things that were in shilling amounts weren't a lot to him.

'I'll find out. Come and look at this.' It was a small octagonal table with an elegant pedestal. The table top was very pretty, with the wood laid in sharp triangles, so that the grain looked like a flower. Her father pressed something and the table lid opened to reveal a conical interior lined with paper that had minute bunches of roses on it – like wallpaper for a doll's house, she thought. Mr Cracknell emerged from the back of his shop holding a shallow octagonal tray papered in the same way, but made with numerous compartments. 'I've been repairing the tray,' he said and fitted it carefully into the top of the cone.

'It's a sewing table, early twentieth century, not very old,' he said.

'Now, Polly, what wood is it made of? Let's see how much you know.'

Polly said she thought it was walnut.

'That's right!' Mr Cracknell exclaimed. He was old,

with steel-rimmed spectacles and greeny-white hair, and he stooped. He passed a splayed thumb over the wood: 'A lovely piece of veneer, that is. Laid as tight as a nut.'

'Do you think Mummy would like it?'

It would only be good for small pieces of sewing: there wasn't enough room in the bottom for things like the winter dressing gown she was making for Wills.

'I should think she might,' she said, and saw her father's expression fade a little.

'Well, we'd better go on looking,' he said.

Mr Cracknell, who knew the Cazalet brothers from their many visits, said he had a rather nice chest on chest that he thought they might like to look at. 'Seeing as you like walnut,' he said. 'Got its original handles too, it has.' The place was so full of things, and so dark that he got a torch to shine on the piece.

Polly could see that Dad really loved it: stroking the wood, gently pulling out a drawer and admiring the craftsmanship. 'See, Poll?' he said. 'They used wooden pegs and dovetailing to make the drawers in those days.' There was a spattering of tiny little round holes in one drawer.

'Worm's dead,' Mr Cracknell remarked; he tapped the drawer smartly, and Hugh nodded.

'If the worm was active, there'd be stuff like sawdust coming out,' he said to Polly. 'And what do you want for that, Mr Cracknell?'

'Well, I could let it go at three hundred.'

Hugh whistled. 'A bit out of my league, I'm afraid.'

In the end he bought the sewing table, and while Mr Cracknell was carrying it out to the car, Polly asked if he would ask how much the writing box was.

'Do you want it, Poll? Would you use it?'

'I want it to give to Clary.'

'Of course. You said. I'll find out.'

He's rather forgetful, she thought; he never used to be like that.

He came back and said, how lucky – it was only twenty-five shillings.

'An expensive present for you, though, darling,' he said.

'I know, but I want to give it to her.'

When they had finished putting everything into the car, she said, 'Why are you smiling, Dad?'

'I was thinking what a very nice daughter I've got.'

When he wasn't smiling, she realised, he actually looked sad.

He said that they would look at the other shops as they were there. It was the old part of the town with narrow streets and seagulls and little whiffs of tar and fish and the sea. In the jeweller's shop, which was tiny and crammed with antique jewellery, he picked out a pair of garnet earrings – long drops.

'Do you think Mummy would like these?' he asked. 'It would go with that necklace I bought her years ago.'

Polly knew that her mother did not like garnets as they did not go with the colour of her hair, and only wore the necklace occasionally, to please Dad.

'You bought her some earrings in Edinburgh; she showed me,' she said. 'I should think she'd rather have something else.' He seemed always to be buying her presents, even though she'd had her birthday ages ago. 'Also, she wouldn't wear them much while there's a war.'

'Practical Poll.' He began looking carefully through a tray of rings. Just as she was going to say that Mummy didn't wear rings much either these days, he picked out a small ring that had a flat green stone set in gold. The back was like a shell, the band was plain. 'Pop it on,' he said. It fitted her second finger exactly.

'What do you think of that?' he said.

'I should think she would love it. I should think *anyone* would love it.'

'Right. I'm going to give it to anyone, then. Take it off.'

'How do you mean "anyone"?' she asked, handing it to him. It sounded bonkers.

'The first person I meet after I've bought it.' He went to the back of the shop and she saw that he was writing a cheque. Supposing, she thought wildly, he met a *postman* outside the shop? Of course, the postman might have a wife, but then again, he might not.

When he came back, he said, 'Hallo, Poll, fancy meeting you here,' and gave her a little box. Inside, perched upon worn white satin, was the ring. 'I knew you'd be the first person I'd meet,' he said.

She was overwhelmed. A ring! And it was *so* beautiful!

'Oh, Dad! It's my first ring.'

'I wanted to be the first person to give you one.'

'It's completely perfect! Can I wear it now?'

'I should be deeply hurt if you didn't. Emeralds suit you, Poll,' he observed when the ring was on and she turned her hand for him to see. 'You have pretty hands – like your mother.'

'Is it really and truly an emerald?'

'It is. It's late sixteenth century – a bit early for paste, I think. Looks like an emerald to me, and the man in the shop said it was.'

'Goodness!'

'You have grown up,' he said. 'I can remember a time when you would much rather have had a cat than a ring.'

446

'The back of it's so beautiful,' she said when they had got back into the car.

'Yes. It's like those drawers in the chest on chest. They just cared about making things beautifully, never mind whether it showed at once that they had.'

Before he started the car, she put her arms round him and gave him three kisses. 'Thank you, Dad, it's the best present I've ever had.'

They went to the front, and walked along past the fishermen's tall thin black huts in which the nets were stored. It was a fine, breezy day with white horses on the empty sea. Barbed wire and concrete pyramids were ranged along the beach making it impossible to reach the sea. They walked, without talking, in a companionable silence. She felt unusually, immensely happy. The double glow of receiving her ring, and the thought of giving Clary her desk box prevailed. 'Breathe deeply, Dad,' she said, 'the sea air will do you good,' and he smiled his gentle, affectionate smile at her and made a ridiculous noise breathing.

'I'm done good to,' he said. 'Let's go and find a nice pub on the way home.'

When they were seated under an apple tree in the pub garden and her cider and his beer had arrived he said abruptly, 'Did Mummy ever talk to you about the possibility of her having to have another operation?'

'Not much. She did mention it, weeks ago, but then when I asked her if it was going to happen, she said they had changed their minds. That was before you went on your holiday.'

There was a silence while he stared into his glass. Mystified, and beginning to feel frightened, she said, 'That was a relief, wasn't it? She never said, but I knew she was dreading another operation as the last one made her feel so rotten. It must have been a relief.'

'Did she say it was a relief?'

'She said—' She thought: it seemed important to get it right. '*I* said, oh, what a good thing, you must be relieved, and she agreed. She agreed, Dad. And she was terrifically pleased about the holiday. She said she was only tired when she got home because she hadn't slept much on the train coming back. And she only asked me not to tell you that because she didn't want to worry you. It wasn't important. She often has odd days in bed.'

'Does she?' He was lighting a cigarette and she noticed that his hands weren't steady.

'Oh, Dad! You worry so much about each other, but you always have. And I think the thing is she really wants to be in London with you. She misses you. I think you ought to let her.'

'I'll think about it,' he said, in a tone which she knew meant he wouldn't. 'Bless you,' he added; it was a kind of full stop.

As they got into the car, he said, 'Are you looking forward to giving Clary her box?'

'Like anything. She gave me a lovely birthday present. All kinds of butterflies in a glass case – for my house. But I think she'll burst into tears of joy when she gets the box. It may make her a bit happier for a change.'

'Is she very unhappy?'

'Oh, *Dad*, of course she is. She absolutely won't consider Uncle Rupe being dead and never seeing him again. She makes up all kinds of stories about him, and she wrote to General de Gaulle because she thought he might be a spy in France for us, and he didn't answer for ages and then she got a letter back saying that enquiries had been made, but no one of that name was known. I thought then that she might face up to the fact that he has died and she won't see him, but somehow she *can't*. She loves him too much to bear it.'

A shock. Her father, without any warning, suddenly broke into dry, almost shouting sobs – put his head on his arms on the steering wheel and sobbed and sobbed. She turned in her seat and put her arms round him, but he didn't stop.

'Darling Dad. I'm sorry. Of course, he's your brother and *you* must mind terribly as well. And I suppose you *have* faced up to it, and it must be awful. It's so final, isn't it? Poor Dad.'

In the end she realised that talking didn't help and simply held him, and finally the sobbing got less and he fumbled for his handkerchief and blew his nose. When he had wiped his face, which he did as though he wasn't used to it (but then, she supposed that he wasn't used to crying), he said, 'Sorry about that, Poll.'

'Don't be. I absolutely understand.'

When he had started the engine and they were on their way home, she said, 'And I shan't tell Clary. It would only distress her if she knew that you felt there was no hope. Although,' she finished tentatively – she did not want to upset him again, 'there's always a *shred* of hope, isn't there, Dad? Don't you think?'

'Must be,' he answered, but so quietly that she hardly heard him.

She didn't have Dad to herself for a long time after that, because of course, to be fair, he had to take Simon out for one morning and, anyway, he spent most of the weekends with Mummy and Wills. Clary wasn't much impressed with the emerald ring until Polly told her that it was Elizabethan, whereupon she asked to hold it. '*Anyone* might have worn it,' she said. 'One of Mary Stuart's ladies-in-waiting for instance. Think of it! It might have been there when the poor thing was executed! I must say, I think that *is* rather a possession.' But she was immediately and utterly thrilled by her writing box, opening and shutting it speechlessly, her eyes filling with tears. 'It shows you must – like me quite a bit,' she said. 'Oh, look! A secret drawer!' Caressing it, she had touched a spring and a very shallow drawer flew open beneath the space for papers. There was a small, thin piece of paper in it folded like an envelope. The paper, opened flat, was covered by spidery writing written in two directions. 'Like letters in Jane Austen! Oh, Poll, what a joy! It'll take me years to read it. The ink's gone all brown. But it might be a very important letter.' They tried and tried to read it, but even with a magnifying glass they couldn't make it all out. 'It seems to be mostly about the weather and how expensive muslins are,' Clary said at last. 'There must be other things, or it might be a *code*, but whenever I get to what might be an important word it runs into the one going the other way and I can't read it.'

Strangely, when they showed it to Miss Milliment, she was able to decipher it. 'People wrote like that when I was a girl,' she said. 'Postage was expensive, and people did not wish to waste the paper.' It *was* all about the weather and the price not only of muslins, but lace, merino, and even a muff.

'Anyway, it is a very *old* letter,' Clary said as she folded it tenderly back into its envelope shape. 'And I shall always keep it in its secret place. Polly, it is the most exotic and amazing thing I've ever had. I'll keep all my writing in it.' She was writing a series of short stories that were linked to one another, by a character from each one carrying on to the next, and sometimes read bits to Polly in the evenings which was far happier than her accounts of Uncle Rupe's life in France, but she only read the bits she wasn't sure were good enough, so Polly never got the whole story. 'You're a *sounding* board,' Clary said severely, 'you're not meant to enjoy the *story*.'

Now, as she hastily swept off all her other things that lay on her dressing table, in order that the desk should sit in state by itself, she said, 'Thank you, Poll. It must mean – you're the most friendly friend.' Then she added, 'It must have cost you an awful lot of money,' and Polly, knowing that this would make Clary feel more loved, replied, 'Well, yes, it did a bit.' She felt that she was getting to be quite good with *people*, which, as she had no other worthy gifts, was something.

'What do you think Miss Milliment could possibly have looked like as a girl?' she asked when they were getting ready for supper.

Clary thought. 'A sort of pear, in pigtails?' she suggested. 'Do you think people ever said, "What a beautiful baby"?'

'They can't have. Unless they were trying to be kind to Mrs Milliment.'

'I should think she must have needed people to be kind to her.'

'Oh, I don't agree. Mothers always think their babies are beautiful. Look at Zoë and Juliet.'

'Jules *is* pretty,' Clary said at once. 'But, then, your mother thought Wills was lovely, and I know he's your brother, but *honestly* nobody could have enjoyed looking at him.'

They were taking an extra amount of trouble with their appearance, because the man who had been Uncle Rupert's friend was arriving that evening in time for dinner. Clary was taking trouble because he was her father's friend, and Polly because she loved dressing up, and brushing her hair a hundred times, and pushing up her eyebrows with her finger and then smoothing them into a fine line, and making sure that the seams of her stockings were straight, and putting on her jewellery. For Clary, taking trouble meant ironing her best blouse and trying to find a pair of stockings that matched, and scrubbing her fingers in a vain effort to get the ink off them. Neither of them mentioned the fact that they were taking extra trouble although each knew that the other one was.

'I wonder what Dad's friend will be like,' Clary remarked with careful carelessness.

'Well, he's bound to be old.'

'What do you mean "old"?'

'Too old for us. Nearly forty.'

'Really, you sound as though you're considering marriage with him.'

'Don't be a fool. He'll be married himself, anyway. People are, by that age.'

'As a matter of fact, he isn't. I happen to know that the person he wanted to marry didn't want him, and Dad said that was partly why he went and lived in France.'

'His life has been blighted, you mean?' Polly couldn't conceal her interest in that.

'Probably. We shall be able to tell by looking at him. So keep an eagle eye out, and we'll compare notes. Archie Lestrange. Archibald Lestrange,' she repeated. 'It sounds like someone in a John Buchan. Archie would be the hero, and Archibald the villain.'

∞ ∞ ∞

He was definitely Archie, Polly thought. He was immensely tall, with a dome-like forehead and fine black hair receding from it. He had heavy lids to his eyes and an expression in them that looked as though he was either secretly amused, or wanted to be.

He'd been wounded and walked with a limp; he also had a slight stammer. The Duchy had put him next to her at dinner and was clearly rather fond of him. They talked about far-off days, before this war, and, Polly thought, just after the war before that when he used to come and stay at the house she and the Brig had had at Totteridge, when he and Rupert had been at the Slade. He seemed to know the family quite well, not only her grandparents, but Dad and Uncle Edward and Aunt Rach. He'd been best man for Uncle Rupert's first wedding to Clary's mother, and he'd obviously met *her* mother and Aunt Villy, although he clearly didn't know them so well. For dinner there was roast chicken and bread sauce and he said how wonderful it was to have such lovely food. 'In Coastal Forces,' he said, 'our ships were just too small to warrant a trained cook, and only the most gormless rating volunteered for the job. Great haunches of lamb would appear either streaming with blood or black as your hat with unspeakable potatoes – all grey and shiny, like frightened people's faces.' Later he said that he'd volunteered for the Trade, but they weren't making submarines to fit people of his size.

Afterwards, when she and Clary were undressing for bed they swapped impressions.

'He's nice. I can see why your dad liked him. Funny-looking, though. Rather *cavernous*.'

'He's been *ill*. I thought he looked rather tragic. People often get a stammer when something terrible has happened to them.'

'You mean his leg being shot?'

'No, stupid. I mean the person not wanting to marry him. I should think that's left him with an awful inferiority complex.'

Recently she had taken to attributing this state to nearly everyone, largely, Polly thought, because it was something difficult to disprove.

'He didn't seem to be particularly inferior.'

'You don't have to *be* inferior, you just feel you are.'

'Oh, well, hardly anyone doesn't feel that.'

'It's funny that, isn't it? I mean you're *with* yourself all the time, so you'd think you'd be clearer about yourself than about anyone else. I mean, look at you, Poll. You're terribly pretty, jolly nearly beautiful, and so kind and nice, and *you*'re always saying you don't know what you're for, and you're no good and things like that.'

'So do you.'

'Oh, well,' Clary said, 'my eyebrows are too thick and I've got awful legs that only bulge at the knees – no ankles like lucky you – and my hair's too fine, and I've got a hideous nature and a squashy nose and claustrophobia – *you* said that so don't try to get out of it now – so I can't see that I've much *not* to feel inferior about.'

'There you are!'

By now, Archie Lestrange was forgotten, and they embarked upon a very enjoyable half-hour's competition to see who could run herself down the most, with the other one contesting every point, until sleep overcame Clary which it always did without the slightest warning: she was talking nineteen to the dozen and then she was suddenly gone.

In the morning Clary said, 'One thing about Archie – he told me to call him that – he seemed awfully shy with Aunt Rachel.'

'She's an unmarried lady. He probably feels shy with all of them, after what happened to him.'

'Oh, yes. Of course he would, poor thing.'

The sad thing that happened in August was that it turned out that Angela wasn't going to get married as she also turned out not to be having a baby. What was sad about this, Polly felt, was that bang went her chance to be a bridesmaid, something she had wanted to be the whole of her life. The first part of this information came through direct questioning: did Aunt Villy think that Angela would have her as a bridesmaid? No, because she wasn't getting married after all. The second part arrived obliquely via Louise, home for the week while her theatre was closed for essential repairs, who got a letter from Nora in which she said how shocked she was that Angela *wasn't* having a baby.

'Extraordinary,' Clary said. 'You'd think it would be the other way round.' Louise refused to discuss it with them for the same old boring reasons that it wasn't their business and they were too young anyway.

'How *can* one be too young for discussion of any kind?' Clary shrieked. She hadn't been at all interested until told that she should not be, then, at once, her curiosity and suspicions were aroused. 'I'm through with Louise. I'm really through. She has gone beyond the pale.' She asked

Zoë what she thought, and Zoë said that she imagined that Angela must have had a miscarriage. 'But the man she wanted to marry *was* married,' she said, 'so I expect it will be all for the best in the long run.' When Clary told Polly this, they both rolled their eyes and echoed 'the *long run*', and Clary said she was all for short cuts and this made them fall about.

It was odd, Polly thought as she picked runner beans for Mrs Cripps to slice and salt down for winter, how frivolous she was. She could make jokes with Clary, and play silly games with Wills, and be fussy about her appearance and all the time the war was going on, and not going very well for the Allies as far as she could see. Hitler was making alarming progress in Russia and people were saying that the Japanese were becoming offensively arrogant, and if *they* came into the war on Hitler's side, it would either prolong it for ever or, worse, it might mean that Hitler *would* win; they would be back to it being as frightening as it had been last summer, the threat of invasion, and all that.

Pursuing her policy of trying to do things to make other people's lives nicer for them, she decided to talk to her mother about her going to London so that she could be with Dad. 'You see, Mummy, *I* could look after Wills in the week for you. And you'd be coming down every weekend. And Ellen would help, I know she would. So why don't you just *tell* Dad you're coming? Or, better still, just go and be a lovely surprise for him when he gets back from the office? I don't mean to be bossy,' she added – she didn't actually think she was being that at all – 'but I'm sure he *wants* you to be there – it's simply that he is being unselfish.'

Her mother was sewing name tapes onto Simon's grey socks and handkerchiefs for next term. 'Darling, I couldn't go when it's Simon's last week of the holidays. You know how he minds going back.'

'All right, but you could after he's gone.'

'I'll think about it.' Then she added, almost petulantly, 'Oh, why can't we just all be together? Simon having to go away to school, and Wills being so young and needing me, and Hugh having to be in London! It's too bad. I'm not much of a cook, you know. I don't know whether I could make Hugh the kind of meals he likes.'

'Oh, Mummy, you could do what Aunt Villy does when Mrs Cripps has her evening off. She reads Mrs Beeton and then she just does exactly what it says. Think of that rabbit stew last week.'

'Well, darling, I really will think about it,' but she said it in tones that meant she would rather think than talk.

Well, Polly thought, she'd done her best. It seemed odd to her, if you wanted so badly to be with your husband, to make a fuss about the cooking.

Teddy and Simon went back to school. Dad took them up on a Sunday evening and out to dinner at his club, and then saw them off on the train the next morning. Teddy went off without a tremor; it was his last two terms and as he hadn't done too well in his exams in the summer, he was to retake some of them, and *then* as he told everybody interminably, he would be able to join up and start learning to fly. But Simon was sick on the Sunday morning and didn't want any lunch and wanted to be with Mummy all day. She played bezique and racing demon and chess with him, but even his easy victory over her with the last did not cheer him much.

Everybody tried to be very jolly and encouraging: 'It'll soon be Christmas,' Polly said to him, 'and you know how you love that.'

'I may have toothache,' he said at tea-time. 'I feel as though at any minute a tooth is going to start to hurt. It's funny, but I'm usually right about things like that.'

But it did not make – as she knew he knew – the slightest difference. When she had to wave them a smiling goodbye, her mother turned and walked slowly back to the house, and when Polly was sent to fetch her for dinner, she said that she didn't want any. She had been crying, her voice sounded indistinct and slurred, and she almost pushed Polly out of the room and shut her door.

Term began for her too, and for Clary and Lydia, and Neville, who went back to his school quite cheerfully, Clary said, because he had learned to imitate Lord Haw-Haw perfectly and was looking forward to showing this off.

Archie Lestrange, who stayed with them for a fortnight the first time, came back in September, and Clary got so worked up about this that Polly wondered whether she was in love. She suggested this possibility to Clary, who got into a frightful temper – said she was mad and trying to spoil everything and she must have a horrible mind to think of anything so idiotic and horrible. Then she sulked, and they had two days and – worse – two tense, silent, icily polite evenings going to bed and getting up in the morning. In the end she apologised in the most humble language she could bring to bear, and Clary, having reiterated how idiotic she was to have thought of such a thing, forgave her. Later, when they were taking it in turns to have the small and tepid bath, she said, 'Actually, I can sort of see why you thought anything so mad. The thing *is* that I do *like* him awfully. And I think he looks nice and he makes me laugh – like Dad does – and I respect him for his opinions on things.'

'What things?'

'Well, pretty well everything. Of course, we haven't talked about *absolutely* everything, but he agrees that women should have careers and that writing is very important and that people being worse than animals is really only saying how nice animals are – and he sometimes tells me things about my mother – he knew her a bit you see. You know my postcard she sent me with her love on it? Well, he was *on* that holiday with her and Dad – he can actually remember her saying, "I must get a postcard to send to little Clary." He told me a *lot* of things. She used to wear blue a lot and she loved a drink called Dubonnet that they drank in cafés, and she couldn't eat shrimps and prawns and things like that, or strawberries, but he said it wasn't the time of year for them so it didn't matter. And do you know the best thing? One evening he asked her if she was happy and she said, "I honestly think I'm the luckiest person in the world. The only thing I miss is not having Clary with me." She must have loved me to say that, don't you think?' Seeing Clary's eyes – a true glass to her heart – and recognising the faithful love that neither time nor misfortune seemed ever to quench, Polly felt too much to say anything.

But when she had washed Clary's back, she said, 'I do see why you like him. I do anyway, but I certainly would even more if I were you.'

Her mother *did* go to London the following week, *and* she didn't tell Dad so it was a surprise for him. Polly felt very pleased at having had such a good idea for them, although she found afternoons with Wills surprisingly exhausting. He was at a really frightful age, she thought. He seemed only to want to do things that were dangerous for him, or destructive for other people, and when thwarted, he lay on the ground, arched his back and howled. 'I honestly think he may turn into a dictator,' she said to Ellen after the second day.

'He just wants his own way,' she said comfortably. 'Just let him lie and pay no attention to him. He'll soon stop.' He did, but he soon started again. In between tantrums, he was very fond of her and gave her charming smiles. But she reflected gloomily that dictators were all supposed to be particularly charming when they chose.

But on Friday, when her parents returned, she was shocked by her mother's appearance. She looked completely worn out – her face had an unusual yellowish tinge, and she had shadowy circles under her eyes. Dad looked grey as well, although they both greeted everyone with a kind of determined cheerfulness before her mother said she thought she would have a little rest before dinner. Polly went up with her to see whether she wanted her case unpacked, or would like a cup of tea, but she said no, she didn't want anything; she was scrabbling in her handbag and produced a very small bottle of pills.

'Oh, Mummy, you're not taking more aspirin? You know Dr Carr said—'

'These aren't aspirin. My back aches from sitting in the car for so long.' She shook two out onto the palm of her hand and crammed them into her mouth.

'Don't you want some water with them?'

'No – I don't need that.' She was sitting on the side of the bed kicking off her shoes. Now she looked up suddenly, and said in a funny half-pleading, half-jocular manner, 'But you won't say a word to Dad about my taking these, will you? He'll only fuss, and I really couldn't cope with a fuss. Promise?'

She promised, but she felt uneasy about it. When her mother was on the bed, she put an eiderdown over her, kissed her hot, damp forehead, and left.

She hovered at the top of the back stairs, wondering whether to go and find Dad – not to tell him about the pills, of course, she'd promised not to, but to see if she could find out why her mother was so awfully tired – they'd probably gone out to theatres and dinners every night . . .

Then she heard voices, coming from the morning room whose door must be open.

'. . . absolute madness, but I had to pretend it was all right, of course.'

There was the sound of a soda syphon being squirted. Then her father's voice continued, 'Thanks, Villy. Do I need this!'

Aunt Villy said, 'Hugh, darling, I'm so sorry. What can I do?

'It's sweet of you, but I can't think of anything.'

'Are you sure she has no idea?'

'She has none. I tested that out this week and drew a merciful blank. She has no idea at all.'

'She's going to need nursing, you know. I mean, I can do all that's needed now – but—'

She heard steps coming towards the door and shrank back against the banisters. But the door was simply shut and then she could only hear a murmur, but not what the voices said.

THE FAMILY

Autumn–Winter 1941

'Potato pie? How very amusing!'

'Amusing? *Potato pie?* I must say, Dolly, you have the strangest sense of humour. Try as I will, I can see nothing to laugh at in a potato.'

'But then, dear, you have never been known for your sense of humour.'

Fifteen all, Villy thought, as she sat at the morning-room desk paying bills for the Duchy. The great-aunts always spent the morning in that room, so named because it did not get morning sun which their generation deemed bad for the complexion, not that the aunts' complexions were in a state worthy of preservation: Aunt Dolly's ponderous cheeks, like a spaniel's ears, were a damp mauve that reminded her of mountains in amateur water colours of Scotland, and Aunt Flo's resembled, as one of the children had remarked, a dog biscuit peppered with flourishing blackheads – due, as Dolly frequently observed, to her penchant for washing her face in cold water without soap. Flo was crocheting a blanket made from odds and ends of wool, and Dolly was mending a winter vest. Villy had managed to stop them appealing to her over their disagreements on the grounds that she was adding things up which had reduced them for a few minutes to a respectful silence. They spent every morning sewing and quarrelling gently, usually, these days, about food. They always knew the menus for the day, having *happened* to overhear or *happened* to see the paper on which the Duchy wrote the results of her morning interview with Mrs Cripps.

'*I* do faintly wonder what a potato pie is made with,' Dolly said, not very much later.

'There must be a distinct possibility that it is made with potato.'

'I do wish, sometimes, that you wouldn't try to be sarcastic – it really doesn't suit you. I meant, if it is a *pie*, will it be the sort with pastry, or will it be like shepherd's pie with mashed potato on top?'

'I should have thought it was fairly obvious that it would have pastry. You couldn't have mashed potatoes above ordinary ones. I mean, why have a pie at all, if that's what you're going to do?'

She said this so accusingly that Dolly retorted, 'It wasn't *my* idea. It was Kitty's. After she read that Mr Churchill has made potatoes one penny a pound to encourage us to eat more, she has been trying to think of new ways to use them.'

Everything that happened was done by Mr Churchill, Villy noticed. Everything good, that is. Everything bad, of course, was done by Hitler. You would think they were conducting a personal war with everybody else on the receiving end.

'Of course, there might be some cheese in it. Just a little, grated, for flavour.'

'I very much doubt it. We had cauliflower cheese *again* yesterday, and macaroni cheese is usually on Sunday nights. You must remember that cheese is rationed.'

Of *course* Dolly knew that, of *course* she did; she really wondered sometimes whether Flo thought she was *mad*.

They bickered on through the classic routine of umbrage, severe umbrage (just reached), to peace-making nostalgia about pre-war food, and back to ruminations about the meals in immediate prospect. Really, Villy thought, they behaved in most respects as though there wasn't a war at all: they would probably have talked about food wherever they were in time or space; they sewed all morning with a longish break for Bovril and biscuits, rested after luncheon, went – if the weather was fine – for a little stroll in the garden before tea, sewed again until the six o'clock news whose contents they were never able to agree upon afterwards, had a little rest before changing out of their jersey suits into woollen dresses and rather painful-looking pointed shoes with marcasite buckles for dinner, and retired punctually at ten o'clock to the bedroom they shared. The Duchy was kind to her sisters because they had never married, and she was of the generation that regarded the single state as a minor tragedy. She also had been heard to say that they had been extraordinarily good to their father when he had become frenetically senile. The Brig regarded them as part of the fixtures of family life and occasionally, when he could find no other audience, told them one of his duller stories.

But then, Villy considered that *her* life was much as it had been. At the beginning of the war, she had imagined herself doing some useful and interesting war work – perhaps training for some job in the War Office or in a large hospital. But it hadn't turned out like that at all. First there had been Roly, the unexpected baby, well over two now but still, she felt, requiring her presence. Even without him, there had been the fact that the household at Home Place had so enlarged that it was unfair to expect the Duchy to run it single-handed, and Rachel, who might have taken over a great deal of it, had been seconded to the family firm where she now worked four days a week. Neither Sybil nor Zoë was up to the sort of chronic, often exhausting maintenance that was needed. Things that would have been replaced now had to be mended; the coke and coal rations meant that more wood was burned and Villy, with Heather to help, spent about two afternoons a week with the big saw, cutting logs dragged from the woods by Wren and the old pony. Drinking water had to be collected from the well and the bottles brought up the hill on a wheelbarrow since their petrol ration was all used for the station and weekly shopping trips to Battle. There was a massive amount of laundry, and getting clothes dry in winter was a nightmare, as there was no central heating – regarded by the Duchy as extremely unhealthy. Villy had devised a line in the boiler room which had been cleaned out by Tonbridge – he had proved useless at sawing wood – and this was always full of steaming clothes. The preserving of fruit and vegetables at this time of the year was also a full-time job. Here Zoë and the girls helped Mrs Cripps. Villy ran the local first-aid classes one night a week and did two nights at the nursing home, as Matron was constantly short of good staff. And now there was Sybil needing help, which was more difficult since so much tact was needed in giving it. She could not, would not, face the fact that she was not able to look after Wills on her own for more than very brief periods, so somebody had to be on hand to relieve her of him under the pretext of his tea, or a walk with Roly or some game the children had devised for him. She was indomitable; the only time she had really confided in Villy had been after the week she had spent in London with Hugh. The house, mostly shut up since Hugh used only the kitchen and their bedroom, had been dirty and thoroughly ill kept: the char she had employed to come three mornings a week was clearly doing nothing but clean the bath and make Hugh's bed plus a little washing-up. She had spent the first day shopping for food and trying to open up the drawing room, with the consequence that she was dead beat by the time Hugh arrived home from work and had burned the careful stew she had made by forgetting it. Hugh had taken her out, but she had been too tired to eat. After that, he had taken her out every night to supper, but the days, spent buying her presents for Christmas, 'It seemed the last chance I would have for that', and trying to clean the house, had exhausted her, and Villy suspected that the strain of trying *not* to seem so tired in front of Hugh must have made it much worse. She told Villy that she had, unknown to Hugh, paid a visit to Dr Ballater, who, she said, had been extremely kind and had prescribed some pills 'that make a wonderful difference'. Only she hadn't been able to take them much in London with Hugh because they often made her feel quite woozy and she was afraid he would notice. 'Only I must say,' she had said to Villy on that occasion, 'I do sometimes wonder when it is all going to stop.' Then, before Villy could reply, or even think how to reply, she had said, 'The thing is, I don't want to worry poor darling Hugh till I – have to. Would you help me about that? You're the only person I can ask.' And she, feeling unable to break her promise to Hugh, found herself making a second promise to Sybil.

Since then, she had once tried suggesting to Hugh that

perhaps Sybil did recognise that she was rather ill and he had instantly agreed, but said that none the less *she* thought she was going to get better and must not on any account be disabused. He knew he was right, he said. Look at the situation: he had to be in London all of every week when all he wanted was to be with Sybil. But Villy knew that weekends were a fearful strain for both of them. In the end, she had telephoned Edward at Hendon and asked him to meet her for lunch in London and he had arranged it for the very next day.

'Anything up?' he had asked after they had kissed. 'You sounded rather serious on the telephone.'

'Yes, I'm afraid so.'

They were in his club and he signalled the waiter and ordered two large gins and Frenches. 'It sounds as though we may need them,' he said; he seemed uncharacteristically nervous.

'It's Hugh and Sybil,' she began and, to her surprise, saw his face clear before it assumed a different concern.

She explained. That Sybil had cancer – what they had all feared when she had had the first operation. That *she* knew and Hugh knew, but that they would not tell each other. 'It all seems so sad, and absurd and unnecessary,' she finished. 'But he does want to be with her and, of course, he can't—'

'The Old Man rang me up,' Edward interrupted, 'not about that, as a matter of fact. He simply said that the business was getting too much for Hugh on his own. We're getting a hell of a lot of Government orders, and with the sawmills still in chaos from the Blitz – only one is working properly – and the shortage of staff, Hugh is having a hell of a time. He asked me to apply for leave to come and sort things out. I'm waiting to hear about that, but the CO seems to think it will come through. God! Poor old boy! It must be utter hell for him.'

'Could *you* talk to him? About talking to Sybil – clearing things between them?'

'I could try, but he's as obstinate as the devil. I've never been able to get him to change his mind about anything. Do the others know?'

'I think they must suspect, but it isn't mentioned. And after Sybil making me promise not to say a word to Hugh, it seemed difficult to talk to anyone else. But I do worry about the older children, though, Polly and Simon, I mean. I don't think it should come to them as a frightful shock. Of course, Polly adores her father which should be a comfort to them both.'

'Lucky Hugh.'

Knowing that Louise was rude and unpleasant to him – yet another reason for being displeased with her – Villy said quickly, 'Lydia adores *you*. You should take her out for a treat – she'd simply love it. She's got a birthday quite soon. Ten! She's growing up, you know.'

'She's a dear little thing,' he said absently. When they were finishing lunch, he said, 'Have you heard from Louise?'

'One letter from Northampton. Entirely filled with her theatre doings. She's completely wrapped up in herself – too utterly selfish for words. She behaves as though there simply wasn't a war. But after this year, she really must buckle down to a sensible job. I'm relying on you to read the Riot Act to her.'

'Oh, I wouldn't be any earthly use at that,' he said. 'Shall we have our coffee in the other room? Then we can smoke.'

After lunch he said he must get back to Hendon, saw her into a cab – although he'd offered to drop her off at Charing Cross – and then repaired to an anonymous and dreary little flat in Sloane Avenue where he had arranged to meet Diana.

Villy, although she had not said so, had no intention of going straight back to Sussex, and since, at such short notice, she had been unable to get in touch with Lorenzo, she had decided to pay a visit to Jessica in St John's Wood. There she would at least get news of him, as ringing his home simply meant a tense, uncomfortable conversation with Mercedes, who never seemed to be out and picked up the telephone on the second ring. She had only seen him once since that heavenly train journey, although he did occasionally write to her. But, oddly, she did not understand why her romantic devotion seemed to flourish with absence: she felt that she knew him better and loved him more for his separation. In fact, she was easily able to enlarge upon and embroider their conversation in the train; she felt she *knew* how he would feel and what he would say, *how* he would listen to her confidences and what his responses to them would be. Sometimes, of course, she did just sorely miss him, but this was simply a part of their fate: the tragedy of previous indissoluble attachments. These conversations that they had took place when she was alone in her bedroom at night. Sometimes he would come even before she had undressed, and she would feel shy about taking off her clothes in front of him. Also, she knew that he must want her dreadfully, and it was not fair on him to make this worse. Sometimes, he waited until she was in bed, and then he would sit on the side of it, holding – kissing – her hand and gazing at her with joy. They would discuss the hopelessness of their situation, and although he at first had been unsure, in the end he had agreed that it was worse for her than it could be for him. His wife's jealousy and general unreason would give him sympathy from the world, whereas it could not be expected to have a grain of sympathy for her. Edward was acknowledged to be a very handsome, charming and generous husband, who had given her four children, two of whom were still very young. In any case, there was nothing to be done. Senses of nobility, self-sacrifice would see to that. So then it would be suggested that they should enjoy the little time that they had, and this would result in delicious mutual confidences and admiration. The evening would end with a reprise of its beginning: nobody else in the world could be expected to put up with Mercedes, and Edward would be devastated if he had the slightest idea of her feelings for another man. What they each had to endure in terms of jealous scenes – with, of course, no foundation – and physical intimacy, which Villy had to regard as part of her marital responsibility, meant that compassion now played a large part: they were so desperately sorry for one another and their powerlessness to provide aid or respite only made them suffer more for each other. In the end, she would become exhausted with emotion, something he was wonderfully quick to perceive, as with one last kiss – on her forehead rather daringly – he would vanish. She would fall asleep, tired, but exquisitely peaceful . . .

The taxi had stopped. She paid the ancient driver and got out. The little gothic house was where darling Daddy had died, where she had afterwards spent innumerable afternoons infested with the boredom that only her mother, it seemed, had ever generated. The dining-room shutters were closed – perhaps Jessica was away? A nuisance if she was as the cab had gone creaking off. Someone was in – she heard feet on the stairs – but whoever it was didn't come to the door. Annoyed, Villy rang again; some instinct made her look up, and she saw Jessica at the bedroom window, but before she could call or wave she'd gone. After what seemed like *ages*, there was only one flight of stairs, Jessica opened the door.

'Villy!' she cried – much too loudly, Villy thought; it sounded like a stage welcome – 'What a lovely surprise! I had no idea you were in town!' She was wearing a kind of smock or overall and her feet were bare and her hair, done these days usually in a small bun on the top of the back of her head, was loose. She looked startled and extraordinarily *young*, Villy thought – her eyes, usually so tired and dreamy – were glittering . . .

'I've been tidying poor Mummy's papers and stuff,' she said. 'I was just going to have a bath.'

'What a funny time to have a *bath*, darling!'

By now they were in the hall, but Jessica did not seem to want them to stay there. She put her arm around Villy and propelled her into the drawing room. 'I *do* have baths at funny times. Any time except in the evening. My nightmare is being caught in the bath with an air raid starting.' She shut the drawing-room door and led Villy to the far end of the room. 'We could almost sit in the garden,' she said.

They both looked out at the small square garden whose lawn, too long, was spattered by livid yellow lime leaves, at the rustic bird table standing at a drunken angle as a result of a nearby bomb, at the black walls and the mildewed Michaelmas daisies and neither of them wished to do anything of the kind.

'I'm not much of a gardener, I'm afraid. And, anyway, I never seem to have time. Sit down, darling, and have a fag, and tell me what brings you to London. You might have let me know and I'd have given you lunch.'

In the brief silence while Jessica lit her cigarette for her, Villy thought she heard the sound of a door shutting . . . the front door.

'Who's that?'

'Nobody. Probably someone putting something in the letter box.'

'Oh. Well, I came up to have lunch with Edward. Then it seemed rather feeble just to go straight back. So I came for a gossip.'

'Well, we can't gossip without tea. I'll pop down and make a pot.'

The kitchen in the basement was large and dark with huge, businesslike pieces of furniture: a vast dresser with drawers as unwieldy as boulders in a dry-stone wall, and willow-patterned platters for family joints on the shelves, a big range and an enormous scrubbed kitchen table on which lay a tray with two coffee cups, a toast rack and two soup plates that had clearly contained baked beans.

Jessica said, 'Don't say it – I *am* a slut,' and quickly moved the tray onto the draining board by the sink.

'I've been so worried about Angela,' she said. 'I simply don't know what is going *on* . . .'

While she made the tea, she enlarged upon this. Angela had become extremely difficult to get *hold* of – one had to leave messages at the BBC and God knew if she ever got them as she hardly *ever* responded. There was no telephone at her flat and the only times Jessica had ever been there, she had been out, her flatmate said. 'I offered to take her away for a few days after she had –

after the D and C, but she wouldn't come. She's become so *hard* and unresponsive!' Jessica complained. 'And, of course, falling in love with a married man, as we all know, is madness!'

There was silence, while Villy sipped her tea and they both had (rather different) thoughts about the madness.

'Of course, she's stopped seeing him—' Villy ventured.

'My dear, she can't! She works in the same department. Of course, she ought to ask for a transfer or join the Wrens or something . . .'

When they had said all that there was to be said – by them – about Angela, they went on to Raymond, Louise and Christopher, who, Jessica said, sounded very miserable. 'He's spent months now levelling ground for a runway near Nuneaton, which is pretty hard, dull work, and the people he does it with only want to go to pubs in the evenings and chase girls.'

'Couldn't he do something else? I mean, he's put in a good stint.'

'Raymond made him. And he knows that Raymond expects him to volunteer for one of the Services; I think making him do this is some kind of punishment. He'd be much happier as a farmer, but Raymond would think that *infra dig*. I do wish he wasn't so frightened of his father. It would serve Raymond bloody well right if he went off with a barmaid.'

There was a short silence. Villy knew that she ought to go if she was to catch the train that Tonbridge met every day, and said so. 'Have you seen Laurence at all?' she asked as they walked up the basement stairs.

'From time to time I do.'

'I thought as you live so near one anoth—'

'Ah, yes, but so does Mercedes! She doesn't exactly

encourage one to pop in. Poor Laurence! I don't know how he stands it! She has the most fearful temper and she suspects every woman in the world of trying to carry him off. To work as hard as he does and then have to go home to a woman who screams like a parrot and smashes things – and if you saw her you'd never imagine she'd be like that—'

'I have met her,' Villy said rather coldly, 'at Frensham, with you.'

'Of course you have. Anyway, I think he's a saint. I often tell him that it would serve her right if he *did* go off with one of those luscious sopranos he rehearses with.'

'I thought you didn't see him much!'

'I told you, from time to time. Darling, do you want me to call you a cab? There might be one on the rank.'

But Villy said she'd rather walk.

'I'll give him your love, shall I?'

'Yes. Yes, do. Thanks for the tea. And do put some more clothes on, darling, or you'll catch your death.' She had noticed when Jessica leaned towards her to light her cigarette, that she hadn't been wearing a bra, and she thought now, as she descended the steps to the street, that this was most unseemly in someone of Jessica's age. She felt the visit had not been rewarding, and she found Jessica's attitude towards Lorenzo irritating: she behaved quite as though he was *her* friend and as though she, Villy, hardly knew him. But then she reflected that secrecy was another part of the price people like she and Lorenzo had to pay; therefore it was natural that Jessica should be entirely in the dark; after all, there was no harm in *her* showing off about her comparatively shallow intimacy – her generally open behaviour about him simply implied her innocence and his discretion. She picked

up a cab, deciding that the next invitation for the Clutterworths to stay need not include Jessica on the grounds
that the house would be too full.

∞ ∞ ∞

Lydia and Neville had put their offer to mind the younger
children in the afternoon to good use, as they had long
wanted to run a hospital and had been deterred largely
from lack of patients. Now they had Wills, Roly and
Juliet, who lay in a nervous row on damp camp beds left
over from the evacuation of the Babies' Hotel. They had
chosen the squash court because it was out of earshot
and, as they had expected the game to be a long one, the
chances of someone crying were quite high. Neville was
a doctor, and Lydia the nurse. On two other beds lay
Lydia's favourite old bear and Golly Amazement. They
were both awaiting operations.

'It's a pity I can't operate on a real person,' Neville
said, 'but I think it would be unwise.'

'It would be horrible as well,' Lydia said anxiously.

'I don't think it would. People are simply made of
skin and blood and bones and things. But we haven't got
any anaesthetic so we can't.' The bear and Golly Amazement were to be given doses of the Brig's brandy, and
tied to bedposts, which is what Neville had read people
did in the old days. Immobilising the others had not
been difficult: they had both attended so many first-aid
classes as patients for people to practise on that they were
adept with splints and bandages, and all three now had
an arm and a leg so dealt with. There had been some
initial protest, but Lydia had cleverly quietened them
down with medicine made up by herself of gripe water,

two aspirin ground up, brandy pinched from the Brig's study, and quite a lot of Crimson Lake from her paintbox to make it look like medicine. Wills had simply loved it, and kept saying, 'More,' until he had fallen into a stertorous slumber; most of the medicine she had given Juliet had trickled down her chin and elsewhere, but she loved Lydia and Neville, and as long as they talked to her sometimes and gave her things to play with, she lay obediently with one stiff leg stretched out. Roly was the trouble. He had hated having his arm put in a sling, and splinting both his legs had made matters worse. In the end, they had to undo the sling and give him a stick of barley sugar which he was now resentfully sucking. The bear, who was to be operated on first, had had his stout, furry legs secured, and Lydia gave him pretend teaspoonsful of brandy before Neville, kneeling by the bed, made a steady sawing cut across his stomach with the bread knife. There were weak crackling sounds, and some straw and sawdust fell out. Neville plunged his hand into the hole and then – a conjuring trick learned at school – drew out a small sheet of paper. 'He'll be better without this, Nurse,' he said.

'What is it?'

'His appendix. It's something that is often taken out of people.'

Lydia took the piece of paper. 'Apendix' it said at the top of the page, followed by some rather boring writing about history, she thought.

'Sew him up, Nurse,' Neville commanded. 'Don't want him bleeding to death.'

Lydia obediently wielded her large darning needle threaded with black cotton, but the bear's rather worn skin was very difficult to sew and the more she squeezed some bits of him together, the more sawdust came out from the rest of the hole. 'You're making me do the far most difficult part,' she complained. But Neville was sawing away at one of Golly Amazement's legs which came off with alarming ease. Roland began to cry and, when no notice was taken of him, to yell. This woke Wills up, and wanting to go to Roly, he fell out of bed. In a matter of moments all three of them were screaming.

'Give them all some more medicine, Nurse,' Neville said. He was wrapping Golly Amazement's stump in one of his socks.

'I've used it all up. Oh, poor Wills! He fell on his head – he's got a cut!'

'Sew it up.'

'I can't! The thread's all in the bear. I'm not enjoying myself! Oh, poor Roly! His feet are all blue. You did the bandages too tight. Oh, do *help!*'

Mercifully for the patients, Ellen suddenly appeared. She had had her doubts about the children minding her babies, and had been searching for them when she heard distant wails. She seized Juliet, commanded Lydia to fetch her mother at once, told Neville to undo Roly's splints while she comforted Wills and Juliet.

Later, there was an awful row. They wanted to know about the medicine, which Neville said Lydia was stupid to mention – he had a row with her afterwards – and they were both sent to bed without supper. Her mother sewed up the bear and Golly Amazement, but his leg was never the same again.

'It seems awfully unfair to get punished for something I didn't even enjoy!' Lydia wept. 'Neville made me do all the hard things like sewing and getting the brandy, and it was *my* bear and *my* Golly.'

'You gave Golly Amazement to Wills,' Villy reminded her.

'I *did*, but I've taken him back because Wills didn't like him enough. I always take my presents back if people don't love them. Neville got an Appendix out of the bear and it was just a piece of paper. That's stupid, isn't it? People don't go about with pieces of paper in them.'

'I *knew* they didn't,' Neville immediately said after Villy had agreed that they didn't and Lydia challenged him. 'Of course I knew *that!* But if I'd taken out a real one – an appendix is a kind of wormy root, if you must know – you'd have been screaming all over the place. I was trying to be kind!' he complained. '*And* I probably saved your beastly bear's life.'

∞ ∞ ∞

The moment he set eyes on Sid, Archie understood what had been a torturing mystery to him for the best part of seventeen years.

Rachel brought her down on a Friday evening; she had had flu badly, and there was nobody to look after her at home, Rachel said, and there was something in her voice of overcasual kindness, that Archie, extremely sensitive to every nuance of tone, gesture or even expression of hers, picked up at once. Involuntarily, he glanced at Sid – and knew. So it had not been personal, after all: it had been both a far more serious matter and one which could have had little or nothing to do with him. The anguish, the waste, the sheer *grudge* of being rejected all those years ago slipped entirely and so suddenly from him that he felt weightless, light-headed with shock. He watched Sid, this small, tired woman in her tweed suit,

her cropped hair, her most carefully tied cravat – saw
the Duchy kiss her, lead her to an armchair nearest the
fire while Rachel went in search of drinks for them. He
was introduced; Rachel returned with a tray, cigarettes
were lit, gin was poured, the family came and went
while the past acquired its perspective. Hugh arrived from
London saying that Edward was coming in the morning.
On Saturdays, Miss Milliment and Heather, 'the lady
gardener' as the Duchy called her, dined with them, and
as he discussed French painting with Miss Milliment –
Van Gogh and his pathetic attempts to welcome and please
the churlish Gauguin, and Signac who painted further
along the coast and whom he had met once or twice. He
could not help watching Sid's tired face with the brown,
very wide-apart eyes, the wide mouth, the senses of mis-
chief and uncertainty and fatigue that crossed her face,
making her look like a noble little monkey, a displaced
person, an unutterably weary middle-aged woman by
turns, then turning his covert attention to Rachel whose
name would now always hold a double image for him;
for at the moment of his discovery she had aged, had
ceased to be the ethereally beautiful, frank and innocent
young girl he had loved so much, and become a charming
careworn woman in her early forties. It seemed extraordinary that he had not *seen* her till now, but it was disillusion
of an unpainful kind. Her reality somehow reassured him;
she was a kind, good, unselfish creature with the same
beautiful, frank eyes, but he knew that now, at least, she
was not frank in one respect, and he wondered whether
he had been the means whereby she had discovered her
own nature – for she had concealed nothing from him, he
was sure. When he had taken her into the garden at the
Lynch House – a lovely still June evening – she had not

known until he kissed her that she had not wanted to be kissed, but had then broken away from him with a small sound of revulsion that he had never been able to forget. At the time he had thought it was fear and had held onto her arm, pleading, reassuring, but at the same time, and he never forgot this either, he had experienced a sense of triumph that he must be the first with her – that if he could win her she would be entirely his, she was wild and he had but to tame her with patience – no mean conquest since she was so desirable and older than he. But she had told him to let go of her with such cold sincerity that he had lost his nerve. He had been twenty-two at the time. And the next morning she had sent for him, had told him how much she had liked him and said that she could never marry him. 'I know that,' she said. 'I expect I should have known it before.'

There must be someone else, he had said. No, she had answered, there was nobody. He began telling her how *much* he loved her – he had been young enough to feel that that must make all the difference – he said he would wait, give her any amount of time she wanted to know her mind.

'I do know it,' she said. 'You are only making it worse for yourself. Poor Archie! I'm so sorry.'

He had left the house that day and, soon after, he had gone to France – to get away from Rupert and his family and their friends, who had all gone about together in a close, carefree set. His father had left him a small amount of money, and he settled in Provence and painted and gave English and drawing lessons and sold some pictures and managed. Rupert and Isobel had spent a holiday with him.

After Isobel died, Rupert had come for a week to stay

with him – a strangely docile, shattered Rupert, who could not even laugh without tears coming to his eyes, who, like an insomniac, could not keep still from his grief, fidgeted endlessly with pencils and cigarettes, kept leaping to his feet and shambling about the studio knocking into things. After the first awful day, Archie took him for three-hour walks and fed him with large bowls of stew: 'You're treating me as though I was an enormous *dog!*' Rupert had exclaimed after the third day of this regime, and as he had begun to laugh at himself, he had burst out crying and been able to talk about Isobel without stopping until the early hours, when the stove had gone out, and cocks were crowing.

The next day when, instead of a walk, they went out to paint together, Rupert said, 'You really are a friend, Archie. Much more of one than I was to you. I always felt bad about that. But I suppose you needed to get right away.'

And after a bit, he added almost shyly, 'But you're over it now, aren't you? You don't mind me asking?'

'No,' was all Archie had said, and he *was* over it. Which had been true, in a sense: he no longer ached for her, and days passed when he did not even think of her, only when he had once or twice seemed to be on the brink of loving someone else, had she intervened and he had drawn back. He had found a succession of girls to paint, and to go to bed with, who cooked for him, and mended his clothes and were sometimes amiable company, but he never got further than affection and lust.

Archie had returned to England in the autumn of 1939 to volunteer for the Navy. He and Rupert had had one hilarious evening in Weymouth when they both got very drunk and then they had gone their different ways, he to

Coastal Forces, and Rupert to a Hunt class destroyer. When he had heard the news of Rupert he had written to the Duchy, of whom he had always been extremely fond, and she had replied, saying that if he had leave and wanted somewhere to stay he would be welcome. So then, when he got shot up and they'd done all they could for his leg, he'd taken up the invitation. He knew Rachel had not married, and he'd wondered how he would feel when he saw her again. After the first evening, he wondered why he had wondered, because he had felt, not exactly the same, but quite as much. She had only to give him her hand, to look at him with her lovely frankness, to speak in her gentle drawl that was so like Rupert for him to be back in thrall to her beauty and the astonishing lack of vanity that had always moved him. If she was in the least self-conscious about their last meeting, there was no sign of it. He hardly ever saw her alone: her job in London – she described herself as 'a kind of stooge at the office' – and her duties at home – she seemed always to be unobtrusively doing something for somebody else – precluded that. It was she who told him how hard Clary had taken her father being missing, and had asked him to deal gently with her determination that he was not dead. On another occasion she had mentioned how passionately interested in painting Miss Milliment was and how she enjoyed talking about it: 'Rupe said she was amazingly knowledgeable as well as perceptive.' Then there had been the Brig, who so much enjoyed having *The Times* read to him. Their rare duologues were always about somebody else. But he discovered that he enjoyed taking Rachel's various hints, and in the autumn weeks that followed, he slipped easily into the family life. His leg still hurt a good deal, especially if he used it much, but he had been told that it was a long business, and when, in October, he had suggested to the Duchy that perhaps it was time he moved on, she had said, 'My dear, what on earth for, and where to?' Unlike the Cazalets, his family was small and far from close knit: after his father died, his mother embraced Gurdjieff and had no time for anyone who did not do the same, and his only sister, far older than he, had married a Canadian doctor and he had seen her once in the last twenty years. She had had five children who seemed identical except for their size, like so many ring spanners, and he only knew this because their Christmas card consisted every year of a family photograph. No, there was nowhere to go and, from his point of view, not only no reason to leave, but a growing need to stay. He had quite decided that he must make one more attempt to get Rachel to marry him but the more he thought about it the more nervous he became about asking her: for once she had said no – *if* she said no (and his confidence was not strong on this point) – surely that would be the end of his chance of love, of staying on with the family? It was too easy to let things slide, to postpone the proposal. He told himself that she was getting to know him again, that it was too soon and so on. He told himself a lot of things that he naturally had wanted to believe.

But now that was all over. He could stay as long as he liked and it would make no difference. During that curious evening, that brought him feelings both of devastation and release, he thought he had recognised something that the rest of the family did not. It *was* a secret, and how hard, he thought tenderly, for someone as direct and innocent as Rachel that must be to bear! Sid seemed accepted in the family: when, after dinner, she had apologised to the

Duchy and said that she did not feel up to playing sonatas, the Duchy had said of course not! She should go to bed with a nice hot-water bottle and a hot drink, and Rachel had instantly got to her feet and gone to procure these things.

In bed that night, he had started to try to examine how he felt: love, it seemed to him, was more painful than it was anything else, and not, he could see, only for him. Rupert's unknown fate hung over them all; upon his strange, gaunt, intense little daughter, upon his wife who once Archie had thought such a frightful mistake. He remembered Rupert saying at the end of their week alone in France after Isobel's death: 'Well, I shall have to marry someone – anyone quiet and homely – who will be a mother to the children,' and then visiting him on his honeymoon with that amazingly attractive, frivolous little pussy with whom he was clearly infatuated. 'This is Zoë,' he had said, as one who is presenting a goddess, a queen, the beauty of all time, and he had seen at once her narcissism, her childish selfishness, her determination to have always and only her own way in everything. She was not like that now. She was paler, less sparkling, tentative about almost everything except the baby. He had been touched when he had said how pretty the baby was, and she had answered at once, 'But she's awfully intelligent – like Rupert. She's going to have a first-class education and a proper career. She's not going to be at all like me.' Unlike Clary, she could not speak of Rupert; one day she had tried, but her eyes had filled with tears, her face contorted, and without another word, she had run out of the room. And the Duchy. When she mentioned Rupert, which he noticed she only did if she was alone with him, he saw her making a steadfast effort to do so calmly. Alive or dead, Rupert was deeply loved, not least by him, Archie. I seem to have lost the two people I have loved most in my life, he thought. Then he realised that his leg was hurting too much for him to get to sleep and hoisted himself out of bed to find his painkillers. 'Maudlin,' he muttered to himself; Rachel had never been his, so in that sense it could not be said that he had lost her, and as for Rupert – why could he not have Clary's faith? Because he knew more about the decrepit, hysterical, *corrupt* uproar that France had become: Daladier and Blum being jailed for life for 'causing the defeat of France', hostages being shot – two hundred of them for the deaths of two German officers – the Vichy Government responsible for the arrest and deportation of thousands of Jews, Pétain blaming British agents for any insurrection, house-to-house searches for any French 'disloyal' to that senile puppet. It would be hard to survive as a foreigner in that, even with very good French. He would need a great deal of support and protection – the cost of being a loyal Frenchman was already terrifyingly high, yet there were such people. Being shot up on the bridge of an MTB was nothing to that, he thought, as he dropped into sleep.

∞ ∞ ∞

Edward woke early with the unnaturally bright feeling that meant, he knew, that he had a hangover. It was the hooch that he'd had to buy in the Coconut Grove. And then when you had been made to buy a whole bottle, you drank more than you usually would because, dammit, you'd paid for the stuff in the first place. He'd taken Diana dancing, because the poor girl got very little fun

485

stuck away in the country with that po-faced sister-in-law and Jamie, now an exhausting three-year-old. But he'd been tired at the beginning of the evening: he had just started back at the wharf and was confounded by the mess they were in there. In the best part of a *year*, Hugh hadn't succeeded in getting the second sawmill working. It was true that the Blitz had wreaked havoc, and one shed had been decimated, but all the same . . . Orders were pouring in for hardwoods, for which they were justly famous, but they had to be able to cut the veneers. The machinery hadn't been too badly damaged, but Hugh had made the terrible mistake of leaving everything exactly as the Blitz had left it so that the damage assessors could see exactly what had happened. Which was no bloody good if you left expensive machinery without adequate protection from the winter elements. It was no good blaming the poor old boy; what with his anxiety about Sybil, and the fact that he had none of the family to support him – except Rachel who, after all, knew nothing at all about the business, but was wonderful with the staff – he had had far too much on his plate. He was obstinate at the best of times, but in the past he and the Old Man had been able to steamroller things when it was really necessary. But what worried him now was that alongside the obstinacy, Hugh had become frighteningly indecisive – more like dear old Rupe. He kept saying he'd think about it when any decision had to be made, and two days later nothing at all would have happened, and Edward found himself having to nag. The result was that every-thing was in a muddle: the accounts department was a shambles since Stevens had been called up; their crane was always breaking down because Hugh hadn't bullied the manufacturers for new parts – in horribly short supply, anyway. Their lorries were in a bad way too. Several of them needed replacing, but there was a fat chance of that and, again, the chap who'd been so incredibly good at repairing the engines had been killed last autumn in the Blitz. The fire-watching was a nightmare. It meant that, in succession, blokes who had worked all day got no sleep at night. The paperwork had trebled since ninety per cent of their business was now Government orders. He'd almost wished at the end of yesterday that he *had* been driving down with Hugh for a nice quiet, unde-manding evening. But he felt guilty about Diana, whom he sensed was relying on him more and more. That husband of hers had become a paratrooper and had not had any leave for months.

As Diana's flat had been bombed, they had gone in the end to Lansdowne Road – officially shut now, but still containing basic furniture. He knew she disliked going there, but a hotel was a bit risky. Ever since that awful evening with Louise he had felt pretty windy about being seen in the wrong place at the wrong time with Diana. A night club was one thing – nearly everyone he knew went to them and usually with somebody they weren't married to since families were so separated by the war – but an hotel was another.

She was fast asleep beside him. Dinner had been fine. There had been oysters, a most welcome addition to their five-shilling meal, and they were given real butter with their bread. 'I know one chap', he had said, 'who asks for a roll, and scoops out all the middle of it and fills it with all the butter on the table and shuts it up again and takes it home for breakfast.'

'Isn't it awfully embarrassing being watched doing it? By waiters and people?'

'He doesn't seem to care a damn.'

'I must say,' Diana had said, 'Goering is the wrong *shape* to have made that remark about guns or butter. He does look as though he gets *all* the butter—'

'And we get all the guns. Darling! Were you very upset about your flat?'

'Oh, well, in a way, you know. It was home. Although I never liked it much. It did have all my things in it. I feel as though I've been camping for years.'

'Is Isla still as stiff as ever?'

'Exactly as stiff. The archetypal sister-in-law. She feels that there must be something really juicy to disapprove of about me, but she hasn't found out what.'

'I can't think how anyone could disapprove of you.'

'She could, darling. And you're the really juicy thing. Actually, I don't know if I can stay there much longer.'

'Does Angus want you to go to his parents, then?'

'Oh, he always wants that. But I simply couldn't *bear* it. Their ghastly Victorian sub-castle is freezing cold even in August, and now they've gone teetotal because of the war.'

'Good God!' He was shocked. 'What's that supposed to do?'

'They feel it's patriotic.' She shrugged. 'Anyway, it's a useful place for the older boys for holidays. I have to go up then, or I'd never see them. Isla, as you know, hasn't got room for all of us.'

That was the first mention she had made of not staying with Isla, but it hadn't seemed particularly important. After dinner, they went to Regent Street, to the Coconut Grove. They were early: it was only about eleven and they parked right outside.

'Whisky or gin?' he had said when they were presented with this choice.

'Gin, I think.'

He ordered a bottle and several tonics, but the gin, when it came, tasted so foul that they decided to add some lime juice instead, and have soda instead of tonic. This took ages to arrive, so they danced. Holding her was a pleasure, both familiar and exciting. She was wearing a violet-coloured dress that, although *he* had not noticed it, matched her eyes; the crêpe clung to her splendid big-boned body and revealed just the right amount of her handsome breasts. They danced slowly to 'All The Things You Are'. 'My promised breath of springtime,' he hummed and smiled down into her eyes, and she glowed.

At the end of the dance, she took his hand, and said, 'Oh, darling! I'm so happy.'

'I'm always happy when I'm with you,' he answered. Their soda water and lime had still not arrived, and he called a waiter to say this, but neither of them felt this mattered as much as he had told the waiter it did. They sipped their gin and tonic; she made a face, and said, 'It might just make us pass out.'

'Simultaneously, two enormous ninepins,' he said. 'They wouldn't like that at all.'

They smoked and watched the other dancers, and soon picked out a very young couple – a guardsman – and a tall, rather ungainly red-haired girl dressed in white. 'A sort of Queen Charlotte's Ball dress,' Diana said. But what made them watch, what was striking about them, was that they were so madly in love – could not take their eyes off each other, were scarcely moving on the floor. They were misty-eyed, intoxicated with desire for one another; very occasionally, he bent his head and his lips brushed her white shoulder and she half closed her eyes, and then they looked at each other again and he would hold her closer.

'Very touching,' Edward said; he *was* touched.

'Poor darlings,' Diana said. 'I bet they have nowhere to go.'

'Surely, if they really want to, he'll find somewhere.'

She shook her head. 'They're too young. And too well brought up. I expect he's asked her to marry him, and her parents have told them to wait until she's older. Even though he may be killed.'

'Do you think we should ask them if they'd like to go back to Lansdowne Road?'

'Of course not. I just feel sorry for them – that's all.' There was a pause, and then she said, '*We*'re not going back there, are we?'

''Fraid so. Darling, I know it's not very comfortable, but it is private.'

'You mean nobody except your wife might find us?'

'I swear she's in the country. I swear she won't turn up.'

'But I want to talk to you,' she said with apparent inconsequence.

'Talk away.'

'Not here. It's serious. I've got to come to some decision.'

When he simply looked at her enquiringly, she said, with the faintest impatience, 'I have sort of told you already. I can't stay much longer with Isla.'

He couldn't see why this was something she couldn't talk about there and then, but knew it would be unwise to say so.

'Well, shall we consider going back?'

When they left, the young couple were still on the floor, entranced. They had not stopped dancing at all except on the brief occasion when the band had a short rest.

'He can't hold her in his arms if they are sitting at a table,' Diana said, as they went out.

∞ ∞ ∞

Lansdowne Road, although possible as a place to sleep, was definitely no longer a place to have an intimate talk. There was nowhere to be, really, except in bed in his dressing room. The rest of the house had been shut up for so long that it seemed full of dust and cold, dead air.

'Aren't you living here in the week?' Diana asked as he told her to wait in the hall while he turned on the electricity.

'No, I'm with Hugh. It seemed stupid to keep two houses open, and the old boy is fearfully lonely. There.'

But the light only showed up the desolation. They went, without speaking, upstairs.

'Oh, damn! I should have turned on the gas as well,' he said.

By the time he had done that, had lit the gas fire and found some linen for the bed, which she made, there was a feeling of tension between them. She sat before the fire, huddled in her skunk jacket.

'Like a drink?'

'No, thanks.'

'Well, I think I'll have one.'

He kept a flask of whisky in his overcoat pocket, in case of air raids and generally being stuck somewhere. The tooth glass had a rim of dried toothpaste; the last time he'd stayed here had been weeks ago, that awful evening with Louise . . . he felt so ghastly when he thought about that, that most of the time he managed not to think about it at all. He rinsed the glass, poured himself a tot and added water.

'Wouldn't we be comfier in bed?' he said, and immediately sensed that that was quite the wrong thing to say. 'What did you want to talk about, darling?'

'I don't know that I want to *talk* about it,' she answered at once. 'I just want to *tell* you, I suppose. I think I'm having a baby.'

'Oh, Lord!'

'In fact, I'm certain I am. So you see my problem.'

He didn't at all. 'Sorry, darling, I'm being rather dense.'

'Isla will know it isn't Angus's.' Then, as though she knew he would ask why, she said, 'I haven't set eyes on him since the beginning of the summer holidays. He joined us at Duninald for a couple of days. And now we're nearly into November. I'm between two and three months gone.'

'My God! I *do* see. You can't tell her you saw Angus in London – something like that?'

'They write to each other *regularly*. She'd find out at once. If Angus found out, he'd divorce me like a shot.'

'Is there anything you can *do* about it?'

'You mean, have an abortion? Where? Don't forget, I've been tucked away in the country, I'm completely out of touch, *I* don't know anybody.'

'I could try and – ask around – you know – there must be someone.'

'I don't want any little backstreet butcher mucking me up,' she said bitterly. 'They're my insides, not yours.'

'Darling, I'm only trying to help. We're both married. I don't see what else there is to do.'

'Don't you? I suppose there isn't anything.' She began to cry.

He put his arm round her and felt for his handkerchief. At the same time the scenario of her having the baby, getting divorced from Angus, and his telling Villy and getting a divorce from her coursed through his mind and he shrank from it. It would take years and be terrible the whole time; he doubted whether they could survive it. At the same time, *not* doing any of that was leaving Diana in the lurch. The thought of being married to her recurred. If only he'd met her years ago! He couldn't start disrupting everything *now*, in the middle of a war, and Roly only two, he really couldn't. But he seemed to be in a position where there *wasn't* a decent thing he could do. Comfort the poor girl, he could do that. He stroked her, and murmured words of love, said he couldn't bear to see her cry, made her drink some of his whisky, and she *did* stop crying – he could see she had made an effort to do that – and it touched him. He undressed her; he wasn't very good at it, clumsy with her bra hooks, but she helped him in the end. In bed, he made love to her as unselfishly as he knew how and, funnily enough, this made him love her more. Afterwards they talked for hours and finished the whisky. In the end he got round to saying that he knew that Villy's sister must have found someone, as her daughter got in the family way not long ago, and it was dealt with. 'And that chap's bound to be all right or she wouldn't have let Angela go to him,' he said.

'For God's sake, don't tell her! She would tell Villy and—'

'Of course I won't. I'll say it's for a young friend of mine in the RAF,' he said. 'I'll manage that – don't you worry.'

'It's probably frightfully expensive—'

'Don't worry about that either. That's the least I can do.'

'You know, I'm practically certain Jamie's yours,' she said. 'It seems so awful to keep having babies without their father.'

She had never actually said that about Jamie before, although he had certainly wondered. What with alcohol, emotion and fatigue she was on the brink of becoming maudlin. He kissed her and said, 'Jamie's wonderful because he's yours. You know I love him. Now, we'd better both get some sleep.'

And she had gone out like a light, but the bed was narrow for the two of them, and it took him time to get off, and then he slept fitfully.

Now, in the cold light of day, and by Jove, it *was* cold, he thought, he'd better make some tea for them both, since there was nothing to have for breakfast. This entailed padding down two flights of stairs to the kitchen and struggling to find tea and the tin of dried milk, which he had no idea how to mix, while the kettle was boiling. In the end, he took the tin up with him, alongside a jug of water. His head was beginning to throb and his mouth felt vile partly because he'd slept in his false teeth. He cleaned them all, the living and the dead, as he called them, and gave himself a stiff draught of Andrew's Liver Salts before he woke her up.

The tea was rather nasty, but she said it was a great deal better than nothing.

∞ ∞ ∞

As he dropped her off at the cottage at Wadhurst, he said, 'I'll ring you on Monday evening. From the office, just before I leave. About five.'

'If you make it half past, Isla'll be at her WI meeting.'

'Right. God bless.'

He drove on, wondering what would be the most tactful way of tackling Jessica about an abortionist. Tact was certainly required: he was not supposed to know about Angela only, of course, Villy had told him, on top of which, Jessica, who was pretty sharp, would not be likely to believe that he wanted one for a friend unless he was very convincing. He began to regret having suggested it, but he'd have to go through with it now.

But he didn't have to, because on Monday morning Diana rang him at the office to say that Angus had been killed – in an air raid on Portsmouth.

'Poor darling. Do you feel—'

'I don't know what I feel,' she said. 'Stunned, mostly. We hadn't been getting on, but all the same it seems a fearful waste. He so loved the Army – a civilian death seems rather a sell.' She sounded brittle with shock. 'He was going to be sent overseas,' she said. 'He was looking forward to it. Apparently it wasn't even a particularly bad raid.' He could not think of anything to say.

'Poor Isla's devastated,' she said. 'Anyway, *you* needn't worry. I can tell her a story now and she'll *want* to believe it.' Then she said, 'I'm going to ring off now: I really can't think of anything else to say.'

He wrote her a letter later on that day. He wasn't used to writing them, but he felt for her. He could see how she must feel guilty, and how difficult it must be to be living with her sister-in-law and having to pretend to feel more than she did. *And* she was pregnant, and money, which had always been tight, would now be tighter on a widow's pension. He couldn't manage to say much of this in his letter, but he told her he would help in any way that he could and that he was sorry. And he sent his love and said he would keep in close touch. It wouldn't help her much, he knew; nothing helped guilt except absolution from whomever one had harmed, and he, of all people, knew how awful it was when you had no hope of that.

∞ ∞ ∞

The platform of the station at Oxford Circus was, as usual, crowded. By this time of night, everybody who slept on it had commandeered their place – the same one every night, Angela had begun to notice. The most favoured slept next to the slot machines that contained a small mirror in which, no doubt, they could comb out their hair in the morning. Many of them slept in curlers. They spread layers of newspaper on the ground, covered it with a blanket, and a pillow, if they had one, and then lay fully clothed with another blanket on top. Over the weeks, they must have become used to the preliminary rush of warm, dark brown air that was pushed through the tunnel in front of each train, arriving with a crescendo of sound that died away to a high-pitched little mechanical ticking. A second's silence; then there would be the hiss of the doors opening and a pause while the passengers got in and out of the train before a weary voice called, 'Mind the doors!' whereupon with a convulsive, moaning lurch it was off again, gathering speed, its rocking racket gradually dying away as it disappeared into the tunnel. Every three or four minutes this happened, and yet people slept through it. When she came off duty after the night shift at six thirty in the morning, there they would be, bleary-eyed, taking out their curlers and dropping them into biscuit tins or brown-paper carrier bags, making up their faces in the slot-machine mirrors or with tiny ones from their handbags, drinking tea out of Thermos flasks, not saying anything much to one another. The men, who were mostly old, would still be asleep since their toilet was minimal: old boys on their backs, their mouths open, snoring, their sparse yellow-grey hair ruffled by the approach of each train.

Outside the station it was utterly dark, and very cold. Angela had always been thin, but since her abortion she had not wanted to eat much at all and had become much thinner, so she felt the cold. She only had to cross the road to reach the Peter Robinson building, now housing the Overseas Service of the BBC. She was the most junior continuity announcer, and had been working for six weeks now. Brian had got her the job – he was quite high up in the administration – and she knew he had pulled strings to get her in. 'I must try and make it up to you somehow,' he had said, on their last private meeting. Although it seemed extraordinary to her that he could seriously equate an admittedly better job with being in love, having his baby and being rejected. She had not *meant* to get pregnant, but when she was, she had told him at once, thinking it would turn the scales, that he would leave the wife he either never spoke of or spasmodically disparaged, and marry her. But he had been appalled by her news and so violent about her *not* having the baby, that she said she would have it anyway – whether he married her or not. So then he said that they might have to wait, but would get married in the end and she had been happy again – and *then*, she did not know how it happened, her mother found out that she was pregnant, and when Angela said it didn't matter, that he was going to marry her as soon as he got a divorce, her mother actually went and *saw* him. But she did not know this until after their meeting. He never meant to marry you, her mother said; he has a wife and children – he would not think of leaving them; he only said what he did because he was terribly worried about you.

They had had one meeting: she had wanted him to come to her bed-sitter in Notting Hill Gate, but he had refused – said he would meet her in Kensington Gardens by the Peter Pan statue. 'Supposing it's pouring with rain?' she said (this was on the telephone). 'It won't be,' he had replied.

It wasn't. It was one of those tremulously balmy September mornings, with a pale blue sky and soft yellow sunlight that had no warmth. The trees were turning and the grass, now that they had taken away all the small railings that had edged every path to use the iron for the war effort, looked very green and faintly crisp from an early frost. She knew she would arrive too early and walked, as slowly as she could bear to, from Lancaster Gate station on the path nearest the Serpentine lake. In spite of everything that had happened, she could not help feeling excited and happy at the prospect of seeing him, and during this walk she moved from being afraid – from dreading – what he might be going to say to her, to wondering what he might say, and eventually to *imagining* what he might say which, of course, miraculously became what she wanted to hear. I shall remember this day all my life, she thought, and, more dramatically, I am walking towards my fate. Their difference in age did not matter (he had said that right at the beginning); he would drink less, she was sure, if he was happier which she was certain he would be with her. If he did not want children, she would not have any. She would do exactly what he wanted, because she wanted to do that.

He was late, but only a few minutes. She saw him coming – along the same path that she had walked – but she forced herself to remain on the bench until he was very near, when she could not help springing to her feet.

She wanted to fly into his arms, but he kissed her cheek, a most non-committal kiss, and suggested they sit.

From the moment that he began to speak – making it clear that the meeting was for him an ordeal – her heart, which had seemed almost in her throat, began to sink, heavily, coldly, in her breast.

He said how difficult it was for him to say the things he had to say. He said he was entirely to blame. He said that he had been carried away – he made that sound as though this was a faintly disgusting, contemptible thing to have been. He said that his wife had been made very unhappy by the affair – she knew, he interrupted her, because he had told her. She had been wonderful about it all, had entirely understood how it had all come about and was prepared to forgive him for the sake of their marriage and their children. He was too old for Angela, and she was so young, at the beginning of her life, that she was bound to find some really nice young man who would be worthy of her (there were fearful echoes here of Rupert, who now seemed so distant, so long ago). He was not going to see her again; he had promised her mother – and then that came out. The shock and humiliation of this – of being *discussed* as though she was a child, by his wife and her mother – was too much and anger suddenly animated the paralysed stupor with which she had listened until then. How dared he go and see her mother behind her back! she'd said. *She* had come to see him, he replied. Pride forbade her asking him how her mother could have known about it, if not from him. Afterwards she recognised that he had lied by not saying things: he had rung her mother up, and *then* her mother had gone to see him. He told her that he had arranged for her to have an audition for the announcing job, and when she said she didn't want it, he had urged her at least to try for it. 'You need something interesting to do now,' he had said. 'The alternative is that you will be called up to do God knows what.' Then he had said how much he admired her courage and that he was taking his wife on a short holiday which he felt was badly needed. He had told her to take care of herself – looked as though he was going to kiss her cheek again, but she turned her face away – touched her hands, a sort of apologetic pat, as she said to herself afterwards, got up from the bench and walked quickly away without looking back. Or at least she did not think he looked back – again her pride prevented her from watching him walk away; one glance had been enough.

She felt utterly betrayed, but the devilish thing was that she still could not think of him without longing. She did not 'respect' him, as she put it – at times she was even able to dislike him – but some part of her hung on to how they had been before all this had happened and longed to go back to it.

She had got the job because she had not really cared whether she did or not, had had no nerves, was calm and

500

cool and collected. She had trailed other announcers for a week and learned the job and then begun. It was two months now since that meeting and she got through the days and nights somehow. Everything, excepting the job, was an extraordinary and pointless effort – travelling, feeding herself, making any small decision, talking to other people. She slept and slept – getting up in the afternoons was always hard, and on her days off she didn't bother sometimes to get up at all.

She had seen him once in the two months – getting into a taxi outside the building. He had not seen her, and she stood and watched him be driven away. She noticed that her heart was aching but it wasn't until the sight of him gave her a little lilt to her spirits, which relapsed as soon as the cab was out of sight, that she realised that it had been aching all the time.

By now she had shown her pass in the hall, taken a lift, which had carried her four floors down, and was walking along the stuffy, soundproofed corridors to her studio. It was good manners to arrive on shift a bit early, so that the other announcer could leave on time. She arrived in the middle of a recorded concert. 'I've logged the records,' her predecessor said. 'Phew! I'm glad to be going home. Our boiler broke down yesterday, and Martin's got flu, I think, and the roof's been leaking ever since the bomb fell in the next street.' Her name was Daphne Middleton and she was married to a producer who worked in Broadcasting House. They did not really know each other, as Daphne's shift had only recently been moved to the one before Angela's. As Daphne gathered up her things, she said, 'By the way, you don't happen to know anyone who wants a room, do you? My lodger's suddenly given notice. Martin's miserable – she was rather a glamour puss, and I'm relieved, but we do need the money.'

'I'm afraid I don't.'

'Oh, well. Have to ask everyone. She's not going for a month. She's got a week's leave and guess who she's spending it with! That producer Brian Prentice. He's married, you know. Aren't some men the end! God – I must fly. You'll have to kick those JPEs awake – they're very slow off the mark.'

Coincidence. She supposed all coincidences must seem extraordinary to their victims, but although for a second she had wondered if it had been malice – if Daphne had known about her and Brian – she knew that it wasn't. She had never spent a week with him, she had told nobody, and she knew that he would not. Until then she had thought that she could not be more unhappy, but the job, continuous, demanding – she must never let there be more than fifteen seconds of dead air in case the Germans picked it up and used it – saved her. By six thirty the following morning, when she came off shift, she felt bitterness and rage, but she was out of love. It was still a desert, but she was free in it. She discovered that she was desperately hungry, and went to the canteen where she had a dried egg omelette, some tomatoes and a piece of bacon.

∞ ∞ ∞

'Mrs Cripps made you this.' She put the steaming mug down on the small table beside the sofa. He looked up at her; he had been staring at his hands placed on the rug in front of him.

'Christopher,' she said gently. 'It's Polly. It's me.'

'I know.' Tears began to course down his face. He often cried like this, making no sound, for what seemed like hours. When he was not crying, his eyes had a hunted expression; he looked haunted, very scared of something, but nobody knew what. To begin with she had thought that the best thing was to take no notice, to be gently cheerful and to talk to him as though he was the old Christopher, but she found this very hard since his unreachable despair, or whatever it was, made her want to cry too. Then she had tried to encourage him to cry more – to cry out whatever was locking him up. But nothing made any difference.

He had been picked up by Military Police in Felix-stowe: they had thought he was a young deserter, a soldier who had gone AWOL. But then they had discovered that he did not seem to know where he was – did not even remember his name. They had gone through his clothes and found his surname on a Cash's name tape on his vest so, in time, his identity had been discovered. Raymond and Jessica had travelled together to the hospital where he was and it was clear that he recognised his father since he made an effort to get out of bed and escape, but he was so weak that he collapsed on the floor of the ward. They had had to give their permission for him to have electric shock treatment, and after a month in the hospital, he had been sent to Home Place to convalesce. The Duchy was extremely fond of him, and Jessica, who now came down every weekend, was grateful to have him out of London in a place that she knew he loved.

But he didn't seem to love it much, Polly thought sadly. He did not love anything. He sat on the lawn, on fine days, heavily wrapped up in front of a bird table that the Duchy had had moved there for him. He *did* watch them feeding sometimes, and once, when a robin chased the others away, he smiled. But most of the time he cried. Dr Carr came, but he was frightened of Dr Carr.

'I think it's doctors he's afraid of,' Aunt Rach said.

'I think it's men,' Aunt Villy had answered, and Polly, who had heard this, was beginning to agree with her.

When it was too cold for him to be out, which it now usually was, they put him in the drawing room. The Duchy, who did not generally allow the drawing-room fire to be lit until an hour before dinner, had it lit in the morning for his benefit, as she said it would give people the excuse to keep popping in to make it up, but it was still cold. He wore a polo-necked jersey that had belonged to Rupert – a kind of indigo blue that sadly matched the deep circles under his eyes. Villy shaved him every other day. Sometimes, in the afternoon, Clary and Polly took him for short walks round the garden. He went obediently with them and they talked to each other, trying to make conversations that he might feel constrained to join, but his contributions were mainly a nervous agreement. He tried to eat some of whatever was put before him. Then, one weekend Hugh brought down a dog – a large black and white mongrel with a good deal of Border Collie in him, middle-aged, that had been found waiting and dazed outside a completely bombed house near the wharf. 'See what that does,' he said to Polly. 'You know he always loved animals.'

'Oh, Dad, that is a good idea!' She and Clary gave the dog a bath, which improved his appearance a lot, and then took him in to Christopher.

'This dog has been terribly frightened by the Blitz,' Polly said; she somehow knew that this would get his attention. He looked at the dog standing stock still a few yards away, and the dog looked back at him. Then it walked slowly up to him and sat, leaning heavily against his legs. Somebody slammed a door and the dog began to shiver. Christopher put out his hand and laid it on the dog's head and the dog gazed at him and slowly stopped shivering.

'What a lovely dog!' Lydia exclaimed the next morning. 'What's he called?'

'Oliver,' Christopher said.

'Is he your dog?'

'Yes. He is now.'

'Darling, you are a brilliant man!' Sybil said. 'We none of us thought of that.'

'Well, he sort of fell into view, poor creature. He's terribly nervous: can't stand aeroplanes or loud noises. I just thought they might do each other good.' If only I could give *you* a dog, and you would get well, he thought looking at her yellowing face, her swollen belly and ankles as she lay on the bed.

'Shall I bring you a spot of lunch up here?' he said. 'I could bring mine too, have it with you.'

'Oh, no, darling, I'm just being lazy.' And he had to watch her hoist herself off the bed and wander to the dressing table where she struggled to put up her hair.

'Sybil! Darling!' He took a deep breath and was ready to plunge into the deep end of truth.

She turned nervously to face him. 'What?' She sounded so defensive, that he lost courage.

'I was wondering,' he said, 'what you would look like if you cut your hair off. It might make an exciting change.'

'I thought you always liked it long.'

'Well, I did, but I can change my mind, can't I?'

505

It would be less tiring for her, he thought. So Villy carefully cut it off which was a great relief to Sybil. She made him stay to decide how short it was to be, and the ground became thick with the long tresses before Villy did the trimming.

Thinking himself unseen, he sneaked a lock from the floor and concealed it, but they both saw him, Villy with compassion, and Sybil with fear, but since she could not stand him knowing, she determined that he did not.

Polly knew, though. Since nobody talked about it, she bore her knowledge alone. She was afraid to talk of it, and every week that passed seemed to make this more difficult. She would not talk to her father for fear of burdening him with more misery – anxiety about how *she* was feeling. She could not talk to her mother, because she felt it would betray him. She did not talk to Clary, because she felt Clary had enough to bear as it was. Everybody else preserved such a bland and consistently cheerful air that she did not know how to approach them. She distracted herself by trying to look after Christopher, who did seem to be slowly on the mend. Since Oliver had appeared, he had begun to stop crying, and Oliver never left his side. Indeed, this was what started Christopher going for walks unattended: Oliver needed exercise, he said. He could be seen wandering round the big meadow, throwing an old tennis ball for Oliver, who was tireless in his enjoyment of this. So, in a way, he did not need her so much. She struggled through each day of getting up in the freezing cold, having breakfast, doing lessons, spending some time with Christopher and her mother, doing her homework, ironing and mending her clothes or minding Wills and Roly for Ellen. The present seemed grey; the future black. She lived in a haze of dread.

One bleak November afternoon Miss Milliment, going to the schoolroom to fetch the Greek primer to set homework for Clary, came in, switched on the light, and discovered Polly seated at the table. She leapt to her feet.

'I haven't done the blackout,' she said, and Miss Milliment could tell from her voice that she had been crying. She turned off the light, and waited while Polly pulled down the blinds. The small paraffin stove had either been turned off or gone out: it was bitterly cold.

'Isn't this rather a cold place to spend the afternoon?' she asked. Polly had gone back to the table and muttered something about not noticing it.

Miss Milliment said, 'I feel something is worrying you very much,' and she sat down at the table opposite Polly.

There was a silence, during which Polly looked at her and she looked back steadily. Then she burst out, 'I'm sick of being treated like a child! I'm absolutely *sick* of it!'

'Yes, I think it must be very tiresome. Particularly at a time when you are ceasing to be one. People always say,' she went on, after a pause, 'how wonderful it must be to be young, but I fear that most of them have forgotten what it was like. I found it quite dreadful myself.'

'Did you, Miss Milliment?'

'Fortunately, whether people like it or not, they grow older. And you will do that. You will get past this tiresome, interim stage and they will have to acknowledge that you are grown up.'

She waited, and then offered gently, 'It will pass. Nothing lasts for ever.'

But Polly, looking away from her, said, 'One thing does. It lasts for ever and ever. Death.'

Her quiet and certain despair exposed a depth of misery that both moved and shocked Miss Milliment. She said, half hoping that it might be so, 'Are you thinking of your uncle?'

'You know I am not.'

'Yes, my dear Polly, I do. Forgive me.'

'It isn't—' her voice trembled, 'it isn't just that they don't talk to *me* about it. They don't talk to each other. They go on pretending to each other that it isn't happening! It makes everything they say a kind of lie. And it must be especially hard for my mother when she feels so rotten all the time – and getting – getting *worse*. It is my father's fault! He ought to start it, so that she can really say what she is feeling. At least, if *I* was dying – that's what I would want.' Tears were streaming down her face now, but she ignored them. 'I think it's wicked and wrong.'

'I agree with you about what you would want if you were dying. I think it is what I would want too.' (For an ignoble moment the thought flashed through Miss Milliment's mind that when that time came for her there would be no one either to lie to her or to discuss the truth.) 'But you see,' she said, 'we are not either of *them*. However much we care for other people, we cannot become them. People can only do as much as they are. It may be more than we could do, it may be less, but very often it will be different. Sometimes that is very hard to bear, as I know you know.'

'But *I* have to pretend with them too!'

'Then you will know how hard it must be for your father.'

Then she added: 'When a person is dying, it must be their choice how they do it. Didn't we agree on that, just now? You are not pretending to yourself, and when you remember that, remember that they are not pretending either. To themselves. What they are doing with *each other* is only and entirely their business.'

Polly looked at the small grey eyes that were watching her with such perceptive kindness and felt *known* – a warm, light feeling. 'What you are saying is,' she said slowly, 'that I mustn't judge other people by my standards – by how *I* am.'

'It always seems to get in the way of love, don't you find?' Miss Milliment said it as though Polly would have thought of this first. 'Judgement's rather a tarnisher in my experience,' she finished. A small smile twitched her little mouth and then disappeared into her chins. 'Now, Polly, I think you should go somewhere warmer. But before you go, would you help me find the Greek primer? The binding is dark green, but the writing on the spine has faded so much that I am unable to read it on the shelf.'

When Polly had found it, Miss Milliment said, 'I am grateful for your confidence. I need hardly say that I shall never betray it.'

So she didn't have to ask her not to talk to other people.

∞ ∞ ∞

Louise sat in her dressing room (shared with one other girl) with her dressing gown over her shoulders – it was cold – the room with its concrete floor and its cracked basin and its small, curtainless window always had a faint smell of damp. She had turned on all the dressing table lights because they gave some warmth. She was between shows, and writing to Michael.

'Memorial Theatre, Stratford-upon-Avon' she'd put at the top of the paper.

MARKING TIME

Darling Michael

It was lovely to get your letter so soon after I got here.
In fact, it was waiting for me. I'm sorry you haven't
got enough guns – or not the kind you want – in your
destroyer – that must be awful. I suppose the people
who give out the guns are never *in* a destroyer, so
they don't really know what would be most useful.

(That was rather good: it sounded interested, and as
though she had thought about it. Actually, his letters
were so full of naval stuff that she found them rather
boring; she wanted him to write more about his feelings
– and, of course, how he felt about her. He always did a
bit, but only a sentence or two after pages about Oerlikon
guns or the weather – always awful – or what his captain
was like.)

Well! It feels quite grand to have got here at all, but it
isn't remotely how I imagined. To begin with, the
theatre seems enormous, and there are whole pockets
of seats where people can't hear a word whatever you
do about it. The average age of the company –
including me – I have worked out is sixty-nine. That's
because two of the actors are in their eighties, and the
youngest one is forty-seven! The younger actors have
all been called up, I suppose. There are only three
women in the company, one quite old, and one sort of
middling. It's the winter season – they don't do
Shakespeare, worse luck. I am the *ingénue* – ugh! I have
an awful part. I'm called Ethyl. The play is called *His
Excellency, the Governor* and Bay played the hero when
he was young a million years ago, and Ethyl was
played by his wife. So that is who I am opposite, but

the whole idea of being in love with someone quite so
decrepit is ridiculous. I have awful lines like 'my hero!'
in it, and I wear evening dress nearly all the time – pale
blue chiffon – and there are no funny lines at all – I
mean, on purpose. It is funny by *mistake* all the time.
Anyway, they are quite kind to me except that some of
the men upstage me rather a lot. My digs are on the
edge of the town kept by an old retired stage hand and
his daughter, Doll. He gets awfully drunk on Friday
nights and swears in Shakespeare: he actually called
me a cream-faced loon last week and turned me out of
the house. But Doll said to wait in the street for a bit
and she'd let me in again. I have 'dinner' – lunch –
with them. Nearly always stuffed sheep's heart and
greens and potatoes and thick brown gravy, but it's the
only proper meal and I eat it all. Otherwise there is a
very genteel tea room where doughnuts cost
FOURPENCE each *and* they are tiny (though delicious).
But I get paid two pounds ten on a rehearsal week, and
five pounds when we are playing and my digs cost
thirty shillings so I have to be careful. There are hotels,
of course, but they have only got five-shilling meals
which are out of the question. [She was so hungry
nearly all the time, that it was difficult not to write
about food.] Occasionally, Bay takes me home to his
flat where his wife, who doesn't act any more, gives us
a wonderful high tea with meat paste sandwiches and
rock cakes and once a boiled egg.

Here she paused. It did not seem a good idea to tell
him about the difficulties of getting home at night after
the performance when she had to choose between being
followed by a pair of Czech officers – there were a lot of

511

them billeted near Stratford and they were working in pairs reputed to rape girls – or being pawed by one of the elderly actors who offered to walk her home.

> My room at the digs is quite small, dominated by a large, creaky double bed with a very thin mattress and one of those eiderdowns that slip off the bed all night. When I get back I sit in it wearing a lot of clothes because there isn't any heating and write my play or learn lines. The river is nice, with swans on it, and sometimes we rehearse in the bar, which has a terrace looking out on it.

She read the letter so far.

> Upstaging [she then wrote] is when the person you're talking to moves further and further upstage (away from the audience) so that you either have to move up too, or speak all your lines with your back to the audience. The old actors do it all the time – to make people notice them, I suppose. One of them used to do a lot of music hall, so when he rehearses he doesn't say his lines properly at all, simply gabbles them in a monotonous undertone. He is rather a fat man, and when he isn't on, he keeps going to sleep on three chairs.
>
> I wonder when you will get some leave, and whether I shall see you? I am only here for three plays. They *might* keep me on, but I don't think so. So I shall just have to go home [she nearly put, 'and be made to do some boring job for the war' but she wasn't quite sure how much he was on her side about that so she ended] and learn to do something useful.

512

Have you read any Ibsen? [she went on] I have
been reading *Rosmersholm* and *The Doll's House*. He
really did understand what a rotten time women used
to have – not allowed professions or careers. His
language is so *modern* that I didn't realise what a long
time ago he wrote – well, *fairly* long. What made me
think of it was that his plays, which caused a scandal
when they were first performed in this country, by the
way, don't seem to have made much difference to
people like my aunts and mother. I actually *met* the
old man who first staged him – and Shaw. He lives
with a fierce housekeeper in a rather nice broken-
down house. He is called Alfred Waring, but he was
too deaf and shaky to have a long conversation with,
and I could see the housekeeper didn't like me being
there so I only stayed half an hour. I told you because
that's how I know about people objecting to Ibsen.
Quite different from Shaw. I should think he *wanted*
people to object to him.

Well [she was suddenly terribly sleepy] – I think
I'd better stop now as this is far too long. And rather
dull, I'm afraid. Much love, Louise.

At the bottom of the page, she added:

If you *do* get leave in the near future, you *could* come
and stay in an hotel here. I could easily book you a
room.

Then she wished she hadn't put that because if he was
going to see her act in a real theatre, she wanted it to be
a better part than rotten old Ethyl.

The letters she wrote to Stella were quite different. In

them she discussed in some detail the relative merits of being pawed by awful leathery old men with bad breath or systematically raped on the towpath by young Czechs, not, presumably, understanding a word they said. She did this because the whole thing frightened her rather – after all, it was six nights a week and even with the Double Summer Time being kept on in winter, it was dark by five, after which the streets in Stratford became extremely, and disquietingly, quiet.

You're frightened [Stella wrote back] and I don't blame you. The trouble is that you must keep the doors open with the old lechers, because one evening, you might really need one of them. I should learn a few blistering things to say in Czech, just to be on the safe side – if there is one! Oh, poor Louise! It's this disreputable profession you've chosen. Actresses used to be fair game for everyone, and as a lot of Europe is behind us in social mores, I expect the Czechs still think they are. Shall I come and see you? Could I share your large, creaky bed, as I'm very short of cash? My father equates lack of money with strength of character – in other people, of course.

And before Louise could even write back saying how lovely, do come, she arrived, without warning, at the stage door after an evening show.

'I haf komm to take you to ze river path to do unspeakable things,' she said.

'Oh, Stella! Oh, how gorgeous! Oh, you are marvellous to come! Come down to my dressing room while I change.'

'Don't you die of cold in your deb's chiffon?'

'I do rather, but I'm getting used to it. It's quite warm on the stage because of the lights. It's waiting to go on that's so ghastly.'

'I saw the play. You were quite right. It is *awful*, isn't it? Poor you.'

'I did my best.' She felt faintly, and perversely nettled that Stella hadn't added, 'But you were good.'

'You want me to say you were good. Well, you weren't bad, and I don't think you could be more than that. Do you have this room to yourself?'

'I do for this play. But in the next one, one of them is playing the lead, and I'm just crowd, so I'll certainly be sharing.'

'In love with anyone?'

'Nope. Are you?'

Stella shook her head. 'I think I'm the kind of person who not many people would go for and then one day just one person will, and I shall be completely bowled over from lack of practice. Unlike you.'

'What do you mean?'

'I mean, my darling, that *you* are the kind of person who millions of people will go for.' She leaned back in the basket chair and crossed her ankles; her thick grey stockings in no way spoiled their elegance.

'I've brought us a picnic,' she said. 'Can we eat it here?'

'No. They'll turn us out any minute. The doorkeeper wants to lock up and go home.'

'At your digs, then?'

'Well, it depends on whether Fred is drunk and up, or out or in bed. And I'll have to talk to Doll – ask her if you can stay and so on. It'll be all right, unless Fred is drunk and up.'

'In which case?'

'We'll be up and out.'

'Well, is there anywhere else we could go?'

'Not really. The towpath by the river, but apart from anything else, it'll be freezing cold. We might just have to eat the picnic very quietly. I must say it's heroic of you to bring it.'

'We may turn out to be heroic to eat it.'

'You ladies finished in here?'

'Coming, Jack.' She spread a face towel over her make-up, picked up her bag, wound her muffler round her neck, and they went back up the concrete stairs and through the swing doors into the pitch dark street.

'Take my arm,' Louise said. 'I have got a torch, but I know the way.'

'He's not back from the pub,' Doll said when she let them in. '*I* don't mind,' she added, when Louise had explained about Stella. 'Why don't you sit in the kitchen and have it, then?' she said when Louise explained that her friend hadn't eaten and had brought a picnic. 'I'll make you a pot of tea. After all, it's not the same as if you were a gentleman,' she said.

'Which of us would have to be that for it not to be the same?' Stella muttered as they took off their outdoor things in Louise's room.

'You, I think. But she's nice, isn't she?'

'Very nice,' Stella answered affectionately. 'Bit frightened of her dad, though.'

When they came down, Doll had laid the table with two cups and saucers, a sugar bowl and a jug of milk. 'The pot's warming,' she said. 'I'll shut the door and happen he won't notice.'

516

She untied her faded flowered overall and hung it on the back of the door. 'I should just lay off talking when you hear him come in. It is Friday, you see.'

She had a tired, kind face that was full of lack of expectation.

When they were alone, Stella said, 'Are Fridays especially bad?'

'He gets drunk on them. He doesn't on the other nights.'

She made the tea, and they sat, rather subdued, eating cheese rolls and apples, and some pieces of chocolate.

'I very nearly wish he *would* come, just to see what it would be like,' Stella remarked, as Louise rinsed out their cups.

'I don't. I vote we go up *now* and get safely tucked up.'

'Is there an indoor lavatory?'

'Yes. It's sort of built onto the back, half-way up the stairs.'

He came back while Stella was in the lavatory, and Louise hoped that she'd have the sense to stay there while Doll helped him up the stairs to bed. But Stella, of course, *did* have the sense. They undressed quickly – Stella had bedsocks: 'My feet are always freezing; they'd be a real hazard for anyone to encounter in the night' – and lay whispering, about nothing very much.

'It was lovely of you to come,' Louise said. 'How long can you stay?'

'Just to tomorrow afternoon, I'm afraid. I've got to put in an appearance at home before I go back to Oxford.'

The next morning they went out early. Stella said she'd treat them both to breakfast at the Swan and Doll said she could manage lunch for Stella.

'Oh, good! Then I'll see her old dad,' Stella said.

'He's quite mild and boring in the daytime,' Louise said, 'and they never talk at meals.'

'Never?'

'Well, pass the salt, but that's all.'

It was a crisp clear day – blue sky, pale yellow sun, rime on the pavements. They went by way of the theatre, because Stella said she wanted to see it in daylight.

'I've heard people say it is so ugly,' she said, 'so naturally, I want to see for myself. Although an Elizabethan theatre would have been stupid, wouldn't it? I must say I think the Tudor houses look frightfully ersatz. They keep reminding me of houses on the Great West Road.'

'I've never really thought about what houses look like.'

Stella always made her feel narrow-minded, but when Louise said this Stella said, 'Well, Oxford has made me notice buildings. It's rather like having a sense of smell, it cuts both ways, but the lovely ones are *so* breathtaking, and noticing the monstrosities might mean that we have fewer of them in future.'

Outside the theatre there were bills advertising Moiseiwitsch playing a programme of Beethoven on Sunday.

'Last time I heard him he made me *laugh* he was so awful,' Stella said. 'Bang, bang, bang. As though he was trying to make Beethoven hear by shouting.'

'How's Peter?'

'Well, he's in the RAF – just. His first week, he washed up a hundred and eighty plates each night. He said his hands got like swollen sausages encased in chammy leather. *And* they expect him to play.'

'To them in the evenings?'

'Oh, no. At concerts. He's joined up in a bit that has a

lot of musicians but the joke is that although the orchestra is composed of amazing professionals – like the Griller Quartet – *they* are all, at best, leading aircraftsmen, so a squadron leader who used to conduct a band at the end of a pier does the conducting. But Peter says they just all take no notice of him so it's all right. They do expect him to play a lot with hardly any practice and his hands are in a bad way. But it could be a lot worse.'

They were walking by the river now – slate-coloured in its reflection of the sky.

'Well? And how do you think the war is going?' Stella asked.

'The *war*? I haven't thought about it much.'

'You mean you haven't at all. I know you. You don't read newspapers, I don't suppose you listen to the news – you haven't a clue what's going on. I suppose you don't know that the *Ark Royal* has been sunk? By Italians, which almost makes it worse. Rather a blow, with the north African offensive.'

'I didn't know,' Louise said. She had no idea what sort of ship *Ark Royal* was. 'A battleship?' she ventured.

'An aircraft carrier.'

Louise suddenly imagined being on a sinking ship. 'It must be frightening. A horrible way to die.'

'They didn't lose many people. Lucky it was the Mediterranean. In the Atlantic it's too cold for people to last in the water long enough to get picked up.'

'Michael is in the Atlantic,' Louise said.

'Are you in touch?'

'He writes to me. Do you mean . . .' she felt hesitant and appalled, 'do you mean that if a ship goes down, the people in her have no hope? Don't they have lifeboats and rafts and things?'

'Of course they do. But sometimes it happens very quickly, and sometimes it is a long time before they get picked up. And sometimes there aren't enough boats, and people have to hang on to them in the water.'

'How do you know so much, Stella?'

'I don't know nearly as much as it sounds. But a cousin of mine was in an escort to a convoy, and he was torpedoed. He told me a bit.'

She did not enlarge upon what he had told her because she recognised that Louise was starting to feel anxious when there would be nothing she could do about it.

When they reached the Swan, who were prepared to let them have some breakfast – scrambled dried eggs, rather muscular sausages and curiously grey coffee – Stella said, 'How do you feel about Michael?'

Louise thought. 'Well, apart from my famous vanity – you know he goes on telling me I'm marvellous, which does make an alluring change, I must say – I don't know. I suppose writing letters makes me have some idea. I write to the family – well, Mummy, because she expects it, and sometimes a letter just saying "dear family". That's one kind of letter. Then I write to you, which is a quite different kind of letter. I mean I can tell you *anything* – you're not going to say I shouldn't be here or order me home. Well, Michael is sort of in between. He feels half like a grown-up, and half like an equal. I suppose that's because he's fourteen years older.'

'Do you think you like him because you have some sort of father complex?'

'Strewth, no!' As she said that, Louise realised that there was one thing that she had never told Stella – and never would.

'I suppose', she said lamely, 'that I just feel sort of safe with him.'

She saw her friend's face, the shrewd, ironical smile softened by affection, and they dropped the subject.

She asked Stella about Oxford, and Stella said that in any other circumstances it would be the perfect place for her. 'As it is, I feel I'm just marking time before I have to do something completely different where everything I've learned will be about as relevant as you and me learning to make a chocolate soufflé was at our cooking place.'

'Except, I suppose, that everything comes in handy some time or other.'

'You mean, like learning to be good with sharks, and *then* getting shipwrecked? I think life is one long shipwreck and you learn about the sharks after you've been rescued. Anyway, my father wants me to be a secretary to an admiral or something respectable like that. My mother thinks I should nurse.'

'And you?'

She shrugged her thin shoulders. 'I don't know.'

'I wish we could do something together.'

'I'd like that. If either of us thinks of anything, let the other one know.'

After a silent lunch of ox liver and onions – Fred was pale but relatively affable and chewed his food very slowly, gazing at Stella with an unfathomable expression – Louise walked to the station with Stella. Feeling the impending separation, they found it more difficult to talk – asked about each other's families. Each said that they were just the same. 'They are, aren't they?' Louise said. 'They just go on in the same old way.'

521

'I expect they change but we don't notice. At least you don't have too many of them to contend with.'

'I was just thinking that at least you have a nice variety.'

She felt sad when Stella was gone. My best friend, she thought. Well, actually, my only friend. This was rather a bleak thought, and she wondered whether it was because she was not much good at friendship. There was Michael, of course, but somehow, his admiration made it rather a hothouse: they weren't exactly *friends*, it was more as though they were playing a game where he knew the rules better than she did. She had thought that Jay was going to be a friend, but when she'd got back from her stay with Michael's family, she discovered that he was sleeping in Ernestine's room; he avoided her, or made faint, gibing remarks that sounded as though they were of a general nature, but she felt were intended for her. He never read poetry to her, or stroked her breasts again. And Ernestine had been noisy and flamboyant about being the only person in the company who was having an affair. Having Stella – even for twenty-four hours – made Louise know how much she missed her. She decided that even a boring war job would be all right if they did it together.

She realised that her throat was sore and that was the beginning of being quite ill, missing three nights of *Maria Marten*, and getting sacked for it.

∞ ∞ ∞

Mrs Cripps and Tonbridge sat side by side in the dark. They were in the next row to the back, and behind them she could hear the heavy breaths and surreptitious shiftings of romance. They were watching *King Kong*, and glancing at Tonbridge, Mrs Cripps could see that he was really taken with it although, speaking for herself, she thought it was all rather silly – a huge great ape soppy about a film star. She would have liked a proper romance, with someone like Robert Taylor or Clark Gable in it, or a nice Fred Astaire-Ginger Rogers film with a lot of dancing. But when he'd asked her to the cinema, she'd said yes without caring what was on. It was the outing that she wanted, and the chance to sit in the dark with him without interruption or anyone knowing who they were. She'd put on her best clothes – her maroon winter coat and her fox fur, where you opened the animal's mouth and it clipped onto the tail, and her best hat, dark-brown velour with some pheasant's feathers draped round the brim and a mustard petersham bow (she'd been asked to remove that as soon as she sat down and now she was too hot, because she couldn't keep the hat *and* the fur on her lap at once). This had been a mistake, because underneath she wore her best sateen blouse – a lovely blue – not a garment she would choose to perspire into but there was no help for it. The ape was wrecking some tall building in New York now – she gave a little gasp in the hope that *that* would get his arm round her, but he only reached out in the dark and patted her hat which, of course, was where he thought her hand would be. He was backward in coming forward, she had to admit. 'It's only make-believe,' he whispered. Her face gleamed phosphorescently at him; it was not possible to tell whether she was reassured.

He wondered what she would do if he reached out and held her hand. He'd missed the obvious opportunity because her hat was in the way. He tried again and this time succeeded. Her hat fell on the floor but she paid no regard to it. Her soft, fat fingers enveloped his – he could squeeze them without feeling the bones. She was all of a piece: the thought of squeezing her anywhere else chirped up his old ticker no end.

'He's only a gorilla,' he whispered; he wanted to add that he'd never let a gorilla near her, but he was afraid of sounding a bit soft.

After the film, she retrieved her hat and they went out into the raw cold. She was glad of it – in her experience ladies did not perspire. He took her to the best tea shop where the individual cakes were threepence each and a plate of scones – with marge and jam – was ninepence.

He said he thought it was a good film and she agreed that it had been very nice. He was wearing his civvies: a dark blue pinstripe suit that was a bit wide on the shoulders and a very smart tie with diagonal stripes of blue and red. The tea shop was warm – the windows being blacked out meant that there wasn't much air – but she could take off the fur and her coat so she didn't mind. The scones were rather heavy, and he was quick to point out that they were not a patch on hers.

'They wouldn't be,' she said, sipping her hot, weak tea. If there wasn't a war on, she would have sent the tea back.

They had never found conversation during meals easy. Usually, she sat and watched him while he had one of his innumerable snacks – and he never put on an ounce, stayed as scrawny as ever.

Feeling the strain, he talked about the war: gave her his opinion about the Japanese and the United States. 'There's no doubt, Mrs Cripps,' he said, 'mark my words, no good is going to come out of *that*. And it's my opinion that there was no call for Mr Churchill to say we'd join in if they go to war. "Within the hour," he said. In my opinion that was going too far.'

'I suppose it was.' She was deeply bored by the war and what foreign countries did in it which seemed to be none of their business.

'But we have to remember that Mr Churchill knows what he's doing.'

'You can say that again,' she said, hoping he wouldn't.

They had finished the scones now, and both had been eyeing the plate of cakes, always a worry, since no two were the same, and one, at least, noticeably more desirable than the rest. He was a gentleman. He handed her the plate.

'Which do you fancy, Mrs Cripps?' he asked. She had seen him eyeing the jam tart, and took the cocoa sponge instead. Then they could both relax, and, she hoped, talk of more interesting things. She knew he'd had a letter a day or two ago, because Eileen had brought it in and put it on the kitchen table. She'd never known him get a letter before, and this one had its envelope typed 'Mr F. C. Tonbridge' and the address on it. As soon as he came in for his elevenses she had pointed it out. He had picked it up and looked at it for a long time before putting it in his pocket. He had never said one word about it. 'I hope you haven't had bad news, Mr Tonbridge?' she had prompted over tea in the evening.

'I have and I haven't,' he had replied. She had later tried saying that troubles shared were troubles halved, but he had seemed, or affected, not to understand her. She watched him chewing, wincing a little as the jam reached his bad tooth, and then a thought occurred to her.

'It's a wicked war all right,' she said, 'and the worst of it is the way it keeps loved ones away from each other. Mrs Rupert without Mr Rupert; Mrs Hugh missing Mr Hugh all week, Mrs Edward hardly ever seeing Mr Edward . . .' she paused, 'and then there's you, Mr Tonbridge. I sometimes wonder if you don't miss *your* wife . . .'

He swallowed the last of the tart, and cleared his throat. 'Mrs Cripps, I wouldn't say this to most people – well, I wouldn't want to let it slip to anyone – but the honest truth is, in strictest confidence, mind – I'm not one for bandying my private affairs in public – that I *don't* miss her. Far from it. Quite the contrary. She's become a weight off my mind. I wouldn't mind if I never set eyes on her again. Which I shan't, if yours truly can help it. She's a – well, you'll have to take it from me, that she's turned out to be not a very nice type of person.'

'What a shame!' She was thrilled.

'A shame it is. I wouldn't like to tell you what she's done. I really wouldn't. It wouldn't be fit for your ears.'

In the end he told her all the same. About George (although not in detail what had happened on that dreadful day, not the throwing of his clothes into the street) – about his going home and finding George there. 'And you remember I got that letter?' he said.

She nodded, so vigorously that a kirby-grip fell onto her plate and she covered it instantly with a wrinkled, dimpled hand.

'Well, that was from a solicitor. She wants a divorce. She wants to marry that bloke. *And* she wants to keep the house.'

'Well, I never! You've no call for the house, though, have you?'

He thought of all the years of service that had paid for it. A home of his own, he'd called it. In reality it had been nothing of the kind.

'I don't think I do,' he said slowly but his voice trembled and it was then that she could see that he'd been through a lot of distress: being bossed about by that London tart, she guessed, and possibly her boyfriend as well. It was too bad, she thought; look at his little scrawny neck and his sad eyes, and his legs were all bandy in his gaiters – he was just the kind to get bullied . . .

'It would mean,' he said, with difficulty, 'that I wouldn't have much to offer.'

'Offer,' she repeated; she was so delighted by what she thought he might mean that she wanted to be sure she hadn't got him wrong.

'I was hoping,' he said, 'that we could have come to an understanding.' There was a pause, while they both waited for the other one to say something. She won.

'I am in no position,' he said, floundering. 'I have no call to say anything seeing as I am, as you might say, a married man. But this letter has cast a new hue on the situation. All the same it wouldn't be right for me to ask you – on the one hand I wouldn't want you to think of me as a bigamist—'

'I should hope not,' she said; she hadn't the slightest idea what a bigamist was, but it sounded very nasty to her.

'But, on the other hand, there's no knowing how long lawyers take over these things?' He ended almost as though he was asking her.

'They take their own time, no doubt,' she said. She had never in her life had anything to do with a lawyer, and was unclear what they were *for* except that she could now

527

see they had something to do with divorce – a thing which so far as she knew was only gone in for by film stars and other people with time on their hands. But she *did* know what an understanding was. It was the next best thing to an engagement.

'I have always thought of you as a fine woman, a real woman,' he said gazing respectfully at her bust.

She could stand it no longer. 'Frank, if you're asking me to have an understanding with you – I don't mind if I do.'

He went suddenly dark pink, and his eyes watered. 'Mabel – if I may—'

'Silly,' she interrupted. 'What else could you call me?'

∞ ∞ ∞

To begin with Sybil was hardly able to believe it – she told herself that she had simply had an unusually good night's sleep, or that the cold weather was making her hungrier. But after a week of not feeling sick at *all*, and her back only aching if she tried to pick up Wills or carry him anywhere, she *had* to believe it. She still felt weak and tired easily, but otherwise she felt as though she was perceptibly recovering. People *did*; she was sure that really wanting to must make a difference, and, heaven knows, she had prayed that she might get better – for Hugh, for the children, particularly for Wills. For as she well knew, losing your mother when you were as small as that was too soon. He would not remember her. Would not have remembered her, she repeated silently.

It was Friday, and the thought of Hugh arriving in the evening had a completely different feeling about it. She was looking forward to him seeing her. She would be very careful all day, have a rest after lunch, and then Polly would bring her the life-saving very weak tea. At her worst, she had craved hot water with a slice of lemon in it, but there were no lemons. But in this last week she had halved her dose of the pills and this, too, made her feel more alert. She would still spend ages putting rouge on her face, and then rubbing it off until she considered that Hugh would not notice that it was rouge, and then put on her newest dress that she had made (she could not bear anything tight round her waist and had taken to keeping her stockings up by twisting a shilling in the top until it was tight round her leg). She wished it were summer, because then she could have gone for little walks with Hugh, but even if there was sun, it was too cold for her to enjoy being out at all. Sometimes Villy took her to Battle in the car for a little outing, but that had been happening less and less often. The house was too cold for her and only a constant supply of hot-water bottles enabled her to get through some days – even in bed.

But now, she said to herself, as she parted her bobbed hair on the other side to see if it looked better, I shall start going for short walks in the weekdays – a little further each day, and when I've got up to half an hour, I shall tell him I'd like him to take me for a walk. He'll be so surprised!

It was morning, and she had woken really wanting to know what sort of day it was. When she had first realised, or thought that she had known, that she was going to die – she had become obsessed with the weather, the season – it had been the end of summer. She had watched the summer flowers dying away; fewer roses, phlox and delphinium becoming seed heads, oaks beginning to become bronzed in the weaker sunlight, swallows leaving, the single old apple tree that she could see from her window becoming portentous with rosy fruit, chrysanthemums, red-hot pokers, and the white Japanese anemone that the Duchy so loved coming to flower in the crisper air, the hint of frosts glinting on the lawn in the mornings, each sight, she had felt, to be her last of that. She would see no more swallows or roses or new green leaves, or mornings when blackbirds stabbed away at the fallen apples. Before that, and almost immediately she had thought that she had only measurable time left, she had forced herself to make the trip to London to equip Polly with winter clothes and clothes beyond the winter, to last her for the first year at least after Sybil had gone. Rachel had urged her to combine this with a visit to Mr Carmichael who had seemed to her a kind, infinitely experienced and practical man. After he had examined her and said almost nothing, she had asked him first whether there was any hope for her. 'There is always hope, of course,' he had said, 'but I don't think you should count on it.' And when, before she had allowed this actually to reach her, she had asked how long she had got, he had said that it was not possible to say – several months, he thought – and as though she was thinking of Simon, he had said, 'Don't worry about Christmas. You have a son away at school, haven't you? If we do the operation, there may be more Christmases,' and she had only been able to nod. He had given her a prescription with strict instructions about how it should be used, and then, when she had got up to leave, he had come round from his desk, put his hands on her shoulders and said, 'I'm so sorry, my dear. You asked me, and lying to you would be no kindness. I'll write to your GP. Your husband—' He had hesitated and she had interrupted him saying quickly that she did not want him to know – yet, and particularly not to know that *she* knew. He had looked at her thoughtfully for a moment and then said, 'I expect you know best.'

He had told her that she could ring him, and even given her his home number; he had been very kind. It couldn't be much fun having to tell people that sort of thing, she thought as she walked down the steps of the large Harley Street house and into the hot, dusty street. To have to tell people that they might die . . . and then it hit her: she realised that she hadn't actually believed it, been able to face the inexorable certainty – her legs had started to give way, and for minutes she held onto the iron railings that flanked the steps. It was then that she realised that she couldn't face going back on the train with Polly and Villy and behaving as though nothing had happened. She needed some time alone. She decided to miss the train, and blessed her own foresight that had made her give Polly her train ticket. Then she walked slowly down through the streets until she came to a pub. A drink: that was the thing to have when you had had a shock. But, of course, it was too early: the pubs were not open. Anyway, she thought, I can't drink *drink* any more – it made her feel awful, and going into a pub on her own without a man would already be an ordeal; ordering a soft drink would make it worse. She saw a cab and asked it to take her to Charing Cross, but when they reached Piccadilly Circus she saw the News Cinema, paid off the cab and went in. It would be dark and anonymous and she could simply sit for as long as she liked.

She sat through the Gaumont British News recited in the usual tight-lipped, slightly heroic tones that so lent themselves to heroics and patriotism, as though the news, any news, was designed both to inspire and to soothe the recipients, two cartoons, Donald Duck and Mickey Mouse, a short film of a munitions factory . . . and then it was the news again which she hadn't taken in anyway. She sat there, mindlessly watching blurred newsreel of the Blitz, now, the announcer said almost triumphantly, intensifying.

As she emerged, blinking, into the street looking for another cab, she thought fleetingly of Hugh, making his way from the East End to their desolate house in London, not knowing that she was still in town, not knowing that she was to die. My darling. What can I do to make it less awful for you? Not tell him, she thought, as she climbed stiffly into a cab. Telling him would condemn him to weeks – or months? (it seemed strange not to know which) – of waiting. It would be like standing on a platform, she thought when she was doing that at Charing Cross, waiting and waiting for the train to depart, to say goodbye; she could spare him that, or at least most of it. Her thoughts were very few, and far apart from one another; what happened between them she hardly knew.

In the train she had fallen asleep.

This morning she remembered again Mr Carmichael saying 'there is always hope'. Of course there was, but also, of course, he would not have felt that he could raise her hopes. It was a beautiful morning with white mist and, above it, a sun the colour of pimento. There were lacy icicles on the window panes. Simon would soon be back from school; it would soon be Christmas. She had made Hugh four pairs of socks and a sweater in an impossibly elaborate stitch and for Polly a party dress, in coffee-coloured organdie. The house was filling up with these innocent secrets. Christopher and Polly were making a dolls' house for Juliet, and Sybil had stitched a minute drawing-room carpet for it in *petit point*. Polly was growing fast which was probably why she looked so pale. She would take her to see Dr Carr who would give her a tonic. She might even take Simon to Hamley's in London to choose his present, she thought, shutting the small top casement window, and suddenly remembering standing there, just before Wills was born, with the Albertine rose, 'look thy last on all things lovely every hour', and thinking that she might die in labour. But she had survived; it had been that poor little twin who had not lived. Well, she would not think that any more; she was going to get better, to live.

That evening, after her first dinner downstairs for weeks, when she and Hugh had retired, at his insistence, and she was undressing, Hugh said, 'Darling, aren't you tired?'

'Do I look tired?'

He leaned over her at the dressing table so that she could see him looking at her face in the mirror.

'You look lovely. And serene. Lovely,' he repeated and put his hand under her hair at the back of her neck. 'I rather miss your neck.'

'I'll grow my hair again. But I don't think long grey hair is awfully attractive, do you?'

'Your hair isn't grey?'

'One day it will be.'

He turned her head towards him and kissed her mouth. 'I'm going to tuck you up now,' he said at the end of this silent gentleness.

'Oh, Hugh! Hugh! Do you realise how much better I am? I can tell you now. I've been feeling awful for so long that I'd begun to think – to be afraid – do you know I even thought that perhaps I might be going to die! Oh!'

She made a little sound between a laugh and a sob. 'It's such a relief to tell you. I couldn't have before, but now – I am so *much* better! For a week now. Every day!'

He knelt to put his arms round her and held her as tears of exquisite relief came and slipped away. When she could look at him she saw unfathomable sadness. He shook his head almost irritably. 'Do you mean you have been feeling all that and not telling me?'

'I couldn't. Darling, I didn't want to distress you. And look how right I was. It would have been needless distress.'

'I want you,' he said, in a voice that steadied as he spoke, 'I want you to promise me that if you should ever, by any chance, feel anything *like* that again, you'll tell me. Don't keep anything from me.'

'Darling, I don't. You know I don't. Excepting that. I couldn't tell you that I thought I was going to die!'

'Do you really think it would be better for me to know – afterwards – that you'd been through all that by yourself? How would you feel if it was the other way round?'

'Oh, my dear love. If it was *you*, I'd know – whether you told me or not.'

She said it with such a certain and tender conviction that he had to dismiss the pain it caused him.

'Well,' he said doggedly. 'Promise me now.'

So she did.

∞ ∞ ∞

'It occurs to me,' Clary said, 'that perhaps people on mountains in the Old Testament really got struck by lightning which turned them from being gloomy and hopeless about destiny into quite bossy, optimistic people. A sort of electric-shock treatment from God.'

They were stacking logs in the porch outside the front door and Christopher, who was bringing the logs in a wheelbarrow, had just told them they were doing it all wrong.

'He's certainly much better,' Polly said. 'But it must be a most frightening treatment. Strapped down on a bed thing and being given shocks.'

'Has he told you about it? I ought to know.'

'He said he felt so awful that at first he didn't really care. And afterwards he had the most terrific headache *but* also a tremendous feeling of relief. But after a few treatments, he started to dread them.'

'He is better, though. He hasn't cried for ages.'

'That's Oliver. Clever Dad for getting him. The trouble is, he's beginning to dread what will happen to him when he is quite better.'

'How do you mean?'

'He's afraid his father will get him sent back to the aerodrome to go on levelling ground for runways or, worse, make him join the Army.'

'I don't think the Army will take him. Not after all that treatment.'

'You don't *know*, Clary. And now Uncle Raymond's working in some grand hush-hush establishment, he's probably got a fiendish amount of influence.'

'That won't make any difference. Louise says that one of the actors in Devon couldn't be called up because he had *flat feet*! I ask you! If they're as fussy as that, it's a wonder they've got an army at all.'

Louise had come back, very run-down, as the Duchy

put it, and Dr Carr had said her tonsils ought to come out.

'She ought to be helping us.'

'She's gone with Zoë to the nursing home. I could see her practising to be Florence Nightingale this morning.'

'Do you think she's in love?'

'With that portrait painter bloke? Haven't the faintest.'

'She writes to him a lot. She doesn't want her tonsils out in case he gets leave.'

'That might not be love. You might want to see *anyone* rather than have your tonsils out. Oh, God! Here come the children.'

Neville's school had broken up early because of scarlet fever. 'I won't be getting it,' he informed everybody. 'I simply loathe the boy who started it all. I loathed him so much I never went within about two miles of him.'

'There aren't two miles in your school,' Lydia said. 'It's quite a small place really.' But she and Neville had become friends enough to run a shop together, which sold what Clary and Polly considered to be such awful and boring things that nobody bought them except out of kindness. 'And I'm running out of *that*,' Clary said, 'quite apart from the cash. How could I possibly want to buy my own last year's vest – outgrown and holey to boot?'

Apart from any clothes they could cadge, they sold insects described by Neville as racing beetles, each in its own matchbox where they quickly died, Christmas cards made by themselves, cigarette cards, old toys, empty bottles, relics from the museum long since abandoned, bead necklaces made by Lydia, shampoo, made by immersing slivers of soap in boiling water and poured into old medicine bottles with labels made by Lydia: 'SHAM POO' they read 'for all hairs'. They sold information cards, each one having six pieces of information on them. 'How to put out fires' – Lydia got that out of Mrs Beeton's *Household Management*. 'Put silver sand into large bottles and store for use,' it read. What to do if chased by a bull: 'Stand very still and take off anything red you are wearing.' The grown-ups bought these, and they began to run out of information. The shop was on the first-floor landing, and Polly and Clary thought it a perfect pest. Lydia and Neville crouched there for hours, cajoling, whining, bullying people to buy things. 'It ought to be against the law,' Clary said.

Now they arrived, very sulky, because they'd been told to help with the logs. Luckily Christopher appeared with another load, and said he would take them to load up the next barrow.

'Thanks very, very much,' Neville said. He was practising sarcasm, but people rather tiresomely continued not to be withered by his efforts.

∞ ∞ ∞

The Duchy was in a bad humour. 'I do not see how everybody is to be fitted *in*,' she said. She was making toast for tea in the morning room with Rachel, the great-aunts, Zoë and Louise. The room was very full of people, and the quantity of toast that needed to be made was flustering her.

'Duchy dear, let me show you my chart,' Rachel said. She was anxious that Sid would not be included and as she had leave at Christmas, this would be awful. 'If we put the younger children on the top floor in one of the maids' old rooms—'

'The windows don't open, and it is most unhealthy for

children to sleep without fresh air,' the Duchy replied, handing out two pieces of toast which her sisters seized.

'Although you never used to eat two pieces at tea-time,' Dolly reproved Flo. 'You always said it spoiled your dinner.'

Zoë looked up from her sewing. 'Duchy, I have been thinking that I really should go and visit my mother. She hasn't seen Juliet since she was born.'

'For Christmas, darling? Are you sure you want to be away at *Christmas*?'

'I think Mummy would especially like that. And it would give you an extra room.'

She did not want to go very much, but she had had a letter from her mother's friend hinting that all was not well, and saying how much her mother longed to see her grandchild. And *anyone* would want to see Juliet, Zoë thought. 'I really do want to go,' she said. 'Apart from anything else, I've never been to the Isle of Wight.'

'The Isle of Wight?' Dolly repeated. 'How, I wonder, do you *get* there?'

'As it is an island, I should have thought it was fairly obvious that a boat would be involved,' Flo said.

'Really, Flo dear, I am not a *lunatic*. It is *because* it is an island that I wondered. I thought that civilians were not allowed overseas. There *is* a war on,' she reminded her sister.

'The Isle of Wight, Dolly, is *not* overseas. It is part of the British Empire.'

'And what, pray, is Canada? Or Australia? Or New Zealand? And incidentally, Flo, you have the teeniest bit of blackberry jam on your chin, to the right of your larger mole.'

Flo flushed with anger, and just as Rachel and the

Duchy were exchanging glances of resigned amusement, put her hand up to her face. Then she made a sudden, shocking convulsive movement, became rigid and started to fall sideways off her chair.

She was caught by Rachel and Zoë who between them levered her back onto the chair. The Duchy said, 'Ring for Dr Carr,' and put her arms round the stiff body. 'It's all right, my darling sister. Kitty's with you, dearest, it's all right,' and gently she removed the red bandana from Flo's head, which seemed locked curiously to one side; her eyes glared unseeingly with a look of outrage and crumbs of toast appeared at one side of her lopsided mouth. When Rachel returned, saying that Dr Carr was on his way, they all three lifted her and with difficulty laid her on the ottoman by the window, and Zoë went to get a blanket.

Dolly sat through this, frozen with shock, but when Flo was on the ottoman she got heavily to her feet and then painfully down onto her knees by it.

'Flo! I didn't mean it! You know I didn't mean it!' She took her sister's unresisting hand, pressed each finger round her own and held it to her breast. Tears were streaming down her face. 'It was just a little joke. Don't you remember our spinach joke? When Mamma said that to you just after you came out and the curate came to dinner? A teeny bit of spinach? And you were *so* upset. But afterwards we laughed together because it was so like Mamma.' With her other hand she pulled her handkerchief out from her wrist band and tenderly wiped the crumbs away from Flo's mouth. Then she looked up at Rachel, who was arranging the blanket, and said in a bewildered, anxious voice, 'She doesn't seem to hear me. Is she very ill?'

'She's had a stroke, Dolly darling. Why don't you—'

'No! I'm not going to leave her. Not for a second. We've always been together – through thick and thin, Flo, you always said, and, my word, we had our share of thin, didn't we, my lamb? Oh, Flo – *do look* at me!' Rachel tried to persuade her to have a chair, but she remained painfully on her knees until the doctor came.

Flo died that evening, of another stroke which, Dr Carr told the Duchy, was a mercy since she had little chance of recovering from the first one. Dolly stayed with her until she died, and the Duchy said she was sure that this was a comfort for Flo, but nobody knew whether she even realised who was with her. After she died, they were going to take the body away, but Dolly, who was otherwise passive from grief and fatigue, became vehement in her refusal about this. Flo would stay in their room until her funeral, in her own bed, at home, with her family. For two days she dusted the room and made her own bed, as the maids were made nervous by the still body with its younger, shrunken face, and the sickly violetish odour of the room. But the Duchy said that things must be as Dolly wished and kept her going by consulting her about every detail of the funeral. Everybody tried to comfort her, but she blamed herself unceasingly and nothing that even the Duchy could say would alter this. She got through the funeral with a thick veil to hide her poor bloodshot eyes, but after it the children noticed that she called them by the wrong names, and she was also liable to break out into often incomprehensible reminiscence, in which, the Duchy said, Flo always emerged as a paragon.

'I should think she should be given an animal to cheer her up,' Polly said, the example of Christopher foremost in her mind.

'A parrot,' Clary suggested, 'a nice Victorian bird.'

'Or a rabbit,' Lydia said: she badly wanted one herself and it wasn't allowed. 'They might let a grieving person have one.'

'You can't keep a rabbit in your bedroom!' Louise said, snubbing her.

'I think you could if you really wanted to,' Neville said. '*And*,' he became inspired, 'we could collect its little pellets every day, and you could paint them, Lydia, and Christopher could make us very *small* solitaire boards for the shop.' But nobody agreed with that.

'You think of nothing but *gain*, Neville,' Clary scolded. 'You are becoming so grasping and horrible that it's quite difficult to like you.'

'*I* do,' Lydia said. 'In fact, I love you. You can marry me if you like. In due course,' she added in case anyone thought she was silly enough to think that people married at her age.

'If you try to marry me,' Neville said, 'I shall shoot you. Or put you in the very middle of an air raid. Or take you to the vet.' The Brig's very old Labrador Bessie had recently gone there to be put down.

Lydia was unmoved. 'You're not old enough for a gun,' she said, 'and there aren't any air raids here. *And* I know the vet. He wouldn't *think* of putting me down.'

By the end of November it was really cold. Washing on the line became stiff with frost; Miss Milliment had the most unfortunate recurrence of chilblains. The pipes froze, Clary and Polly put Plasticene round the edges of the window in their bedroom to stop the draughts of icy air and begged Villy not to tell the Duchy. Ellen's rheumatism was so bad that she could not start the day without four aspirin and a cup of strong tea, and everybody kept saying that at least it was slowing the Germans down in their advance on Moscow although that seemed to Polly as though it must mean that the war would simply last longer.

Archie Lestrange felt the cold too. He slipped and fell on the icy path outside the front door one morning, and when he tried to get up, the pain was so excruciating that he simply lay there; Clary, running out of the front door moments later to see if there was any post for Louise, nearly tripped over him.

'Archie! Oh, poor Archie!'

'Do you think you could help me up?'

'I could, but I don't think it would be wise. First aid says never move a patient until you know what's wrong with them. What's wrong?'

'It's my gammy leg.'

'Oh. You may have broken it again. You need hot, sweet tea for shock.' And sped away before he could stop her. There was always tea in the kitchen at that hour, and she was back very quickly, with Polly carrying a blanket.

'I don't see how we give him tea lying down,' she said.

'Look,' Archie said. 'Just help me up, you two. I'm perfectly all right, really,' and he made another attempt to move, but he couldn't make it.

'You'll make it worse. Get Aunt Villy.' She propped up his head and put the cup to his mouth. He obediently swallowed some and scalded his tongue.

When Villy came, she told them to get Christopher. 'Must get you in the warm,' she said. 'I expect you've just jarred everything.'

In fact, he turned out to have done rather more than that. He had to go to Hastings for an X-ray, and proved to have cracked his already damaged bone. He was sent home in the ambulance, and told to lie up. He had been

542

thinking that really he ought to make a move – have another go at the Admiralty for a desk job of some kind and find himself somewhere to live. Now he was confined to bed. This delighted the children, who had started to like him when he told them they could all call him Archie. 'Even *Wills*?' Polly had said; hierarchy died hard with them, but he had said everyone – even Oliver. They took turns to bring up his meals, played chess, dominoes, Monopoly and bezique with him, acted charades for him, told him about their Christmas presents – the ones they were making or giving, and the ones they hoped they'd get. They confided: Christopher, about his pacifism and his hostile father; Louise, about Michael and her not wanting to stop acting; Clary – there was a great deal of this – about her ideas of what her father was doing; Polly, about her mother and what she *had* feared and no longer did since her mother seemed so much better; Neville, about being bullied at school (something that nobody else knew at all); Lydia, about how much she wanted a dog of her own. Wills brought him a very large and random selection of toys and often any other portable object he came upon that he could reach. Oliver brought him his bones, rolled-up newspapers – he was not fussy about their date – and once what Archie described as a fantastically dead rat. Mrs Cripps made him treacle tart. The maids took turns to do his room because they both thought he was so lovely. The adults came too, of course. Sybil saw that his dressing gown was torn, and after she had mended it, suggested going through his clothes to see if anything else needed doing. 'I'm afraid you may find that everything does,' he said. 'Now that sailors no longer make sails, they aren't so handy with a needle.' Zoë brought Juliet. The Duchy paid a daily visit, often bringing tiny vases of berries and, occasionally, a spectral rose that had survived the frost. Even the Brig arrived one day and told him a quite frightening amount about elephants in Burma. Only Rachel, he noticed, never came by herself, but always with a child or Sybil or Villy. She was kind, as always, and solicitous, brought him a special pillow to prop up his leg, and a better bedside lamp. She also persuaded the Duchy that he needed a coal fire in his room which made it extremely cosy. Lydia and Neville roasted chestnuts on it and burned the carpet.

'But it's a patterned one, it just looks like a bit of blackish pattern,' Lydia said. 'I don't think we need to mention it, do you?'

'I think not,' he said. It was this kind of thing that made him so popular.

At the beginning of December Zoë left for her visit. She had decided to go before Christmas, after all, influenced by pleas from the nursing home – and particularly Roddy, who had been away for another operation and returned to recuperate. She had been surprised as well as touched that they counted on her so much. And Juliet, she felt, ought to spend Christmas at home. She went to say goodbye to Archie on the morning that she left. She looked very pretty in a dark green cloth coat with a black fur stand-up collar and a hat to match.

'You look like a Russian heroine,' he said.

'Rupert bought me this outfit,' she said, 'when he joined the firm. I've hardly worn it, but trains sometimes are freezing, and I expect the boat will be as well.'

'When are you coming back?'

'In about ten days, I think. Before Christmas, anyway.'

'Have you left people a telephone number? I mean, so that we can get hold of you—'

'I have, but there won't be any news,' she said. 'It's only Clary who thinks that one day there'll be a call from him, or he'll just walk through the door.'

'And you don't?'

'I *pretend* to – but I— Sometimes I wish we *knew* that he was dead. I know that's awful of me, and please don't tell Clary that. I don't want her to feel let down by me. I have Juliet, you see. She has nothing.'

'She has you,' he said.

'Oh, Archie! You don't know how selfish I was or you wouldn't say that!'

'She has you *now*.'

Unable to respond to that, she said, 'What do you think? Do you think there's any chance?'

'There's a chance, but a very small one, I'm afraid.'

'It's too long for him to have been taken prisoner?'

'Far too long.'

There was a silence. Then she said, 'It isn't that I wish he was dead. I just wish I *knew*.'

'I know. Of course I know that.'

She tried to smile at him then; there was something piteous in the attempt. He was moved.

'Kiss the poor invalid, then,' he said.

She bent and kissed his cheek; she smelled of rose geranium and he felt a completely unexpected frisson.

'Get better,' she said, and was gone.

∞ ∞ ∞

'Mummy, he can't not come *now*! I can't get hold of him. It's only for two nights anyway.'

'I simply can't understand why you didn't come and ask first!'

545

Louise hadn't because she had been afraid that they would say no.

'It was a long-distance call, and I was afraid of getting cut off,' she said. 'I should have thought you'd have wanted him to come. You always say you want to meet my friends.' To vet them, she privately added.

'It has nothing to do with not wanting to meet him,' Villy said, exasperated. 'It's a question of where on earth he is to sleep. You seem to have forgotten it's the weekend the Clutterworths are coming. The house will be bursting at the seams and it will upset the Duchy.'

'Can't he have Zoë's room?'

'The Clutterworths are having that. Really, Louise, you are so thoughtless. You think of nothing but yourself!'

'Well, Clary and Polly and I could sleep in the squash court, and he could have our room.'

'Well, you *must* go and ask the Duchy before you do anything. I'm not prepared to shoulder your selfish blunders.'

She gets snappier and snappier, Louise thought, as she went to find the Duchy. She said she was sorry, and all her mother had replied was that it was a bit late to be sorry. What was the use of apologising if the other person didn't accept it?

However, when she found the Duchy, she decided to start by saying how sorry she was for not asking first, and that worked. The Duchy said that everybody made mistakes, and that she would be most interested to meet Michael. She agreed to the squash court plan provided they used sleeping bags on the camp beds, which she said should be brought into the house to be aired before they slept on them. Then she had Clary and Polly to face, and they were nice about it until they discovered that Louise wanted to clear up the room on a scale that suited neither of them.

'I'm bloody well *not* taking all my things to the squash court for two nights,' Clary stormed. 'He can't need all our chests of drawers for *two nights*. *You* can clear yours out for him.'

Polly also hated the idea of her things being disarranged, although she was not so vehement about it. 'I don't suppose he'll notice his bedroom much,' she said. 'I don't think men do.'

But Louise found herself looking at the room and, indeed, the whole house with new, and severely critical, eyes. She looked at the worn dark green linoleum, the chipped and yellowing white paint, the absurdly old-fashioned wallpaper that had tulips and Indian birds on it, the black iron bedsteads, and felt that none of it was good enough for Michael. In the end, she pinched (with his kindly consent) the rug from Archie's room and put it over the worst worn places on the floor. But the whole house worried her. The loose covers in the drawing room were faded and patched, the large and ancient Aubusson was in places actually threadbare; even the packs of cards, she felt, let her down. They were dog-eared with use, and frequently the joker was chalked with some number of a card that was missing. The lampshades, of parchment, had gone coffee-coloured with age, and the hall, where the children ate – the hall! It was full of gum boots, and tri-cycles, tennis and squash racquets, and even some of the garden furniture – spiteful deckchairs whose hinges had rusted, and caterpillars pupating on the dusty canvas. Wills' and Roly's toys abounded; one stumbled over pieces of Meccano and bricks (they no longer had a day nursery as it had been turned into their bedroom). The skylight leaked, and enamel buckets and bowls were placed at strategic spots. The bathroom also caused her despair. Nothing had been altered there since she could remember. The bath contained a long greyish-green streak where water had dripped from the old brass taps for years. The dark green tongue-and-groove pine walls had blistered and flakes of paint often fell on anyone having a bath. The mirror was spotted with damp and the basin taps, white china, had been chipped so badly that there was an art to using them without cutting yourself. The lavatory, next door, contained an impassioned note in ink so faded that no stranger would be able to read it on how to pull the plug. She knew it by heart. 'Pull sharply down, release, wait and then pull again. The lavatory should then flush.' Should, but often didn't. She began to wish he wasn't coming. 'I've got forty-eight hours,' he had said on the sudden, amazing telephone call. 'And then I have to go to Newhaven. It struck me that it would be lovely if I could come and stay a couple of nights with you, and then go on from there. *If* that would be all right with your family.' There had been a noise of hammering in the background and his voice was faint. When she had said yes, it would be fine, he said, 'There's a four-twenty from Charing Cross that I could just catch. Won't be a minute,' he said, to somebody else. 'Oh, darling, I can't wait to see you. I have to go,' and he was gone.

She started to worry about meals. Meals always used to be wonderful, but in the last two years they had got steadily duller. She began with the Duchy.

'I was wondering,' she said with what she hoped was pensive sweetness, 'whether we could possibly have roast goose on Saturday night. As a sort of treat for everybody?'

The Duchy shot her a sharp look and was not in the least deceived.

'My lamb, we shall be at least seventeen for dinner that night, eighteen if your father comes and that would mean three geese. Mrs Cripps couldn't get them all in the oven – even supposing we could get them in the first place.'

'Pheasants, then?'

'We'll see.'

'Well, not rabbit,' she said.

'That will be for lunch on Sunday. Mrs Cripps makes very good pies, you know that.'

'Do you think she would like me to help her at all? After all, I can cook a bit.'

The Duchy was clearly pleased. 'I think that might be a very good plan. But you will have to do exactly as she says. It is her kitchen.'

'I promise I will.'

'I'll speak to her this morning and see what she says. You may just have to be a kitchenmaid, you know. Is that understood?'

Louise took some of her worries to Archie, who listened, as he always did, with imperturbable gravity until she had finished. 'Well, darling Louise, I take your point, but I shouldn't worry *too* much. If I were Michael, I'd be far keener on seeing you and your exceptionally nice family than the sofa covers. Which, anyway,' he added, 'are rather nice. I only like things if they look used.'

This point of view hadn't occurred to her, but because it was presented by Archie, it made her feel much better.

∞ ∞ ∞

Villy, too, was in a state of high tension about the weekend. It was something she had wanted for so long, it had been put off so often, that even now, on Saturday morning, she felt that something might go wrong at the last minute. And when she wasn't worrying about that, she was feeling anxious about it happening. Meeting Lorenzo with his wife – and possibly with Edward there as well – he still wasn't sure whether he could get away, although she didn't know quite *why* he couldn't know – was going to be a peculiar strain. The chances of being alone with Lorenzo for a minute were remote, and even if they occurred, the likelihood of interruption was so great, that nothing could be said. She had managed to telephone Jessica to say how sorry she was that they would not be able to have her that weekend but, to her surprise, Jessica had said that she would not have been able to come anyway. She expected Raymond up for a weekend's leave from Woodstock, and she knew the house was very full, so both of them coming was out of the question.

Villy, immensely relieved, said, 'I'll give him your love, shall I?'

'Who?'

'Lorenzo.'

'Oh. Yes, do do that.' She seemed about to laugh. 'But not Mercedes, I think,' she said.

∞ ∞ ∞

Saturday morning was turmoil. Clary and Polly spent it moving themselves to the squash court. The maids made up the beds for the visitors, did all the bedrooms, lit Mr Archie's fire, washed the extra china and glass needed and were hardly through before dinner time – twelve thirty – in the kitchen. There, Mrs Cripps had made four pounds of pastry, plucked and drawn four pheasants, made two rice puddings and three fish pies for lunch that day, and a huge pan of bubble and squeak for the kitchen dinner, jointed, floured and fried five rabbits for the Sunday pies, made two pints of onion sauce and two pints of bread sauce – she allowed Louise to help with these. Edie scraped fifteen pounds of potatoes, cleaned five pounds of leeks, and five pounds of Brussels sprouts, scraped three pounds of carrots, washed up breakfast, middle mornings and laid the table for kitchen dinner. Ellen, in the smaller children's night nursery, ironed the clothes of Wills, Roly, Neville and Lydia – she missed the baby very much, but it was a blessing not to have all those nappies to air. Christopher took Neville and Lydia to the spring to fill up three dozen bottles with drinking water which then had to be put in a wheelbarrow and taken back in batches. They soon got bored, and played with Oliver. 'He has turned into a very nice dog,' Lydia said approvingly. 'Aunt Rachel said that people got to look just like whatever dog they had.'

'No, she didn't,' Neville said. 'She said dogs got to look like their person.'

'That's a very boring way round.' She stroked Oliver's black and white forehead and touched his grape-coloured nose. 'It would be much more interesting if Christopher had topaz eyes and a black nose.'

'She meant it in a manner of speaking,' Neville said loftily.

'When people say that they just mean that it isn't what they meant.'

'Come on, you two. It's your turn to fill some bottles. My hands are freezing. Stop quarrelling and help.'

'We weren't quarrelling. We weren't *quarrelling*.' Neville was outraged. 'We were simply talking about a subject.'

∞ ∞ ∞

Villy went to Battle and did an enormous shop for the household, and also collected prescriptions from the nursing home, had them made up and returned them. She collected their quota of paraffin for the cottage and the Brig's study, and paid the monthly accounts at the garage, grocer and Till's, called on the piano tuner, who had missed his last appointment, and then returned to mend the carpet sweeper, a fuse in the cottage – poor Miss Milliment had spent the previous evening with no light – and finally braved the stables to put new batteries into the wireless Wren had been given by the family last Christmas. He had received it without expression, but he played it all of every day when he was not asleep or at the pub. *He* had started the morning by sawing wood as he had been told to do by McAlpine, but he soon got tired of it and set about repainting the stable door. But as he couldn't be bothered with sanding down or with undercoats and was simply slopping another coat of gloss on top of the old one, it was rather a mess and he was just deciding to give it up when Villy appeared. He was incapable of putting in the new batteries himself. His skills with horses – no longer wanted – had once made him a cocky, belligerent little man; now he had retreated into a sullen ineptitude. He still retained respect for Mrs Edward, though; she never forgot him, unlike some – 'some' being everybody excepting the Brig who, on red-letter days, he took riding on a leading rein since the poor gent had lost his sight. He was kept going by his burning hatred for motor cars and the Germans, and his salary, which he drank. Mrs Edward, having made the contraption work again, offered him a cigarette. He took it, touched the side of his forehead like a nervous tic and put the cigarette carefully in his waistcoat pocket. He would have it with his dinner, he said. He did not eat at the house. Edie put a covered plate outside the stable door every day; it was usually stone cold by the time he fancied it.

Such a sad little man, Villy thought as she walked away.

She didn't ought to wear trousers, he thought watching her across the courtyard. He never wore them himself, and despised anyone who did, although he had had to admit that when Mrs Edward took to riding astride, he'd had less trouble with saddle sores. Still, breeches were one thing, trousers were quite another.

In another five and a half hours he will be here! Villy thought as she ran upstairs to wash for lunch.

∞ ∞ ∞

Sybil spent the morning playing with Wills and Roly, who were beginning to play with each other. This cut both ways: they took toys from each other and there was spasmodic rage and grief. 'You can't have that – it's too *important* for you,' Wills said once, wresting a red-painted engine from his cousin. Roly did not fight back; he simply wept and nothing would please him until suddenly something else did. In the afternoon they would have rests, and then Ellen would take them for a walk. Sybil would have a delicious sleep and then it would be tea-time and then Hugh would come. There were all those other people as well, but it was Hugh who would make her day. She smiled as the thought occurred to her that she was looking forward to his coming – and they had been married now for nearly twenty-one years – quite as much as Louise could be looking forward to her Michael.

Dolly spent the morning trying to find her bottle-green cardigan, the one Flo had made her – it must be ten years ago. It was only after she had been through all the shelves and drawers twice that she remembered that Ellen had taken it away to wash. She also wrote a letter thanking somebody she hardly knew from Stanmore who had seen about poor Flo in *The Times* and written a very nice letter. 'She will be greatly missed,' she wrote back in her large, spidery hand. A few sentences took up all the paper. Their house at Stanmore had been shut up for a long time. I suppose I shall never go home, now, she thought. But then she would not wish to do so alone – without Flo. She did not want to do anything without her, but now she had to do everything. She had been such wonderful company. Dolly often found herself having conversations with Flo who, no longer there with her own opinions, now agreed with everything Dolly said, but somehow this made the conversations shorter, and not so interesting. She did try once or twice disagreeing with herself, but she never felt she quite caught the *flavour* of Flo's mind. She had been taught from a young girl to bear adversity, and she did not complain or mourn openly to anyone, but this simply left her with little or often nothing to say. The Duchy had kindly suggested that she might like to change her bedroom after Flo died, but no, she would never do that. The room was where she could best remember her – except, of course, at dear Stanmore where they had lived all their lives, with both, and then one parent, and finally by themselves. She thought sometimes now that they had lived all their lives on the sidelines, as it were, in the slipstream of other people's events. Being bridesmaids at Kitty's wedding, rejoicing in the schoolroom that Papa had been made a Fellow of the Royal Society, comforting their mother when their younger brother Humphrey had been killed in the war, nursing their mother, comforting their father, and finally nursing him . . . there seemed to have been nothing direct, no circumstance entirely belonging to them. And now she was left, and so fortunate that Kitty had married well and could take her in. But if there hadn't been a war, she thought with sudden fear, I should have been at Stanmore and I should have been entirely alone with only Mrs Marcus coming three times a week and Trevelyan mowing the lawns on Saturdays. It was Flo who had been so good at opening tins; modern food had been a blessing although not always easy to digest . . .

There was a knock on the door and it was a child telling her it was lunch-time. The child was Lydia.

'Thank you, Louise dear,' she said.

'She ought to *know* I'm not Louise, because I don't wear lipstick,' Lydia said to herself, as, there being no one looking, she slid down the banisters to the hall.

∞ ∞ ∞

Edward and Hugh drove down together. Diana, rather to Edward's relief, had gone to Scotland to spend a lugubrious Christmas with her parents-in-law. She had, of course, taken Jamie, and the older boys would be joining her when they broke up. It did simplify things – temporarily.

'I suppose this will be just the weekend when Goering will arrange another nice little blitz.'

'I know, that's why I thought we'd better take the car. One of us can get back if need be. Unlikely, though. I think they've got their hands full. They're not doing so well on the Russian front, are they? Do you remember how bloody cold it was in the trenches? A Russian winter must be twice as bad. And a lot of the time we weren't even trying to advance.'

'It always seems amazing to me,' Hugh said, 'that Napoleon got as far as he did. How the hell did they even feed the horses – let alone the men?'

'Dunno, old boy. I should think they ate the horses.'

'I must say, though, I preferred being frozen to the awful thaw and all that mud – and stench.'

'At Hendon,' Edward said, 'I never told you, but they brought a crashed German bomber, and when I went into it, the smell was exactly the same as when one went into a German trench. The same sweet smell – entirely different from ours – my God, it took me back.'

'I remember that. Sausage, garlic, cigarettes, latrines . . .'

'I suppose we smelled just as different to them.'

They had crossed the river and were threading their way through streets of terraced houses, gaps in them where there were heaps of rubble and parts of walls with torn wallpaper, and sometimes lavatory cisterns and fireplaces still intact.

'London's getting pretty shabby,' Edward remarked. 'It's funny to think that there are cities lit up with all the buildings untouched. I've always wanted to go to New York.'

'I don't. I just want London back like it was. But if the Americans go to war with Japan—'

'You think they will?'

'I think Japan is determined that they should. God knows why.'

'If they do, it means we'll have the Americans on our side.'

'Roosevelt doesn't want war with Japan.'

'Surely *we* don't want war with Japan? We've got enough on our plate as it is.'

'But it would be a help to have the Americans sharing the plate with us,' Hugh said. Some time later he asked, 'Do you still want to go back into the RAF?'

'Well, yes, but I don't think it's practicable. The firm really needs the two of us. Managing the Old Man is a half-time job. The older he gets, the more he seems to want to interfere in everything.'

'He *is* going to be eighty-one any minute. And we wouldn't have the best stock of hardwoods in the country if it wasn't for him. Remember how we used to argue about him buying too much?'

'I do. I just wish he'd make a proper job of retiring, bless his heart.'

'Well, he won't. I'll be glad if you don't go back. I need you.'

Edward, glancing sideways, thought how very much older his brother had got in the last year.

'It's marvellous that Sybil is getting better,' he said.

Hugh was silent. He didn't hear, Edward thought, and then he thought, of course he did. He looked quickly at Hugh again. He was fumbling with his cigarettes – balancing the packet against his stump, so that he could pull one out.

'No – she's in remission,' he said flatly. 'Her doctor told me it often happens.'

'Dear old boy! Does she know?'

'I don't think so. No,' he repeated, 'I'm pretty sure she doesn't.'

Edward found he couldn't speak. He took a hand from the steering wheel and touched Hugh's rigid shoulder. They did not talk at all for a long time after that.

∞ ∞ ∞

'Well,' said Clary as they trudged with their torches, some time after dinner, in the dark to the squash court. 'What did you think?'

'About what?'

'The guests, stupid. I thought Mrs Clutterworth looked as though everything that she didn't like had happened to her.'

'She did look rather broody. Of course, not being English, it's hard to tell. She might be just homesick for her native land, wherever that may be.'

'She's Spanish.'

'She didn't *look* Spanish. But actually,' Polly added truthfully, 'I don't know what Spanish people look like – except in pretty old paintings. She liked Uncle Edward.'

'But she kept on watching Lorenzo. Laurence he's really called. I noticed Aunt Villy called him that. Lorenzo must be a secret joke between her and Aunt Jessica. What did you think of him?'

'I simply can't imagine *anyone* being in love with him.' Then she remembered them on the train. 'But I suppose some people have to be in love with the unlikely ones. But his teeth stick out, and his hair's all greasy and he has a red mark between his eyes when he takes off his spectacles.'

'The Duchy liked him,' Clary remarked.

'The Duchy likes talking about music. Anyway, let's get on to the other one.'

'The famous Michael Hadleigh?'

They had reached the squash court, Polly unlocked the door and they were assailed by the odour of warm rubber balls and tennis shoes. They climbed up the stairs to the gallery where their beds had been placed by Christopher that afternoon. They still had to use their torches because the blackout wasn't much good.

'Well,' Polly said, 'he wasn't one thing or another, was he? I mean, he wasn't quite one of *them*, and he certainly wasn't one of us.'

'Wasn't he sort of in between – like Louise?'

'Not quite. Louise was acting frightfully grown up, and he was treating her as though she was a terribly clever child.'

'Patronising her!' Clary snorted. 'Catch me being in love with anyone who did that!'

'She got bored when he talked about the war. Which he did, rather a lot, I thought. But then he went off with Louise after dinner.'

'She took him to see Archie.'

'Well, I bet that was only partly what they did. I bet she found some nice dark corner so that he could kiss her.'

'Do you really?'

'She took him to see our room.'

'She did that before dinner.'

'Well, she took him afterwards as well. I must say,' Clary said pensively, 'this would be a ghastly house to be in love in. There's nowhere to be with the person at all.'

'And I suppose one needs to be.'

'Of course. It's because people in love say such idiotic things to each other that they'd be afraid of other people laughing.'

'How on earth do you know that?'

'Think of Gerald du Maurier in *Punch*. "Darling!" "Yes, darling." "Nothing, darling. Only darling, darling!"'

'I honestly don't think people go on like that now-adays!'

'The modern equivalent. Listen! Is that her?'

They listened, but there was no sound of Louise, due to join them at some point.

'Do you think he wants to marry her?'

'She wouldn't be allowed: she's too young.'

'If she did, we could be bridesmaids.'

'I don't want to be a bridesmaid!' Clary said with vigour.

'Well, I do.'

'Oh, well, you'd look nice and everything. You know how silly I look in tidy clothes. After the war I shall go abroad because I've never been. Archie said I could stay with him.' She fell silent suddenly, and Polly knew that she was thinking about her father.

'I want to say something to you, Clary,' she said. 'I know *you* know that the family all think he's dead. I'm afraid I think that as well. What I wanted to say was I do *admire* your faith about it. Whatever happens, I shall always admire it. It's the most faithful thing I've ever known.'

After a silence, Clary said, 'How did you know I was thinking about him?'

'I think I always know.'

'I do – every day. And in the evenings as well. But I've stopped talking about it, because everybody else has run out of things to say. Even Archie.'

'Yes.'

'Good night, Poll. Thanks for what you said.'

Much later, and long after they were asleep, Louise joined them.

∞ ∞ ∞

'I still do not understand why we are *here*.'

'They asked us, darling.'

'And who is they?'

'Viola. Edward's wife. They have asked us before, you remember.'

'I remember with perfect clearness. I still do not know why.'

There was a pause while she unclipped her painful earrings and began to unpin her hair. 'Viola is that woman Jessica's sister, is she not?'

'Mercy darling, you *know* that. I thought you would like a little social life. It was an excellent dinner, didn't you think?'

'It was certainly good,' she conceded. 'And Mr – Edward – was a very nice man.'

'Mercy!' He ruffled her hair with an attempt at lightness. 'I expect he was charmed by you. But I must warn you, he is in love with his wife.'

'Is that so?'

'It is so. As I am in love with mine.' He put everything he could into that, and watched her dark eyes soften at the idea. 'To bed! To bed!' he cried, with all the fervour he could muster.

'You know,' she began, 'that I would not dream of looking at another man. I am not made in that way.'

'Of course I know.' He had heard it all before – a thousand times. The thing was to get her to bed before she started to compare her nature with his – to his serious disadvantage. 'I do not wish to wait,' he said.

'You would not come here if you were serious about *her*?'

'My darling, I haven't the least idea who you mean, and I told you, her husband is in love with her. I am hardly the type to wish a duel.'

'Oh ho! So it is both of them that is on your list? I am not to be deceived.' She was away – and twenty minutes later, he was out of love with Jessica, with Villy, and more dangerously, with her. It took hours for her to vent her jealousy, forgive him, and then persuade him to make love to her. He liked the attention, so in the end he was able to do so.

∞ ∞ ∞

'He's a bit too old for her, isn't he?'

'She's too young for him. She's too young for anybody.'

'I expect you're right.' Edward undid his sock suspenders and put them on his bedside table. Villy was taking out her teeth and scrubbing them with that powder stuff she used. As they both had dentures, they had developed an unspoken ritual whereby whoever had their teeth out was not expected to do the talking. Now he said, 'Nice bloke, though. Very keen on the Navy. I should think he'll go a long way. He told me he was to take command of a new gun-boat building at Cowes. He seemed really excited by the prospect – wasn't at all your usual arty type.'

'In any case,' she had put them back in now, 'Louise should stop messing about trying to work in an over-crowded profession where everybody is more experienced than she is, and get down to some sensible war work. I wish you'd speak to her about it.'

'She's got plenty of time, surely? They're not calling girls up until they're twenty.'

'They're not calling them *up*, but it would be better if she volunteered, and anyway, if she did a shorthand-typing course, she's far more likely to get a good job. At present she has absolutely no qualifications of any kind.'

She sounded so acid, that he looked across the room at her image in the mirror: her camisole lying over the flat but, even so, sagging breasts. From that distance with her short cropped hair, her heavy eyebrows and face devoid of make-up, she looked like a sour little boy. The uneasy thought occurred to him that she actually didn't *like* Louise, but he dismissed it as nonsense. She was just tired; everybody was tired these days – there was too much work and anxiety and not enough fun. He wondered whether she would notice and mind if he didn't make love to her – he certainly didn't feel like it.

'I'm really fagged,' he said, 'let's talk about it tomorrow.'

She was already putting on her pyjama jacket, had taken to sleeping in them in preference to nightgowns because of the cold, and now he got up and walked over to the basin so that he wouldn't see her without her camisole.

'The Clutterworths are heavy going, aren't they?' he said wanting to get onto a neutral subject.

There was a slight pause, and then she said, 'You were awfully good with her at dinner.'

He had taken out his teeth now, and didn't reply. Villy went on, 'She's not at all easy, I know.'

When he had cleaned his teeth and put them back, he said, 'Oh, she wasn't *too* bad – rather dull, but perfectly amiable. It was him I couldn't stand. Oily little feller – looks like the Mad Hatter – he kept saying how wonderful everything was, whether it was or not.'

Villy was in bed now, had turned onto the side that would be away from him. 'He's a very good musician,' she said, 'and the Duchy has been longing to have him to stay.'

'Bless her heart. I'd put up with *anyone* for her.'

He opened a window, then got into bed and switched off the light.

'Night, darling. Sleep well.'

'And you.'

But in fact sleep eluded each of them for some time: she, because she found it impossible to conjure Lorenzo when he was sleeping a few yards away from her with another woman, and he because, not given to either thought or anxiety once he was in bed, with or without a woman, found himself worrying about Louise, who still treated him to small, glassy smiles and avoided being touched by him, about Diana, now husbandless and pregnant, and finally about poor old Hugh, who he loved as deeply as he loved anyone and for whom, now, he felt he could do nothing.

∞ ∞ ∞

Louise had let herself out of the front door without making a sound. It was a quarter past one in the morning. All the evening they had been surrounded by the family, and although she had initially been pleased and elated to see how well he got on with them, she longed to be alone with him. Eventually, after they had listened to Mr Clutterworth and the Duchy play Bach on two pianos, she had suggested to Michael that they play a game of billiards.

'I don't really play,' she said when they were safely in the large, rather dark room.

'I did wonder,' he said. 'I don't either, as a matter of fact.'

She looked round the room; the only place to sit was a rather hard bench. 'I'm afraid it's pretty cold in here.'

He took off his uniform jacket and draped it round her shoulders.

'Won't you be cold?'

'Not after the North Atlantic. Anyway, I have my love . . . I have you, haven't I?'

They sat on the bench, and he kissed her quite a lot and she liked it, and in between they talked. He hadn't told his mother he had this leave, he said. It was so short that it would have meant not seeing Louise if he had gone home. 'So don't, for heaven's sake, ever tell her,' he said, half laughing, but she felt he was serious. They heard people going to bed, and he said, 'I feel awful about your giving up your room for me. Won't the squash court be frightfully cold?'

'I don't mind. Some of this house is probably quite like the North Atlantic.'

'Couldn't you come up to my/your room for a bit?'

'We'd have to wait until everybody has really gone to bed.'

'Let's wait, then.'

'I'm making up to you,' he said during this time. 'You know that, don't you? You're such a darling, amazing girl. I'm afraid I'm falling in love with you.' And he kissed her a great deal more.

It was half past eleven by the time the house was quiet and they crept up the dark stairs, she holding his hand, and along the gallery passage to her room.

They lay on the narrow little bed and he undid her blouse.

'There's a perfectly delightful bra,' he said moments later, 'that undoes in the front.'

'Do you want me to take mine off?'

'Well, it would be rather *nice*.'

They were speaking almost in whispers. Louise suggested turning off the light, but he said that he couldn't bear not to see her. It was exciting to be loved and wanted, and very soon when he asked her if she loved him – just a little – she said of course she did, she really loved him, 'enormously,' she said, and saying it made it seem real – and true. It was lovely to be with someone who admired and approved of her so much, and although she didn't feel that she felt exactly the same about him as he seemed to do about her, she imagined that this was yet another of the mysterious differences that one did not discover until they happened. Men weren't supposed to be beautiful – rugged, handsome, manly, all that sort of thing, but not possessing faces that encouraged the sort of adjectives he used about hers. Eventually, he groaned, and said that she must go, he could not trust himself, she said, 'Need you?'

She was lying on her back, naked to the waist, and he had sat up. He looked at her, then he picked up her blouse, and said gently, 'Put it on, there's a good girl.'

She sat up then, and put it on. She didn't bother with her bra.

'I'll see you to your squash court,' he said.

'No, don't. You see, I know the way, and you might get lost coming back. I'm all right, honestly. I've got a torch . . . You're not cross with me, are you?'

'I'm certainly not cross with you. I'm just trying to be responsible, which is not something I'm particularly good at in this context. Have you got a coat?'

'I'll get a jersey out of the cupboard.' When she had put it on, she said, 'Michael! If you wanted to – to sleep with me, I wouldn't mind. That's what I meant just now. I can't say I'd love it, because I don't know what it's like, but I *might*. Anyway,' she felt a bit shy now, 'I'd rather try it with you than anyone else I know.'

'That's the nicest thing anyone's ever said to me.' He put his hands on her shoulders and kissed her forehead. 'You'd really better go.'

So here she was, in the utter darkness, walking very carefully, round the house, past the tennis court, through the little gate in the middle of the yew hedge into the kitchen garden. It was very cold and there was a delicious misty stillness that went well with having an adventure. He had a wonderful voice, she thought, even when he was almost whispering – it charmed her. It was amazing to have somebody of one's *own* caring so much. She was beginning, she felt, to see the point of love.

∞ ∞ ∞

'Seventeen days to Christmas!'

'Eighteen.'

'Wrong, wrong, wrong. What's the date, Ellen?'

'I don't know.'

'Ask Archie.'

They pounded upstairs.

'Seventh,' he said. 'What difference does it make to you, anyway?'

'Longer to wait,' Lydia said.

'Shorter for people to get presents,' Neville said. He was quite worried about this. With Dad gone, and Zoë away, and the aunts hardly *ever* going to Hastings, he couldn't see how any decent presents would materialise. There probably wasn't a single thing he would want to be got in Battle. He felt the outlook was grim.

They spent the morning collecting holly to make Christmas things for their shop. 'But it doesn't really want to be made into *anything*!' Lydia said, as she licked the blood off her pricked fingers.

Music went on the whole of Sunday morning, with Sybil and Hugh and Villy listening. Mrs Clutterworth sat crocheting a lace collar and keeping an eye on her husband. Edward took Michael rough shooting, so Louise, rather reluctantly, went too. 'Supposed only to shoot vermin on a Sunday, but luckily rabbits count as that and if you happen to encounter the odd pheasant or partridge, they're always useful for the pot,' Edward said. He was duly impressed when Michael shot four rabbits, a brace of pheasants and the only partridge that rose from the stubble of one of York's fields.

'Although what I am supposed to do with one partridge, I do not know,' Mrs Cripps said when she received the morning's bag. Miss Milliment read the paper to the

Brig, interrupted by the hourly news bulletins on the wireless to which he had become addicted. Rachel spent a patient two hours with Dolly, and then rang Sid, who didn't answer, and she remembered that Sid did Sunday duty at her ambulance station and felt sad. But she'll come at Christmas, she thought. She, too, was counting the days.

Sunday lunch: the rabbit pies, followed by tarts made with bottled plums were consumed, after which Villy organised an expedition to Bodiam Castle for the benefit of the Clutterworths. The younger children clamoured to go too and the expedition ended up, as they so often do, not being at all like their perpetrator had envisaged. Everybody else dispersed to read, to rest, to write letters.

Clary and Polly had a row.

'If I'd known you were going for a walk with Christopher, I'd have gone to Bodiam,' Clary stormed.

'You never said you wanted to go.'

'I didn't know you were going for a walk.'

'You could come too.'

'I loathe walks, you know I do. I wanted us to do our presents.'

'We'll do them after tea.'

'Oh, Polly! You are maddening sometimes! I've got something else I want to do after tea.'

'What?'

'Shut up. This is a typical boring weekend. I'm going to wash my hair. That shows you how bored I am.'

By the time she got out of the house Polly saw Christopher disappearing down the drive with Oliver. For a moment she felt cross with him; then she thought that was silly, she could easily catch up. It was a beautiful winter afternoon, with silvery sunlight and silent birds rustling through the piles of fallen oak leaves at the sides of the drive.

A taxi suddenly appeared round the bend, and she waited, because this was extremely unusual and interesting. It stopped at the house, and one of the smallest men she'd ever seen in her life got out of it. He was wearing a naval cap and greatcoat that reached almost to his ankles. I suppose he's a friend of Michael's; oh dear, she thought: she knew Michael had gone off somewhere with Louise. The small man paid the driver with some notes, and then turned to stare at the house. The driver was trying to give him some change, but he seemed not to notice.

Polly advanced. 'He's got some change for you,' she said.

The man spun round on his heels, acknowledged her, and took the change from the driver.

'I'm Polly Cazalet,' Polly said.

'Cazalet,' he repeated, with evident pleasure. He had sparkling black eyes, a charming smile and, surprisingly, a heavy French accent.

'I come,' he said, 'for Madame Cazalet.'

'Which one?'

He looked confused and said, 'My English is not good. Do you speak French?'

'Not much, I'm afraid.' She remembered Archie. 'Come with me. I'll find you someone to talk to.'

She took him up to Archie's room.

'Archie. A French person wants a Madam Cazalet. Could you find out what exactly he wants?' As she said this, she suddenly thought of Uncle Rupert, and her heart dropped like a stone.

The small man broke into torrents of French, and Archie interrupted him to ask questions, which he answered.

Then he drew from his pocket two very small, thin pieces of paper and handed them to Archie who read them, and then said, 'Fetch Clary, Poll – now.'

∞ ∞ ∞

'I can't come – my hair's dripping wet!'

'Clary, you must. Never mind your hair. Archie wants you.'

'Oh! All right.' She lifted her dripping head out of the basin, smoothed some of the water out with her fingers and together they ran to Archie's room. 'He's all right, isn't he?' Clary asked. 'I mean, nothing awful?'

But not feeling at all sure of this, Polly did not answer. The small man had taken off his greatcoat and was sitting in the visitor's chair, but he sprang to his feet when they entered the room.

Archie said, 'This is Rupert's daughter. This is Sub-Lieutenant—'

'O'Neil. Pipette O'Neil. Not real name, you understand – from telephone book I take.' He smiled at Clary, kissed her hand and said, '*Mademoiselle Clarissa. Enchanté de vous voir.*'

Clary stood, stock still, staring at him, her eyes, in a face gone very white, had an expression that nobody in the room could bear.

'I was friend of your father,' he said.

'Sit down,' Archie said gently, patting the bed. 'It's a long story,' and pushing her sleeked-back hair from her face, she did as she was told.

He told her that Lieutenant O'Neil had met her father hiding in an orchard, that a family had kept them for nearly three months in different outbuildings on their farm. O'Neil had been on leave from the French navy when the Fall of France overtook him, and had been determined not to stay in France but to get to England and to join de Gaulle. But it was too soon for there to be any established network for escape; he and Rupert had to rely on their own wits, invention and luck. Their plan was to get to the coast, and there try to steal or bribe some fishing boat to take them across the Channel. The first farmer passed them onto a friend, a man who made cider, but there they got stuck: the cider manufacturer seemed unable or unwilling to find a reliable contact for them further west. They took turns in the daytime to pick apples for him while the other kept watch for Germans. Pipette tried to persuade the cider maker's daughter to get them some papers, but although she agreed to try she was so obviously terrified that they decided it would be foolish to persist. In the end they got her to get prints of snapshots they took of each other, alongside a lot of other pictures, and she bicycled to the nearest town to get them developed. They borrowed an identity card belonging to the farmer, and Rupert copied the layout and forged papers for them both that they hoped would pass if they got asked for them. Then he said they hadn't agreed about the next step. He was in favour of acquiring a couple of bicycles, but Rupert thought they would be better off on foot which meant that they could abandon the road more easily. They needed a map. Pipette had some money; Rupert had none, and he had given his watch in exchange for civilian clothes to the first farmer. But now it was winter, not the best time of the year for sleeping rough, but they knew they had already out-stayed their welcome at the cider farm. So one morning, armed with bread, cheese, meat and a bottle of Calvados, they set out. Their plan was to use only small roads or lanes, to walk during the early hours of the morning when it was still dark, to lie up in the day, and to walk again after four o'clock. And thus they proceeded. There were many, many stories about this time, Archie said. They reached La Fôret – a small place south of Quimper – last April. Here, he said, they had another argument. Pipette was for them trying to find a boat together; Rupert said they should part and try their luck separately. But he, Pipette, had been adamant that they should at least try first to see if they could go together. By now their money had long run out and they were reduced to stealing – food, and sometimes things they could swap for food. They slept in a barn outside La Fôret where a woman found them one morning when she was going to feed the chickens. She was intelligent and quickly understood they were on the run and she offered to help them. Her fiancé had been shot by Germans when he had tried to stop them taking chickens from their farm and she seemed anxious for any kind of revenge. They would have to go to Concarneau for any chance of a boat, she said. There were a few fishing boats there but occasionally other boats would put into that port for a day or two and then leave. She had no idea where they went. She offered to go to Concarneau for them to see what she could find out. After she had gone, they got very anxious, and left the barn in case of betrayal, but kept it in sight and, sure enough, she came back alone that evening. There was a boat that had arrived that morning – what incredible luck! – and she thought it would be easy to slip aboard. When they asked her why she thought this, she answered that she herself had done so, had peered down a hatch into the forecastle where two men were snoring, and had then walked along the deck to the galley where she had taken a knife – and she showed it. It seemed too good to be true, but it *was* true. Their ill luck came from another direction. Their long walk had made their shoes unwearable. Pipette had come by some boy's boots that were not too bad, but Michèle had got some shoes for Rupert that proved so large that he could hardly keep them on his feet. They had to set out for Concarneau in the early afternoon, because Michèle did not know the precise hour that the boat would sail, and they had not gone far before they heard a lorry approaching which was all too likely to be Germans. To get off the road they had to jump a ditch and then climb a bank to the field. They ran, but when Rupert jumped he landed badly. The others were ahead and did not realise this until the lorry had almost reached the bit of road they had left. They listened, but it did not stop, and when they emerged, they found Rupert lying face downwards in the ditch. He had rolled there as the safest cover, as he said he couldn't walk. Michèle bound up his ankle in one of her stockings soaked in ditch water but although he could hobble painfully, he could not make any distance.

Here Archie stopped and said, 'That's as far as Pipette has got with his story. So from now on, it will have to be me asking questions and translating for you.'

There had been a furious argument. Pipette did not wish to leave Rupert; Rupert said he should go. The woman joined in here. She had not gone to all this trouble, she said, to have it all come to nothing because of sentiment. At least one of them should get away. She would look after Rupert, and *he* would get away when his ankle was restored. She became quite angry and, in the end, Pipette gave in. They helped Rupert up to the bank and settled him behind some bushes. Michèle said she would fetch him on her way back.

'And then,' Archie said, 'Clary, he gave Pipette this,' and he handed her the flimsy piece of paper.

She read it under her breath. 'Darling Clary, I think of you every day. Love, Dad.' She read it again to herself and then bent her head over it. Then she looked at the paper again. 'Oh! my beastly hair's spoiling the paper!' Her eyes, that had become like stars, began to stream. 'The second piece of paper! The second piece of love sent!'

'The second piece is for Zoë,' Archie said, not understanding.

'She means the postcard her mother sent from Cassis with her love on it,' Polly said.

She was trying to blot the paper with tender, anxious, nail-bitten fingers.

'It's in pencil, Clary, it won't run,' Archie said.

'So it is. When did he write it?'

'In the barn, at La Fôret. He asked me to deliver it if I should get to England. Not to post. To go – to come – myself. That was eight months ago. I do not know—'

Archie held up his hand, and Pipette fell silent, but a shadow of the old anguish crossed Clary's face; a momentary darkening of the incandescence in her eyes came – and went. She read the piece of paper again and when she looked up at Archie he saw that her loving faith had been resolutely resumed.

'It's just a question of time,' she said. 'That's all it is. Waiting till he comes back.'

∞ ∞ ∞

The news about Rupert spread fast. That evening Hugh and Edward carried Archie down for dinner, to drink the champagne that the Brig produced from his cellar. Pipette was to stay, of *course*, the Duchy said. An atmosphere of determined relief prevailed – if Rupert had been alive eight months ago, then they would find no reason why he might since have met misfortune. His excellent French, the intelligence of the woman Michèle, his nearness to the coast, the fact that Pipette had made it – all these factors were optimistically discussed, and more stories of Pipette's and Rupert's adventures came to light. Once he felt at ease with the family, Pipette was a wonderful raconteur and sometimes very funny in a manner which was endearingly like Rupert. On one occasion, he said, when the Germans suddenly turned up at a farm where they were lying up and where there was nowhere safe to hide, Rupert had put Pipette into a wheelbarrow: he only had time to say 'You are a complete *idiot* – understand?', as he began, with a pronounced limp, to wheel him past the German lorries that were disgorging their occupants. Here Pipette flung his legs over the arm of his chair and lolled in it with a vacant smile and his tongue slipping out of the side of his mouth, then springing to his feet to become Rupert limping and conducting a monologue of contempt and hatred for this idiot brother, while at the same time managing to imply that he had a screw loose himself. He was taking his brother to the doctor for his fits, he told the German officer, although a vet would be more suitable since he was hardly more than an animal. The officer had shrugged and turned away; the men had stared, and one of them had even looked *sorry* for him, Pipette said. The Duchy was crying with laughter and wiping her eyes on her little handkerchief. Pipette said they had to keep it up for ages, as the road to the farm was long and perfectly straight, and they could not be sure that the farmer would not come out of his house and give the show away. There were many stories, he ended, turning to Archie, who had interpolated translation where necessary for the non-French speakers of the party.

That evening though, after dinner, they listened to the nine o'clock news and heard that the Japanese had launched a massive surprise attack on the American Fleet in Hawaii at a place called Pearl Harbor. As this had happened only an hour before, details of damage had not come through but clearly a state of war was imminent, if it did not exist already.

'How *can* it have happened an hour ago when it's evening now and they said the attack was seven o'clock in the morning?'

'It's the time difference, Poll,' her father said. 'What with double summer time and it being the other side of the world, we're hours and hours ahead. It's breakfast time there, and bedtime here – for you.'

Sunday evenings were always early, because the London contingent had to leave so early in the morning, and everybody dispersed soon after that.

∞ ∞ ∞

Somehow, that day, that evening, was a watershed, a turning point for many of them. The Brig, when he had made his way to his bedroom and slowly divested himself of his many clothes – his jacket, waistcoat, flannel shirt, woollen vest, trousers and braces, long johns, polished brogues, prickly woollen socks speckled like a thrush's breast – groped about on the bed until he found his thick flannel, widely striped pyjamas, thought wearily that there was little or no chance now that he would see the end of this war. He was eighty-one, and it seemed to him that with the Japs and the Americans in, it could last twice as long as the last war. He'd been on the sidelines for that one as well – a position he intensely disliked. Still, he had got Hugh and Edward back the first time, so perhaps there'd be a third stroke of luck with Rupert. But the idea that he might not live to know this disturbed and depressed him. It won't matter to Rupert, he thought, one way or another. It matters to me. He did not pursue this: he had never been any good at using words about love – even to himself.

∞ ∞ ∞

Sid, in London, rushed home after the news came through at her ambulance station in case Rachel rang up. There was no particular reason why the news would make Rachel ring, but irrational hope persisted, and she sat, in her now very dusty sitting room (she loathed housework) eating a Spam sandwich, and making up and then changing her mind about whether *she* would ring. Just to hear her voice, she thought. She had nothing much to say, and she thought that perhaps there would come a time when she had nothing at all to say to Rachel, since she was not able – would never be able – to say what lay nearest her heart. She thought of all the people in the world who were in love, to whom that would simply come as a joyous and natural asseveration: 'I want you. I want your naked body in my bed, your flesh against my flesh, your need to be my pleasure, your pleasure to be my joy.' She had long become used to concealing herself from other people – it was second nature to her now – but she never got used to disguising herself for Rachel. It made her feel like some secret agent or spy; her true identity in this endless alien land would mean death.

That evening, as she sat and waited and the telephone did not ring, was the first time that the idea of not loving Rachel came to her, not as some terrible limbo, but as a possible release.

∞ ∞ ∞

'He didn't write to *me*,' Neville said to Lydia as they lay in bed.

'He might have, and that French person might have lost it and felt too embarrassed to tell you.'

'No fear.'

Lydia could sense he was deeply hurt. 'He didn't write to Juliet, either,' she said.

'Of course he didn't! Write to a horrible little baby who can't even read! Even Dad wouldn't be as silly as that. Well, all I can say is that when I'm grown up and doing a lot of interesting, dangerous things, I shall write to—' he considered, 'Archie, and you and Hitler and Flossy. And not to him. *Then* he'll see.'

She was so flattered at being included that she did not mention anything about cats not being able to read.

'I should treasure your letters,' she said. 'And I should think Hitler will soon be dead and not worth writing to.' Then, when he didn't say anything back, she said, 'I'm honestly awfully sorry, Nev. I know how important he is to you.'

'*Important?* I hardly ever think about him. He's a distant memory. Soon he'll just vanish like a puff of smoke. He's just a little tiny weeny thing I'm nearly forgetting. I wouldn't have thought of him at *all* if he hadn't written a letter to Clary.' His love and disappointment raged on until, worn out by it, he eventually fell asleep.

∞ ∞ ∞

The Duchy sank gratefully onto the stool before her dressing table and bent to unstrap her shoes. The evening had tired her more than she would admit, even to herself, and her fatigue increased her apprehension. The news about Rupert – though it was a hundred times better than no news at all – was still uncertain, incomplete. He had been alive eight months ago. But since then anything might have happened. He could not escape without some help, and people had to risk their lives to do that. It was because of this that she had said that Zoë should not be telephoned. They could not tell her he was alive and safe, and therefore it was better to wait the few days until she returned and could be told the whole story. Is that what I would want? she thought. Yes. I should not like not being told at once, but I should be grateful all the same. That was that.

She took off her sapphire and pearl cross that was slung round her neck and held it in her hand for a long time before putting it on the table.

∞ ∞ ∞

Diana, having padded along what seemed like about a quarter of a mile of stone corridor to the only loo on the bedroom floor of the Scottish baronial Victorian castle that her parents-in-law so imaginatively, she thought, called home, crept thankfully into the enormous dark and, of course, cold bedroom. Its stone walls were adorned with an uneasy mixture of weapons and watercolours. Some quite vicious coconut matting provided an occasional contrast to the stone floor. The deeply recessed gothic windows had been deemed too small to merit curtains, so fresh air, in the form of draughts, was unchecked. The huge bed was superlatively uncomfortable. It stood very high off the ground and was furnished with a thin horsehair mattress, a bolster fit to dam a dyke, two soft thin pillows that smelled of violet hair oil and blankets of the kind that rich people threw over the back of a horse that had won a race. She slept in her dressing gown and bedsocks. It was the room they had slept in when Angus was alive, and would always be hers, his parents had said. They had tried to be very kind to her, especially when they learned that she was pregnant, but even two days with them had her screaming with boredom. Naturally, they assumed that she was hardly herself from grief (their phrase), and, poor dears, *they* were hard hit, and she knew it, and made extra efforts. Already Angus seemed to her to have died a long time ago, but in fact it was just over three weeks. With the older children soon to be home from school, she had no choice but to go to Scotland for the holidays. At least, apart from getting there, it meant she didn't have to spend any money, which now, she knew, would be tighter than ever. And there would be a fourth baby. She adored the others, especially Jamie, but if she had another son the financial situation would be dire. If it were not for Edward, she supposed she would sell the London flat (supposing she could find anyone who *wanted* a bombed flat in London in the middle of a war), and rent or buy somewhere very cheap in the country. Even so, the prospect of two more sets of school fees seemed bankrupting. These thoughts were foremost in her mind, because after the news that evening about the Japanese bombing the American Navy, everybody had agreed that the war was obviously going to be a very long one, and her father-in-law had offered a permanent home with them. She recognised that this was noble of him, since he had never liked her, but she knew that she would rather die than accept. It would mean never seeing Edward again, and without him, she felt she would sink into a morass of isolated responsibility. If only he was here *now*, she thought, as she climbed miserably into the icy bed. He would make even this place fun. If only he was with me all the time, she then thought, after she had turned out the light. This thought did not go away; it prevented her from sleeping, and towards the small hours it began to seem so essential to her that for the first time she began to consider how on earth it might be achieved.

∞ ∞ ∞

Michael Hadleigh had at once offered to share his room with Pipette, who now lay asleep in the bed next to him. They had not talked much, as Michael's French was rudimentary – he had gone to Germany as an art student – but he gathered that Pipette had had a pretty rough time getting to England. They had tried to talk about the Japanese attack, and had agreed that the damage had probably been awful because of the element of surprise. Then Pipette had said good night, rolled himself in his bedclothes and become silent. His coming had prevented Louise from spending another evening with him as she had yesterday. Just as well, probably, he thought. The last one, although extremely enjoyable, had been a severe strain. She was so young – almost too young to have an idea what she wanted. She was beginning to love him a bit, but it would not be fair even to try to sweep her off her feet unless he knew he was serious. Was he? Mummy always said she wanted him to get married, and he knew she passionately wanted a grandson. Usually, she had found good reasons why the girls he brought home would not do, but she had not done that with Louise. He hadn't talked to her about it directly, but the subject of the grandchild had come up again at the end of his last leave. 'Don't leave it too late,' she had said, and then pretended that she had meant until he was too old, but he knew what she meant: don't get killed without having begotten an heir.

Tonight, listening to that stark piece of news and knowing that it contained, or would contain, terrible statistics in terms of ships and human life, he had thought seriously, and for the first time, that the possibility of getting killed was something he had to take into account. Until now, he had led a charmed life, always been lucky; in a sense that had seemed to him to be courage, and he took his own courage very seriously. It ran in the family: he must be as brave, or braver, than his father. Now, imagining those American sailors in their mess at breakfast being shockingly assailed by screaming planes that rained down bombs upon them – a colossal, hideous ambush of thousands of unsuspecting and innocent men, he felt real fear for the first time in his life. How would he have behaved under that sort of fire? Would he have been a survivor even? Would poor darling Mummy have to go through all that again? First his father, then him: the two people she had loved most in the world? The ship that he was going to command – the MTB building now at Cowes – was as vulnerable to air attacks, mines, torpedoes as any other vessel, but it was gunfire that picked off the coxswains and the officers; it was the people on the bridge who most often copped it. And that was where he was going to be. Again, he felt a cold, sick fear of the apparently imperturbable hours he must spend there. That evening he recognised that fear was an essential element of courage, as he also saw that the chances of his getting killed in his new job were quite high. Mummy, as usual, had been right – he could easily leave having a son until it was too late . . .

∞ ∞ ∞

On duty that night, Angela, among her other tasks, spent her shift reading the hourly news bulletins from which more and more information about the Pearl Harbor attack emerged. Five battleships seriously damaged, over two thousand dead, two hundred aircraft destroyed. There had also been attacks upon the American base in the Philippines and two islands in the Pacific. Japan had declared war upon the United States and Britain. It seemed very odd to sit alone in the tiny room with the heavy glass panel separating her from the JPEs so that they could not speak to one another, and to read aloud these violent and distant events in much the same calm and professional manner that she would have used to announce an increase in the price of potatoes. In between, when she was not logging the records played or announcing them – when, in fact, there was a concert running that gave her some free time – she made lists of all kinds of things. Qualities that she thought most important in men: 'honesty,' she put; 'kindness. Straightforwardness,' (but that was like honesty). 'Loving,' she put. Then she made a list of what she wanted most in her life. 'A more interesting job. Travelling. Someone to love.' Then she got stuck. She thought of a list of what she wanted for Christmas, but nearly everything was unavailable; things she wanted to happen next year. 'The war to be over.' Fat chance of that: it was simply getting to be a bigger and bigger war; it would be all over China and Africa and India soon – like a plague. Perhaps people whom she might love and who might love her, whom she had never known, were being killed at this minute. Everything she thought of – even different kinds of lists – always seemed to come back to the same thing. It's all I want, she thought sadly. I don't want anything else.

∞ ∞ ∞

Christopher lay on his narrow camp bed in the attic with Oliver using up most of the space. If he tried to move, Oliver gave a deep sigh and shifted his bulk as though he was giving way to Christopher, but he always ended up by taking more of the bed. Tonight, however, Christopher wasn't noticing Oliver as much as usual. The news had appalled him. The behaviour of the Japanese had not only shocked him, it had brought up new and distinctly alarming questions of conscience. How would *he* feel, as an American, if this had happened? People who could attack in that way were capable of anything. So, if he was an American, would he not feel that he should rush to defend his country from more of the same thing? More than that: did he need to be an American to feel that? He had been against war because he didn't want anyone to kill anyone else, but the fact was that that was what they were doing. Perhaps one could not adopt a superior attitude to nearly everyone else while at least a number of them, who also disapproved, were mucking in and doing the dirty work. In all his conflicts and misery during the last year or so it had never once occurred to him that he might be wrong – not wrong in an intellectual sense, but wrong to separate himself from his own species. He thought now of his father's jibes; at the way the other youths levelling the runway where he had been for so many weary months had scoffed, and argued with him and eventually left him alone, so that sometimes days passed when nobody spoke to him except his sour-faced landlady with some complaint. She had cheated about his rations, taking his book and giving him bread and marge for breakfast, so that practically all of what he earned went on sandwiches in the only pub within reach of work. Through all that he had sustained himself with being *right* – which, of course, had meant that practically *all* the others were wrong. But now, as he thought of all those sailors who had not been fighting but had simply been suddenly bombed to death, he began to feel that even if he *had* been right, it was wrong to be right in that kind of way. It implied a kind of moral superiority that he secretly knew now did not belong to his nature. Look at how he had fought Teddy years ago when Teddy had wanted to join the camp he had made in the wood. And if he was no better than anyone else, he had no business behaving as though he was.

After the really bad time – when that landlady had turned him out of the house without warning because she claimed to have been told he was a nancy boy, and he had said it was nonsense because it was, she'd said, 'Are you calling me a liar?' and he felt he had to say yes. That had been *it*. She'd summoned her husband out and he'd sort of elbowed him out and down the steps into the street. He hadn't even fetched his things. It had been very cold and it must have been Friday because he had money. He'd gone to a pub and drunk two whiskies to stop him shaking. Then he'd walked – he had a vague notion of catching a train and he must have caught one but he couldn't remember anything more at all – until two men in uniform, wearing armbands, were shaking him on a bench by the sea, and asking him a whole lot of questions he simply couldn't answer, and each time they asked a question, he went on finding out more things that he didn't know. He knew he was alive because he was frightened of the men, and something else that lurked just out of the reach of his mind. They kept asking very strange things about regiments and leave and stations, and also much less strange things like what was his name, but he didn't seem to have one, or at least he couldn't remember it then. They took him off and shut him in a very small room. Someone brought him a cup of tea – the first kind thing that happened, it seemed to him, in this new life where he wasn't anyone. He'd started to cry and then he couldn't stop. He didn't *want* to be anybody at all; he wanted just to pass out, stop, not feel anything. Then he was in a hospital, and they told him who he was, and it was no better knowing. His parents came and the fear that had seemed out of reach was suddenly all around him. They'd given him the electric shock treatments. The first time hadn't been so bad, because he hadn't known what they were going to do when they strapped him down on the high table. He'd come round after the first time with a splitting headache, but also a great sense of relief. But he had begun to dread the

'No, Poll, he thought you were beautiful. Besides, you've got the right kind of hands for kissing; mine must be one of those hazards that I suppose Frenchmen have to face.' She held out her rough, nail-bitten hand critically. 'I should think I'd better not marry a Frenchman.'

'If you marry one, they'd kiss you in other places, silly. It's only strangers' hands they kiss, instead of shaking them.'

They were in the bathroom at Home Place, cleaning their teeth and washing before repairing to the squash court. Clary, sitting on the side of the bath, said, 'I've got a headache.'

'It's the excitement. Have an aspirin. I won't tell the Duchy.' She looked in the bathroom cupboard but there weren't any. 'I'll get one from Mummy's room.'

But she came back a minute or two later and said, 'Sorry, Clary. The light's out and there's not a sound. They must have gone to sleep.'

'It doesn't matter. I expect the cold air will make me better. Anyway, I don't mind. I don't mind anything.' She put her hand in her jacket pocket, and Polly knew she was touching the piece of paper.

'Clary, I want to tell you something. I didn't want to talk about it before, because you were so worried. I didn't want to make it worse.'

'What?'

'Well, in the autumn, and quite a bit of this winter, I thought Mum was dying—'

'Poll! Did you? Why did you think that?'

'Well, I sort of overheard Dad and Aunt Villy, and that's what it sounded like. It was so awful! You see, Dad didn't know what I'd heard, and he didn't tell *me*. People *ought* to tell you really important things like that, oughtn't they?'

'Yes,' Clary said slowly, 'they always should. As a matter of fact, I got pretty worried about her too. I didn't *hear* anything,' she added hastily, 'it was just that she seemed so awfully ill, and getting worse, not better. But she has now.'

'Yes, thank goodness.'

'You should have told me, Poll. After all, I'm your best friend. Aren't I?'

'Of course you are, but you didn't tell me.'

'I see what you mean. There's a sort of trap, isn't there? You don't tell people things out of love. But actually, I think, the more you love people, the more you should tell them – even the difficult things. I think it is the best sign of love to tell them.' She put her arms round Polly. 'You're never to bear things by yourself. Promise!'

'OK. You promise as well,' said Polly.

'I do. Any not telling is a sign of not love.'

And Polly answered in the Duchy's voice 'I *do* agree, my dear.'

∞ ∞ ∞

By the time Edward and Villy had helped Archie up to his room, and he had collected his crutches and limped down the passage for a pee and back again, he felt exhausted. Apart from the emotions involved, hours of translating and spending an evening with so many – albeit now well-known and much-loved – people had been unexpectedly tiring. And then the news about the Japs, who would really spread this war, he thought, so that in many places the British were going to be pretty thin on the ground, or at sea, let alone the air.

Dear old Rupe! I hope you're all right, wherever you

are, he thought, as he eased himself carefully into bed. What a piece of luck it was Rupert! None of the others would have got by on their French if this evening was anything to go by. He'd allowed himself to be infected by the family's optimism but, alone now, and privy to far more of Pipette's information and views than anyone else, he recognised that Rupert's chances, at best, were no more than even. It must have been very lonely, lying in that field with his friend going away. Pipette had said that they had early made a pact that they would not emulate the three musketeers – the all-for-one-and-one-for-all principle. Pipette was entirely professional: it was his duty to get away so that he could fight the Germans from England. Rupert, although he was only 'wavy Navy', had felt the same. So, of course, when it came to one of them going and the other staying, neither felt they had a serious choice, although Pipette said he had felt so bad about it that he had tried to stay.

Then he thought of the whole family sitting round the dinner table; with Pipette on one side of him, he had found Rachel on the other. When toasts were being drunk, to Rupert, to Pipette, and Pipette's reply, 'To the family,' and people were turning to one another to clink glasses, he had turned to Rachel. Touching her glass with his, he had said, very quietly below the general family jollity: 'Here's to you, dear Rachel – and to Sid.' Her eyes had widened a moment as though with shock, and softened. Then she had given him a wholly enchanting, slightly anxious smile and said, 'Bless you, Archie.' It was the very pleasant, very end of falling out of love.

Love: Clary immediately came into his mind's eye. What an extraordinary, intense and changeable face she had, that was always such a mirror of her heart! He went

591

The Cazalet Series of Novels

Elegantly constructed and told with exceptional grace,
The Light Years is a modern classic of twentieth-century
English life and is the first novel in Elizabeth Jane
Howard's extraordinary, bestselling family saga
The Cazalet Chronicles.

Every summer, the Cazalet brothers – Hugh, Edward and
Rupert – return to the family home in the heart of the
Sussex countryside with their wives and children. There,
they are joined by their parents and unmarried sister
Rachel to enjoy two blissful months of picnics, games and
excursions to the coast.

But despite the idyllic setting, nothing can be done to
soothe the siblings' heartache: Hugh is haunted by the
ravages of the Great War, Edward is torn between his wife
and his latest infidelity, and Rupert is in turmoil over his
inability to please his demanding wife. Meanwhile, Rachel
risks losing her only chance at happiness because of her
unflinching loyalty to the family.

'Charming, poignant and quite irresistible . . .
to be cherished and shared' *The Times*

The Cazalet Series of Novels

Beautifully and poignantly told, *Marking Time* is the second novel in Elizabeth Jane Howard's bestselling Cazalet Chronicles.

Home Place, Sussex, 1939. As the shadows of the Second World War roll in, banishing the sunlit days of childish games and trips to the coast, a new generation of Cazalets take up the family's story.

Louise, who dreams of becoming a great actress, finds herself facing the harsh reality that her parents have their own lives with secrets, passions and yearnings. Clary, an aspiring writer, learns that her beloved father is now missing somewhere on the shores of France. And sensitive, imaginative Polly feels stuck – stuck without a vocation, stuck without information about her mother's illness, stuck without anything except her nightmares about the war.

'The Cazalets have earned an honoured place among the great saga families . . . rendered thrillingly three-dimensional by a master craftsman' *Sunday Telegraph*

The Cazalet Series of Novels

The Cazalet Chronicles continues with *Confusion*, the third instalment, set in the height of the Second World War, in which chaos has become a way of life for the Cazalet family.

It's 1942 and the dark days of war seem never-ending. Scattered across the still-peaceful Sussex countryside and air-raid-threatened London, the divided Cazalets begin to find the battle for survival echoing the confusion in their own lives.

Headstrong, independent Louise surprises the whole family when she abandons her dreams of being an actress and instead makes a society marriage. Polly and Clary, now in their late teens, finally fulfil their ambition of living together in London. But the reality of the city is not quite what they imagined, and Polly is struggling to come to terms with the death of her mother and manage her grieving father. Clary, meanwhile, is painfully aware that what she lacks in beauty she makes up for in intelligence, and is the only member of the family who believes that her father might not be dead.

'She is one of those novelists who shows, through her work, what the novel is for . . . She helps us to do the necessary thing – open our eyes and our hearts' Hilary Mantel

The Cazalet Series of Novels

The Second World War has finally ended and so begins a new era of freedom and opportunity for the Cazalet family. Elizabeth Jane Howard's magnificent Cazalet Chronicles continues with *Casting Off*, the fourth novel in the saga.

The Cazalet cousins are now in their twenties, trying to piece together their lives in the aftermath of the war. Louise is faced with her father's new mistress and her mother's grief at his betrayal, while suffering in a loveless marriage of her own. Clary is struggling to understand why her beloved father chose to stay in France long after it was safe to return to Britain, and both she and Polly are madly in love with much older men.

Polly, Clary and Louise must face the truth about the adult world, while their fathers – Rupert, Hugh and Edward – must make choices that will decide their own, and the family's, future.

'She is the most amazing storyteller because she makes you care' Elizabeth Day

The Cazalet Series of Novels

All Change is the fifth and final volume in Elizabeth Jane Howard's bestselling The Cazalet Chronicles, where the old world begins to fade from view and a new dawn emerges.

It is the 1950s and as the Duchy, the Cazalets' beloved matriarch, dies, she takes with her the last remnants of a disappearing world – houses with servants, class and tradition – in which the Cazalets have thrived.

Louise, now divorced, becomes entangled in a painful affair, while Polly and Clary must balance marriage and motherhood with their own ideas and ambitions. Hugh and Edward, now in their sixties, are feeling ill-equipped for this modern world, while Villy, long abandoned by her husband, must at last learn to live independently. But it is Rachel, who has always lived for others, who will face her greatest challenges yet.

As the Cazalets descend on Home Place for Christmas, only one thing is certain: nothing will ever be the same again.

'A family saga of the best kind . . . A must' *Tatler*